# THIS LITTLE WHATEVER

## NICOLE FORCINE

Dreamspinner Press

Published by
Dreamspinner Press
5032 Capital Circle SW
Ste 2, PMB# 279
Tallahassee, FL 32305-7886
USA
http://www.dreamspinnerpress.com/

Cover Art by Paul Richmond
http://www.paulrichmondstudio.com

Cover content is being used for illustrative purposes only
and any person depicted on the cover is a model.

ISBN: 978-1-62798-131-6
Digital ISBN: 978-1-62798-132-3

Printed in the United States of America
First Edition
September 2013

To Don, for withholding my favorite indulgence until I pressed the Send button. I love you.

To Kaje, Yeah, I kept "hunk-seeking dowsing rod." Thank you.

CHAPTER ONE

# Tired

*Six months ago:*

"YOU have one new message. Message sent at 6:43 a.m."

> *"Morning, mijo. Yes, I know, it's nearly seven and you're not even awake yet, but I've been up all night trying to think of a way to tell you what I need to tell you.*
>
> *"Remember when I told you I was napping more and more lately, feeling all tired and run down, and we thought maybe I caught the flu from one of the patients? Well, I finally got to the doctor, and I had some tests run. Something about being safer than sorry or some shit. I'm not even sixty yet, and I'm getting treated like an old woman. Can you believe it?*
>
> *"There's no nice way to put this, boy, so here goes: your Mama's liver is a little fucked up. Biopsy says that it's cirrhosis. Have I ever told you how not fun it is to attend a biopsy? It's not so much fun receiving one either.*
>
> *"Don't you dare try to call me right now. I'm also not flying your ass to Peru to baby me so don't even think about it. Just listen to me. I won't answer any calls until tomorrow, and I mean it, boy. Just. Listen.*

*"We caught it early, and I should be able to finish the contract before I go into serious treatment. I'll be staying in Peru until it's safe for me to travel. We don't know the cause for it yet. It could be the drinking biting me in the ass after all. It could be a lot of other things. We know it's not any of the alphabet hepatitis, since I got my boosters a year ago. Are you current on your jabs? You should check up on that. Grab the HPV one as well, and don't 'aww Mama' me. If you need the cash to cover it, I'll wire some to you. No argument.*

*"How are you on condoms? Need to get more? Wait, never mind, you're not sixteen anymore. You can buy your own. And you better be.*

*"And about your health, here is why I wanted to speak to your voice mail instead of you, because the voice mail interrupts me less. This... I want you to... God, mijo, I would be lying if I am not a little scared, but not for me. I am scared for you. I know, you're grown and taking care of yourself, but we both have our excesses, you know that, and the thought of you having to deal with anything like this later in life, when I might not be there to help you, scares the shit out of me. Sooo... I want you to think about yourself right now, while you're young and can't fuck it up too badly. Try to cut down a little, you know, on the drinking and the drugs and the men—don't 'aww Mama' me again. There's probably a man in bed next to you right now. I know you. If you are anything like me before I had you, I hope you're not listening to this with a hangover as well. Let's just say that. Consider doing it for your mama, okay?*

*"Call me tomorrow, around three in the afternoon, okay? I love you."*

"Hey, Jonathan, you coming out of the bathroom any time soon? We're packing a new bowl."

I hit the button to save the message without even seeing the numbers. Or the phone, for that matter. The rest of me didn't feel like moving much.

My mouth worked automatically. "Sure, Rach, be right out."

At the promise of oblivion, to forget what I'd just listened to, my body got into gear, and I rose from the floor, heading for the door.

*Present:*

I NEEDED sleep, badly. Crimson Dream Tribal had a show that next night, and while it was going to be just a few hours at the local Greek place to liven up the Friday night baklava-munching crowd, it was still a gig. A paying gig. After that would be the usual throw down get-together house party that was already getting started downstairs and all around the house, but it wasn't the noise that kept me up. I've slept through tornadoes louder than that.

The orgasm I'd just had wasn't easing me to sleep either.

My bedmate made short work of the condom we'd just used, tossing it in the general direction of the trash can before slumping next to me, already drifting into the land of Nod. "'Night...."

I smirked, tousling his straight blond hair before lightly smacking him upside the head. "Gonna wander. Don't steal the pillow."

"Ow." His voice was too sleepy to sound upset. He even chuckled, half muffled by the pillow. "Jackass."

Moving from the facedown position I'd collapsed into after we came, I ignored the twinge of discomfort in my ass and slowly rose to my feet. I attempted to smooth down my hair as I looked around for whatever I'd been wearing before Patch got his hands on me—a black canvas kilt with metal studding around the waist—and put it on sans underwear. Millions of Scots couldn't be wrong; regimental was the only way to wear a kilt. I was no Scot, but who really gave a shit?

I took one more glance at Patch on the mattress. He slept deeply, looking as young and innocent as he very fucking well wasn't. Envy overtook the lust that earlier overtook the buzz I had before we hit the sheets. Normally, once I got to sleep, I was out cold, but it was damned hard to get there lately, while Patch could nod off at the drop of a hat, like he had nothing on his mind, no worries. Asshole.

Thankfully, there was no one in the upstairs bathroom, one of the few places in the house where anyone got any alone time. I grabbed a washcloth, not caring who it actually belonged to, wet it in the sink, and quickly wiped under the kilt so I wouldn't have "itching like a son of a bitch post coitus" to add to the reasons why I couldn't fall asleep. Tossing the wet washcloth back where I found it, I looked in the mirror and spotted a large crack that nearly took one of the top corners off. Fuck, that wasn't there when we moved in. There goes the security deposit on this piece-of-shit hovel.

I stepped to the side to avoid the crack and got a better look at myself. The face that blinked back at me looked as tired as I felt. Outside, I played the role of exotic-looking rake to a T. My skin held the natural mocha tan of Hispanic heritage only slightly diluted by having a gringo for a dad. From him, I got my eyes, still bright green through the haze of exhaustion. My thin mustache and goatee both remained tightly groomed, though I'd need a shave in the morning to take care of the shadow creeping up on my cheeks. My hair, long enough to hit the small of my back, didn't look half as bad as I expected after our tussle. Patch loved to grab handfuls like reins nearly as much as he liked calling me "papi" while pounding into me.

Annoying habits, both, but at least I liked having my hair pulled. I haven't broken him of the "papi" habit yet. He found it ironic and funny, a result of a freshman Spanish class he didn't finish. In trying to call me an "old man," he completely ignored the fact that "papi" implied something much closer than what we actually were. He was also nineteen, so that said a lot for what he found funny and ironic.

At closer inspection, the bags under my eyes looked enormous, and there were those damned lines, small ones at the corners of my mouth. Laugh lines, my ass. I didn't feel like laughing too much when I saw them. Did I look this tired to everyone, or was it just me?

Next points of inspection were my ears, and more importantly, the two newest additions to the line of silver hoops that adorned the curves of both, three on one ear, four on the other. No redness, no swelling, no nasty gunk, they were healing fine. Maybe next time I could afford to visit a piercer, I'd finally get my lobes done. Or maybe not. I'd cross that bridge should I ever come to it.

One quick leak later, I headed downstairs toward the noises, thanking every god I knew that no one had started a drum circle at this hour. While I could have stood a few hours of dancing, at least enough to wear me out, the neighbors got bitchy if we drummed more than once a week, and our once a week was planned for tomorrow. Or today. Whatever.

A gaggle of bodies sat chattering across beat-up couches and the dirty carpeted floor of the living room in front the TV that played some horror movie I'd never heard of. A few faces turned to acknowledge my presence, and a couple of people waved, smiling faintly like they knew me, but most were riveted to some poor sap's CGI-assisted mauling. I didn't bother waving back, not recognizing any of their faces in the dim, flickering light of the ancient TV. Who were they again? Why were they here at stupid early o'clock? Fuck it, I needed air.

I got to the glass sliding door leading to the back deck and pushed it open before realizing what a terribly stupid idea it was to choose this door instead of the front one. The hazy pot smoke screamed "beyond lies temptation, Jonathan" like a flashing sign. A group of six girls, all topless, passed around a well-used purple glass bong. We'd named it Grimace, after the big purple McDonald's mascot, and also after the look someone would have before coughing their lungs up if they weren't careful with the toke. At least I knew some of these girls, three of them, in fact. One, my svelte, pale best friend, peered up at me through black-and-red-striped bangs.

"Where's Patch?" Bloodshot eyes slid over my equally topless form as she arched an eyebrow to punctuate the question.

"How am I doing, you ask?" I barely held back the sarcasm. "I'm doing fine, Rachel, and you?" I broke eye contact to smile cordially at the other girls, taking a seat near the circle. The house's walls were absurdly thin; the answer to her question had been pretty damned obvious. You couldn't fart in one room without the people downstairs hearing it, never mind get your freak on quietly, so no one really bothered with discretion.

One of the other familiar girls, a tiny little redhead named Chrissy or Carol or something, elbowed the other familiar girl, tall, brown-skinned Tam, and they both gave knowing laughs.

"Guess you wore him out." Tam chuckled at me, took a hit from Grimace, and passed it along the circle.

Rachel, to her credit, said nothing more about it, but kept staring at me, wide gray eyes trying to see through my words, and waiting.

There wasn't much I could do about her scrutiny right now, at least until the bong made its way in my direction.

I brushed a loose bit of hair from my shoulder and winked at Tam, who dutifully blushed. At least everyone else on the deck thought I was charming. "You know me. I'm a loud man to keep up with."

Ah, the familiar sex boast, as easy as putting on a broken-in pair of Docs. Surrounded by curious ladies most of the time, I've accepted my role as the rainbow-colored sexual oddball, just man enough to be sexually frank and play-flirt with, but too gay to be a threat. Hell, they seemed to get more enjoyment out of mine and Patch's sexing than their own with men actually interested in bedding them. Ah well, it's good to have a niche.

"You know, if you ever feel like using up all that energy to make a girl happy...." The redhead—her name was Cindy, I was sure of it—waggled her eyebrows, much to the amusement of the group. Except for Rachel, who glared at her and shoved Grimace and the lighter into her hands.

I kept acting as if I didn't see the glare. "I'm flattered, really, hon, but there's a small problem. Well, I wouldn't call it small, but see, even with all this boobflesh around...." I paused and lifted the end of my kilt to the view of the gathered. No shame here. You didn't live in this house with this group without seeing my lanky ass stride about sans pants at least once, and it was only fair, with all the tits about. "Not even the slightest twitch. I stopped lusting after tits shortly after I started eating solid food."

The whoops and giggles that followed should have made my little exhibition all the more worth it. I usually liked dancing on that line between friendly and just plain outrageous. But now, I felt utterly tired. And Rachel's little "too cool for this" eye roll didn't help, turning the annoyance into pissed. We'd been at the weird little emotional impasse for a while now, since I got the voice mail from Mama, with neither one of us willing to talk about it. Easier to play our parts for the sake of the little band of misfits we called our family.

Cindy passed me Grimace and lighter, and my stomach dropped as I released the kilt back to take it. I remembered Dr. Spaulding's words, reminded myself that, while weed wasn't addictive, I needed to cut down, if not completely stop, and that I could actually say no. I was a grown man, after all. Rachel's stare bored into me as I checked the bowl, smiled, and with fingers that slightly trembled, passed it right along to the next girl without saying a single word. This was normal, Jonathan. Saying no was perfectly normal. It wouldn't help me sleep anyway. I chattered my face off when I got high.

"You're tired." Rachel's dark gaze had a flicker of something in it: anger, disappointment. What the fuck did she have to be disappointed about? My pass meant more for her when it got around. No way was I going to ask that out loud. That would only kill the group's buzz, a bigger sin than me being tired and her being pissy.

Best to keep deflecting for now. "Who are those guys?" I jerked a thumb behind my shoulder to the group watching the movie.

Tam, fresh from her two hits, little clouds of pot smoke steaming from her lips as if the weather had suddenly grown cold, happily answered, "We met them at the craft fair today, and they seemed cool. They know Lala, you know, that British hula girl?"

Oh yeah, the friend-of-a-friend vouch. I felt the urge to suddenly run back upstairs and make sure my shit was still where I kept it. I can be friendly around strangers, but I'd learned the hard way about trusting them.

Rachel huffed at me, reading my weird theft paranoia with the ease that came from knowing me for damn near ten years. "She's Welsh, Tam. Jonathan, you were there when we met them. If you had a problem with inviting them, you could have said so."

Suddenly everyone's eyes fell on me. Some of the other girls, the ones I didn't know, were probably part of the group we were discussing right now. Fuck me, way to look like a jackass. And extra points to Rachel for helping me into the jackass costume. Double fuck me for even bringing it up, knowing full well that even if I had a problem, it wouldn't have mattered if Rachel wanted these people over. Besides, it wasn't completely my fault for not remembering any of their faces among all of the other people I saw at the fair. Someone had to mind the booth we had set up while Her Highness schmoozed.

No, that was a shitty excuse. The real reason wasn't any better, though. I didn't notice these people at all because I didn't even care. They were just new entries into the catalog of nameless, faceless joy seekers I'd met before and would never see again. If any of them had anything worth noticing, I would have remembered some names. Like if one of the guys was cute enough to look at twice.

Since I was firmly wearing the jackass costume, I decided to make myself scarce. "No problem, Rach, was just curious. I'm going to see if I can wake Patch up again for round two."

I added a lecherous grin and got exactly the reaction I wanted, more hoots and catcalls, one suggestion about how to give him head—like I needed the help—and I headed back inside and up the stairs. If Patch was awake, it wouldn't take much convincing to get him hard and inside me one more time. To hell with being able to walk the next morning. But once I really thought about it, I wasn't in the mood for the pacifying effect of another orgasm any more than I was in the mood for getting stoned or even drunk. I'd been good all day. Only a few beers, and I'd slowly nursed those. I wasn't even buzzed. Maybe that's what was wrong, why I was so tired. Dr. Spaulding would think differently, but she didn't have to come home to this after each counseling session.

Back in the room, Patch was curled up on his side of the mattress, snorfling softly like a little puppy having a dream, still looking angelic, save for the stitch tattoos on his back and arms. He was a fucking baby, too much swagger and sex appeal for his own good. He'd woken up in my absence, given the two white pills that lay on the pillow he thankfully didn't completely take over for his own comfort. They came from his secret Valium stash, located only God knows where, because I could sure as fuck vouch for it not being up his ass. He always had some, although he didn't deal it, and as far as I knew, I was the only one he shared with.

I looked at the pills, and my brittle resolve to not have any more chemicals tonight completely dissolved. Screw it. At least this would calm down the gnawing in my brain enough to sleep. I would pay penance to Our Lady of Recovery, Saint Spaulding, next time I spoke to her. It had been long enough since the last beer that I wasn't courting a bad interaction, so I simply popped the fuckers dry. After shucking out of the kilt, I stretched out on my side of the mattress, closed my eyes, and waited for drug-assisted oblivion.

Sorry, Mama. I couldn't do it today. Again.

CHAPTER TWO

# *Shimmy*

THE dining room and lobby of Kouzina were already getting pretty full when the dancer contingent of Crimson Dream, that being Rachel, Tam, Cindy, and myself, rolled through to the back area reserved for a changing room. The servers and hosts politely greeted us on the way there, and I got a small salute from Mike, the bartender. By the time we finished our set, he'd have a scotch and soda waiting for me. A godsend, that man. Damn shame he was happily married and not into dudes.

I dropped my duffel in my usual corner and started pulling out costume bits, listening to the girls chatter. The bag was a freakishly large military-issued thing I scored at a surplus store for cheap years ago. The room was damned small with no mirror, so the girls had to share Rachel's compact to make sure that little details, like bindi crystals and eyeliner, were applied neatly. Thankfully, other than the eyeliner I'd donned before we left, I didn't bother with much flair. I didn't need to. Just me stepping out onto the dining room floor would attract attention enough. Male belly dancers were just that rare in the Midwest. I could go as natural as I liked, keep my hair loose, only a shiny belt of pressed silver coins around my hips as jewelry. Add a pair of dark-green dance pants that looked so nice hugging my thighs and ass and flared out at the ankles, with a matching green vest, and I attracted attention enough.

I almost envied the girls that much bling, all the coins and bells adorning what little fabric they wore to keep their tops modest. Below the waist, to a woman, they all wore similar skirts with splits up to their thighs and sashes and belts of coins. We joked once that I should get a skirt set of my own, but I refused to shave my legs for any reason. I barely grew any body hair below my neck, only a few pluckable stragglers on my chest, light wisps of armpit hair, fine growths on my arms and legs (thank you, Gringo Daddy, for the genes that didn't render me a Sasquatch), but I wasn't going to submit to razor-bump torture for a couple of giggles. I wore the face fuzz just to prove to myself that I had the testosterone to do it.

"Are we bothering with zills tonight?" Tam asked, helping Rachel with her bra top.

I looked up from buttoning my vest. "I asked Anah the other week, and it was a go, remember?"

"Oh?" Rachel murmured, leaning forward and shaking her chest to get the girls to settle in her top properly. "I talked to her two days ago, and we decided not to do it."

The door opened, and the members of the Caress troupe, polished, professional, enviable, entered before I could ask just when did Rachel plan to inform any of us about the change in props. For crying out loud, I was co-leader, and it wasn't like we didn't spend nearly every waking moment around each other. Rachel promptly shifted to nice mode to talk to the more traditional dancers we shimmied with monthly at Kouzina, and I let it drop, sliding my smile on tight until I finished dressing.

I couldn't stay in the dressing room and make friendly for too long, though. Sleep finally came late last night, but that morning and afternoon left me so out of sorts, with the same worries, mixed with the guilt of taking those pills when I'm supposed to be quietly "recovering." Yeah, recovering so quietly I haven't bothered to inform anyone in our troupe of it.

I pulled my phone from my discarded pants pocket to check the time. I had seven minutes before showtime and smiles and remembering short routines, and that was just long enough to rush to the restroom to make sure I was dancing on empty, so to speak.

"I'll be right back," I announced before heading out, the coins around my waist jingling like bells on a sleigh. I didn't stop to hear anyone respond.

I burst through the door and had to stop short before I bowled into some tall wall of muscle leaning over one of the sinks. I looked up and up and up into eyes so hazel they glowed gold. Like, lions of the Sahara, gold eyes. Coin belt shade of gold. Those eyes were highlighted by thick framed glasses and below those were.... *Holy Christ, Jonathan, we don't have time to ogle the lips of a man you nearly knocked over, though as tall as he was how the hell was that possible and....*

"Sorry!" was all I could mumble before ducking into the first stall I could get to. Better to make it look like a hell of a hurry than having to deal with some dude getting pissy at the jingling fag that ran into him.

"S'not a problem," a deep rumble replied over my stream. My ear promptly zeroed in on the sound. His voice sounded... strained. He probably got too close of a look at me and didn't know what to think. It was okay. Hopefully, he was leaving Kouzina before the dancing began. I'd have hated to see those eyes looking at me the same way some dudes in the audience did, all disturbed and disgusted. They were too striking; that brief glimpse promised to be a complete distraction.

By the time I got out of the stall and was frantically washing and drying my hands, the mystery man had left the bathroom. I didn't have time to think about him, anyway. I hurried back to the changing room in time to see Anah, the leader of Caress, stepping through the curtains the staff had put up to make the area we would be dancing in more like a stage.

"I think I should be the one introducing us," Rachel whispered to me once I got in place, standing next to her. "I'm louder."

"You could have asked earlier while you were talking about the zills." It was hard keeping the resentment out of my voice. "Or mentioned it to me when I talked to Anah."

She ignored me, and it didn't matter because Anah had already started the CD that held the traditional Middle Eastern tunes every belly dancer knew. Rachel might have been louder than Anah, I would never doubt that, but the piercing trilling ululation that we heard from Anah's throat gave Rachel's a good run for its money. The sound shot a thrill of anticipation and joy through me, and I threw my head back and opened up my mouth to return the cry with one of my own as we moved past the curtains and onto the dance floor.

After that, nothing else mattered. The music was so primal, drums, flutes, and woodwinds flowing and melding with the sound of a dozen sets of coined waists jiggling and shimmying in time. Bared feet moved fluidly across the hardwood floor, hips swayed and rotated, and there I found my peace once again.

It was funny that, with all the drink, all the drugs, all the fucking, it was in the act of bending my spine and arms like a snake while keeping my hips shaking at a ridiculous rate of speed that I found my connection, where the world shut up for a little while and let my mind focus. I could focus on the steps, on the way I moved, the ways I could move, on the audience looking in wonder and delight at all of us moving together, crying out and yelping together, clapping together. Sometimes I questioned my choice to found and run Crimson Dream Tribal, but all I had to do was look to these moments to remind myself why I stayed. Where else could I feel this grounded, this connected to everything?

With each twist, I showed off my joy and my pride, my talents and my body. Ten years of work went into making sure each move was precise, yet flowing. When I turned to the side and rolled my spine like the letter *S*, flashing the small galaxy of inked stars that dotted both my flanks, when I made my belly flutter until the snake circling my navel quaked, I knew I had eyes on me. Some would be genuinely surprised that a man could move this way, others appreciative of the effort at the very least, and a few, in a haze of too much *ouzo*, would wonder where the topless chick with the mustache misplaced her tits. It didn't matter. I would drink in their energy to replenish what I was giving from my dancing.

We had a good routine going, coming out all at once to start the show. Then four of us would make our way around the tables of the diners, gracing them with smiles and a little up-close action while allowing those remaining on stage more room to really work their assets. It was on my first pass that I found the man I'd seen in the bathroom. My stomach twisted in anticipation and dread. Just my luck that I stood near his table with Tam on the other side.

First thing I noticed were those eyes again. In the candlelight, they looked damn near chocolate brown, but they blazed with a heat that hit me low in my gyrating belly. Stop the presses. This man wasn't simply watching, wasn't just enjoying the show, he was enjoying me. Well, shit. It was rare that I got such attentions from any man at these gigs, so I was going to enjoy the hell out of it with every pass I made near his table. It was damned hard to check out any more detail with the low light, other than the glasses and that his hair was some sort of dark red-brown mass of curls, and he was blushing hard enough to melt those frames every time I looked at him. Cute, interesting. And apparently very interested.

I was so completely into his reactions, that when he finally broke into a barely there smile, a beautiful, brief curl of lips, I missed a goddamned step. I was looking over my shoulder at him, preparing to take a series of turns, and that smile made me pause long enough to miss my cue when Tam started to spin. I recovered quickly and was fairly red-faced myself when we finally returned to the stage to finish to a roar of applause, a few people standing, tons of whistles.

My eyes darted around as the dance haze was fading and found Gold Eyes still watching me. He wasn't standing, and I hoped to God it was for the same reason I rushed backstage to get into something a lot less tight around my dick.

LATER, I leaned one hip against the bar and watched the patrons file in and out, sipping my waiting scotch and soda and offering a pleased, slightly goofy smile to anyone who looked my way. I was still riding on the wave of endorphins that always followed a good set. The smile had to look damn strange on me, clashing with my regular clothes. With my eyes still lined, long-sleeve mesh shirt, tight jeans, and battered Doc Martens, all black, I looked so Goth I could shit bats on command. The smile didn't really belong with the outfit, so big on my face, full of pleasure and joy. I wouldn't be standing there long, just until Rachel, Tam, and Cindy finished standing outside Kouzina's lobby handing out flyers advertising our big show at the Point Theater in a few weeks.

I'd be happy to be out there helping, but the last time I tried, a pair of assholes took one look at me in costume, thought I was advertising for a gay bar, and threatened to kick my "faggot" ass. It took the combined intimidation power of me, the ladies, and two subtly concealed blades to convince them to move the fuck on. That altercation made the managers of the restaurant nervous, so I opted to stand at the bar and wait, watching our bags. The management even offered me free drinks at the bar, so it was a fair deal. I could have this one drink, maybe another. Maybe enough so that I wouldn't need to drink at the party. I might be able to get away with it this time.

Swishing the ice in my drained glass, I knocked back a scotch-flavored cube and let it slowly melt, savoring the taste as the water slid down my throat. Tonight, I fucked up my own rhythm because of a face I could still see when I closed my eyes. The dude outright eye-fucked me every time our gazes met. Eye-fuck, no, that wasn't enough. By the end of the performance, "eye-fuck" became "eye-undress, eye-fuck, eye-cigarette after." I'll be damned if any man had looked at me like that during a performance before, and I'd bet my ass that I've jiggled it in front of more than a few gay dudes in my time. I wished I'd gotten a closer look, made sure the face I thought I saw was as handsome as it was in my fevered dance-induced bliss. He blushed, didn't he? Didn't the gene for blushing die out when a man put on a certain amount of muscle? Not that I was complaining. It's a compliment on top of more compliments. I liked having that effect on him. If I could have gotten away with it, I would have climbed into Mr. Eye-fuck's lap, brushed back those curls, and plundered that smiling mouth. He looked so well put together that I ached to rumple him up something fierce.

My eyes scanned the lobby to see if I could get a glimpse of the guy on his way out, all thoughts of dancing and parties or getting another drink shoved out of my mind. Was he single? He didn't seem like he was "with" anyone, not the way he stared. More importantly, why the fuck should I care? Nothing wrong with a little peek at him from afar.

All the gods that ever existed had to be smiling on me, because it didn't take five minutes before I saw Mr. Eye-fuck walking out of the dining room and into the lobby. Jesus, was he really that tall when I ran into him at the bathroom? He looked about six and a half feet, and very, very well put together in tan slacks and a black sports coat, opened, revealing a dark-red button-down. His hair was more of a reddish-blond under the lights of the lobby. I watched him smile and say good-bye to a bunch of people who were probably sitting at his table. I was too busy looking him over to even notice anyone else. That smile was even more radiant than the one he gave me, and that just wasn't fair. I wanted that big smile aimed at me. Want? No, I needed it.

It had to be the excess of postperformance energy that got me off the bar and sauntering toward the lobby. Either that or temporary insanity. What I intended to do once I got up to Mr. Eye-fuck, I had no idea. I was guaranteed to get away with a casual face-to-face hello, and that became my goal. Best to keep these things simple. Again, I wasn't sure if he was gay, bi, taken, or not even out yet, and outside my little circle of friends, it was *très gauche* to cram my tongue down an admiring stranger's maw in lieu of a hello. Of course, the last time I said hello that way, I got into Patch's pants, but that boy was easier than Sunday morning.

My thoughts were promptly interrupted by the sight of the man walking right in my direction, too busy looking at his cell phone screen to even notice where he was going. If I'd had any common sense, I would have moved out of the way before he crashed into me, instead of risking being run over by wide shoulders that looked better suited to that padding football or hockey players wore. Then again, if I made the crash look like an accident….

The impact wasn't as hard as I thought it would be. He wasn't moving quickly, and I braced myself to take most of the hit. What I wasn't expecting was his hand to grab my shoulder, keeping me upright. His grip was tight, his eyes wide with heart-melting concern. Bingo. Achievement Unlocked: Mr. Eye-fuck's Undivided Attention.

"Damn, I'm sorry." He looked me over, keeping his grip tight, and shoved his phone into his pocket to grab my upper arm with his other hand.

His deep voice was made for an alpha-male jack-off, but the worry that laced it softened the tones and turned it into a sound that caressed my ears like warm velvet. He wasn't pushing me aside; that was a good sign. He gave a shit about almost knocking over a stranger, an even better sign. It would be worth letting him off the hook, since I hadn't gotten the smile I wanted yet.

I stood up straight and gave him my best rakish grin, laying a hand on the one on my shoulder. Smooth skin glided against the pads of my fingers as I gave it a little stroke. "My mistake, man, I should have been paying attention."

Both his hands flexed against me but didn't move away, and a flush darkened his very uneasy face. "If I wasn't trying to walk with the phone in my face at the same time, I would have seen you first. You're one of those dancers, aren't you?" He gave an embarrassed huff, and he shook his head. "Damn, I could have hurt you. I'm sorry."

"Hey, hey." I tried a charming smile, drinking in those features from up close. Strong, clean-shaven jaw, broad nose and beautiful lips, wide where mine were full, currently tight, drawn down into a frown. Still no good. I wanted that smile, dammit. "No worries, handsome. Can I get you a drink?"

The man opened his mouth, then closed it, then tried again, looking like a damned fish before actual words came out. "Actually, I was just going to the bar to double check the address for this place. For my GPS." He took his hand off my arm and motioned to the suit pocket where the phone had been stashed.

Well, that only meant we didn't have a lot of time for me to get my flirt on a little, boost my ego by a lot, and, if I was lucky, get a phone number for some fun later. Mr. Eye-fuck may have been looking at me earlier like I was on the menu, but it wouldn't do to ask for more than that tonight.

I took the hand on my shoulder into mine, savoring the bob of his Adam's apple as he swallowed, and led him back to the bar. Mike already stood there, waiting for an order. I released my captive's hand to slide my empty glass toward Mike.

"I've got this," I told him. "He's just looking for the address. I'll give it to him." Mike nodded, gave me one of those encouraging smirks that made me want to smack him, and headed back down the bar to take care of the other customers.

"Thank you," Mr. Eye-fuck said once we were relatively alone again. "The show was really something. I haven't seen anything like it before. You looked like you had fun. I mean, all of you. Having fun, that is."

If that wasn't admitting to all the blatant staring, I didn't know what was. Mindful of the bags around our feet, I turned to look at him, committing his face to memory. I could definitely get lost in those eyes, and I did for a few seconds too long before I remembered it was my turn to speak. "It's a lot of fun. Even more when I get to dance for someone as into it as you were."

I lost his attention when he looked down as I called him out. Way to go, Romeo. Before I could fully mourn the loss, he extended a hand to me. "I'm Dean."

My night had truly been made. Not only did I get a name, but I got to touch him some more too? I didn't know how to deal with this weird, kind-of-bashful pose of his, though. He had to know how hot he was. How wasn't he used to being appreciated this blatantly? I wasn't known for being subtle. Damn me, it was even more appealing. It was insanely appealing. I hadn't flirted with anyone this appealing, and there was no other word I could conjure up for how I saw him, in a very long time.

"Jonathan." I took his hand, notched my smile up a few watts, and hoped I didn't look too predatory. His palm was slightly damp with sweat as I curled my long fingers around it and we shook, and I completely forgot to give my little mini-speech about how I liked to be called by the full name. Not Jon, or Johnny, or Joe, and for fuck's sake, not José. I hated it when people I barely knew shortened my name. That was too familiar. A few select folks were aware that Jonathan was my middle name, those few being my family and Rachel. But anyone attempting to call me by my first name, Esteban, who wasn't the woman that birthed me, risked me kicking their ass.

"So, Dean," I continued once my brain kicked back into gear and decided skipping the speech was a deliberate move on my part. "You're not in a hurry to get home, are you? Got a lady friend waiting or something?"

Dean—a name as short and sweet as he was tall and hot—looked down at our still-joined hands and didn't make a move to pull away. "Lady friend? Never. No boyfriends either, in case you were going to ask." There was another long pause, as if he were steeling himself to speak. "How about you? I bet you have to beat them off with a stick after a dance like that."

If Dean didn't want to let me go, I sure as fuck wasn't going to break the contact either. It got me a front row seat to the smile that finally broke onto his face, friendly and warm, contrasting with the heat in his eyes. He was eye-fucking me again—I knew it and reveled in it. Yeah, handsome, look at me, enjoy the view and my company and stay a little longer and talk to me. The need for his company churned inside me as my belly fluttered in a way that was unfamiliar. It was completely unexpected in the wake of the physical desire I was beginning to feel.

Not wanting the flutters to ruin my fun, I shoved the distracting thoughts aside and brought my own voice down to purr, "Just between you and me, I'd rather beat them off with my hand."

My fingers ran over the soft skin of the inside of Dean's wrist, and he shuddered slightly. I wasn't sure if it was because of my voice or my touch or both, and I didn't care. If I played this right, pushed a little further, danced on that edge I knew so well, I could have Mr. Dean Eye-fuck eating out of my hand and anywhere else I asked him to.

Desire flared through me at the thought of Dean eating out any part of me, and wasn't that just the best damned idea ever. I'd gone from only wanting a little tease, a little notch on the ego post, to wanting a notch on a completely different sort of post. Maybe I would get luckier than I expected earlier.

He spoke again, voice soft as he echoed, "Between you and me?"

My own lust was catching. His eyes dilated, that broad chest heaving and lips parted, all hints of worry or shyness gone. Thank fuck, because I dove in for the kill.

I stepped over a bag to stand chest to chest with Dean, up on my toes, letting my lips brush against his. I wanted to do so much more than talk, but I needed to ask, "You're not in a rush to leave, right?"

Yes, I'd asked something like that before, but that was way before this little spell sparked up between us, and I hoped the answer would be different.

My answer came in the form of Dean closing the millimeter gap between us. My mouth opened the second our lips touched, and two things instantly became clear as we started our teasing, tasting kiss. One, the man tasted delicious, so good that someone should bottle this flavor, call it Taste of Hot Guy Number Five, and put it on the market for me and only me to buy. No one else deserved a single taste. Second, Dean knew what the hell he was doing. I wasn't going for some sweet, virginal press of lips when I got all close to him, but it was as if a switch got thrown and turned him into a pro. A pro who gave me a run for my money in keeping control of our kiss. It made it hard for me to mind, the way Dean's tongue tried its damnedest to lick my tonsils. My knees buckled, and I felt his arm move around the small of my back to hold me upright, close to his body, as our tongues brushed, bumped, and tangled together. Through the fabric of his jacket and shirt, I could feel his hard muscles, and the desire to touch them almost blazed out of control. I swore I heard a whimper in my own voice. How had this little seduction of mine turned into this kiss, this kiss that held so much heat and want and the promise of sweet satisfaction that I had to pull away, my lungs burning for air, my mind reeling out of orbit?

"Holy shit," I gasped. One kiss and I was whimpering like some kind of virgin. My fingers gripped the front of Dean's sports jacket like it was the only thing keeping me from slipping to the floor. When did I do that? It didn't matter, because I needed another taste. "Do that again."

"Yes, sir." His husky voice rasped against my cheek, and I shuddered again. Sweet Jesus, and he takes orders? Somebody pinch me. I mean, we both looked like we'd tear each other's clothes off any second. At that point, he could have picked me up, bent me over the bar, and had his way with me, and I would have completely thrown caution to the wind and let him have me. But I'd made a demand, and he'd complied. It was so un-alpha-male jack-off. Maybe I should stop expecting him to be anything but delicious and sleepy-eyed and kissable.

Our next kiss got interrupted by an exasperated and all too familiar voice. "Seriously, Jonathan?"

I didn't bother looking Rachel's way as my jaw tightened with annoyance. I was having a good time, and I didn't want to let it go this soon. Sadly, Dean broke our eye contact to glance over at her. I could hear the coins on her belt as she moved up to us and repeated. "Seriously?"

I knew it wasn't the fact that I was making out with someone while I waited. It wasn't even that it was a guy. It was because Dean didn't look like one of "our" people. His ears weren't pierced. I'd bet good money that he didn't have a single line of ink on his body. He looked "straight" in every way except sexually. Normal. Nice. Boring?

Not with kissing skills like that. Oh God, there was nothing boring about the past couple of minutes or hours or however long we stood near the bar making out.

"Rachel." I finally turned my head to look at her annoyed face. "This is Dean. He loved our show. Be nice."

Rach didn't seem remotely impressed by the new information and looked as if she'd smelled something awful. The death stare was so effective that I felt Dean's arms unwind from around my back. Fuck that. I wasn't going to move my hands at all, wanting to stay close and savor his heat. With Rach came the awareness that we would have to head out soon to the house and the party. I'd have to give up having him pressed against me, and that just made my entire body go into mourning.

She slipped on the same patient and fake smile we have when we deal with guests and fans, reaching into her purse. "Here, let me find you a flyer and you can see him on stage for our upcoming big show. I hate to sound rude, but tonight's show is over and we have to go, right, Jonathan?"

I quickly counted to ten in my head to hold back the urge to smack my best friend. "You'll have to pardon Rachel. She's strictly business when she's tired." I turned back to Dean, an idea popping into my head, crazy enough that it might work. "Say, you could come along with us. We throw a party at our place after these shows, hang out with a bunch of friends. It's a real laid-back sort of thing. Interested?"

"For fuck's sake, Jonathan, are you serious?" Rachel sputtered, thrusting a photocopied flyer in Dean's direction. I couldn't help but savor the annoyance in her voice. Let her not get her way just this once. That idea vanished as I felt Dean's heart race under my hand. He looked flushed for more reasons than our kiss, that jaw set extra tight as he stared not at Rachel or me, but down at our feet. Dean stood up a lot taller as she spoke, and I hoped we weren't scaring him away. I didn't like it one bit. Was it anger? Shame? I could understand anger. I was pissed at the interruption and Rachel's attitude. He was a potential ticket, and she was being bitchy.

I sighed. "Yeah, I'm perfectly serious, so chill. Go on and take the van. We'll follow. You want help taking the bags out?"

There, the gauntlet had been thrown. If Rachel left right now and Dean relaxed a little, then we could continue where we'd left off and take it wherever it was meant to go. At least that's what my fevered libido wanted.

Rachel thankfully relented with a snort and a frown and got the bags, leaving my duffel behind. "No, I'll take the fucking bags. Try not to get lost."

As she stalked out of the bar, I finally released Dean's lapels and looked up at him. Before I could even speak, he did, rubbing the back of his neck, looking utterly embarrassed. "Jonathan, I'm sorry I pissed your friend off."

I did a double take, and not just because my name on his lips sounded damned good. "What? Are you kidding? You don't have shit to apologize for. She was being... tired." I smiled, smoothing my hands over his chest. Those muscles were so firm that I wanted to lay my head on his chest and fall asleep and not think about spoiling Rachel's plans for our usual Friday night revelry. "And since my ride just left, I guess that means I'll have to ride with you, right?"

My plan was pure genius. Sure, the plan was me taking him to our hovel of a home and trying to get him onto my cramped little mattress for a screw. Okay, not the mattress, he wouldn't fit on that thing. Would he settle for a BJ in one of the bathrooms? Maybe this wasn't a good idea in the first place. Hot kisses or not, there was no way this guy, this fit, clean guy with the amazing mouth, would want to follow me to my bed. And then there's the issue of what Patch was going to do with himself while I was busy....

The look on his face before he spoke made it plain that the answer was going to be no, and I started mentally plotting bus routes to get me home. "Yeah, about that, I suck at crowds. I'm not a big partier, but I'll drive you back to your place."

"You know, you don't have to drink or anything there." I had to give at least a token attempt to insist, for my ego's sake. "You can just focus on me, promise."

"Just focus on you?" Dean asked, one russet eyebrow raised, and I could hear the stirrings of heat. "You seem very sure that's what I want."

"Oh, you don't want me?"

"I didn't say I don't want you...."

I didn't let him finish, aiming straight for that opening, pressing up close against his body and growling into his ear. "Good, because I don't bullshit, and you don't look like a bullshitter, Dean. I want you too, and unless you tell me no right now, I'm going to have you, even if

I have to pull you into the bathroom and ride you in the first stall we land in."

It was bold, going for broke. I knew I was approaching the point of being a pushy dick, but fuck, I wanted him too bad to give up. The longer we stood close and touched and breathed together, the more I didn't want to accept defeat in the Battle of Getting into Dean's Pressed Pants. I had to try.

Dean closed his eyes and exhaled deeply. "God, a ride sounds good."

Success! Sure, the managers would be incredibly pissed if we got caught, but I was too far gone to care. I tried to pull him away from the bar, but he stopped me with a hand on my arm.

"But not with an audience and not in a goddamned bathroom." Dean pulled me back to his chest and brought his mouth to my ear to whisper, "Come back to my place. I live a little ways out of Belle Point, but I promise I'll drive you home."

Home? He wanted to go to his place instead? Unease gnawed at the back of my mind. I couldn't remember the last time I went home with anyone. Was his place as neat as he was? And if it was, he had to be insane to want a scruffy, sweaty son of a bitch like me there.

At the same time, though, it sounded right. Felt right. I bet he had a bed that wasn't just a mattress on the floor, and it would be big enough for us to roll around. And if he didn't want me mucking up his sheets, I was sure we could make use of the rest of his place. If he had a home, he probably had a couch, walls, a shower. I'd started this little adventure, no time to chicken out of it now.

I brushed my nose against his cheek, followed by my lips as I moved to his ear, licking at the lobe. "Let's go. I hope your neighbors don't mind noise."

HAPTER THREE

# Una Noche

IT WAS when we got out of the city limits that I started to worry a little. He said he lived a ways off, but I still expected we would drive to a little apartment or even a condo. He looked like a condo sort of guy, wanting to own a home but not wanting to have to deal with a lawn. We were a little farther off than I'd thought, and every PSA about not going anywhere with strangers popped into mind. Was I going to be horribly murdered in this guy's wooded cabin?

I wish I could have said that it kept my hand off his thigh, but it didn't. I could take care of myself, carried a blade in my pocket. I quit smoking cigarettes two years ago, so my lungs were as awesome as they were going to be if I needed to run. Still, I looked out for landmarks in the headlights just in case.

"Sorry about the distance," Dean said, biting back another gasp as my fingers brushed against the sizable bulge in his pants. Shit, he felt huge, and I wanted it. I thought about getting my face down in his lap, but nothing screamed "death wish" like a crash on an unfamiliar shoulder while giving road head. So I would be a good boy and wait my turn.

I chuckled, keeping the nerves out of my voice, and grazed him again. "S'long as you keep this ready for me, it's all good."

The car slid a bit to the left, but Dean regained control quickly and sighed deeply. "I haven't done anything like this in a while."

That was enough for me to ease up on the foreplay, leaving my hand on his thigh. "Really, now?"

"Yeah." A hand touched mine briefly. "I hope I don't go off too early. It's been two years."

I choked on my next breath. Two years? In what universe is it possible for a man this achingly hot to go without ass for two goddamned years? Was he insane? Or was the gay male population of Belle Point and surrounding counties insane and/or blind? Well, I was full-on determined to make this little private show of ours worth the trouble. Even if it meant my grisly murder afterward.

I thought about sending Rach a text, let her know of my change of plans. Nah, she wasn't my mother, as much as she tried to take that role. Mama would have rooted me on, at least before the voice mail. If she hadn't taken a chance on a complete stranger in a bar, I wouldn't have been conceived.

We pulled into a long driveway that cut into more woods, dotted with those little solar-powered lights, and ended at this adorable little house on a huge patch of lawn. There was no other word I could think of to describe it. It was freaking adorable. Two-car garage on the bottom floor, one story on top. I guess that made it a two story or something, I don't know, but it was cute and compact and way too small for the land I could barely see in the dim lights and the man slowly pulling into the garage. He had to be earning some serious cash to afford a house like this on so much land with no lady friend or boyfriend around. I couldn't even see another house nearby. No one was going to hear me scream, from passion or gruesome murder. This both worried and turned me on, twisted fucker that I was.

One side of the garage was space for the car, and the other was a mini gym with some basic weight equipment, a treadmill, and a bench, not enough room for another car, so he could have been telling the truth about there not being another person living with him. I couldn't wait to see the fruits of his gym labor up close and personal, though. The moment the engine was silenced, I hopped out of the car, grabbing my drab-green duffel bag from the backseat.

Once I followed him up the stairs and into the house, I had to temporarily postpone my thoughts of ravishing this poor near virgin upon seeing the inside of his place. The concept of one person having all this space to himself was mind-boggling to someone like me. I didn't even get a bed to myself. There was so much room, from the open-space living area and kitchen with a breakfast bar separating them, both looking very much lived in and not ready for company, from the flashing timer on the coffeemaker to the dishes still in the sink, to the dark-green overstuffed plush couch in front of a wide screen TV to the DVD clamshells to the wine glass on the coffee table. The colors screamed warm and masculine, greens and reds and browns, from the big, thick curtains to the rugs on the dark hardwood floors. Farther beyond was a long hallway, and I stalked down it without asking permission.

"Sorry about the mess," Dean called behind me. "I wasn't expecting company."

The house still looked tidier than any house I'd seen since I was a kid. No holes in the wall, no unidentifiable stains on the carpet. The bathroom had a wet towel curled up on the floor near the tub, the only thing marring its neatness. I stopped myself before exploring the other doors, remembering some form of one-night-stand etiquette. It'd been so long, I couldn't remember how to act in someone else's home.

If we'd gone back to my house, I'd have had it all down. First, tell Patch so I didn't get an extra party involved, unless that was the first party's kink, then game on, we'd show him a hell of a time. Next, get something fermented in him, one drink, maybe two, enough to relax the inhibitions but not cause any problem with consent. Offer something more illegal, be gracious if refused. Dance around the drum circle with extra grinding until he was in a lusty haze, blow him wherever we ended up, then back up to my bed for more. Simple, but effective. Here, my game wasn't going to work.

"Are you sure you don't have a wife, husband, roommates, anything?" I returned to the kitchen area to drop my duffel next to the bar before nosing around in the cabinets. Each housed a bunch of funky gadgets that I had no idea what they were used for. He had to be some sort of executive pulling the serious figures if this was all his.

Dean had stayed leaning on the bar as I took my impromptu tour, graciously allowing this nosy slut to check his stuff out like some overexcited kid. He had his sports jacket off, hanging on one of the bar chairs, leaving only that dark button-down between my eyes and his chest. "Nope, it's only me. Would you care for something to drink? I don't have a lot to offer, wine and beer, but...."

"No thanks," I answered entirely too quickly. No more booze for me tonight. I wanted to be fully aware of what we were doing. Saying no still felt odd in my mouth. In the car, I'd talked up the Tribe and the craziness of our weekend parties, revealing enough to make it perfectly clear what my image was, the sort of guy I'm known to be, hard drinker, hard partier, shameless cocksman. Dean was so different from my usual that I needed to make sure he wasn't entertaining any crazy thoughts of more than what I was here for.

I breathed an inward sigh of relief when he didn't push the drink offer, and promptly regretted it as I looked around the house again. This nice, clean house made my skin itch. It was far nicer than anyone like me deserved. I wouldn't stay long. He'd promised me a ride home after I rocked his world, so all I needed to do was give him that tumble, be his walk on the wide side, and get gone to let him fumigate his sheets of "bad boy" and go on with his life. If I really wanted to make it final, I could use the address on the bills on the fridge to figure out where I was and walk home. I wouldn't inconvenience this guy.

My insides gnawed with a sudden attack of nerves, and it was time to get the show on the road before "nervous" became "uncomfortable" became "unable to get it up." Cocky smile in place, check. Saunter at the ready, check.

And, action.

I stopped right in front of him, my hips popping with every step, eyes narrowed like I'd just spotted prey. "Actually, big guy, I'm more interested in having some more of you."

His lips crashed into mine the second I tipped my head up, and the taste zinged through me once more, like a hit of a long-missed drug. It soothed a craving in me that I didn't know I had been carrying since we left Kouzina. That first kiss was no fluke, and my knees buckled again as I remembered the effect those kisses had, sending my control fleeing for the hills. Dean wrapped his arms around me again, and I could feel all of him, chest to hips to gloriously hard cock. A small part of me kept up the game, and I spiced up our grind by twisting my hips to and fro, a figure eight of motion perfected by years of dancing. The moan I swallowed was so deep, and pride amped up my desire. I did that. I made him make that sound. I was going to draw out more of those sounds and leave him a gasping mess on his bed before the night was over.

Dean's grip on my hips stopped my little dance, and it was my turn to moan when he pulled his lips back out of my range. "No audience here, remember?" He moved from my hips to my ass and squeezed it hard. His hands fit so perfectly there that I did stop and trembled slightly. "You don't have to show off for me."

He was insane. Had to be insane. Here he was, breaking a two-year sex fast, and he didn't want me to show him a good time? What the fuck did this guy want? My argument died on my lips the moment his found my neck and started to perform the same magic there that made my lips tingle.

"My bedroom's the last door on the left," he added with another generous squeeze on my ass.

Well, looked like he was getting straight to business, and I really liked him for it. I took his hand and started down that hallway, head full of steam, regaining control of this encounter. Now that he wasn't kissing me, I could think straight. Or start to. I couldn't afford to see too much in this guy's passion. It helped to refer to him as "this guy" in my head, not use his name too much. For all his assurances that I didn't need to show off, that bed was going to be my stage. He was getting my best, or my name wasn't Esteban Jonathan Mendoza.

Oh good, I could still remember my name after all.

"Last door on the left," Dean reminded me as I walked into the first open door I saw, another bedroom, and then put a hand on my back, his skin hot against the mesh. He touched me right through it, and that fiery caress damn near liquefied my legs again. It didn't even feel like I wore a shirt. I hurried down the hall and through the doorway before I gave up my control completely and leaned into his arms. Gotta keep my eyes on the prize, after all.

The master bedroom looked just as lived-in neat at the rest of the house, some clothes thrown about, dresser topped with knickknacks, and a closed closet door, but my attention zeroed in right on the bed. King sized, wrought iron posts for a headboard and footboard, light-tan sheets and pillow with a brown cover unmade in such a way that screamed only one person slept here. I threw myself at the mattress before I could stop myself.

Soft, so soft, this mattress didn't have a single lump to be found, and if my back could cry in joy, it would have, just lying on such a luxury. The sheets I rubbed myself against smelled like man and detergent. When the man in question didn't promptly follow my leap and bear down on my body, I felt extremely aware of what I was doing. I'd been dancing up a sweat over an hour ago, and there I was rolling around on these probably dry-cleaned sheets like a damned oversized, nasty, yet sexy as hell tomcat. Dean would have been well within his rights to toss my grungy ass right on out the front door.

"You look really good in my bed." His full mouth twisted into a big grin as he stepped out of his shoes and worked on the buttons of his shirt.

I should have called him out, reminded him of the rules of these sorts of encounters, and how silly saying shit like that, sweet, kinda possessive shit, was simply Not Allowed, but he opened that shirt and slid it down strong, rippling shoulders, and the words shriveled up and died in my throat. He'd obviously been working hard on that equipment in the garage to be so cut. Pale skin shone with the moonlight pouring out the window, stretched across perfectly defined pecs and a carved six-pack, dusted with a happy trail of light-red hair. It was enough to make any sane human forget who was trying to turn on whom here, because I felt like panting and begging just looking at his body.

It wasn't until I felt a hand on one of my still-booted feet that reality caught back up with me. I could speak and move again, flinching at the strong grip around the ankle. "Whoa, there, big guy, don't scuff the Docs."

I've had my black Doc Marten's since high school, and they've treated me wonderfully, fashionably scuffed, on their fifth set of laces, and these were tipped with little skull beads. My pride and fucking joy.

"Wouldn't dream of it." Dean gave another infectious grin and started unlacing. His delight made me want to ask if he had a thing about feet. I wouldn't have minded, God knows I've heard of weirder fetishes in my usual crowd, but every little bit of info about what made him hard would help me give him a good time.

"I can take off my own shoes, you know."

"Yes, but you'd have to get up to do it."

I couldn't imagine a rational argument to combat that logic. He wanted to help me get more naked, and I liked lying there and getting an eyeful. It was the perfect arrangement.

He carefully pulled the boot and sock free, and before the sock could hit the floor, Dean pressed his lips against the arch of my foot so reverently that I couldn't do anything but gasp. No one, and I mean no one, had ever so much as offered me a foot rub, never mind kiss the damned things as if it was some sort of honor. The effect blew what little of my mind I had left, and even more when he freed and kissed my other foot. By the time he set down both my legs to dangle over the edge of the bed and started to unzip my pants, I was more than ready. My dick was about to tear its way free of the dark denim if it stayed trapped any longer.

I lifted my hips to allow Dean to bare me, and then I pulled my shirt up, off, and then tossed it over Dean's shoulder in the general direction of where my other clothes were being tossed. Some sensible part of me considered this a good idea for when tomorrow rolled around and I needed to find my clothes. It would be incredibly rude to leave something behind, in case he had any regrets.

The look on Dean's face once I was completely naked, all hot and hungry, gave me back some of the power I had been losing in the face of his strange caring. I lifted my feet to the edge of the bed and spread my knees apart wide. There it was, all on display: my cock, long and lean and so hard that it bobbed like some obscene flagpole in barely discernible wind, my hole, puckering with every pulse of my heart, my entire body, ready to wrap around his and welcome him into me. It was everything I had to offer, everything of value, Dean's bad boy fuck toy for the night.

Yes, to the small voice in my head that sounded very much like Dr. Spaulding, saying shit like this in my head is self-defeating. Ask me if I care.

Dean raked his eyes over my body as if I were a buffet he couldn't believe he got to partake of. But there was a sweetness behind the heat that was odd. A lusty "want to grab my hair and pound me into the mattress" heated gaze was the appropriate response when Jonathan Mendoza got all naked and inviting, not the adoring stare thing he had going on. It was against the rules, Not Allowed. It was not how a one-night stand was supposed to be. I felt less like dinner and more like something I refused to acknowledge, because I really needed to get those thoughts out of my mind right the fuck now.

"Like what you see?" I teased, flexing my stomach muscles to make my dick jerk upward, right into my waiting hand. It had to be shyness that kept him off me. And the cure for shyness in this particular case was to ramp up the heat until he had to have me. I had to be careful with my strokes, keeping them slow and easy so I didn't shoot right then and there. Each slow stroke drew out drops of precome that pooled around my foreskin. That's right, Mr. Eye-fuck, look damned close at me, watch me bring myself off if that does it for you. I moved my hand faster, widened my legs, and lifted my hips with a deep groan as more wetness dripped down my hand, and I squeezed my eyes shut to try to hold it all back for a few seconds more. I couldn't remember the last time I even had the opportunity to jack off like this, slow and hungry with an appreciative audience.

The touch of a tongue on my balls made my eyes fly open in surprise. Dean was on his knees, mouthing and nuzzling and making me cry out. I let go of my dick, and he took over: licking until it gleamed, tracing the vein, tasting fresh drops directly from the slit, going back down to mouth my sac. His mouth was everywhere on me. My surprise grew at his skill: just like his kisses, perfect and breathtaking. Dean was an oral dream come true, and he worked my dick like it was the best thing he'd ever tasted. It only got better when the entire wet heat of Dean's mouth closed around me and he bobbed his head up and down, taking me down to the root, then back up until he trapped the head between those tight lips. His hands squeezed my hips, urging them up, urging me to fuck his mouth, and I happily obliged, crying out at the tight swallow of his mouth and throat. God, he took me down deep with practiced ease and barely a shudder.

I swore my heart stopped for a few beats, my mind racing, my body sweating all over again as I gripped those thick curls on his head and hung on for dear life. "When did you learn how to do... oh shit!"

It took a special mouth to take me in that deep, and this guy didn't seem the type. Not bragging, but I'm pretty damned hung. Not very thick, but long enough to give someone who tried to go deep a run for his money. Usually.

Another deep swallow stole my breath. One more made me go blind as I came, surging right into that amazing mouth. It was too fast, too soon, too much for me to take, and the thought of suddenly becoming a minute man, okay, a five-minute man, scared the shit out of me. If Dean could do that to me with just his mouth, what could he do with his cock? No doubt, I wanted him in me even more, but anxiety colored all the lust addling my brain and made me second-guess myself. I thought I'd brought my "A" game to this, but it wasn't sex as usual if this guy, practically a virgin as far as I was concerned, with his dry spell, was bringing me off like I was having my first BJ.

While I had this mini mental meltdown, Dean licked me clean, then licked me until I'd gone completely soft, then nuzzled my thighs, looking up at me. His gaze was worshipful, and I released his hair, loving the slide of his curls against my fingers. I couldn't help savoring that feeling, memorizing the feel of his eyes on me. I wanted that image in my mind forever, something to remember this man by. I swallowed back the sudden weird tightness in my throat to speak, but Dean beat me to it. "So, this is what you look like when you're not showing off. I think I like it."

His smile made my heart do that stupid leaping thing I was starting to hate. For the sake of my dignity, I needed to get this man into the same state he was trying to leave me in. It was a matter of personal honor, for fuck's sake. "Oh, man, you haven't seen me show off yet. Get up here."

Dean didn't argue as he stood up, removed his glasses, and worked on opening his belt buckle. He didn't move like a man in a hurry. *That's okay, pal, let's not wrinkle those nice pants or anything.* I hung on to that thought, let some contempt rise within me. Next morning I'd be leaving this clean, boring house with this clean, boring man who neatly placed his slacks over a nearby chair. A clean, boring man who sported a very unboring bulge in white boxer briefs, the front wet with proof of how badly he wanted me. There we go, Mr. Clean and Boring, you're just as normal and base and dirty as I am. Get on the bed and wallow in me.

I was done being polite. "I'm doing the honors." It was not a request, and I didn't wait for an answer as I grabbed his hips and hauled him closer, pinching his waistband between my fingers and yanking the underwear down. I was greeted by a cock as thick and cut as the rest of him, nestled into well-trimmed fuzz around the base. I should have known it would be gorgeous. Leaning forward, I pressed my nose against the hair and inhaled, my antagonism just fading away in the face of sweet sweat and musk and Dean. The plan was to prep him, get him on the bed, and go hog wild, but the urge to gorge myself on his length rose and twisted in my belly. I had to pick one. There was no way I was going to stay for a round three. He was going to give me everything his balls had one way or the other.

I used my tongue to distract myself, licking the tender skin that connected Dean's hip to his body, adding that taste to my little list of things about this man that rocked my world. His navel and the happy trail beneath it got added to the list soon after that, as was the feel of his bare ass in my hands and the deep groans I could not only hear but feel from this close.

He was busy above me, leaning over to the side, straightening, and then dropping some things next to my thigh. I tore my eyes away from mapping his entire pelvis to see an unopened box of condoms and a half-full pump bottle of lube that I instantly recognized as some high-end brand. Figures the son of a bitch even jacked off in comfort. Yeah, bring back that resentment, Jonathan, keep the edge. I needed to remember I was just a quick little snack to tide him over on his search for the perfectly compatible boyfriend that met his high standards. His standards had to be damned high if it had been this long since he'd been laid, and that still didn't explain why he was slumming with me.

"I'm still prepping you." I looked up at him, only meeting his eyes for a second so I didn't forget myself before I gave the cut mushroom head still jutting out in front of me a lick, getting a little taste and moaning at the bitter flavor on my tongue. He had no right to taste this good.

He had no right to cup my cheek and run his thumb over my lips either. Or to say, "God, you're beautiful."

I started a chant in my head then, "Don't pay attention, don't listen, this was just a fuck," as I brushed my lips against that palm, then nudged it out of my way before he could touch me again. I quickly broke the seal of the box, nimbly grabbed a foil packet, and stuck it between my lips to hold it so I could get some lube on my hands. I anointed the silky skin and drank in his low moans. His hands closed on my shoulders, tight, but not enough to bruise me, and they felt like blessings once I got that packet opened and drew the latex over him. It didn't matter anymore that he was breaking the pickup rules by being nice. We were so close to what we both needed.

I backed away toward the head of the bed once he was good and ready, getting some distance so I could remind myself that the niceness didn't matter. He didn't spare a second this time, climbing right behind me with the ferocity of a bull charging a matador. Yes, I had finally been triumphant in getting this guy too worked up. Now he was going to pin me and spread me and screw me silly....

Or cover me with his big, strong body and slam me with one of those maddeningly heartfelt kisses that made my entire body tremble. I didn't have time to even think about it before I was surrounded by all that wonderful power, exchanging moans and meeting every thrust he rocked into me. His latex-covered cock rubbed between my own and the crease of my thigh, slick and hot. His hands moved everywhere: gliding over my flanks, my hips and thighs, taking handfuls of my hair and gripping hard at the back of my neck to keep my face against his. My hands flailed for seconds before finding his broad shoulders to hang on to. Dean was both the cause of my spiral out into space and the only solid thing that existed that I could hold on to at the same time.

Before I could see if it were possible to telepathically move something of his—his fingers, his cock, his tongue, his elbow, anything—inside of me, Dean had one finger, slick with that very fine lube, pressing against my entrance. He held me close with his free arm curled around my shoulders, peppering my face and neck with kisses.

"God, yes," I hissed and pushed back against that finger. "More!"

He obeyed immediately, pulling out from that tentative press, and brought two fingers back to push past my tight ring of resistance. I wanted to tell him it wasn't my first rodeo, that I didn't need that much prep. Hell, I'd been fucked last night. I wanted to say something, but between his strokes, finding and grazing against my sweet spot until I saw stars, and the gentle embrace, I was well on the way to losing my mind. I stopped hating him immediately for every slight my mind had tried to cook up.

I freed an arm and gave his shoulder a hard push. "Fuck me from behind," I moaned, kissing him hard and quick before rolling out of his grasp onto my stomach.

My answer was another hissed "yes" that made my spine tingle, and he covered me once again before I could get up on my hands and knees properly. I wanted to complain, to tell him to wait until I was up and could give him something to bang against, but I felt Dean's blunt fingers part my cheeks, felt the invasion of something way thicker and more amazing than fingers, and the need won. He sank inside and I welcomed it. His size brought me to the edge of pain, even with the lube and the prep. Good. I needed those jolts to focus. This position would have to do. At least I couldn't see his face as he slid me past discomfort and right into ecstasy.

His face? Fuck, it was better that he couldn't see mine. I couldn't control anything anymore. It all shattered the second he was fully seated inside me. He paused then, letting me feel the pulse of his cock, his heartbeat against my back, competing with the crazy dance mine was doing in my chest for speed, panic making it slam harder against my ribs. I hoped facing the heavenly pillows would quell the weird sensations I was having. If the bastard would let me up until only our lower halves touched, his cock in my ass, hands on my hips or in my hair, achieving minimal physical contact, I could get my hips into the game, just like earlier, shimmying as we slammed together until he lost his mind. Dean had a decidedly different concept of doggy style, lying completely on me, our legs entwined, keeping me trapped between his bent arms.

"Move!" I yelled, bucking uselessly against him and earning a deep, rumbly chuckle as he finally started thrusting. I could breathe again, but only to gasp and yell louder with every single steady shove as he proceeded to fuck me until I didn't care about anything anymore. Dean was right; there was no audience. I didn't have to show off. There was no one to judge or perform for. I could lie here, under this man, and let him have whatever he wanted. I'd been fighting it all night, and if I kept on, I would miss out on everything he gave me. Every slide of his sweaty skin against mine, each press of his lips on my shoulder and neck, every nuzzle into my hair, the gasps and groans filling my ears, I would miss out on enjoying all of this. I managed to find a rocking rhythm to meet him, and the sounds of our flesh smacking together added to the sexy soundtrack we created between my cries and his moans and our pants. I heard him whisper my name, and while I've had my name whispered, grunted, groaned, and screamed more times that I cared to count, the way Dean said it, with that same reverence he'd been bestowing on me, made me want so much more. No one had ever made me feel like this in bed before.

"You feel so good," I felt more than heard him say against my shoulder.

"Dean!" His name was a plea, and I couldn't say anything more than that. I didn't want it to end, wanted him to stay inside me until we collapsed, until the world stopped, until what made us different didn't matter. I couldn't find the words to beg for that.

I got even louder in my appreciation when Dean suddenly shifted, sliding his legs under mine. With one meaty arm wrapped tight over my chest, he smoothly pulled us up until I sat on his lap, leaving me impaled, with his weapon of choice striking me just where I'd needed it. I was going to pass out. I knew it. I would pass out before either one of us came. This was too damned much. We had as much flesh touching as when we were lying down, his arm holding me tight, free hand gripping and stroking my dick fast and hard. My hands tried to go for the headboard, but it was out of range from our firm embrace, so I sank one hand into his hair, the other tight on his shoulder. From there, I could move, twisting and swaying my hips between the buried cock and generous fist, give him as good a ride as he was giving me.

Being free to sway while being fucked mattered a lot less to me than it would have minutes ago, though his moans told me he appreciated the effort. I turned my mouth against his neck and bit down, getting a broken grunt that pleased me even more. I wanted to show him a good time, but it was getting very clear that his good time involved making me crazy. One insane Jonathan coming up... and coming quickly.

My cock pulsed in his hand as I spilled, bucking like a barely contained mechanical bull. I could feel him inside as I squeezed him hard enough for him to stop moving, stock still, his dick pulsing inside me. "Oh God, Jonathan!"

Oh yeah, my name sounded best when he came. I whimpered again as the thought of how he would feel flooding me and not the condom passed through my mind. That would have been hot, so hot, and we shuddered together, clinging tightly, waiting for those ripples to subside.

Slowly, carefully, I pulled away, freeing his spent cock, and then fell on my side on the mattress. He followed right behind me, arms around me, holding me close, and gasped, "Winton."

"What?" My eyes narrowed in confusion, not sure what that even meant, or if I had heard him correctly.

"My last name." I felt him pull away for a moment, heard the gooey slide of a spent condom being pulled off and tossed away, and felt him return to my back before I could even miss him. "It's Winton."

"Oh." Interesting pillow talk he had going on. Both our brains had to be out to postorgasmic lunch, because that sounded perfectly sweet. Winton was such a fancy name, made me think of manor houses and shit. Oh well, it wasn't as if we would ever see each other again anyway. "Mendoza. E. Jonathan Mendoza."

"E?"

My mouth kept moving even as my brain wondered why the fuck I gave him even that much personal information. "Esteban. Mom's side of the family hails from Guadalajara."

"Pleased to meet you." A chuckle blew across my neck, and the arm around me flexed, hand on my belly stroking at the mess I'd made. "I hope you're not in a hurry to get back to your place. I'm not even sure if I can see straight right now."

"That's because your glasses are on the table." Check me out, having enough brain to make a funny. "Take your time, I'm pretty.... I'm pretty cozy right here." Cozy was the best way to describe this entire thing. Cozy, thy name was Dean Winton.

Dean's arm flexed once again, and I swore he was lightly kissing my neck. Figures he'd be a cuddler. I couldn't conjure up enough annoyance at the strange post-sex behavior because damn, it had been too long. I had to get my bearings and quickly, and think of some way to politely extract myself from "cozy" before I did something stupid. Like beg to stay in this bed like this, comfy and sex-sticky and satisfied, forever. But I was too damned tired, between the dancing and the fucking and how good Dean felt surrounding me.

I would think of something after a little nap. Not even forty winks. Just twenty. Maybe ten....

"AND then you crept out the next morning."

"And then I crept out the next morning."

I leaned back on the couch, looking at my lap, fingers busy with pliers, turning a cloth bag of stainless steel loops into a chain four rings thick. Keeping my fingers busy made it easier to talk about feelings and shit. And I got some satisfaction out of getting something tangible done in relative peace.

Dr. Spaulding reminded me of Mama most times, carrying that vibe that screamed "You will tell me anything. Resistance is futile." She was warm, with a smile on a slightly wrinkled face, long blonde hair kept in a ponytail at her neck, all sweetness and light until I attempted to bullshit. Good thing she was female. I was less likely to make myself look appealing and fuckable during our twice-monthly forays into my issues.

Her office had little homemade accents, a knitted blanket folded over the couch, funky sculptures on her desk, hand-beaded necklaces around her neck. I owed her a chain-mail tunic, one made for some kind of live-action role-playing thing she did on the weekends, in return for listening to me ramble on, but I couldn't work on her tunic while looking at her. The chain I was working on was a belt for myself, and I didn't have a lot of time to get it finished before the upcoming show.

After I got that voice mail from Mama, I only told Rachel, and then I spent about two months constantly fucked up, drunk, high, or in some combination of all three, incapable of dealing with reality for a little while. I couldn't believe that Ms. Carmen Mendoza, a regular Wonder Woman and the most chill parent in all of existence, could be ill or ever leave me. Given what I did for fun, I all but assumed she'd be burying me first.

But after those months and another phone call to Mama that I only remembered because it was full of equal parts weeping and screaming from both sides, I started to try to slow down the boozing and drugs and the random fucking. I didn't bother telling Rachel or anyone else about my little attempt at a lifestyle change to something a lot more lucid, because I didn't want to harsh their grooves, and besides, who the fuck would believe me? I'd nurse one drink, pass the bong or cig, dance myself to exhaustion so I could claim being too tired to sit and indulge. One time, out of sheer desperation, I took a few tabs of acid, then pretended to be sick so I could run to the bathroom, shut the door, and nearly shove my entire hand down my throat to make myself puke to get it all out of my stomach before the walls started melting.

I relapsed and overdid it over and over again before we moved to Belle Point, and once we got a regular gig and a reason to stay for a while, I secretly searched for outside help. Dr. Spaulding was the first who was willing to barter. Who knew there was so much crap behind my need to check out from reality so often? The woman was clearly determined to unearth it all, whether I liked it or not. I was getting better. I didn't even list "meaningless sex" as a vice anymore, now that I only fucked Patch. Was only fucking Patch until a few nights ago. Now I had this other problem.

"But he offered you a ride home." She cocked her head in that way I'd learned meant I'd done or said something she couldn't quite understand. "Are you sure he didn't do anything to you I should know about?"

I looked up from my work and lifted a shoulder. "I was completely consenting, and he didn't hurt me. It was just strange, okay? Guy had no clue how to treat a one-nighter."

"Jonathan, you're going to have to give me a bit more context here." She stood up from behind her desk and moved around to lean against it, closer to me. It was the rules of how these encounters worked—when she got up, it was time for me to get real.

I felt like I was trying to explain some weird foreign culture to her, so I looked up from my work to focus. "Look, some assholes think because you're not going to call them back, they can treat you any way they want. It wasn't like that at all. You can be nice without being... nice."

"And this guy was 'nice'?" Oh God, she even did the air quotes with her fingers.

"You don't treat a lay the way he treated me, okay? I mean, damn, Doc, I kept getting thrown. Mentally, not physically," I added quickly as she looked at me with alarm. "Every time I thought I had the upper hand, he pulled some 'nice' shit, and I got all confused again. It scared the shit out of me."

A smile crossed her lips, and she nodded slowly. "And so you fled the first moment you could."

"Man sleeps like a rock," I snorted, remembering the morning after.

It almost physically hurt, wiggling out from under his arm and out of those covers. He must have thrown them over us when I passed out, another "nice" thing to do that made me want to burrow in closer. Which is why I had to go.

Walking through the house in the dull gray of the early morning, earlier than I've ever been up unless I didn't bother sleeping, I got to see how much of a "home" it was. Pictures on the hallway walls of people being all family-like with Dean in various stages of life. There was one rather appealing one of him in a rugby uniform, holding that weird white football thing they use. I'd expected he'd gotten that body from all that working out, another surprise for me. No other kids in the photos, only child?

Just as I hoped, the bills on the fridge confirmed his name and, most importantly, address. That helped me figure out where I was and how I was getting home. The walk back into town took me two hours, and I hopped a bus the moment I found a stop and navigated my way to a house that was still mostly asleep. Must have been an awesomely hard party.

Dr. Spaulding was quiet a moment, then cocked her head again. "Define 'nice shit'?"

"He kissed me."

"You're not a prostitute, Jonathan. I'm sure kissing is allowed in a one-night stand."

I shook my head. "No, no, it wasn't that he did, it was how he did it." I closed my eyes, and the memory of those toe-curlingly thorough kisses made my entire body feel warm. "You kiss a lover the way he kissed me, okay? He was doing it all wrong."

"All wrong?" She straightened and picked up the notebook she used during our sessions, scanning her notes. "Let's see, he refused to have sex with you in a restaurant bathroom, offered you his bed with the promise to drive you home, respected your decision not to drink once you got there—I'm proud of you for that, by the way—kissed you 'like a lover', and you enjoyed it. What was wrong with being treated with a little respect?"

"The hell are you going on about?" I glared up at her, feeling the usual anger that welled up whenever we even approached the very word "respect." Time to tamp down that conversation before we had it yet again. "I'm respected in the Tribe. I helped *found* the damned thing, so fucking spare me the 'respect' speech today, all right?"

She stayed calm as usual, flipping through her notebook. My name and patient ID were written on the front cover, and within were all the notes she had taken the entire time I'd been seeing her. I knew what was coming and braced myself, looking back down and resuming my work on the chain belt.

"When was the last time you got completely wasted?"

"Two weeks ago."

"The circumstances?"

"It was a party. You drink at a party." My fingers moved faster, and I feared I was going to drop the work. I remembered two weeks ago too clearly.

She stopped at a page and read, "Patient expressed concern with previous weekend's excesses, states he was 'overwhelmed' and 'people kept shoving drinks at me'. Last time you took an illegal substance?"

Technically, it had been the Valium Patch gave me to sleep, but I hadn't mentioned it to her this session, so it wouldn't be in her little book of truths from my own mouth. "Last month, when we hotboxed in Thor. I wanted to get out and dance a bit, but Rach gave me The Look, so I stayed." My gaze returned to my lap. "Some dude offered coke, and I refused, because that shit will mess you up if you get hooked. I got The Look again, and up my nose it went. But only one line." That line had been enough to satisfy Rachel's expectations and not kill the vibe in the van.

She flipped to the appropriate page and nodded. "You can't get clean if saying 'no' has no meaning to those around you, Jonathan. Have you even told any of your friends what you're doing here yet?"

I had to laugh. She really didn't get it. It was a sellout thing to do, wanting a clear head, to no longer see the appeal of a life lived between dance and dazed. To not make my mother disappointed now that she had bigger things to worry about. None of them would get it. Rachel would have a fit about me even going outside of the Tribe to seek help for anything. Even if I told her I was doing it for Mama, she would be so hurt, and that was one more person on my conscience I didn't need. It was easier to scurry to Spauldy's office in secret and make it look like I was wandering around town, taking advantage of what little freedom I had being Rach's best friend.

"Perhaps what is weirding you out about this guy is that, for someone you'd only known for a few hours, he showed you more regard and care than the group you've been running for... how long again?"

"Nearly ten years," I answered numbly. We'd gone through this over and over again, and I clung to the thought that I could handle being around this group as if nothing were different and not lose myself in the excesses anymore. The strain and discontent that kept me up nights would pass, I knew it. I hoped, anyway.

She put the notebook away and walked around to the desk, signaling the end of my hour. "Are you going to see this guy again?"

"Nope, I didn't leave a number, and I only have a name. It's better this way, less complicated. No way he'd want another go."

I ducked around her disapproving look to slip the pliers into the repurposed Crown Royal bag that held hundreds of steel rings and opened my duffel to tuck it back in. It was something else we warred with, my inability to agree with her that I had poor self-image issues or anxiety about anything. Yeah, a guy that shakes his ass on stage once a week or more while wearing enough flash to make a cameraman jealous having a low opinion of himself? Who'd'a thunk it? I wasn't in the mood to talk about it now. It made me feel too raw to drop the bravado.

"See you next time, Spauldy." I turned on the charm with a big smile that wasn't returned. Oh well, we'd hash things out next time.

Now I had to get home before anyone wondered too much about where I wandered.

The bus had just pulled up to the stop in front of her office when I dashed out, giving me barely enough time to fumble in my wallet for the two bucks to get me across town. It was the middle of the day, plenty of space for me to take up two seats for me and the bag, and I took the one next to the window. The trip wouldn't take long, no need to whip out the rings, so I leaned my head against the cool glass and settled in for what was becoming a weird new hobby of mine, thinking about Dean.

I didn't even give his name to Spauldy. Once people started waking up after I got back from our night together, Patch was the only Tribe person who even smiled at me and wanted juicy details: looks, size, and stamina. I'm comfortable with that kind of talk; it was easy and expected. Rachel gave me more of those looks, disapproval and disappointment, and didn't talk to me the entire day until I apologized for "worrying" her. Like everywhere else, there were rules here too, and I had broken a big one, making my bestie upset on purpose.

As the bus pulled away, I glanced over at the familiar little office that was probably once a single-family abode, and I did a double take. A familiar figure walked down the street, toward the office, up the stairs, and through the door. Very familiar, tall and broad, with red hair and thick-framed glasses. Shit. As the bus pulled away from the curb, I pressed myself tighter against the glass to get a closer look, heart twisting in recognition and worry. Jesus, I knew Dr. Spaulding saw other clients, clients who paid with actual money instead of little trinkets, but how had I never caught a glimpse of Dean before now? More importantly, what the hell did Mr. Perfect have to speak to a shrink about? Guys like him aren't allowed to have problems. Life was good if you had a house and a car and a steady job to afford both, or if you were big enough to pound whatever was troubling you into mush. I tried to conjure up some annoyance, some indignation from seeing the man with his unknown shrink-worthy flaws, but just like all my attempts the night we met and fucked, they crumbled under the weight of curiosity and... concern?

CHAPTER FOUR

# *Chained*

THE mini show at Kouzina went off well as usual, despite my deep, deep annoyance. I was missing a bracelet, one of my own design, another chain-mail work made from brown steel accented with bronze. Bronze rings cost more. It had been a little treat for me to use a few rings left over from making some lady an honest-to-goodness chain-mail bikini top.

And it was gone, right out of my bag. Had been gone all week. I was sure some son of a bitch managed to get into my duffel and take it while I was taking a piss or a shower or something. It was one of my greatest worries with living with so many people—someone making off with any of my stuff.

"One scotch and soda. Do you ever drink anything else?"

I turned to Mike and took the drink, rolling my eyes and stuffing my irritation back deep in my gut. Wasn't his fault I would have to carry my duffel in the bathroom now to avoid any more fucking thieves. "I wouldn't want to confuse you with anything more complicated."

Mike tossed an ice cube at me with a snort. "Asshole."

I could have told the truth, that it was fancier than any of the stuff I could drink at home, but it was more amusing to be an asshole. Once he made his way out of striking range, I went back to thinking of horrible fates for the son or daughter of a bitch now wearing my bracelet—may they have a serious allergic reaction and the metals turn their fucking wrist green until their hand falls off. It kept my mind off of watching the lobby like an idiot.

I wasn't looking for the ladies to come back inside after flyer duty. No, and I had to be honest here, I was looking at the groups of people milling in and out on the off chance that I'd catch a glimpse of you know who.

I hadn't been able to shake my curiosity since seeing him enter Dr. Spaulding's office. I wouldn't be speaking to her for another two weeks, and even then I couldn't very well ask the woman to spill about someone else's damage, but it didn't stop me from wondering. If anything, it somehow made him even more appealing to know he was a little bit fucked up too. Or maybe a lot more fucked up. Although I did manage to survive the night without grievous stab wounds or being tied up in a basement like some horror movie victim, so he couldn't be that much of a head case.

I kicked myself for not staying the entire night now. I knew he would have made good on driving me back into town the next morning. If I were really lucky, I could have convinced him that another round would have been a great idea. Yep, that was the entire reason I wanted to stay. It had nothing to do with how it all made me feel, how Dean made me feel.

Good Lord, let's get home and drunk soon. Sorry, Spauldy and Mama, but nothing short of getting completely blitzed and then blown was going to get Dean out of my mind completely.

The dancers from Caress walked past me on their way out for the evening, and we exchanged polite waves and smiles. I rather liked the name of their troupe. Next town, we should steal it, become Crimson Caress Tribal instead of Crimson Dream Tribal. Oh, the eye rolls that suggestion would earn me. Would be worth a laugh. I invited them to one of our after-parties the first week we started dancing with them, and earned more than an eye roll from my cofounder. One could never know what to expect from a "norm," a "mundane," or whatever we were calling non-Tribe folk this week, she reminded me once we were out of earshot. I gave her credit for at least waiting until they couldn't hear us first.

The lady in question and the rest of our crew were done and at the bar by the time I polished off S and S number two. Rachel's dark eyes were already heavy-lidded and bloodshot. Looks like someone remembered her after-dance flask this week.

"Jonathan!" she called out cheerfully, arms around my waist and giving me a squeeze. The smell of brandy on her breath, someone's home brew, confirmed the whole flask thing. It made all the smiling while passing the flyers out bearable, she told me once. "It's so good to see you alone this time."

I didn't rise to the bait, kissing the top of her pigtailed head, and left the glass on the bar to gather my bag. "Let's ride, ladies."

"Why do you even bother with the bar booze when we've got shit at home to drink?" She let me go to do the same.

I threw my arm around her shoulders as we walked out of the bar. "The ones here are both good and free, and we can't afford decent scotch, and if we did, some pig-fucker would down it before I could enjoy it." I could almost taste the bitterness behind my own cheerful tone, visions of the bracelet thief's hands falling off, both of them, just for extra malice, bouncing in my brain.

"You could always stash it somewhere that isn't in the kitchen."

"The only safe place to stash anything in that house is up my own ass."

She rolled her eyes and snorted. "Oh please, everyone knows your ass is the last place anyone could call safe."

"Yeah, but only Jonathan could fit a bottle of booze up there," Tam piped up behind us. Even I joined in the fit of laughter. Being the literal butt of any and all anal sex jokes was par for the course.

I could give as good as I got, though. "Whatever, you *putas* are all just jealous that I'd be able to hold a bottle up my happy place without it falling out."

"Better hope Patch isn't into scotch," Rachel jeered, "or that Boy Scout of yours. You'd be shit out of luck."

And it was my turn to roll my eyes. While she wasn't speaking to me, she had been speaking to anyone who would listen about how I was unfaithful to Patch by having slept with a "boring, overgrown Boy Scout." For the life of me, I couldn't see where she even got the comparison from. He was too good in bed to be morally straight, or whatever was in that chant those tiny fascists had to recite. "Jeez, Rachel, give it a rest. He wasn't that bad."

On the contrary, he was very, very, oh so very good.

"Bad enough that you stayed out all night instead of being with us." We stood outside the restaurant now, and Rachel was looking up at me in concern. "You know I worry when you're not around. You're too cute to go out by yourself at night."

Which was why we tended to leave the house in groups of varying sizes after dark. We refused the gig here at Kouzina unless all four of the dancers could perform at the same time on the same nights. It was nice for protection's sake, but it got damned stifling at times. I was the outlier, "allowed" to wander occasionally during the day because she trusted me to come back and to not screw the Tribe over. Rachel never got in my face about it, as she would with anyone else under our command. I worried, sometimes, that all this group togetherness made us all more insular. I know I needed air from time to time, but Rachel seemed to crave the family-like closeness. It made up for what she didn't have growing up. I knew that from years and years of many drunk and stoned confessions. The Tribe was her family.

I adjusted the duffel strap and moved toward the van. "You worry about me with a 'Boy Scout'?"

She stood in front of me, looking down her nose in that lovely expression that insisted that she was right and I was dumb. Given she was five inches shorter than me, it was always amazing when she managed it perfectly. "He reminds me of Patrick Bateman. You know, kinda twitchy and straitlaced, this close to flipping out and throwing a chainsaw at you."

Anyone with fewer than two piercings was considered "straitlaced" in her eyes. We'd had that conversation constantly over the time we'd known each other, and I'd be damned if I was going to have it again with her. "Okay, I'm kicking the ass of whoever brought *American Psycho* in the house. It's got you all paranoid. Let's go, party's a-waiting."

Cindy pointed one skinny arm behind me. "Um, Rach, Jonathan? Do we know that guy? 'Cause he's coming this way."

Fuck me. My eyes had to be playing tricks. Dean walked from the other side of the parking lot, eyes set on me, face pensive, nervous, one hand in the pocket of the same suit jacket he'd worn last week. Screw talks about Boy Scouts and compatibility and wondering why he was seeing Spauldy. All I wanted to do now was tackle him for one of those kisses again. The desire was so strong that my palms itched with the wanting.

"Oh, no, we are not doing this shit again," Rachel snarled and moved to stand in front of me with her arms crossed over her ample chest, like my little gothy guardian that I sure as hell didn't want right now. "He's some kind of stalker. I knew it." She called to Dean in her best dominatrix impression: "We're taking him home."

Dean stopped short, just long enough to move out of the way of a car leaving the lot and onto the sidewalk that ran in front of Kouzina. Few could resist the domme voice. Smart man. She's been known to bite, and we've joked about getting her a rabies vaccine in the past. He raised one hand in some gesture of peace and pulled the other one out of his pocket, holding a folded white envelope. "It'll only be a second, I promise. I just wanted to return this to Jonathan."

The way Dean said my name made me so stupidly happy inside. It sounded like a wonderful multisyllabic purr that made my lips curl into a smile. That smile got bigger when he opened the envelope and pulled out a few inches of very familiar chain. Worries about his mental state quickly forgotten, I walked around Rachel and toward him. "Holy shit, I've been looking all over for that!"

Bless my own sloppiness, for it brought him this close again. Our fingers touched when Dean handed me the envelope, adding a little extra zing to my joy. I glanced up at him, reading the satisfaction in his eyes. He didn't look hurt or upset about my disappearing act last week. "Nice frames. I think I liked the thick ones better."

Points to me, I got his cheeks to burn a little. It was strange, but I loved it all the same.

"Thanks, I've got a few pairs to switch around. This bracelet was on the kitchen floor. Beautiful work."

"It should be. I made it." Pride welled up, mixing with all the crazy mishmash of emotions in my gut. I looked back down at the opened envelope and got a third surprise: a phone number written on the top flap.

"Jonathan, we're leaving," Rachel singsonged from behind with barely restrained annoyance. "You've got five minutes before I drag you to the van by your dick."

Ever classy, that girl. I glanced over my shoulder to see them walk off for a moment. "She really isn't this bad, normally...."

"She's tired, then?" The curl of his lips made me want to kiss him. Again. More. "I've only seen chain like this on bras in fantasy comics. Didn't know you could make jewelry with it."

"I've made those too, on commission. Usually I do more delicate stuff for ladies, but for the stuff I wear, like this, I like things a bit thicker, tougher...." My mouth went dry as I looked Dean up and down, thinking of what parts of him were thick and tough. "Surprised you came out of your way to give it back, really."

Dean flushed even harder and looked away, his smile shy. "It was this or try to get it to you at your show next week. I thought you might want it sooner than that, and yeah, I hoped that I'd see you."

He was cute all flustered like that, but I wanted his eyes on me again, showing me the passion behind this bashful demeanor. If I only had a few minutes right now to just be near him, I wanted some new memory to take with me.

The touch of his lips on mine would do nicely for now. Funny how I was so happy to see him again, face to face, that all thoughts of conjuring up resentment to temper my need flew right out of the window. I stepped forward and briefly kissed him, getting his attention back where it belonged. "So you're still coming to the show?"

"Yeah, but I wasn't sure if you wanted me to be there after last week. You left without a word. Lucky you left that behind."

I could hear the hint of being rejected in his voice, and I wanted to kiss him harder and make it all go away. It wasn't him, I wanted to say, it was completely me. "I guess we both got lucky, then."

A loud car horn made us both jump, and I knew that particular noise well. Sounded like Rachel was reaching a new level of bitchy for the night if she leaned on Thor's horn that hard. I gave Dean an apologetic smile and glanced back into the envelope again. What was the fastest way to show him that there were no hard feelings, that I wanted to see him again? I could have told him, but I'm more of a "show" guy.

The idea popped up so fast that I was already taking the bracelet out of the folded envelope and tucking the paper in my jeans pocket before I could fully form the plan in my head. "Do you trust me, Dean?"

His eyebrow arched up over his frames, but he nodded, and I didn't allow him to say anything more, taking his arm with both hands and his lips with my own at the same time. I felt his gasp against my mouth. Then his tongue met mine as I secured the bracelet around his wrist, then brought my hands back to his thick hair, pressing him closer, quietly demanding that wicked SuperKiss that I knew Dean had in him. He eagerly obliged, and I was instantly transported back a week ago, back to his house, his hands on my bare skin, kissing me just like this. And then he drew it out like a slow burn, not a kiss fuck buddies were supposed to get. It promised so much more than another good roll in the hay, but I craved it. I melted at the impossible prospect.

We parted with reluctance, and I licked Dean's lips playfully. "I better get going before she makes good on her threat." And with the semi-boner I sported, she would have something solid to drag me with. I placed my hand over the metal now surrounding his wrist. "You're borrowing this until you see me at the show."

"What if I decide to keep it to remember you by?" His voice was all raspy and deep.

"You're too good to steal, big guy, and you gave me your number." I patted my hip pocket. "I'm gonna use it, so don't worry."

"And your friend? She doesn't seem to like me much."

"What about her? She's my friend, not my owner."

Another loud blast from the van made a liar out of me, and we had to chuckle at the irony. Man, of all the places I'd rather be, it wasn't in that van at all. "Take care of it. It's a unique work of art."

Dean pushed his glasses up his nose and grinned. "So's the man that made it."

I knew he watched me walk away, and if it wasn't for the large duffel covering up the view of my ass, I would have put an extra strut in my step. Standing ovations may make me feel like King Fuck of Awesome Mountain, but what Dean had said was the ego-boosting cherry on top.

Rachel glowered at me from the front window, and that gaze was only broken once I swung into the backseat. "Jesus Christ, is 'boring-looking straitlaced roider' some sort of new fetish of yours?"

That wasn't going to ruin my mood in the least. "Yep, and you have to respect my kink, no matter how weird you find it."

"Oh please," she grumbled, taking a swig out of her skull-emblazoned hip flask as Tam got the rust bucket on the road. "Doesn't mean I have to like it. You're just doing this to annoy me, aren't you?"

I leaned back in the seat to unlace my boots, and keeping my tone joking and light, as if we were simply teasing each other, was a struggle. "If I wanted my sex life to have anything to do with you, Rach, I'd be straight."

"Eww, not even if you were the last man alive."

"Likewise," I grumbled right back, and I said no more as we drove past Dean heading for his car. The sight made me want to step out of the van and beg to go with him. Longing? No, it had to be lust and the appeal of something new. I wanted to lick him all over, not lie with him wrapped around me like we did last week, no matter how good it felt to think about doing both. That was it. Only lust.


OUR current home base, that we simply called The House, was already hopping by the time the van pulled to the side of the road. It was an old duplex, the largest house in the entire crappy neighborhood. Signs of wear and tear were obvious in the peeling paint, rusty rain gutters, and plastic sheeting over some of the second floor windows. A good strong breeze could have knocked it over. We were renting it super cheap for a reason.

It was a perfect place for us to settle in for a few months, or even up to a year, before trouble between local cliques or other dramas compelled us to load up Thor and our smaller station wagon we called Loki and move on to the next town that would take us. It got harder as the years passed, harder still thanks to the Internet and all the potential for gossip, so we've been holing up in places longer and traveling farther out to find new places to settle. Hell, we'd been in this town for six months, and that was long for us.

The sounds of the indoor drum circle greeted my ears once we ambled inside. All sorts of people milled around the house, performers who already lived and performed with us, some locals, whoever they invited along and more, dancing around the drummers in the living room, toting plastic cups of whatever alcohol someone brought along, either store-bought or home brewed. There was some sort of strange symbiotic relationship between tribal/spinner/burner types and home-brewed booze.

Most of the folks attending were locals, drawn to our group through the performances and mutual interest in dance, juggling, hooping, body modifications, or some other weirdness. When we moved on, we took the core group with us, and maybe a new friend or fuck buddy tagging along. If they had any marketable talent, they became one of us. Leaving the Tribe meant you'd fucked up royally somehow, gotten arrested, knocked someone up or gotten knocked up, or made the mistake of crossing me or Rachel.

She and the girls skittered up the stairs the second the scent of pot hit us, Rachel taking my duffel up with her. I headed into the kitchen, giving a smile and a nod to everyone who greeted me on the way. I was hungry and buzzed from the two drinks. But if I got something in my stomach before the inevitable pressing of more drinks, I should be fine.

It didn't take long for me to find someone's leftover veggie wrap in the fridge, and I was halfway through it when hands wrapped around my waist and a drunken slur filled one ear. "Heeeey, *papi*, had a good time?"

I turned my chin to nuzzle pale-blond hair, taking in the familiar scent of cig smoke and lamp oil. An odd combination normally, but on Patch, it was completely him. I had known it wouldn't take long for him to find me. "Sure did. Keep yourself busy tonight?"

Patch let me go long enough for me to turn and face him. He was several inches shorter than my six feet. He also was too twink for words, skinny where I had some definition, his hair cut to give him a long emo bang that couldn't hide his brilliant smile, a metal ring in one nostril and a stud next to his mouth à la Marilyn Monroe, eyes lined in black, and pillowy lips made for sucking cock. He was in his usual uniform, long cargo shorts and boots—he rarely bothered with shirts—showing off tats that that resembled stitches on his wrists, elbows, around his neck, and down in the shape of a Y that reminded me of an autopsied body on those crime-scene shows. Brilliantly blue eyes already showed signs of booze and God knows what else that made his head loll to the side.

"Got some cash playing freaky fire-eater at a party tonight." He grinned, then grabbed my hand that held the wrap and took a huge bite with teeth slightly stained from his nicotine habit. Oddly enough, that one minor flaw made him seem more human, clay feet contrast to the lanky Ganymede standing before me.

I pulled back with a growl. I was hungry, dammit, and I stole the wrap fair and square. "What do you mean 'playing'? You are a freaky fire eater."

"Yup, and Rach suggested I come down and remind you how freaky I am." He leaned in even closer, pressing me against the fridge and kissing my throat, running his wicked pierced tongue over my skin.

I coughed around my next bite in surprise, feeling damned horny and damned not at the same time. When we got together, although those romps were rarely bad, those emotions never stopped roiling inside me, horny and not—"should I be doing this?" and "oh God, need to get off now" conflicting in my brain. After my last failed attempt at a relationship ended up with me sporting bruises I didn't ask for (damned closeted jackass), Patch had kinda just fallen into my lap in the last town we'd crashed in. He was a wanderer like us, a juggler who busked his way from place to place, a grown-up foster kid who ended up on our couch after a few up close and personal introductions. He could do awesome stuff with fire too. He ate it, twirled it on the ends of staves and swinging poi, spat fuel on flaming torches to make balls of fire, generally did things that made his already pale eyebrows nonexistent from time to time. We hit it off instantly, and much to my surprise, Rach practically ordered him to come along with us to this next town to keep me well distracted from the relationship disaster. He was no dancer, but we could use the variety, and the fact that he was young, liked to party, and knew how to use his freakishly thick cock to make me hit the high notes, were bonuses.

The downside was that Rach treated him like my "gift" and my appeasement, as if getting me an appropriate play toy would keep me focused on the Tribe and grateful to her and away from trying anything like dating ever again. I suppose nursing me through a broken face and heart scared her worse than I thought. Unfortunately, she wasn't all that nice to the kid once we got him on the road either, but Rach tended toward cranky by default. There was a good reason why pot was her drug of choice, after all. Patch sure didn't seem to mind, and if I were honest, it was nice having a steady piece on the side.

He began to slide down to his knees, but I stopped him with a hand in his hair. "Later, I'm hungry and need a drink."

"Need a drink" fell out of my mouth before I could even stop it. Compared to going upstairs and getting high, I'd rather drink. It was a fair compromise tonight, I told myself.

Dick-sucking lips poked out in a pout when he stood up and shrugged. "You're in luck. Marigold brought a jug of mead. Stay put."

And like that, Patch was gone, leaving me alone in the kitchen and wondering who the hell Marigold was. There had been a few other folks hanging out in the kitchen with us, but they must have made tracks when Patch went for my dick. We're an all-inclusive sort of crowd, but not everyone was cool with being an audience, and I totally understood. I'm mostly surrounded by women, which meant I saw more naked vagina than any self-respecting gay man should, and I didn't want to stick around when any of the ladies were making use of theirs any more than they wanted to watch Patch's special sword-swallowing trick.

Speaking of swords, mine wasn't responding properly, not even the slightest twitch at the thought of getting blown right here in the kitchen. I frowned, looking down at my pants as if visual disapproval would be enough to get Little Jon to do his duty. Damn, I must be tired. Or hungry. Or sober. Once I had taken care of some of those needs, I was sure my body would come around. It was wise not to look a gift Rachel in the mouth, and making the walls shake loud enough to scare some of the houseguests with our bedtime racket might be enough to get her off her "Ew, Boy Scout" kick. For now.

Much to my surprise, the slightest mention of Dean got my blood moving in the proper direction. Seriously, body? Dean's mouth was nothing like Patch's. His was wide, with lean lips, and yet the thought of that mouth on me made me moan out loud. My tongue glided over my own lips, as if I could catch the slightest taste of our kiss there. I should have asked for another go-round tonight.

Patch came back right away with a plastic cup of sweet-smelling booze. I wasn't a fan of mead at all, not able to get past the rancid, sweet taste, but I drank up anyway. My palate was getting spoiled by Mike's higher-class selections. I was supposed to appreciate the work of homemade brew. Even if it was gross. I hoped I wouldn't run into this Marigold person and have to lie about the taste.

I managed to keep my disgust out of my voice when I thanked Patch, who bounced along on the balls of his feet, head bobbing to the beat of the drums in the next room. He was gone, pupils turning his eyes almost completely black and leaving me guessing as to which party favor was on offer tonight. Not that I wanted to partake. I'd been a very good boy with that illegal shit. Hadn't had so much as another Valium since speaking to Spauldy. I should start demanding gold stars from her.

"I'm gonna go dance," Patch said suddenly, coming out of his daze so fast I jumped, and like that, he was out of the kitchen. He may have been high off his ass, but he'd figured out quickly that, until my pilfered meal was done, there would be no sword swallowing, and I wasn't in much of a chatty mood yet.

I made quick work of the wrap before the kid came back to steal another bite or, worse, the actual owner of the wrap discovered me eating it. Two guests sauntered in carrying a bottle of rum, and my cup was refilled without me even asking. So it began, but I had a plan. I would drink enough to maintain my buzz, no more. Whatever kept my head in the party, and that would be it.

Dancing would help too, so I made my way into the living room and through the press of bodies writhing to the drumbeat. Loud whoops greeted me, and I returned the call with an ululation of my own.

Much to my dismay, my cup kept refilling in the press, and my buzz transformed to a haze far faster than I'd hoped. Talented hands pounded on tom-toms and djembes, producing a beat that was downright primal, adding to the spell. We danced hard, swaying and writhing for what felt like hours, like some sort of ritual to cast out the demons of the week. I felt hands on my body, stroking, some groping. I didn't mind—dancing this close pretty much guaranteed you were going to get really personal with all sorts of people. Bodies, music, alcohol, the scent of humans and pot and the essential oils this crowd used over cologne and aftershave, were all the components in a spell that should have taken me out of body and mind and helped me find my peace.

A hand cupped my cock. I looked around for the source and saw the familiar blond head bobbing over my shoulder. I gripped his hip against my ass, and we moved together. My dick was slow to respond, though, until I had the thought of that hand belonging to a certain tall redhead. Then my cock grew big enough for Patch to stroke through my jeans. I threw back my head and moaned out loud, the sound drowned out by the drums, and let my mind wander.

Oh yeah, if that was really Dean grinding up against my willing body, I'd let him do me right here in the middle of the group. Not like anyone would notice until things got messy.

*"But not with an audience."*

Shit, that memory of his voice, horny and rough but firm with restraint, killed my fantasy. Dean wouldn't fuck me here, where other hands groped and pawed at me. He'd want me all to himself, alone. Before I could acknowledge how I liked the idea, I forced myself back to the here and now. This was my real place, with my people, and Patch was still fondling my now-flaccid prick. He was the sort of guy I deserved, just as debauched as I was. Maybe if I had another drink, I'd get back into the groove, maybe let the kid bring me off, maybe drag him off to a corner and let him finish the job face to face with anyone who cared to watch looking on.

It wasn't working. Like a little mosquito buzzing at my ear and ducking every swipe, the feeling of this not being "right" niggled at me. I shouldn't be this drunk. The room smelled wrong. The hands on my body weren't big enough. No one's voice was as deep as the one I wanted to hear. Fuck, no one was tall enough. No one here was Dean. It was all wrong, and it splashed over my peace like cold water.

Without so much as another word, I shoved through the crowd, needing air to think, hoping the bedroom was empty so I could get my churning thoughts together, figure them out, and get my groove back.

The sharp sound of laughter from one of the other rooms upstairs changed my mind. Maybe some more sedate social time would work, and nothing screamed "sedate" like a room full of potheads.

I didn't bother knocking, just opened up and was promptly hit by a cloud of hazy, familiar-smelling smoke. A few bleary faces, most belonging to people sitting on the floor chatting and passing Grimace around, a few on the beds, turned to greet me.

"Jonathan!" Rachel waved to me from the bed, then beckoned me over, moving off the dude she was straddling. Him, she gave a little push off. "Get us some beer, okay?"

Thank fuck, quite literally, they were both still clothed. The last thing I needed was a live sex show. My brain and dick were confused enough this evening, thank you very much. I tiptoed through the circle and climbed up on the bed and into my best friend's waiting arms. It was like old times.

"Who's your friend?" I asked, motioning to the deposed dude who stepped out of the room as Grimace got passed up to us.

"Michael? Micah? Does it matter?" she smirked before putting the mouthpiece of the bong to her lips and taking a hit. "If he brings me the beer I asked for, I might fuck him later, if not, his loss. You look like you need me now. And some of this...."

I didn't even think about refusing. I was already drunk as hell, so the acrid THC-loaded smoke filling my lungs wasn't that much worse in my list of sins for the night. Rachel looked pleased as I passed the bong over, and she pulled my head onto her lap. "What's wrong? Patch too wired to get it up tonight?"

It seemed as if our little tiff in the van was forgotten in the haze, and I tried to embrace it and actually talk. "He gave me his number. He's coming to the show too, by the way."

"Who?" Her hands combed through my hair. "Wait, that Bateman Boy Scout dude? Why?"

"He's got ten bucks to spare on a ticket? I'm so good that he wants to see me twice?" I was getting tense and longed for Grimace to make his round back this way. "Does it really matter?"

I felt her sigh deeply, and I quickly added. "He's not Rafe, Rachel."

"You don't know that. Do you even know if he's out or not?"

She had me there, because I sure did not know that. "If we're just fucking, why does it matter?"

Tam, lying on her back across the room from us, raised her hand like a very stoned kid in class. "Who's Rafe? I don't remember a Rafe…."

"Right now, Tamera," Rachel snarked, "I'd be damned surprised if you could remember where your tits are."

That got the room laughing as Tam gripped both of said tits and stuck out her tongue at us. Grimace got passed to us next, and I sat up for my hit while Rachel kept talking. "It's not that big of a deal, really. Some mundane asshole thought he could put his hands on my Jonathan. We kicked his sorry ass. End of story."

I had to struggle to keep from coughing up my well-earned lungful at how casual she made it sound. Truth was, I was lonely, had just heard the news about my Mama's sick liver, and had a crazy idea that someone to hold me at night would make some of the shock and grief less painful. Enter Rafe, some college junior hockey player who came to a few of our drum circles. Much to my surprise, we hit it off really well. I spent a few nights at his place, and he liked heading off campus to see me perform.

"Was that why we left frat boy town so fast?" Tam asked.

Rachel nodded. "Well yeah, didn't want the asshole to try to press charges, if he was even willing to admit that he'd gotten his ass handed to him by a chick and a fag."

Tam saluted with Grimace. "Good move. Homophobic dickheads deserve to get their asses kicked."

"He wasn't really homophobic," I corrected, and felt Rachel glare right at my temple. "Just closeted."

"Doesn't matter." Rachel sniffled daintily, pulling my head back on her lap and resuming her hair petting. "He shouldn't have touched you."

We were both right, of course. Rafe was so deep in the closet that just seeing me at the same bar made him freak out. (Of course, he'd never bothered mentioning that he wasn't out to his buddies between hot fucks at his place and mine.) Rachel had followed us to the alley and got there just in time to see him backhand me into a wall. That was all she wrote, and before we were done with the guy, I was pretty sure his perfect Roman nose would never be straight again. Also, his balls were probably still aching to this day. It wasn't my proudest moment, to be sure, but I refuse to say that we were in the wrong. The local police would have probably thought differently, so we had Thor and Loki packed up in a matter of hours. We were gone before dawn.

I wish I could say I didn't regret being with Rafe, though. It was really nice having someone regular, even a closeted jerk, so nice that my heart hurt long after the bruise on my face cleared up. Rachel wanted to make up for that, and since there was no way we'd fuck, she did the next best thing.

"It's not all bad." I smiled against her thigh. "Any other way and we probably wouldn't have gotten Patch."

Before anyone could reply, the door opened again, and Michael/Micah/whatever came in, holding three beers. I rose from the bed and yanked playfully on one of Rachel's pigtails. "Sounds like this one's a keeper. I'm gonna go lay out for a bit, 'kay?"

Rachel didn't look too satisfied that my mood had been lifted, but she let me leave. I turned down one of M-dude's offered beers and crossed the hallway to our bedroom.

It was empty, bordered on two walls with an actual full-sized bed—Rachel's—and a twin-sized mattress topped with a white sheet and a gray unzipped sleeping bag—mine and Patch's. There was a trunk at the foot of her bed that contained her possessions, exactly like my huge canvas duffel, only not as portable. She had a lock on it to keep anyone from helping themselves during these sorts of shindigs, where I was perfectly content to carry it all with me, including the toolbox that contained all I needed for my little commission business. If people didn't see it, it would be less of a temptation to swipe.

My bag was thrown on top of the trunk, and I assumed Rach had been in a hurry to get Grimace in her hands, or it would have been lying on my bed. I picked it up and carried it over, set it on the mattress, then sat down to shuck off my boots. Maybe I could lie down for a minute to sort myself out. I could even attempt to sleep a little. Okay, fine, I would make use of the number burning in my pocket. Maybe calling Dean would ease me enough to party... or sleep. Suddenly I felt so damned tired, just by sitting on something relativity soft.

Shirt and pants followed next, leaving me bare as I stuffed them into a grocery-store bag in the corner, already full with this week's laundry. I opened the side zippers on the duffel and pawed through a horde of smaller gallon freezer bags, all tightly packed to keep my belongings organized, dry, and clean. Each one had a label, though with time I needed to get them out in the moonlight to read them—Daily, Dancing, Club, Silks, Toilet, Hair, Underwear, all written in fading marker. Underwear was empty. Damn, it looked like I was going commando until I could head to the Laundromat, sometime this weekend. I might have to borrow some of the Kouzina money for the trip.

I placed the bag in the usual spot between the head end of the mattress and the wall like some sort of makeshift headboard, then shoved the sleeping bag to the foot of the bed and lay down, phone in hand, checking the time. I'd been dancing for hours; it was close to midnight. Since I didn't know if Dean would be asleep by now like a normal person, I sent a text instead of calling.

*Hey, it's Jonathan. You awake?*

I pulled the sleeping bag over my waist and rolled to my stomach as I waited for something, anything. Anticipation and nerves tangoed in my belly with the booze, and for a second, I thought it was time for a naked dash to the toilet to hurl before the phone buzzed.

*Mostly. How's the party?*

I shouldn't have been this happy about getting a response so quickly, never mind at all. I really shouldn't have been. *Not bad, but I'm beat.*

*So you're texting me instead of going to sleep?*

*Yeah. Didn't catch you busy with anyone else, did I?* I typed with not a little bit of apprehension. The guy was hot enough to have someone over any day of the week, especially now that he'd broken his sex fast. I really shouldn't begrudge him if he did. I had Patch, after all.

*Anyone? Just me, a glass of wine, and a DVD. Usual Friday night.*

I wrinkled my nose and willed my heart to stop doing that stupid skippy thing at the fact that Dean was by himself tonight. That should have sounded like the most boring thing ever, but as I looked around the empty room, the drums and whoops still going on downstairs mixing with the sounds of other people on the second floor loudly yapping and laughing all around me, it sounded really peaceful. If I could be honest with myself, I could accept that I had the need for quiet, for peace, for air in a house that always had more people in it than ought to fit.

*Wine doesn't sound like something I'd expect a Boy Scout to drink.*

*Boy Scout?*

I pressed a hand to my face and groaned. That was the booze talking. I did *not* just tell Dean the name Rachel and the girls had bestowed upon him. *Sorry, my friends have taken to calling you that. No offense.*

*None taken. The ladies at work call you Jingle Boy.*

I cocked my head at the phone, wondering when any ladies from any work had ever seen me jingle anywhere. *My turn—Jingle Boy?*

*I was with some people from work last week. One of the girls was really interested in learning how to dance, btw.*

I shrugged a shoulder out of sheer habit. It was normal for a few wannabes to go and find a class after seeing us do our thing, and I really couldn't give a fuck right then. I didn't even notice he was sitting at a table with other people from work. And I wanted to talk about just him now. *What are you watching?*

The Devil Wears Prada. *Don't laugh.*

I actually liked that movie, and the thought of a dull Friday night with decent booze and a few campy, funny movies on that overstuffed couch sounded better and better. *Nice. Still wearing my bracelet?*

The door to the bedroom opened while I waited for a response. I didn't bother looking up. Rachel and I had a standing agreement about the use of our shared bedroom, since we always shared a bedroom. The first person in for the night, for sleep or sex, trumped the other person's need for sleep or sex. If that was her with Michael/Micah/whatever, she'd find somewhere else for them to go fuck without me having to say a word.

Patch landed on the side of the mattress as the phone buzzed, one hand going underneath the covers to cup my ass. "Was wondering where you ran off to."

"I'm calling it a night. I'm tired."

"Getting old?" The cover was pulled back to expose my ass to the air. "Or just soft?"

"Fuck you. I still can out-party your ass on my worst night."

I didn't look at the kid as I read the response. *Of course I am. It's gorgeous. Still can't believe you gave it to me.*

A snort. "Sure you can, *papi*. That's why you're up here ready for bed at midnight instead of showing everyone how partying's done."

I rolled my eyes as he kept molesting me. "And what the hell are you doing here, party boy?"

A snort puffed against the small of my back. "You know why I'm here. Her Majesty wanted me to look after you, but you bolted."

I knew what sort of looking after she wanted him to do, and I rolled over to my back as I typed away. *Not give. Borrow. You have to see me again to give it back.*

Patch gripped my cock, and it was the direct simulation that got it waking up to do its duty. I could have said no. I knew I could, but that would have meant more pissiness to deal with in the morning, should Rach find out. With the determination in his face, eyes locked on my cock, lips slack and panting, I told myself that refusing one of his blowjobs would just be cruel. He must have scored some "E" tonight to be literally this hard up, and I've always been that easy.

It was worth one token objection, though. "Patch, I'm kinda in the middle of something."

He snorted, leaning down to lap at the crown, circling with his round tongue stud. "So?"

There, I'd made an objection. It was brushed aside. That should keep the guilt from bothering me right away. Patch liked to suck cock, specifically mine, so this was like ordering a hungry kid to eat a bowl of ice cream. He'd get what he wanted, and I'd be less "cranky," as Rachel had been calling my current down mood. It would make it harder to concentrate on the conversation at hand, but I could use the challenge.

*Still surprised you wanted to see me again.*

That warmed my chest as much as my groin was warming up under the tender mercies of Patch's talented mouth. I wasn't looking down, but could feel the wet, hot slide gliding up and down my entire length, and when the tip hit the back of Patch's throat and he swallowed it down, I couldn't hold back the moan, even as my fingers typed away. The mattress shook as Patch probably jacked off at the same time. Horny little fuck. *Face like yours? I'd pay to see it.*

It took some time before I got a response, long enough for me to run a hand into Patch's soft hair, just resting, not guiding, as he brought me even closer. The anticipation of that reply was just as strong as the wait for my orgasm. Patch grabbed my hand and slid it down to his neck, enough of a sign that he wanted that guidance, so I gave in, gripping his warm skin tight and moving his head up and down. The moan, muffled and low, told me that I'd understood him perfectly.

I read the reply though slitted eyes struggling to stay open. *Could we get together before the show? How about dinner?*

It had to be thrilled surprise that gave me the extra push over the edge. My eyes slammed shut as I trembled and tensed up. Patch fought my grip, pulled away long enough to take a deep breath, then lunged to take it all in again, throat working the head. The thought of Dean doing the same to me again, or me on him, was glorious, and that led to the memory of what his come tasted like. Oh yeah, there would be a next time, and I would be on my knees with him down my own throat, and that was just the visual I needed to make me come hard enough to damn near black out.

It took several deep breaths to be able to see again, and by then Patch had wordlessly curled up naked on "his" side of the mattress, wiping a hand stained with his own come on the sheet. Offering the mattress was a fair trade, better than attempting to sleep on the couches that were lumpier than bad gravy. And in the middle of a party.

"Not going back down?" I gasped. I didn't mind. Patch was actually decent, and fooling around with me kept him away from any other assholes who would really use him. Having him close meant I could keep an eye on him. That was what I told myself, anyway.

"Nah, too loud. 'M tired too," he murmured, rolling over so his back faced me, the mattress a little snug with two bodies on it. He wasn't a cuddler, didn't like it, and it wasn't my place to show him how nice it could be. Hey, maybe that explained why I was so strung out on Dean after one night. I had to be missing the joy of having another man wrapped around me. Last time was with that Rafe jackass, and I sure as fuck didn't want to give him another thought tonight, not with a much better lay within texting distance.

Speaking of Dean, I turned to my side to give us both some space and fumbled for the phone I'd dropped. "Try not to snore too loud, okay, kid?"

"I don't snore, you dick." He was fading fast, his drawl extra thick, ready to drop into that insta-sleep I so envied. The post-orgasm bliss would help me rest tonight, though, a better aid than all that I'd ingested that night.

"'Night, kid." I had to reread the last text Dean sent, since I'd forgotten what it said while I was coming my brains out. *Not this week. We're doing rehearsals until showtime.*

Rehearsals and practices were one of the few things Rach and I both took damned seriously. Shows like this, big ones that featured a lot of acts, were our bread and butter. Everyone would practice their routines for hours, which were afternoon and evening hours since nothing productive happens in the House before noon. Given that Dean worked some sort of nine-to-five downtown, there would be no time for me to sneak off to see him.

*I understand. Can't wait for Saturday, anyway.*

*You'll love it.* He'd better love it. I had two solos, one duet with Rachel, and a group number that I'd been working my ass off to get right, and that was while playing co–stage manager and making sure everyone else hit their marks. Now that I knew at least one member of the audience would be intently appreciative of watching me at work, the pressure was on to make it all better than good.

I typed out a quick good night before closing the phone, letting it rest near the bag, and drifted to sleep with Patch's body pouring off heat. The last spare thoughts my tired mind tried to process involved wishes of having Dean here instead. He'd hold me, same way he held me last week, and a feeling I could barely describe nearly stole my breath. Longing. That's what it was. I longed for him, couldn't wait to see him again.

Tomorrow. I would think about it more tomorrow.

HAPTER FIVE

# *And I Burn*

DESPITE what I told Dean over the phone, our rehearsal schedule wasn't work, work, work every waking moment. We would have driven each other insane, and with swords, fire fuel, ropes, chains, and other props at easy reach, it would have quickly ended in a stress-induced bloodbath.

So with that in mind, on the Wednesday before the show, I woke up, looked up at the beautiful sunshine streaming into the bedroom that promised a lovely midafternoon outside, called to a barely awake Rachel, and suggested a picnic at Atterro Park. It was a big enough patch of green, right in the middle of downtown, more than perfect for a group of ten to stretch out and relax before the show on Saturday. Much to my surprise, Drill Sergeant Rach muttered something like an agreement, rolled out of her bed, and left the room, already barking orders and banging on doors.

I got off my mattress, shoved Patch off his side to wake him up, and wandered into the kitchen with a towel wrapped around my waist to see what we could throw together for food.

Tam, Cindy, and two more boarders I barely knew were already there, putting sandwiches together and loading up bottles of water. Guess they had been awake or knew how to say "how high" when Rach told them to "jump," because I knew it hadn't taken me that long to roll Patch's skinny ass out of my bed.

"Afternoon, folks." I dug into a bag on the counter and pulled out an apple that wasn't soft and pitted, a rare find from the local food bank. "Need a hand?"

Cindy frowned and snatched the apple right out of my hand before I could take a bite. "That's for the picnic."

"Rachel is a fucking genius. We totally need a break," said Tam as she stashed foil-wrapped sandwiches in separate canvas bags by meat content. "Did she tell you which park we're heading to?"

Did Rachel? It was *my* idea, but saying so just wasn't worth the effort. "Atterro. Do you guys need a hand with setup?"

"Nope," Cindy replied, "We've got until Rach is out of the shower and ready to go before we head out, so we're covered. You better get dressed."

It was then that I noticed I was also the only person in the kitchen not dressed to go outside. With all of ten people in the house in various stages of wakefulness and possible dress, it was going to take longer than the half hour she normally took to get ready to get all of these people washed up. Most importantly, it was going to take me a bit longer. I grabbed the apple back from Cindy, ignored her indignant squawk, and turned to rush back to our bedroom, heading straight to my toiletries bag.

Patch had rolled back onto the mattress in my absence. "What's the hurry, *papi*?"

"Quit calling me that. I'm not introducing you to my mama anytime soon." I took a bite from the apple and sat it on Patch's stomach. He obediently put it to his mouth without me saying a word. I think I was getting used to the pet name, creepy as it was. There was a ten-year age difference, but I'm no one's father figure. "And if you don't want to go to this picnic smelling like my jizz, hurry up and grab a shower with me."

"There are worse fates," was the groggy response, but Patch managed to stand up and follow me to the downstairs bathroom. Sure, the water would be much cooler since Rach was in the one upstairs, and she'd be pissed as hell the second we started the water and fucked with her pressure, but there was no way I was going out that door with stubble and crazy hair, looking like I just rolled out of a sweaty, sticky bed. I had some standards.

The ladies in the kitchen giggled and wolf whistled at the full monty view of both Patch and me trudging from the stairs to the bathroom, exchanging the apple between us. Not only was the water ice cold in the cramped little stand-up shower, but the pressure was for utter shit, rendering hair washing all but impossible. I was sorely tempted to step out and flush the toilet, just to give the lady upstairs a shock of this oh-so-delightful experience. Although actually, it would be nice to have a "discussion" that didn't involve how much she didn't like Dean or the fact that we'd been texting and calling each other fairly often when the Tribe wasn't busy.

Some of her arguments made sense, of course. Dean was not my typical pick. Never mind the lack of body art or the whole nice stable life thing, he had never heard of Van Canto or Covenant or Cruxshadows or any of the bands we swore allegiance to. He may lose interest in me once the novelty of sex wore off. She'd have to deal with my heartbroken ass, and that was apparently a fate worse than death. All very true and very ignored by my mind and my dick.

Even under that freezing, pissing rain of a shower that chilled me to the bone, the very thought of Dean made me smile. I wondered what he was doing. He told me he worked as a mailroom supervisor for a largish company in town. By now, he'd be at work, going about his day in a nice boring suit. A boring suit that probably looked damned good over his broad shoulders and narrow hips. That man could wear a potato sack and look utterly fuckable.

"Dammit!" Patch's growl brought me out of my lust-addled reverie. "It's too fuckin' cold in here to deal with your cock. I'm getting out of here before my nuts try to hide in my throat." He shoved me into his place in front of the dribbling showerhead on his way out, driving away not only all rational thought for a few seconds, but the start of an erection that he had no doubt felt against his back.

The very moment Patch left the bathroom, still sputtering, cursing, and naked, the shower pressure suddenly increased, giving me a face full of boner-killing spray that drove me out of the shower as well. Rachel had to be done with hers, and that meant there wasn't much time left. She would leave stragglers behind and, for all I knew, me too.

I toweled off my hair, leaving it damp. There wasn't time to toss more than a quick handful of some conditioner through the locks, and hopefully the weather wouldn't heat up too much and turn it into straw. If there was anything stereotypically gay about me, it was the attention I paid to personal grooming. I had product, used moisturizer, and I wasn't ashamed about it. My hair was my pride and joy, one of what we coined our "moneymakers." A performer had to take care of their moneymakers: their bodies, their costumes, their props, anything that made them stand out on stage. It was one of our rules, and treating my number-one moneymaker so shittily on someone else's schedule was pissing me off for the first time that morning.

A few quick swipes of a razor to tame my stubble and keep the hair I actually wanted on my face neat, and I was out of the bathroom and back up the stairs. Rachel was the only one in the room and didn't look very happy as she dressed. "Did you really have to shower at the same time?"

"Did you really have to give everyone such a short time limit to head out?" I gave myself points for managing to sound neutral. "I mean, it doesn't take you that long to get ready. You know they're gonna need more time than that."

"There's how many people in the house? By the time they all got ready, it'd be time for dinner."

I knelt on my mattress and rifled through my casual baggie for a clean shirt. "And? I suggested a picnic, something nice and casual, no pressure. The wait's just the downside of having all of these people around."

"I'm sorry. Should we get rid of some of these people?" Rachel crossed her arms, now fully dressed, and glared at me. "Would that make it easier?"

My head jerked up and at her. "The fuck? When did I say that ever?"

We needed those extra boarders to keep the rent of the place as cheap as possible. We needed them as much as they needed us for a place to stay, even if they had to double and triple up in the rooms, share two bathrooms, and put up with our troupe's quirks.

"Because I could." It was as if I'd said nothing. "Just say the word, Jonathan, and I'll tell the most useless of the boarders to take a hike tonight. Then we can have all the hot water and shower time and

food and time for everyone to get all prettied up before we have
random outings. Would that make you happy?"

She would do it too. And tell everyone that, unlike the awesome
idea of a picnic in the park to relax, evicting people she found useless
would totally be for my sake. I would look like the bad guy, the selfish
one. I don't know how I managed to see her moves before she made
them. I guess I owed Spauldy for all these clues, and for trying her best
to teach me coping skills when it came to moments like this when I had
to be reasonable. Mostly it was for ways of refusing offerings of drugs
and shit, but it could work for making my friend see reason.

I took a very deep breath before speaking again, boxers still in
hand because I was too busy what-the-fucking to cover my ass. "That's
not what I'm saying at all, Rach. Let's give everyone who wants to a
chance to wash up before we go. That's all. What's the rush?"

"What's the rush? We've got a show in a couple of days, and
we're going to fool around at a park." Dark eyes bored into me, even as
she pitched her tone low and quiet enough that we couldn't be heard in
the other rooms. "Am I the only one taking this seriously?"

That wasn't the proper response to my attempt to be reasonable. If
these shiny new coping skills weren't going to work with something
simple like a picnic, then they weren't going to be worth shit when
someone offered me something I shouldn't be indulging in. Fuck.

I put my boxers on, feeling a lot less vulnerable with my bits no
longer dangling free, and gave it another shot. "Really? One day will
not ruin the show. We're pros. We've got this shit down to muscle
memory. I can do my routines in my sleep and probably with a dick in
my ass." I swore I hummed Metallica's "Fuel" last night, but Patch was
too out of it to notice while he pounded me. "If you had a problem with
my brilliant park idea, why the hell didn't you say so instead of
rounding up the troops like this was your plan?"

Before those words tumbled out of my mouth, I knew her answer.
"Patch was in here. They can't see us disagreeing, Jonathan. Not even
him. You know that."

Which was why we saved the disagreements, most of them,
anyway, for the bedroom. Which was why we always shared a
bedroom. We both had serious fears of the Tribe succumbing to
internal drama and falling apart like scores of other troupes we've

heard of in our travels, and that lead to our merciless tag-team style of management. It was very simple. If you were with us, the words of Mama Bear and King Fuck were law. If you didn't like it, you could find the door.

If only things had continued to run as smoothly as they did when we were both insane art students who cooked this idea up in our shitty apartment ten years ago. Now it was more Mama Bear's law, with King Fuck simply going along because it seemed easier than fighting. It didn't help that no matter what beef I could have with Rach lately, she'd never admit to anything being her fault.

In her world, if something was the matter, that meant I needed to get laid, needed another drink, needed another puff or pill. Maybe some other useless asshole was actually bothering me, and they needed to go. Rachel, dear, generous Rachel, would take care of it all, no matter what. So I had little reason to complain, right?

I swear, if it wasn't for Patch's fascination with my balls, I could be easily convinced that I didn't have them anymore. Then again, when the only other option was going it alone without Rach, maybe my balls were a fair enough trade.

I turned, breaking the eye contact, and found pants. "Just give 'em another half hour, okay? Then we can go with fewer smelly hippie types bouncing around Thor."

Rachel snorted, the tension in the room finally dissipating, and stood, the sound turning into a chuckle. "Fine. You know, for a guy whose grandma hitchhiked to Woodstock from Mexico, you sure got a hate-on for hippies."

"I've got nothing against hippies, just the lack of hygiene." *Abuelita* Carla loved to grace anyone within earshot with tales about her experiences in the counterculture of the 60s and 70s, including how many days her commune would go sans a bath to conserve water. It never failed to make my skin crawl, even as a kid. "The mainstream may be optional, but washing your ass should never be."

The sun was just as awesome as promised, and had burnt off any hint of morning chill by the time we arrived at Atterro and settled in. Someone had made calls to other partiers and performers, and those partiers and performers brought more food, turning the impromptu picnic into a gathering. People were clustered on the grass in clumps, eating or talking or dancing or drumming or playing with various juggling props.

We found a spot under a huge oak tree to place our blanket and made it the official Tribe hang space. I lay there, watching the girls dance in the middle of a circle of drums, my own hips aching delightfully after going a few rounds myself. Patch's lap made an awesome pillow to chill on.

"Can't believe we can't light up the fire poi here." Patch's lips pouted up as he changed the batteries on a set of LED poi he had brought along to spin. "We're professionals. We wouldn't have set anything on fire that wasn't meant to be."

"I know that, you know that, we all know that. The cops don't know that." I had my cell out, greeting Dean and telling him what I was up to. "And we want as little to do with the cops as possible, right?"

Dealing with the cops was another big no-no to us, and the fact that there wasn't a damned thing we could do if a local got stupid at this little shindig was a concern. Unless we were visiting other piles of people or dancing or spinning, Crimson Dream and our boarders stuck to our own blanket, within sight of the van, just in case. Patch had a hard time getting the separate part through his skull, and had been looking forward to hanging out with some of the locals he'd been getting to know. I couldn't blame him in the least.

The park banned alcohol unless there was a festival going on, but I knew for a fact that Rach had brought her trusty skull flask, and a few people were pretty clever with smuggling booze. Thankfully, no one was stupid enough to bring anything blatantly illegal or had the sense to get high before arriving. Atterro Park was surrounded by tall office buildings, a huge patch of green, and trees to break up the concrete jungle. Folks in suits walked around our little gathering, some curious, some sneering. I know. Who had time to lay out when there was so much work to do?

*Atterro? I work a couple of blocks away.* Dean's text brought me out of my own little sneer, turning my mouth up into a wide grin.

"Lucky, lucky you." Patch had been reading over my head the entire time I'd been in his lap. I didn't mind. He'd been the only person I could even talk to about Dean without judgment. He seemed honestly happy that I seemed so thrown over the guy, probably because that meant he had implied permission to break away a little as well. "You gonna see him?"

"I can't tell him to leave his job in the middle of the day."

I typed back, *Which building?*

"It's lunchtime, dumbfuck. There's food carts everywhere."

Dean's reply buzzed in my hand before I could change my angle to smack Patch anywhere I could reach. "Dumbfuck" was less stupid than "papi," though.

*Trenton Enterprises, off Main Street. Was just heading out for lunch.*

I ignored Patch's fist pump of triumph and replied, *Awesome.*

His fist pump turned into a smack on my shoulder. "That's all you're gonna say? The fuck is wrong with you?"

"Do you seriously want him down here?" I dreaded the very thought, not sure who I was more worried for if Dean came over to this crowd.

"This is a huge park. You can go over to him and make stupid eyes together, and I can go spin with Lala's group without getting eye daggers from Her Majesty for ignoring your crazy ass. Sounds fair to me." The smirk on his pretty lips took much of the sting out of his words. We were friends and very much aware that we'd never be more than friends with benefits, but the friend part, the protégé part, was more important that the getting off together part. "Oh yeah, Lala's been asking about her necklace."

"Tell her I'll have it in her hot little hands at the show." The hooper was one of the featured performers, and I'd been working on her wire-worked pendant for about two weeks now. I couldn't wait to have a little extra me-cash in exchange for it. "And I do not make stupid eyes."

Patch moved then, back and fast enough that I had to roll to the side to keep my head from smacking on the blanket-covered grass. "Bullshit. You make stupid eyes at your phone whenever you talk to him, like some teen chick talking to her crush."

"Yeah, I bet you'd know exactly what that's like, kid." I frowned up at Patch as he turned the LED balls on, the spheres blinking and flashing with multicolored lights. The fucker was laughing at me, and I didn't like it. "Jackass."

"Yeah, whatever, *papi*. Now go see your man and let me go play." He bent down to brush a kiss against my lips and then ran off, leaving me shaking my head.

"He's not my man!"

That got some eyes of the nearest gathering looking over at me, confused and amused. Patch was halfway to the small group of people already twirling their own poi, tipped with the same LED lights or lengths of ribbon. Me, I simply smiled and checked my phone again.

*If you're not busy, could I treat you to lunch?*

My heartbeat could have rivaled the drummers in speed and strength. He could have asked me to tap dance naked to the mayor's office, and I would have been all for it. I imagined Dean walking to the park, in that boring suit, just to meet me. In my tight silver shirt, black jeans, and Docs. I looked down at my clothes and frowned. I looked like I really wouldn't belong walking next to him.

*I'm not dressed for a sit-down meal.* My eyes roamed the bordering streets. Main was to the right of the picnic, off a ways, with enough trees and people already there to make it hard to find me if anyone from the Tribe looked over there. I hoped.

*Can't really do a sit-down for lunch anyway, but that's okay. I'll see you at your show.*

I could let this opportunity to see and talk to the man mostly alone go, or I could accept it and damn the risks, like Rachel suddenly approaching the blanket.

*I'll meet you on the Main Street side. I'm in a shiny shirt.* I had the message sent and the phone closed before she collapsed with a happy-tired huff. "Hey, lady, taking a breather?"

She smiled as she rummaged in our bags for a bottle of water, looking like the girl I've always known. Dancing did wonders for us both in setting our moods right. "Saw Patch wander off. You done resting?"

"Yeah, I'm done." If I made this getaway seem perfectly normal, she would buy it. "I'm gonna get up and wander around the park for a bit, stretch my legs."

It was lame, but she sent me off with a wave of her hand. "Don't be long. We'll be here a few hours, or until the food's gone."

"Good thing people brought more grub, right?" I smoothed my hair down and yanked at the ponytail to straighten things out after my lie-down. "Not a bad collective effort at all."

She took a pull of her water, and, as if by magic, her usual sour expression returned. "More like offerings to stay in our good graces, but I'll take it."

And she was in "Queen of Fucking Everything" mode, a horrid mutation of all of our attempts to shore up our confidence in our skills when we first started out. Act like we were the shit, dance like we were the shit, and eventually people would recognize that we were the shit. Now she had little patience for those that didn't recognize that fact right away. The only cure was time away from any local folk, as she was doing, and it worked well to keep us in the good graces in any town we ended up in, if only for just a little bit longer.

I said nothing to that, got up and headed for the Main Street park entrance, schooling my walk into a relaxed swagger. It wouldn't do for me to look too eager, not for anyone watching me leave and not for Dean. It was a little annoying, the excitement that welled up in me, the desire to see and touch and kiss. I really wanted one of Dean's kisses again, if just for the novelty. Who was this guy to get me, of all people, this excited? Even after ducking out on him, he wanted to see me again, gave me his number, and put the ball in my court.

And I took that ball and ran with it, despite all common sense telling me no good could come from it. Running right to the lone unused bench that gave the clearest view of the street before me.

While I considered the best way to position myself on the bench to convey anticipation, but not too much, Dean practically materialized out of a clump of pedestrians crossing Main Street. How a man that tall managed to do that, I didn't know. It could have had something to do with him not being dressed the way I'd been fantasizing since I woke up. Not in a boring suit, looking like a corporate clone, but straight-up business casual in a pair of khakis and a dark-blue polo shirt. Today was dark-framed glasses day, and that little detail made me grin like an idiot, even if they weren't worn for me specifically. Dean returned the smile once he saw me and came right over. My face ached from smiling so hard, and the grin somehow grew when I noticed a gleam on one of his wrists. He still wore that damned bracelet. I was sure something so unusual couldn't have been allowed in any business' dress code. Concern didn't stop the rush of heat that flared through me at the very possessive thoughts that filled my mind at the sight. Possessive thoughts I shouldn't be thinking. He wasn't mine, but damn, seeing that bracelet didn't help my thudding heart or the dry squeeze in my throat.

"Hey, you." I got my throat to loosen up enough to make words, crossing my arms and leaning back on the bench, radiating all the slack I wasn't feeling as he got closer. "Where are you taking me for lunch?"

"I've got a half hour, so where would you like to go?" He grinned, offering a hand to me.

He was close enough to touch now, and I wanted to take complete advantage, take that hand, wrap my arms around some part of him, his waist, or arm, or neck, and never let go, but I didn't want to risk any of Dean's coworkers seeing us, just in case he wasn't out. No need to mess up his job with this little whatever we had going on. I opted to take the hand and let him pull me to my feet, suddenly remembering Patch's suggestion. "There's food carts all over the park."

Most of those carts served food I didn't eat, variations of beef, pork, and chicken in the not-egg form, but the walk was worth it when he pressed his hand on the small of my back. So much for worrying if he was out or not. I didn't even care that I'd had a couple of sandwiches an hour ago. He could have led me into traffic with that hand on me, but the line of the Greek food cart was good enough.

"Hey." I motioned to the bracelet. "You're not gonna get your supervisor up your ass for wearing that, are you?"

"There's not enough yoga in the world for me to get up my own ass, and I don't think Richard would be interested." He chuckled as we moved into the line and drew me even closer, one hand curling around my hip. It was a damn perfect fit, especially when I brought my arm around his waist. "We're both supervisors, so don't worry about it. He was there at Kouzina too, looking like you'd bite him if you danced too close."

I had to laugh, relieved that he wouldn't get some asshole in his face for any reason having to do with me. "I hope he wasn't too traumatized."

"After he got his share of breasts, he recovered just fine enough to tease me about you that Monday after."

"No one at work cares that you're into dudes?" Best to get this question out of the way before we went any further. I would not put up with another "Rafe" situation.

"Those who know don't, or they at least don't bring it up. I had to tell Richard so he'd stop trying to set me up with women from the office."

We got to the head of the line, where Dean got a gyro for himself, and we decided to split an order of falafel and a lemonade. We found a bench nearby, far enough from the Tribe that I couldn't see them off in the distance, so I got to finally relax and simply talk.

"What got you into dancing?" Dean lifted the straw to his lips and smirked. "And let me know if you're sick of hearing that question."

I shrugged, so happy to be talking to him that I didn't even care what he wanted to talk about. "No worries. The story isn't that interesting. Rachel wanted to go to belly dancing lessons while we were in sophomore year of art school, and she didn't want to go alone. The bug bit me from the first class, and that was all she wrote. That was ten years ago."

"Ten years? How old are you?"

"You know it's not polite to ask that, right?" I couldn't hide my grin before popping another warm fried ball of glorious chickpea mush into my mouth. I answered with my mouth still full. "Twenty-nine, you?"

"You're joking." Dean looked honestly surprised. "You don't look almost thirty."

"I come from a line of Latin beauties who age gracefully." I tossed my ponytail back over my shoulder, grinning like an idiot. "And since I'm an only kid, I got the full dose of the gift. You're not going to make me feel like I'm robbing the cradle, are you?" One "kid" fucking me was enough in a social group that got younger and younger every goddamned year.

"Not if you don't count twenty-six as 'in the cradle.'"

I sighed in relief. Four years wasn't as big of a deal as ten was. "That's not too much of a gap." Thank fuck. "Any siblings?"

"Nope, there's only me. My folks traveled enough with just one kid." He suddenly looked down at his half-eaten gyro before blurting, "I don't know how to ask this without just coming out with it, so here goes. If you'd like to come back to my place after your show, you'd be welcome. No pressure or anything, just thought I'd put that out there. I had a great time with you and…."

I shut him up with a kiss, short and sweet, because it kept me from saying something stupid in return. The smile I got once we parted lips was pure acceptance. The rest of our lunch passed in comfortable silence. We watched people passing, couples walking the paths, kids running about, dogs pulling at leashes. It was nice to relax with Dean nearby, and my hand didn't move from on top of his, crinkly hair on the back of his hand, the inside of his wrists soft and warm under my touches. Dean didn't make any move to close the gap or move away, and that was fine with me. It gave me enough space to think about the man next to me without lust overloading my mind.

We were downtown, and Dr. Spaulding's office was a couple of blocks away. I could be incredibly nosy and ask Dean about her. He could be seeing her for a lot of reasons, and I warred with my curiosity until it was my turn to blurt out something. "You said you don't do crowds. Is this okay?"

Dean looked around the crowd and nodded. "It's fine. There's more than enough space, I can see ways out, and well, I know you. It's when the crowd is packed in and I can't find an exit that I get weird."

"Weird?"

"Yeah. Sometimes it's just a little sweat and stammer. That's when I'm lucky."

And here I thought the sweat and stammer of the first night was standard "Jonathan is flirting with me" response. That was a big old hit to my ego. "Kouzina's way crowded on Friday nights."

"I could see the exits, and I knew the group I was with. Sorta. You missed me sweating it out in the bathroom. Usually it's in my car. Oh, wait." He turned to me, eyes narrowed for a moment. "Wait, you did see me. You almost knocked me over."

I beamed up at him with a playful shrug, squeezing his hand and wondering how the hell that was possible. A truck couldn't knock the man over. "Well, when you gotta go, you gotta go. How about when you're not lucky?"

"I keep 911 on speed dial." He spoke quietly, passing me the lemonade. He was watching the people again, shoulders hunched. "It feels like I'm having a heart attack. But I'm not. It only feels that way. Worst thing happens is that I pass out or something, but that's not happened in a very long time."

And that would explain why he was seeing Spauldy, I guessed. I tried to imagine Dean in the middle of a full-blown panic attack, and I couldn't. "Really, you're kidding, right? That's just crazy."

His back went stiff, his neck turning a little pink, and I knew that was the completely wrong thing to say. It didn't look good for the future harmony of our conversation. "You think I'm crazy?"

Time to run interference. "Well, no, not like you're gonna bust out with an ax and hack me to pieces or something. I can't see a dude as stable as you like that at all. You've got yourself a house, car, and a steady job. That's pretty solid, despite… you know. You could be a gigantic loser like me. I haven't had a steady job in years, and…."

"You'd think so, right? A lot of people think so. Guess I'm a little too messed up." Dean suddenly stood up, not looking at me at all, his back stiff and voice pinched. "I gotta get back to work."

I frowned, going over what I'd said one more time. I gave him what I thought was a compliment, put myself down, and he was still upset. Was stable another word for massive tight ass or something?

I shouldn't have given even the slightest fuck. If he couldn't take a simple question about his "crazy" condition, then screw him. I should just let him walk his tight ass back to his little nine to five, turn around, find Patch, blow him in one of the park toilets, and chalk this up as a failed walk on the norm side.

That's what I should have done.

But Dean wasn't looking at me, and that felt wrong. He didn't even seem willing to toss me a parting "Get stuffed, you insensitive asshole." It hurt. Not the being a tight ass, but the fact that he was withdrawing from me. I didn't want him to walk away.

I got to my feet. "Look, Dean, I run off at the mouth sometimes—"

"You didn't say anything I don't tell myself. Don't worry."

"Doesn't make it fair for an ass like me to say it, though. I'm sor—"

"You don't have to apologize, Jonathan." He turned and started walking away, too fast for me to grab him and make him stay put and listen to me.

"Will you look at me already!" I was loud enough for passersby to glance at us, but screw 'em.

Dean stopped, and a few breaths later, he turned around and faced me dead on, flat amber eyes sad and his face a bit flushed. Embarrassment. He was embarrassed, and with good reason, I supposed. He'd shared some of his damage with me, since I'd asked, and I'd called him crazy. To his face. Way to fail, Jonathan.

Now that I had him looking at me, I had to do something about it. It took three big steps to close the gap, and my hand circled his wrist. "You can tell me when I'm being an asshole, you know. Sometimes I don't realize it until I've opened my fucking mouth."

"You're not a bullshitter, right? That's what you said the night we met."

Those words would be carved on my tombstone one day. Right after someone killed me in some bullshit-related fit of rage. "Doesn't mean I can't mess up. I'm sorry. I don't think you're crazy, I mean, other than for wanting to see me again." At least I hoped he wanted to see me again. I wanted to tell him how I understood, that we had the same shrink. For chrissakes, we were practically brothers in arms.

My heart sank when he pulled away again. "Look, if I don't get back to the office, I'll have Richard burning up my line. It's his turn. I'll see you Saturday, okay?"

There was a smile on his face when he turned around to leave the park and me, but it didn't go up to his eyes the same way, and my sunken heart twisted with guilt. Man, can I do anything right? At least Dean was still coming to the show, he hadn't taken back that invite to go to his place after, and he hadn't told me where I could shove the bracelet. I would make it up to him then.

SATURDAY night rolled around, the place was packed with a paying audience, and I was on fire. Not in the flamingly gay way. I literally had fire in my hands.

It was my first solo, and with it being only me on a relatively large stage, I do love to make a spectacle of myself. I brandished a pair of metal spoke fans, each tipped with lit Kevlar, my hips flexing and writhing to the face-melting guitar shred of Metallica's "Fuel." The crowd was quiet, staring, with only a few bursts of cheers or applause, as if the fans would go out if someone sitting there watching me breathed wrong.

I loved it.

I couldn't move as quickly as when I'm belly dancing, nor was my focus on the crowd, other than to make sure I was in the sweet spot—not too close to them, not too close to the dark curtains that hid the backstage area from view. My costume, simple black pants and a dark-red tank top, was damp, as was my hair, pulled back into a ponytail, then coiled at the base of my neck, simple safety procedures that took some of the worry out of fire work. Gave me more brain space to concentrate on making this dance look good.

And it looked damned good. The heat of the flames made a light sheen of sweat pop up over my bare skin as I drew first one fan in front of my body, then the other, then brought them both over my head and held them there, swaying like a leaf in the wind, eyes locked on them adoringly. I loved playing with fire; the reward was always worth the risk.

I knew Dean was in the crowd, knew where he was sitting too, front row, stage right. Far stage right. I thought at first while I was sneaking peeks through the curtain before the show began that it was a weird place for a guy who sucked at crowds to sit. Then I realized that from there, he could see the red exit light backstage, he didn't have to see the crowd behind him, and most importantly, he could see me. Given how our last conversation ended, I was surprised that he showed up and sat so close, but I was going to grab that blessing with both hands and squeeze it for dear life.

But I couldn't look up at him during this routine. It would have put a real damper on the night if I looked up, caught a glimpse of hot amber looking back at me, and accidentally scorched myself. First and second degree burns are so not sexy. If we were still getting together afterward, I needed to be in one piece. One hot, lightly sweaty, unburnt piece.

The audience's silence ended right on the heels of the last note, leaving me with arms out, head back, drinking in the wild applause with the hunger of a vampire at a blood bank. I drew from that energy, took it into myself, would feed on it for the rest of the night, and I could finally look over at Dean, whose smile outshone everyone else in my eyes. That wasn't the smile of someone still annoyed with me, I hoped. I floated backstage on a cloud of anticipation.

The house lights rose, signifying both intermission and my need to find co-stage manager Rachel to go over things for the second half, making sure everyone and everything was ready for finishing this awesome night on a high note.

Patch peeked through the curtains, holding our shared bottle of fuel in one hand and a heavy blanket over his shoulder. "Your man is so out there somewhere. I could see you straining not to look at him from here. I bet I know which one he is, too."

"He's not my man." I rolled my eyes, took the blanket off him, and rolled it up. It was our first line of defense, should whoever was on stage playing with the shiny, pretty flames fuck up. Patch had blanket duty when I was on stage, and I would have it when we came out of intermission, for his spinning routine. "Do you have your shit together?"

"As always. You know, Rach bitched about him looking like a jock, but I don't see no jocky-looking anything out there."

I raised my hand in preparation to smack him if he didn't change the subject quickly. "Patch, I need you to focus."

He kept looking out the curtains. "I'm all yours. Are you sure you don't want a little peek? We've got time enough for you to show me what he looks like."

I gave in, if only to appease Patch and get him back on track. That was what I told myself, anyway. I moved behind him and peered over his head, expecting Dean to have followed the crowd to grab a snack and/or a piss, and I was wrong. He was still in his seat, relaxed, gorgeous. A petite little blonde with a coin scarf tied around her waist sat next to him, chattering away at him merrily. "The redhead over there."

"Bingo, I knew it!" Patch cried out and then whistled. "He's hot as hell. Damn, didn't know glasses turned you on, *papi*."

I gave in to the smacking urge, savoring the yelp it got, not bothering to admonish him on the nickname again. "Go soak your hair already, unless you want to torch it."

"Ten minutes, people!" Rachel called out as she walked over to us, fire extinguisher in hand.

We replied with the customary "Thank you, ten!" without even thinking about it, along with the stagehands and performers also zipping about backstage.

"Patch, why are you still dry?"

"Don't worry, lady. I've already been nagged. I wanted to see the hottie Jonathan bagged." He chuckled, with a lopsided grin. "Check me out. I should go into poetry."

"You're a regular fucking Neruda," Rachel groaned, also looking through the curtains. "Oh look, and there's his beard. She was with him when they bought tickets, you know. And check out that scarf she's wearing. God, we attract wannabes like shit draws flies."

I frowned and took another look. They sure did seem really friendly. But I'd been in Dean's house. There wasn't the slightest hint of residual estrogen in the place that I noticed. I saw a guy on her other side listening in. Not much to look at, brown hair, dark eyes, average looks, but he was leaning toward her as she babbled on. He was also holding her hand, and I pointed it out with a satisfying sense of triumph.

"Maybe she's just easy," was all Rachel said before giving Patch the side eye. "Shouldn't you be a little more upset about this?"

Patch kept looking. "Yeah, I'm upset I didn't meet this dude first. Does he bottom? Bet he's got an ass like a drum."

The kid deserved a medal for being a shining example of how to be cool about this sort of thing, and it didn't even seem to be an act. He really shouldn't have been that impressed by my taste. I did know how to pick 'em.

Rachel yanked him from the curtains by his belt loop. "Don't be stupid, and go soak your head."

He balked, but I added a sharp smack to his ass to get him moving. As much fun as it would have been to stare at Dean all night, we did have a show to finish.

"By the way, I switched your and Lala's acts," Rachel said the moment he was out of earshot.

"The fuck?" I just stared at her. "When did we decide that? Is there something wrong? We told everyone we had the set list in stone yesterday."

Having a solid set list was like a lifeline for performers and props people and us to cling to during showtime. We'd talked it over and over again this week, making sure we had a good balance between acts. It was one the things we did as stage managers that I really enjoyed.

She coolly shrugged and blinked up at me as if I had a brain injury. "Didn't you hear the crowd out there? They like you, so they're gonna get you sooner. I bet it would really please your 'friend' out there too, so don't bitch, okay?"

I didn't like how she said "friend" in the least, but I wasn't going to rise to that bait. "I thought Lala was okay. A lot of those folks out there are fans she brought in on name alone."

"Why should we care? You're a better performer with better stage presence, and you know that. I thought I was doing you a fucking favor."

I felt my face harden in unpleasant surprise. She had never done me this kind of "favor" before. Switching the script in the middle of things for no good reason was downright unprofessional, and we prided ourselves on being good when it came to our bread and butter. I didn't want to know what Lala was thinking about this switch. It would be on me to be the asshole and bear the bad news, I knew it. "A favor without bothering to check in with me? What was the point of working on this together if you were just going to change things up for before we're back on? Does she know?"

"Done and done, and you're welcome." She turned on a heel, her words so frosty that I expected clouds of air to cling behind her. Was she honestly expecting my thanks? "Five minutes, people!"

The "thank-you five" was out of my mouth before I could stop it. Damn Pavlovian response.

"And the prop table?" I called out at her retreating back, and got no answer for it. Wheels, silks, poi of the fiery and glowing sorts, anything a performer used during their set was placed on a table right next to stage left in order of the set list. It made it easier to keep up with all the crap—you just grabbed the object sitting closest to the stage and went on. Nothing would fuck up my groove further than to rush on stage with a pair of blinky hula hoops that I had no clue how to make look interesting.

And thanks to my best friend and fellow talent wrangler doing me a favor that would make me look like a dick and a diva, because it was my set that got bumped and Rachel sure can run her mouth, my mood was downright shitty. I prayed Lala didn't mind. No one wanted the diva rep. It made collaborative shows like this much more difficult to arrange if you're known for pulling shit like Rachel did.

Patch was at the table, checking over his torches and poi, hair slicked back, with wet droplets clinging to his nose. "They already bounced the house lights."

I glanced past his props and saw that the switch of mine and Lala's was already made. Well, I supposed I should thank Rachel for covering that much.

Without even waiting for me to respond, he turned and darted over to stage left. Time for me to get my head back in the game too. I peeked out to see Dean, who looked as if he hadn't moved from his seat during the entire intermission, still relaxed and looking amazing. The sight made me settle a little, and reminded me that, even with the backstage shit, we still had an audience to finish utterly rocking.

Performers scurried to their places, the green room, the dressing room, just out of the fucking way, and both backstage and the seats grew silent. I hunkered down at stage right, blanket at the ready, and saw Rachel walk on to scattered applause. She had the voice for emceeing, able to be heard out in the parking lot when she really wanted to get loud. It suited her perfectly, and I never fought her for the role during these shows. I spoke better with my body, anyway.

"Ladies and gents in the first three rows, I do hope you took care of potty breaks during intermission." She gave the crowd a naughty smirk that caused a few chuckles. "For our next performance, for your safety, we are asking you to stay seated. Because if you thought my boy Jonathan's dance was hot… wait until you get a load of Nightmare…."

And I groaned at yet another attempt by Patch to give himself a cool stage name. When we moved to Belle Point, it was Fieyro. When we first met him, he went by En Fuego, and he wore a luchador mask. Thank God I got a very up-close look at the pretty face behind the stupid thing later that night and convinced him to lose it. Rumor had it that Rachel quietly tossed it in a bonfire while I had Patch good and distracted. It was for the boy's own good, really. The audience could focus less on the goofy gimmick and more on his skill.

The crowd was awed as he swung the lit poi around his body, the speed turning the ends into rings of flame. No shimmying here, Patch let the props do the dancing, moving from one side of the stage to the other, kneeling, rising, making the rings small, then large, whipping them around his body until the trails looked like butterfly wings. Whoops filled the room when he extinguished and exchanged them for thin torches that he twirled between his fingers. He looked like a creepy, macabre doll with the heavy and dark eye makeup and all the stitch tats that I knew went all the way down past the long, baggy shorts. Normally, I'd be as hard as a rock watching him work, eager to get him backstage and in a corner so I could lick the sheen of sweat that made his pale, decorated skin glisten and jerk him off until he came. People backstage would leave us alone, some giggles, some rolled eyes, but hey, it was us, and we were utterly shameless.

The urge to jump him wasn't there, and that was weird. One glance past the twirling, flashy twink with the twirling, flashy flames right at Dean, and it was as if I'd never had that desire for backstage grappling. I didn't want a quick hand job in the dark. I wanted to climb into Dean's lap and kiss him until we both trembled with need, then have him in a bed. A real bed. That smelled of him. His bed.

I gripped the blanket tight, bringing myself back to focus, ready to up and run if Patch's next trick failed spectacularly. I watched as he opened his mouth and placed one of the torches inside, then closed his lips, extinguishing the flame. On the other side of the stage, Rachel held the bright-red canister tightly, ready for the next part and, like me, hoped nothing went wrong. I think Patch named himself Nightmare due to the nightmare of a liability his shtick could be. I love my fire fans, and I can swing a poi with the best of them, but I'm no expert at taking a mouthful of fuel and spitting it over a torch, creating a huge explosive fireball that ignited over the audience's heads. Luckily, it seemed that the first three or so rows heeded Rachel's warning, and no one caught on fire.

Patch swallowed the flame of the second torch, winked, and bowed low as the crowd not only clapped, but seemed to breathe a sigh of relief, as we did backstage. Another risky performance done without a hitch. I had to beat feet to the dressing room to prepare for my own. Instead of the fifteen minutes I calculated with the former set list, I would only have about eight or ten. Thanks, Rach. Such a pal.

Passing Tam and Cindy at the door for their upcoming set, I found myself alone in the dressing room with Ms. Lala herself. Her hot pink pixie cut was hard to miss. Hell, she was a real-life pixie as far as I was concerned, a pixie who came to earth from the faraway land of Wales to make the world a more awesome place. Everything about her was tiny: her build, her height of barely five feet, her weight of under one hundred pounds, even if you counted the scraps of shiny gold lamé she called her costume and dunked her in water first. I wanted to check her for wings every time we met. I'd find them, all right, butterfly wings that graced her entire back, beautifully inked in black, pink, and purple. If I ever decided to bat for the other team, I'd fall on my face to ask Lala out, if she hadn't been already happily married, of course.

She stood at one of the huge mirrors that took up two parallel walls, touching up her purple eye shadow, and glanced over to me as I walked up. "So, got the news about the switch from your friend."

Oh boy, she didn't sound happy at all, all icy and strained. It made her accent even more pronounced. "It was a surprise to me too."

She waited until I walked past before rounding on me. "You think you're better than me? Because she sure as hell implied it."

I was going to kill Rachel, if I managed to live to make it to my set. "No, and if Rachel told you anything like that, she's talking bullshit, Lala, really. It's the stress, makes her crazy, and it makes her say shit she doesn't mean."

"Oh really?" The woman held up the baggie with her commission from me inside, a single strand of silver chain with a square-cut rose quartz pendant the size of a quarter dangling off it, held fast with delicate loops of silver wire. She provided the gemstone and told me to go to town with the design, only to keep it simple enough for her to wear at her day job at the local metaphysical shop. Her payment was twenty-five bucks, a new black eyeliner pen from her hookup at the MAC store downtown, and two more commissions from her coworkers. "Give me one good reason I shouldn't ask for my cash back, tell you two to fuck off, and leave now. I didn't know I was working with a pair of prima donnas."

"We're not, I swear. Rachel's talking shit." I motioned to the used eyeliner pencil sitting near my stuff. "I don't think you can exchange that, because I've already used it, but you can keep the necklace even if you want your money back. You've got people out there. They want to see you. I want to see you."

I could have used that cash, was hoping to have a little more to eat than plain ramen, eggs, and rice until the next commission came around, but if it would ease the drama I didn't even cause, so be it. Rach and I totally needed to have a talk, one where I reminded her that pissing off the local talent was always a bad fucking idea.

Lala turned back to the mirror and shrugged a shoulder. "You're lucky I like the pendant. Keep the money."

I sighed in relief, looking at my bag as if I could see the folded twenty and five dollar bills tucked into one of the pockets. It was going to stay right where it was, Lala was going to perform, and I needed to get changed right away. "Just don't wear it while hooping. It won't take that kind of beating."

Lala hula hooped with her entire body, hips, arms, legs, neck, chest, using two hoops that were sturdier and heavier than what you could buy at a toy store. They were made even heavier by the power packs for the LED lights inside, installed by her lovely husband Mark. Like Patch and his fire, once she got those suckers whirling around, she would look downright magical.

I waited a second, my guilty-by-proxy conscience nagging me as I removed my shirt. "Hey, dollface?"

She turned her head, blusher sponge in hand, and drawled, "Yeeees?" I could hear the lifted eyebrow.

"You know I wouldn't fuck you or anyone else over on show night. I am going to talk to Rach later about not messing with the set list like that, maybe get her to maybe smoke up a bit before showtime so she can relax a little, deal?"

Lala slowly grinned, nodded, and turned to finish her makeup. I felt a bit more relieved to get smiles, and lost myself in my own prep. One solo setup next, then a duet with Rachel in the same garb. She was currently all coined up for a more traditional dance, working the harem chic, while I was going for a look a lot less so. For starters, dancing villagers in the Middle East would never dream of wearing as much chain as I had wrapped around my waist. My black dance pants were worn dangerously low, but they were tight enough around the hips to keep me from accidentally flashing my dick at people. Falls of red scarves sewn below the knees would flare out with every turn I took. Even my chain belts had red and purple scarves tied to some of the links, all directing attention to my lower body. My chest would remain bare, showing off my snake and stars, save for two purple scarves tied around my upper arms. My hair had dried a lot since I wet it down for my last set, and I let it fall loose down my back.

I gave my eyeliner and face fuzz once more look over in the mirror, leaned back and gave my hips an experimental shimmy, loving the way the scarves bounced against my legs. A familiar excitement pulsed up my spine, speeding up my heartbeat. I couldn't wait to get out there. No stage fright here. If anything, I got a stage semi-boner just thinking about soaking up the adoration. I'll admit it. I'm an attention whore.

"Break a leg," Lala called to me as I hurried out of the dressing room, hearing the last of the girls' song and the applause and knowing I had to be at the prop table right now. Tam and Cindy passed by me, and even in the low blue backstage lights, I saw the happy, satisfied looks on their faces, the relieved glow of a job well done. All that rehearsing had been put to good use, and even taking a day off to frolic in the park hadn't affected anyone's performance. So far, so good.

Patch was crouched next to the props table when I got there, tucking the last of the fuel and fire toys into a knapsack. He looked up at me and let out a playful growl. "How do you manage to make jiggling around like a girl look good?"

"Because I'm awesome," I whispered, checking the table for the tightly bound length of cloth I would need, my Wings of Isis. "Is that all of the fire things?"

Patch nodded and took advantage of my crotch being so close to his head and gave my dick a brief nuzzle. "Dean's a lucky bastard, you know that?"

That was unexpected. Not the dick nuzzle, but hearing Dean's name come out of Patch's mouth. I looked down at him. "You're not jealous, are you, kid?"

"Are you sure you want to call me 'kid' when my teeth are this close to your dick?"

"Good point. Now answer the question."

Patch kept rubbing his cheek against my pants like a cat. "Yeah, but not because you fucked him. We're not like that. But man, you didn't see him look at you when you were on stage. I mean, I had him pegged just by the way he was clocking you."

"You were watching the audience? Weren't you supposed to be watching me in case I went up like the Human Torch?"

"Please, you know what you're doing better than I do. But yeah, that's what's got me all weird, I guess. He looked at you like you were the only fucker in the house. It was… nice."

I tucked the still-rolled-up fabric under my arm and gave Patch's hair a pat. He was such a younger me, so much that sex sometimes felt like masturbation. I hoped like hell I was being some sort of a decent role model. Sometimes, though, he totally surprised me. "That's kind of what I'm going for anytime I'm on stage." This heart-to-heart shit was so very unlike Patch. Then again, we weren't exactly "normal."

"Don't fuck with me, Jonathan. I ain't dumb, and you know what I'm talking about. Have a look yourself." He then leaned forward and brushed his nose against my crotch again before standing up. "Just, you know, we don't want to piss Rach off too much if she thinks you're leaving me for him or some shit."

"Don't worry about her, okay? You're with us whether we're fucking or not. You don't think I'm gonna kick you off my mattress because...."

I paused, my brain catching up to what my mouth was saying. It all sounded as if Dean and I were an item already. We'd only had one night, for crying out loud. Sure, we might screw again tonight. I definitely wanted us to do it again. I'd been dreaming about it ever since, which was a pain in the balls when there was barely privacy to rub one out at the House. But that didn't mean we were any more than what Patch and I had.

I kissed his cheek. "Relax, okay? You did good out there. Now wish 'papi' luck."

"I thought you hated it when I called you that." Patch laughed and slung the sack over his shoulder. "Break a leg."

Rachel rushed by me as I moved to center stage behind the curtain while carefully unrolling the fabric. The Wings of Isis were made of a long curved length of transparent black lamé attached to two long clear Lucite wands. The very center of the fabric had a chain that I attached at the neck, wearing it like a cape, and I took the wands in hand, extending both arms out to the side to make sure I hadn't somehow twisted the fabric behind me.

Between the curtains where I'd be entering the stage, I could see the lights dropping low, leaving only a spotlight for Rachel to stand in and reintroduce me to a loud burst of applause. The spotlight moving with her off the stage was my cue to step from behind the curtain and into the dark, one arm up, the other down and pointing to the stage floor, feet ready for the first note of the song, "Black Wings of Hate" by Van Canto.

And I began to spin. The wings gave me a larger-than-life presence once the lights were up and the crowd could see me, turning in circles with a spiral of black coiling with me, first clockwise, then counter as I spun in the opposite direction. Both arms raised up high, displaying my body as my hips twisted and turned. My feet shuffled quickly across the stage, wings undulating with my hips. Every twitch of my body was felt and shared by the fabric. I rocked to the rhythm of the fast pounding drums, then suddenly swayed my arms to the time of the vocals, movements going from controlled and fast to gentle and smooth in the space of the few measures. It would be so easy to just get lost in it all, to let muscle memory take over.

I couldn't do that, though. I couldn't let rote memory be my only guide in this dance. Dean was out there. I may not have much to offer him, but I had this, my body and what it could do. Despite my misgivings, I did seek out his brilliant amber eyes when the routine led me spinning to that side of the stage. It was muscle memory that kept me from falling over or missing another step at the intense gaze. His gorgeous face was open, lips slightly parted. It was appreciation of a completely different sort. Patch's words echoed in the back of my mind. I was the only fucker on stage, true, but Dean looked at me as if I was the only fucker in the entire theater.

I had to tear my own eyes away to work the other side of the stage, but I swore I felt Dean's gaze on my back, and the crinkled fabric could not protect me from it. I couldn't think about it now, as the song moved to the bridge, no drums, just voices. I slowly lowered my arms in time to the singing, released the wands, then unlatched the chain around my neck, letting it all drop behind me. The whoops of the crowd made my smile grow wide. Yeah, everyone tended to get all excited when there was less cloth in the way of the view of bare skin. Arms out, I quickstepped to the front, turning to the side, and slowly undulated, turning my body into exaggerated S's. Patch called my dancing "shimmying like a girl," but to me, dancing was one of two moments I felt truly masculine, the other being when I'm having sex. I was completely in my body, and could stretch it long and lean, work my hips fast enough to turn the decorations there into blurs, show off my flexibility by bending backward until the ends of my hair touched the stage floor. My stomach wasn't completely cut, with a six-pack on display, but the muscles were tight and allowed for flutters, and no one's complained about them yet, not here.

I finished up with a set of turns, one, two, three, and stopped in stance, arms thrown behind my back and smirking at the crowd, and I couldn't continue that thought due to the drowning waves of applause that washed over me like a baptism of praise or a coronation. All hail King Fuck of Awesome Mountain. Long may He reign.

The rest of the show passed in a blur, and soon we were all done, all on stage for final introductions and thanks and bows. I didn't bother turning around to walk backstage, just rushed over to Dean and stood in front of the man, drinking in that huge smile.

"You were amazing." He shifted in his seat as I approached, the slight darkening of his cheeks noticeable even under the house lights. "I'm really glad I got the best seat in the house."

I couldn't help myself, patting my own ass and winking. "Oh no, this is the best seat in the house. You should know that."

It took the cute blonde giggling next to us to keep me from telling Dean to come get a handful of the best seat in the house. "Wow, Dean, he's even cuter up close!"

Dean turned to her, and the flush increased. "This is Bette and her husband, Robert. Bette and I work together, and she came along to Kouzina that first night."

I offered my hand, charming smile in place. "Nice to meet you, Bette, I'm Jingle Boy."

Now it was her turn to blush to the roots of her hair. "He told you that?"

"I'm flattered, really. Nice scarf, do you dance?" I winked at her and offered my hand to Robert. I could guess the answer to that, since we danced with the only other professional troupe in town at Kouzina, and I'd never seen her before with Caress. It was a polite thing to ask, anyway.

She shook her head. "I'm only taking classes, and just a few so far. I'm not nearly brave enough to let anyone see me but my instructor."

At least she didn't assume she'd be stage ready with so little instruction, the usual irritation I had with a wannabe. I had to admit, without the Tribe girls to be bitchy at my back, I couldn't conjure even hidden contempt. Bette was too enchanted, and Dean made me too relaxed.

She and Robert said their good-byes and left us in the quickly emptying seats. Both Dean and I had opened our mouths to say something when I felt a sudden weight hop on my back, pitching me forward. "Come on, *papi*! The sooner we get out of here, the sooner we can go party!"

Fucking Patch. The momentum of his pounce shocked Dean enough to hold his arms out to catch me, bringing me close against his chest. Patch bounced back just in time to keep me from being the center of a hunk and twink sandwich I didn't order. He overshot by a lot and stumbled back to fall on his ass with a grunt of pain that made me feel a lot better. "Jesus, if you wanted to meet him, you could ask like a normal person, shit!"

Patch looked right up at us from his sprawl, his smile unrepentant. "Oh no, Brer Rabbit, don't shove me into that hot guy's lap. Heya, hot guy, I'm Patch. A friend."

"Dean." His arms tightened around me, as if Patch's words made him realize where I sat, I suppose. "Also a friend?"

"Yeah, definitely a friend." Now that we were this close, I didn't want to move. But Patch had a point about getting the place shut down quickly. "Look, kid, I'll be backstage in a sec. Scram."

I didn't move once Patch picked himself off the floor with a loud bark of laughter, running behind the curtains, and Dean didn't make any move to let go. I took that as a good sign and wound one arm around his neck, laying my free hand on his chest, feeling his warmth seeping into me from everywhere. I'd have to thank the kid for shoving me on him after all. After I smacked the brat.

Dean pressed his nose into the crook of my neck. "You smell so good." The tickle of his tongue brushing against my skin made my toes curl.

"I smell like a racehorse. Stage lights are hot." I wanted to smack myself for not being able to think straight, but I was busy unfastening one of Dean's buttons, eager to feel his skin, and I stopped caring about anything else but warmth and smoothness and the feel of a racing pulse beneath my fingers.

Dean cupped my hip and pulled me tighter, kissing behind my ear and making me completely forget who was supposed to be seducing whom yet again. He was damned sexy all relaxed. "Your friends must be really ready to rip it up after that show."

I had two buttons loose and bit back a moan when my hand slipped inside his shirt, in and down and stopping to graze over a pebbly nipple. I wanted to know what that tasted like, and its twin. I wanted more than a taste of his cock. There wasn't enough time for me to do what I wanted to him, not even if we had until the heat death of Earth. A question niggled in the back of my mind, however. "I'm sure they're going to have an awesome time. I'm still invited to your place? I know I was kind of an asshole to you earlier."

"It's okay. It's something I'm still really uncomfortable telling people about. I shouldn't have gotten so pissed." He ran a hand over my thigh, and I moaned. "Forgive me?"

I had to be sure that forgiveness equaled invitation. "Let's get back to your place, and I'll show you how forgiven you are."

"God, I hoped you'd still want to come with me," Dean replied quickly, in a hot rush that had the edge of a moan. Thank fuck I wasn't the only one here that was so needy. "You can stay the whole night if you want, the whole weekend. I want to see more of you. I… just…." A low chuckle gusted across my neck, raising goose bumps. "Could I sound more desperate?"

It really did seem like all was forgiven from our last face to face, and I wasn't going to complain. I leaned back to look at him for a moment before leaning in to kiss his grin. If it wasn't for the lingering crowd and the impatient performers, I would have been more than happy to start our postshow celebration right there. Just sink down to my knees and undo his pants….

"That makes two of us," I rasped honestly, forcing that naughty thought out of my head. "Let me change and grab my shit, and I'll meet you in front of concessions." I paused for a second, considering what I knew about him and crowds. "Things should be emptyish out there by now, but you can wait here too."

He raised an eyebrow, and I mentally kicked myself for what I'd said. I was trying to keep him in mind.

"I appreciate that, but you don't have to look out for me. I'm learning how to deal. In front of concessions is okay."

"I do it because I want to, big guy, and because you're dead sexy all relaxed." His smile told me it was okay, and I slid off his lap, thrilling at the slight bulge I left in his pants. It sure matched the one I was sporting.

HAPTER SIX

# *After-Party*

I RETURNED to the dressing room with the biggest, goofiest smile I've ever smiled plastered to my face. The sooner I could get ready, the sooner I could go back and show Dean my appreciation.

It wasn't as if I didn't appreciate the Tribe. In lieu of finishing our degrees in art college, Rach and I had turned a small ever-changing group of disaffected performers into a traveling troupe of twenty-four-hour party people. It was work and time and more than a little drama, but in the end it was worth it in how my people paused and lifted their heads, nodded to me, smiled, patted my shoulder, didn't object to my smacking Patch upside his head. If I asked, I'd have no problem getting someone to fetch me a drink, a joint, pills, a blowjob. I had respect and status here. I was co-top monkey of the totem pole.

Still, there were issues—people not familiar with how we worked who liked to mess with one of the obvious faggots of the main group. And I carried my meager belongings with me like a turtle or snail because I couldn't trust anyone to not rob me blind. And there was the not-so-minor issue of Rachel becoming more and more controlling as I'd gotten more and more distant, with all the worry about my Mama and so on. It wasn't anyone's fault, I thought, just what happens with time and the constant chaos that was our way of life.

Of course a clean-cut guy like Dean would appeal to me. He was solid, different, and I was the one who chose him. I wish I could say that Patch was the first toy boy "gift," instead of just the first that had a talent we could market, the smarts to keep from doing something stupid to fuck it up for everyone, and the maturity to not expect more from us. Our little chat before my set surprised me. He understood better than he let on, and he knew to keep up that brainless-beauty pose in public. He did it so well I wasn't really surprised that Rachel was pissed at me about the whole Dean thing. Patch was the closest she'd come to a perfect fit for me, at least in her eyes.

And she remained pissed, glancing at me as I walked to my corner and started removing the chains and scarves. She hadn't even put on a clean shirt before ripping into me. "Why are you even wasting your time with Boy Scout? You know he's going to drop you the second someone else more his type comes along."

"And what's his type, Rach?"

Her petite nose wrinkled in disgust. "Someone more mainstream. Someone more normal. Not you."

I couldn't tell if that was supposed to make me feel better or not. I couldn't pinpoint when shit like that started to be the norm, or when that started to be aimed at me more often than not. We could argue about this tomorrow, not around people. "Funny, he seems to like me just fine."

"Damn it, Jonathan." Her furious whisper was an impressive contrast to her stage voice. "What if he's a closeted piece of shit? You saw that bimbo wannabe hanging over him. He can have in her pants with a blink. I'm looking out for your ungrateful ass."

I swallowed the lump of anger that bubbled in the back of my throat like bile, feeling quite protective of that "wannabe." She was polite and eager and, most importantly, married to another dude. "Bullshit. If you thought for one second that he was a closeted piece of shit playing me, we'd have to pull you off him. You sure as fuck wouldn't be standing there speculating on nothing."

I had her, and she knew it. Before whatever was happening between us started happening, Rachel would have kicked the shit out of anyone who dared hurt me, and I've earned my black eyes and bruised knuckles doing the same for her. That gave me a brief thought of Rafe's bloodied face, and I had to smile just a little. Rach and I had each other's backs.

She bristled, eyelids fluttering, bared breasts swaying, and grumbled. "I thought you wanted to handle this yourself, since you're acting like we're not good enough for you anymore."

Her eyes moved over to where Patch was happily chatting with Lala and a few locals before returning to look at me, and her meaning was clear. Patch assumed Rachel thought this was some sort of infidelity. From the looks of it, she seemed more miffed that it looked like I was turning down her very generous blond and hung gift. But I wasn't having this conversation tonight. "I like this guy, and it's got nothing to do with the Tribe or Patch or you. Jesus, are you not getting laid enough that you're pulling this clingy shit?"

We both knew that wasn't it. Some days I wished for her luck with men. Rachel was short, voluptuous, had a wicked smile and no interest in dating, a perfect combo in this crowd for a chick who moved around a lot. Not one for relationships, that girl. She looked away and yanked a black shirt over her head, one with Hello Kitty's skull on it, red bow and all. That gave me a moment to stash away my costume in a "to be washed" bag and get boxers on. We so had to start having these conversations with both of us fully dressed.

Her voice was calmer when she spoke next. "Look, I'm worried, okay? I worry when you're not nearby. I don't know this guy, and I don't want him to hurt you."

I sighed in relief, glad that we'd gotten past the bullshit to the actual point. "You've gotten a good look at him. Does he look like someone who would even try it?" That was a ridiculous question, and I knew it. Dean was half a foot taller than me; of course he looked like he could do damage if he wanted to. I needed a better argument, and one leapt out of my mouth before I could stop myself. "You know me better than that to wander off with just anyone. He's got his own issues and shit. Hell, Rach, crowds make him wig out."

There, I could make him look more human, and for a moment, it seemed that Rachel was actually mulling it over before turning to the attitude. "Do I really know you? Really? Because I swore tall and boring wasn't your type…." She stopped, took a breath, and tried again. "Okay, I don't want to fight. We'll go home, get hammered, and celebrate a good show, okay? Safe and sound at home, yeah?"

As usual, no apology from her, but I also wasn't going to apologize for keeping my plans, because I knew what would happen if I did show up at the party after this little chat. We wouldn't talk about anything, she'd make sure my cup never ran empty, that my lungs never lacked pot smoke, and have Patch take care of me. I didn't want that tonight. I shouldn't have wanted it any night, but I remained too much of a wimp to go into the details with her. At least not right now, because I knew my refusal was going to make her very, very upset, and I didn't want to make matters worse. "Not tonight, Rach. I'm going over to Dean's."

Hurt flashed over her face, but outrage frosted her pretty features. I saw it, though, and felt like a tool. Oh, this wasn't going over well. If looks could kill, I'd be splattered against the back wall. "What?"

The others had noticed the angry whisper fight by now and stared at us, worried and curious and confused. I hoped we could hold off on this tiff until we could be alone. Now wasn't the time for it, not where we could ruin everyone else's good vibes, not when I was so very, very close to having Dean within my grasp. My palms ached to touch him again.

"You heard me." I surprised myself at how calm I felt. I had made my decision, and saying it out loud was easy. Saying "no" was easy. Who knew? "I like him. A lot."

She shook her head in disgust. "Fine." Her whisper was ragged. Then she snatched up her bag, wheeled around, and headed for the door. "Hurry the fuck up or you're all getting left behind!" she snapped before the door snicked shut.

All those eyes were on me in the uncomfortable silence that followed. Just like little kids witnessing a fight between their parents, everyone else looked toward the remaining one for reassurance that everything was okay. Most of them, anyway. Tam and Cindy looked both scared and pissed at me for daring to upset Mama Bear and getting away with it. Patch just looked confused. I tugged my duffel over my shoulder, as cool as I could fake it. "You heard the lady. Get your asses in gear before all the booze is gone."


I WAITED until everyone else had left the dressing room and made sure the place was neat so the volunteer staff would have less work to do and more reason to invite us back. Rachel would have gotten our take of the ticket sales, after paying the theater and our featured performers, so I didn't have to mess around with carrying cash myself. With the packed house we'd had, we'd have rent covered this month. Go us.

Dean kissed me hello, pulled away, and then kissed me stupid enough to barely hear him say, "We could stop by the party, if you wanted to."

I shook my head, raking my gaze over his face to make sure he wasn't joking. "You said it yourself, Dean, you suck at crowds, and this is not your ordinary crowd."

If he'd been standing there the entire time I'd been backstage, I could only imagine Rachel's face as she passed him, probably all pinched, like he smelled bad or something. He smiled, though, grabbing the strap of the duffel. "I don't think an hour or two will hurt. I can't get used to crowds if I don't try to be in them, and I don't want to come between you and your friends."

"You're sure about that?"

Dean nodded. "Yeah, Rachel actually invited me over. She didn't look happy about it, but she did."

Shock threw me off enough to let him take the bag. Maybe Rachel was trying to be understanding. It made me feel hopeful. "You sure it won't be a problem for you?" I had to know.

"There's only one way to find out." He easily hauled the bag onto his back. For the first time that night, I saw the bracelet. Still there after a week, and boy did that make my gut do somersaults. The brown and bronze really suited his eyes, like it was made for him all along. I'd wait until tomorrow to ask for it back. Maybe.

My hand wrapped around his wrist tightly, feeling the metal press into our skin, my eyes boring into his to show him I wasn't messing around. "The moment, the very second you start feeling uncomfortable, overwhelmed, whatever, you're going to tell me. And don't think that I'm not coming home with you still. You're not getting rid of me that easily."

It wasn't a request. Now who was sounding desperate? I wanted so badly to make it clear that I was going home with him tonight, for more than carnal reasons, if I was being completely honest. I was a little worried, though. The thought of him freaking out on my watch made me want to freak out too.

His smile dimmed by a couple of notches, his eyes became serious, and he moved his hand until my fingers drifted from the chain mail to twine with his, then lifted our hands to his lips, brushing them against my fingers. "Of course."

Gah, those two simple syllables of acceptance with no question turned my knees into Jell-O and my cock into steel. I had to kiss him, and hoped I was giving him some incentive to make the hour at the party a very, very short one.

THE crowd that ended up at our place after a big show tended to be humongous. I've often wondered how we could cram that many people in the place without it bursting at the worn-out, tired old seams. I could see Dean getting pale just driving past the house as we looked for a place to park.

Once we paralleled ourselves into a spot about a block away, I took his elbow, clad in his usual sports jacket, and gave it a firm squeeze. He felt a lot warmer than I did, and that made me regret not hauling my trench coat out of the duffel to deflect the icky drizzle that pissed down on the world outside of the car. "Just say the word, and we're gone."

He nodded, and we made our way into the misty night. I looked up at the house, mind racing with plans, seating arrangements, typical crowd formations, figuring out the best place for the two of us to sit and chill without overwhelming him. Finding Rachel to see if she was all right was the secondary goal, but it was a party, so that meant she would be upstairs or on the back deck making out with Grimace and someone else's pot stash until she couldn't feel feelings anymore. She'd be easy to find once I got Dean comfortable.

After confirming that cig smoke didn't bug him, we settled on the front porch, the usual den for those who like to light up legally. A glance and a jerk of my head got two people sitting on the swinging bench to get up for us, which was one more than we needed because my plans involved that nice rain-damp lap of his once I'd dashed inside to get us something to drink. It would be a lot easier to mind my intake with Dean nearby, as much as the cravings gnawed at me. I had to be mostly sober for him, or I'd be the one embarrassing myself.

A few folks side-hugged and back-slapped me, congratulating me on a show well done, complimenting my sets, introducing me to starry-eyed people they'd brought along. I made those moments brief, but my ego ticked up a few points, mostly since I wasn't getting the cold shoulder for the little spat in the dressing room. Although maybe that was because the majority of the folks there were fans and friends of boarders who wouldn't have even heard about that incident. I didn't see Patch on my way into the kitchen or back outside, and made a mental note to check in with him before we left. He'd be thankful as fuck to have the mattress to himself for a night.

"No labels, it's a home brew, lager, I'm told." I presented one of the two bottles to Dean and slid my happy ass onto his thighs with the ease of putting on my favorite pair of pants.

For the most part, we were left alone by the smokers, with just a few questions about where I snagged the hottie. I enjoyed watching Dean's full-on blush. No way he couldn't have known how good-looking he was to be this embarrassed about others bringing it up.

"How are you doing, baby?" I asked him, shuddering at the endearment that slid out of my mouth naturally. I couldn't even blame being drunk; I was only on my second beer. Dean had refused another since he was driving. It shouldn't have made me admire his restraint, but it did. Hell, if I were in his shoes, surrounded by strangers, prone to freaking out, I'd be trying my best to drink myself into a stupor.

Dean curled his arms around me even tighter, speaking right into my ear. "I'm good. Everyone sounds like they're having a great time."

"Yeah, we're real weekend warriors around here. It's not usually this full, but you know, special occasions and all." Suddenly, and I should have asked this before, the question was on my lips. "Hey, Dean, got a personal question for you—"

"More personal than have I ever bottomed?" I could feel that grin against my ear, and it was my turn to grow a little warm under my tank top. Didn't Patch ask me this same question already? I was so fucking drunk the night I texted that question to him, drunk and horny and very happy with the response—yes, and he liked it. "Or have I ever had sex in public? Boxers or briefs? Been with another uncut guy?"

"Jesus, I asked all of that?" No wonder people considered drinking and texting a bad idea. I must have sounded like some sort of sex-obsessed über-slut.

Dean nipped at my earlobe, hard enough to make me gasp. "Yup, so what do you want to ask me now?"

"Do you do anything more dangerous than that occasional glass of wine or this beer? Pot, coke, pills?" I couldn't remember if I had mentioned to Dean that all of that shit was probably on order right behind the front door or not. If he did, and if he was game, I'd be a shitty host to not offer, right?

It was a dangerous question. The last thing I wanted was him thinking I was a total druggie as well as some sort of sex-obsessed über-slut. Spauldy didn't like it when I called myself any of those names, and I didn't want him thinking it of me.

He was quiet for a sec, then nodded, his nose brushing against my cheek. "Years ago, nothing like that now."

Oh, that was a surprise. A relaxing, ass-unclenching surprise. "You used to party?" I almost asked him if that was another reason why he was seeing Dr. Spaulding, but that would have required admitting I was also seeing her. Not right now, not when I had no idea how to deal with it.

"Yeah, in college, before I got... sucky... around crowds." He looked up over my head at everyone else, and I laid a hand on his chest to get that attention back where it belonged, on me.

"I bet you've got some crazy stories. I wanna hear them." I turned my head to mouth at Dean's neck, feeling good, buzzed, not remotely drunk, but good enough to openly flirt for all to see.

The taste of rain and sweat and him drove me crazy, and I kissed the skin there, nibbling before he stilled me with a hand on the back of my head. "Sure, as long as you share a few with me. What are they doing out there past the porch?"

I lifted my head reluctantly and gazed over the porch railings. Even with the misty weather, you couldn't keep a bunch of firebugs from playing. Patch, ever shirtless, stood in a circle of five, spraying all their hands with a mister filled with a clear liquid. "Oh, he's spraying Everclear. They're going to pass the flame around."

"Pass the what around?"

"Just watch."

Once everyone's hands were misted with the high-octane grain alcohol, a girl flicked her lighter and set her hand on fire. There was no other way to describe it. She touched the lighter to her hand, and it caught. Quickly, she pressed her flaming hand to her neighbor's, igniting his hand, and he moved to Patch, who moved along, and so on until the fire went out. They laughed and whooped as Patch unhooked the mister from his belt and started spraying hands again.

"That doesn't hurt?"

"Only if you're dumb enough to sit there and let the alcohol burn out." I chuckled. "You'd have to be way out of it to let that happen."

"You've done it before? I mean, let the alcohol burn out…."

"Count it as one of my crazy party stories. I was young and stoned out of my mind, and fire's pretty."

We watched a few rounds of flame passing before the group wandered around the house to the backyard. As they went by, I returned my attention to Dean's neck. Without booze and drugs sending my mind into a foggy daze, I was getting restless as hell. He'd never replaced the buttons I'd unfastened back at the theater, so I took advantage, removing two more and sliding my hand inside. The skin under my fingers was still very warm, the sensation like lightning shooting right to my groin, making it harden like the nipple I found and toyed with. He moaned roughly, his arms squeezing tighter around me. If anyone on the porch noticed, they said nothing.

He was hard against me, and I rubbed against the bulge with my hip. "Do I need to convince you that it's time for us to go?" I said, sounding raspy, "I mean, I could undress and molest you some more right here, but I'm feeling a little territorial."

I wanted to kick myself the second "territorial" came out. Being around Dean made all kinds of stupid shit come to mind and right out of my stupid mouth. This man was not mine. I should not be feeling territorial about him or anyone else. I didn't have the right.

"I think I could be convinced," Dean whispered, cupping the back of my head and drawing me close for a SuperKiss, the slow and sexy "I need you in my pants, but I'm going to take my sweet time with it" version. Otherwise known as the "drive Jonathan out of his mind until he humps your leg" version. I went for how long without that kiss, only a week? Dean's kisses were worse than any drug I'd ever contemplated taking.

When I pulled back to take in air, I saw the front door open, and Rachel stepped out, coming right for us. "We've got a problem, Jonathan."

"Problems" could be anything, but if they were bad enough to get Rach downstairs, it required both our attentions. Someone was dumb and got hurt, or got sick, or some drama we didn't ask for was happening in our home and we had to get the participants the fuck out before they ruined the groove for everyone. We didn't do 911 unless someone was dying, because nothing spelled "groove killer" like the presence of cops and EMTs.

I was on my feet, out of those arms before she finished speaking, and turned to Dean. "I won't be long, okay baby?"

He looked a bit lost for a second, still in that lust fog, but eventually nodded with a big, sexy smile. The way his lips looked, all red from our kiss, made me moan out loud. I could have kissed him again for not giving me shit about it, and I tucked that idea in mind for later. I followed Rachel back inside, pushing my way to the stairs. She pointed up. "Our room, I'm getting some water. You can thank me later, by the way."

Oh goody, I guess someone had too much to drink. Drunk or not, if this mystery loser puked on my mattress, I was going to stomp a mudhole in their ass before throwing them out the door.

I took the steps two at a time, slipped into the room and looked around for a downed body, and found no one there but a very confused-looking Patch. Other than the confused look, he seemed fine.

"Hey, kid, you okay?" I kept looking around, just in case he came up to help with our "problem."

"I thought you were here with Dean." Patch had sauntered up to me, close enough that his bare chest brushed against my clothed one. Normally it'd be sexy as hell, but given the situation and the odd look in his eyes, I was unmoved, so to speak.

"I am, but Rachel told me there was a 'problem' in here, and hey!" I backed up as Patch started working on the button of my fly. "The fuck are you doing?"

"If you stay still long enough, you," he murmured, no heat behind his voice as he cupped the crotch of my pants.

I stopped his lunge with both hands on his shoulders. "Patch, what the hell is up with you? What's going on?"

"Rachel said you looked tense with your guy out there, and well, you know…."

Just like "problem," me "looking tense" was another bit of Tribe-code for me "needing head so I wouldn't be a buzzkill." So, that was the "problem?" Rach saw me making out on the porch and squirming on Dean's lap, so I had no clue where she got the idea that there was any sort of tension other than in my pants. What was really screwed up was that she invited Dean over and was trying to pull this shit. "And why did you decide to go along with it?"

"'Cause the only person in the house that can say no to Rach and not get tossed is you, man." His head dropped between his shoulders, the bang hiding his face from me. "The last thing I wanna do is piss her off. More."

I gave his shoulder a little shake. "Hey, look at me. You knew I wasn't going to let you do this if you did want to. What's really going on?"

Patch looked up, the spray bottle still at his hip banging against mine with how badly he shook. He didn't sound like himself, all tight and angry. "She don't want him around, but she couldn't do a damn thing about it with you right there."

He looked fucking miserable. While I couldn't blame him—he didn't have a place to go in this town if Rach threw him out—a small part of me wanted to deck him for going along with this anyway. Luckily, the rest of me had a better idea. I grabbed a fistful of blond hair and crashed his lips into mine. This wasn't a gentle kiss. I wanted to get those lips red fast and brought my teeth to bear, to bite and bruise. The horny little bastard whimpered but didn't pull away until I was good and done, pushing him away to check out my work.

The effect was perfect, full lips made even more full and lush and red. I even managed to draw a bit of blood. With the mussed-up hair and passion flush all over his face and chest, Patch looked ravished in a matter of seconds. I pointed to the spray bottle. "Gargle a mouthful of that. If anyone asks, *papi* got a little too rough with the blowjob. Got it? I fucked you up."

The near-pure alcohol could roughen the throat of even the staunchest alkie. Between the croak he'd have and his face, he'd look okay enough for Rachel to believe the ruse. Hell, it could even get him some pity. He could stay here, sleep here, and I'd be the cock-gagging bastard who tried to get off quick and then left him sore before running back to the unwanted party guest. I could live with that. Patch would know the truth, and that was all that mattered right now, because I had to get to Dean before whatever Rachel was planning to do got done.

Patch looked confused for a second, then grateful, but before I could tell him to hurry the fuck up with the shot, I heard a sudden rush of noise from downstairs. Either someone just brought more booze, more drums, or there was a very real "problem" going on.

I ran out of the room, not bothering to stick around to see Patch obey my command. Downstairs, it looked as if the entire party population had concentrated itself in the living room and hallway, loud and boisterous. The front door was open, with more people filling the doorway and the porch. My heart dropped at the thought of how many people could fit on the porch. All those people plus Dean equaled very not good things.

"Did you see that guy?" someone said as I pressed through the crowd, hoping like hell it was some other guy. Mentally, I ticked off the little list of situations Dean needed to be comfortable. There was space on the porch, an exit Dean could easily see. He'd be fine. I'd grab him and we'd be out of here, and then I'd tear Rachel a new one in the morning.

"Ran like his ass was on fire."

"I thought we were going to say hi!"

"What a pussy!" That someone had me grabbing the front of her shirt, hauling her up, her smirk gone.

"Who's a fucking pussy?" I kept us moving toward the door as I snarled at her.

Before she could answer, Tam was at my side, pulling me off her. She seemed immune to my anti-laughing glare, still looking too amused as she led me from the door and down the hallway by the arm. "Jonathan, we've got a problem with your friend."

"What happened, Tam? He was outside when I left him."

She shrugged, stopping us in front of the closed bathroom door. Rachel and Cindy busily shooed people away, looking competent even with the pot stench reeking off them both.

"You got to get this loser out of here." Rachel shook her head. "He's going to ruin the vibe."

My head throbbed. "Where is here and what the fuck happened?"

She shrugged. "He's in the bathroom, and this wasn't our fault."

"Really?"

"This is one of the biggest parties we've had here. I can't believe it." Rachel grinned at me with pride. "We couldn't even fit everyone on the front porch."

The throbbing sharpened to wedge itself right behind my eyes, and I looked at the door. Dean was behind it. I couldn't hear anything, no screaming, no crying, nothing that told me he was freaking out. "You got a bunch of people to just... rush the porch?"

"And say hello to your guest," Tam chuckled. "Then he got all weird and red and bolted in the house."

Cindy rubbed her side. "I think he got me with an elbow."

"You did grab his ass." Tam rolled her eyes and looked back at me. "I mean, we took turns. Good job, Jonathan. He's really hot, for a psycho."

I saw red, hot, steaming red. They touched him? They touched what was mine? Didn't they have a house full of straight guys to fondle? I felt like doing some closed-fist touching right about now, and Rachel's oh-so-very-smug face rocketed to the top of the list.

Then it hit me as if I'd punched myself. Didn't I tell Rachel he wasn't good with crowds? And she invited him over and did this rushing/touching thing that we never do. She'd done this shit on purpose. I knew it, but there wasn't time to bawl her out about that.

"When did we start deliberately being dicks to people? When did we start touching without their permission?" I said through clenched teeth, each word a slow growl. "Was there another change you haven't told me about yet?"

She didn't look fazed. "Hey, we're touchy-feely, and if he's going to hang around, he's gotta get used to us. If he can't, then I just did you a favor, fucko. Now get him out of the damned bathroom and send him on his way before we have people pissing off the deck."

I lost it, getting into her face, and screamed loud enough to be heard on the other side of the house. "What the fuck, Rachel! What part of 'I like him' are you not fucking getting?" When that got her staring at me as if I had hauled off and smacked her, I added, not even bothering to quiet down, "If you don't want me calling 911 to help him, get the living room and the porch cleared. Right. Fucking. Now."

I threw the door open and stepped in. Dean, looking huge in the tiny bathroom, sat on the floor, back against the wall across from the toilet, knees up. His chest was rising and falling scary fast, and his face was the color of a freshly spanked ass, red and blotchy, his pale skin not hiding any of his distress. Eyes closed, mouth opened, and finally I noticed his throat moving, but only a soft strangled noise poured out. A noise easily hidden by the four loudmouths, if I counted myself, outside the door. Shit, he said something about these things feeling like a heart attack, and he was there, suffering in near silence. I knew that, if the tables had been turned, I'd be running around screaming "It's the big one!" like Fred Sanford until some motherfucker helped me out.

I didn't wait for a response from the hallway before closing the bathroom door in the girls' faces and wheeling around, kneeling next to Dean, not touching him. I had no idea how to help him come back down, and I was scared I would have to make good on my threat no matter how many people were left on our path out. Thankfully, the door didn't open with round whatever of this little battle Rachel and I were having that had just come to a serious head. That wasn't important right now.

"Dean? It's me, Jonathan."

He shuddered hard, and his head lolled to face me, eyes opening, revealing dark hazel, wide and unfocused. No tears, I noticed, though his eyes shone with the promise. His eyes slowly regained focus the longer he looked at me, and his lips moved again, voice raspy. "Sorry, Jon."

"No, baby, you got nothing to be sorry for." I stamped down the hot swell of anger that tried to overwhelm me and didn't even think about the shortening of my name, other than joy that he could recognize me even in the midst of a panic. He could have called me Princess Johnny Jinglebutt for all I cared. "Not your fault. What can I do to help?"

"Just talk." Another shudder and a gasp for air. His expression reminded me of the haunted look someone in the movies got from watching a friend get torn apart or before they start raving about the war. The thought of Dean actually having PTSD scared me a bit. If he lashed out in this tiny room, I'd be screwed, but hell, I'd let him lash as long as he needed. This was completely my fault for not watching him better, and if he needed to come back swinging, I could afford to mar my handsome looks with a black eye or two.

Okay, he wanted me to say something. I wasn't sure what exactly, but I knew how to babble, so I went for the first random thing that came to mind. "We travel a lot, right, so there's some stuff we kinda go without, like pets. It's a shame, because I really like animals. I tried to have a pet once, a goat, petite little sucker, black with a white diamond on her head. I named her Marilyn because, you know, 'Diamonds Are A Girl's Best Friend'? Well, okay, that and 'Marilyn, My Bitterness' is one of my favorite songs. Have you heard it before? The Cruxshadows are a pretty awesome band. Anyway, she—the goat, Marilyn—was an awesome pet. Pygmy goats are pretty smart, and for a couple of months, she traveled with us."

"What happened to her?" Dean gasped as if the words hurt to say, sticking his hand into the inner pocket of his jacket.

"Goats are herd animals. Keeping only one around, even in a van full of weird humans, was kinda cruel. She went a little crazy, chewed on anything she could get her mouth on: costumes, props, people. So we... ah... we stopped near a cow pasture and put her on the other side with a herd of cows. Not sure if the owners would keep her, but it was a lot safer than just giving her away, and there was a ton of grass and other animals to keep her company. I miss her sometimes."

While I babbled, he lifted his hand and put a bit of red plastic to his mouth, an inhaler. Two puffs and his breathing eased a bit. I was glad as hell I hadn't thought about convincing him to leave the jacket in the car.

"Just give me a sec. I'll be on my way soon."

That didn't sound right. He was obviously still in a weird headspace. "Good. I told them to clear the hall so we could get out of here. But take your time."

"We? You're coming with me?" His eyes were slowly returning to their beautiful honey color, which dulled the ache in my chest at his question. I could have railed at him for the assumption, but this wasn't the time for me to waste being hurt by that.

"I told you. You're not getting rid of me that easily." Putting on the confident act helped. "'Sides, I can't let you get back on the road like this alone."

By rights, Dean could have told me and this whole house to go to hell. It would hurt, seeing him get in his car and leave me to this chaos, having to tuck my tail between my legs and declare Rachel the winner and myself the utter loser. I'd finally lose my vaunted "best friend who can get away with shit" status, if I was lucky, but without Dean, and I couldn't believe I was thinking it, but without Dean, it wouldn't matter. It would hurt too much to see him go. A hurt I maybe deserved, but it would still be there.

"I made an ass of myself, Jon. You were right, I shouldn't have come."

There it was again, that "Jon." I'd thought I would hate anyone calling me that, but on his lips, it was as intimate as a kiss. "We were fine until they wanted to mess with you. You didn't ask for this, none of it. I'm glad you tried."

"I don't want to come between you and your friends. They're important to you."

"Yeah." Despite my inner conflicts, I did talk a good game about how the Tribe was like family and how close the inner circle was and blah, blah, blah. "But, fuck, so are you."

I couldn't take it back. It looked like he needed to know that as much as I needed to say it. It was stupid, but that was the truth, if I had to be honest. And I could be honest with him, technically being alone with no audience to play to in this dingy little bathroom.

Dean's gaze was steady. "We barely know each other."

*That's it, baby, be the smarter one of this odd pair. I'll keep being the idiot.* "So we'll learn."

"I suck at crowds."

Thanks, Captain Obvious, was the first thing on my tongue, but I allowed myself to tell the truth. "You think I can do crowds all the time? Everything gets all crazy and whirly and it's hard to see which way is up. We all need something solid sometimes, to ground us until the whirling stops. Shit, does that help, or am I sounding like an asshole?"

"Yeah, it's helping. You seem more real like this." Dean's lips quirked in a small smile that faded to a more serious glance. "Will you let me be your something solid? You sure have been for me tonight."

"It's not a quid pro quo thing, Dean. I'm doing this because I fucking like you a lot." Did I just say that? Fuck. I had meant, "I like fucking you a lot," hadn't I? Okay, that was also true, but really inappropriate for right now.

"Didn't mean it like that. I wouldn't have been here if I didn't like you a lot too."

"Oh, and here I thought it was the promise of my fine ass that brought you into this hell." I grinned teasingly at him.

His arm, the one still holding the inhaler, wrapped around me and pulled me into a hard sideways hug. "There's easier ways for me to get sex if that was all I wanted. Trust me. It's not just your ass I'm interested in anymore."

Fuck me. Okay, so maybe I did want this, want him. I'd been slavering over the thought of having him buried to his balls in me all week, but this urge to return the hug and stroke his hair and revel in the joy of him wanting to be something more than a casual thing, more than one or two nights, was damned scary. Scary, but it felt so right.

"Can you stand up okay?" I murmured into his ear, giving it a kiss. That felt right too. I hoped it was enough to let him know I felt the same way, because I couldn't trust my words anymore. He nodded, and I kissed his ear again. "Let's get outta here. I think we both could use some grounding."

CHAPTER SEVEN

# *The Room*

THE small crowd still on the porch required another break near the car for Dean to take another hit from the inhaler. I insisted on driving his Grand Am, following the reverse directions from his GPS. Driving with one hand, I clung to his fingers over the middle console. Things were a lot more muted compared to our first trip to Dean's place.

"I haven't had an attack that bad in a very long time," he finally said once were we out of the city limits. "I should have listened to you."

"That was not remotely normal." I sighed deeply, deciding for now to leave Rachel's name out of this, since just thinking about it made my jaw clench. "You're not having second thoughts about... this... are you?" I squeezed his fingers tighter to define what "this" was. I needed to know, because there was no way I'd go back to the House tonight if he wanted me gone.

"It'd be kind of an asshole move to have you drive me home and make you leave, wouldn't it? I'm more worried that I've scared you off. I mean, I'm a grown man cowering in a bathroom like a child. Not my sexiest moment."

The conversation at the park came back to me. I'd said nothing that he hadn't told himself, what he was telling himself and me now. The shame nearly choked out the air in the car. "You don't have to tell me how it happened, but whatever it was that got you like this, it was fucked up and not your fault."

"And you know this how?" There wasn't any anger there, just resignation.

"I just know, okay? Unless you got this way drowning kittens or baby goats or something, then well, you deserved it all, but I don't think you're that kind of guy."

"Jonathan, we barely know each other. I could be a gigantic jackass who has the occasional panic attack."

"Nah, my gaydar may need work from time to time, but my jackass-dar is well tuned. Tell you what. We'll get to know each other, starting now. What are you doing tomorrow?"

Dean leaned back against the seat, his hand flexing in mine. "My original plan was you."

I couldn't help but grin, bringing our joined fingers together to kiss his. "I like your original plan."

"Doing yourself? You must be quite flexible."

"Dean, baby, you have no idea." One lone street light filled the car just in time for me to catch his upraised eyebrow, and I confessed. "Okay, I sucked my own dick once, drunk and on a bet, and I'm blessed enough to not require that much of a bend in the first place, as you well know. Your turn."

I didn't need to see to know both eyebrows were up from the confusion I heard. "My turn?"

"That was a crazy party story. Your turn." I grinned at the road, hoping he could hear it in my voice. It was a nice change of subject, and the mood in the car lightened considerably as the weather outside got even suckier, the rain beating down on the roof. I swore I saw lightning up ahead.

"You gave yourself head at a party?"

"It was that kind of party, now spill."

Dean was quiet for a second, and I almost thought he was ignoring me. "Icy Hot. There was this one time with Icy Hot. Can't remember how drunk we were to even try something so damned stupid."

I winced. "Icy Hot where?"

"On our cocks."

I winced even harder, and if my legs hadn't been busy making the car go forward, I would have crossed them. "We?"

Another silence. "Friends back in college. About six of us, trying to see how long we'd last before tearing up or running screaming for the showers. I didn't win that one."

"Were you out to anyone there?"

"Nope. There was one guy, though. He did the dare and offered to make sure it was all washed off, with his mouth, but I turned him down. I wasn't ready for the team to know yet. That wild enough for you?"

"That is pretty damned wild." The sense of relief I felt when he said he turned down a guy was stupid. Even if it was a former lover he'd tried something that nuts with, I had no right to feel that relieved, not with how I was the boy that didn't say no in my own sex life.

We finished the trip in silence, hands intertwined until I slid the car into the garage. Years of taking turns driving Thor made me very aware of how a vehicle could take more space than I realized, so I was happy I didn't accidentally ding the car against the sides of the garage opening.

"Where are you taking my bag?" I wanted to snatch it away as he pulled it out of the back and took it to the kitchen door. I was okay with it being in the car during the party, but now I wasn't at "home," and someone else was touching it. My palms itched with the need to hold it myself, to know where it was going.

I guess I sounded a little too sharp, because I saw him flinch when I stepped into the kitchen. "Bedroom. I mean, if you want it there. For convenience."

Oh, well, that made perfect sense. Perfectly awesome sense. He really wasn't going to turn me out after all. "You are way, way too sweet for words, you know that?"

Before Dean could make words come out of his open mouth, mine was there, lips against his, kissing him hard. I heard the thump of the bag on the hardwood floor and felt arms circling my waist, pulling me close. The kiss became desperate instantly, and we clung to each other hard. I wanted to erase the past couple of hours from our memories, replace it with what was going to happen, what should have been happening instead. Us, in his bed. Him, taking me hard and fast. Me, spending over and over until I passed out.

"Shower?" Dean gasped before bending his knees to dip down to my neck, kissing me there. I could feel his inhale. "Not that I don't love the way you smell right now. God, it's driving me crazy."

"Not yet." The teeth grazing against my neck made me moan loud and deep. My hands clung to his shoulders and slid up into his hair, keeping him there to explore as much as he wanted. His glasses bumped against my nose a few times, but I didn't care. He was kissing me, licking from one side of my neck down to the hollow of my throat and up the other side, sinking into my flesh with greedy teeth. Yeah, I wanted him to leave marks, and leave a few of my own. I felt his hands move up my tank top, over my back, then down to cup my still-covered ass.

I let go of his hair to pull my shirt off and then his. That meant Dean had to stop nibbling my neck for a few seconds that felt like hours of deprivation, but once those were gone, we crashed back together, moving down the hall until he pushed me against the wall next to the bathroom door, his hands on my hips, digging in tightly as we kissed over and over again. I got my chance to bite, leaving a few beautiful red marks on his neck and shoulders that I couldn't wait to see turn into bruises marring his pale skin.

Yes, he's mine. All mine. Take a good look everyone, past, present, or future. I've claimed him as mine.

Dean aimed his kisses lower, one right on my collarbone, another between my pecs, licked down my belly and dipped his tongue into my navel. As much as I would have loved to look down and see him swallow me again, it was my turn to get my mouth fucked.

"Baby, wait…." I fisted his hair and pulled his face away from my suddenly opened zipper. The light of the open bathroom door reflected on his glasses, but I could still see his eyes, darkened with lust that reflected my own. "I've been thinking about sucking you off for days now. Come up here and let me have you."

A little sound of need pushed its way out of his throat, zinging down my spine and straight to my groin. I helped him back onto his feet and against the wall, kissing him again and again before copying the same trail down his body that he did to mine, taking a detour to each of his perked rose-colored nipples, sucking them between my teeth until that little needy sound turned into an outright yell. I committed those sweet spots to memory.

"One sec, need to kiss you again," Dean murmured, capturing my face in his big hands and pulling me into another kiss that quickly turned into one of those sorts of kisses that almost made me forget what I was heading down to my knees for.

I allowed it for a few long, sweet moments before pulling away and nipping his bottom lip hard, my fingers getting to work on opening his jeans. "No more distracting me with one of your SuperKisses…."

"SuperKisses?"

"Don't look like you don't know what I'm talking about." My mouth kept going even as I knelt down in front of him, distracting myself by grabbing the waistband and hauling his jeans down his powerful thighs. "Fuck, you kiss me like the world's ending and it's the last thing you'll ever do. You gotta know how that affects a guy."

Dean wore black boxer briefs, noticeably damp right at the crotch, and I reveled in that reaction. The wet bulge brushed against my nose as Dean stepped out of his pants, filling my nostrils with his pure and primal scent that made my own cock throb.

He said, "It's been a while since I've kissed anyone. Tell me how it makes you feel."

"Don't make me talk about that now," I whispered, eyes on the prize. "I've got a face full of your cock, and I want to concentrate on making this good for both of us."

My answer came in the form of Dean hooking his thumbs into his underwear and pulling them down to midthigh, making the behemoth he called a dick graze against my chin fuzz and then my cheek on its way up and out, smearing fluid on my skin. Holy hell, it was bigger than I remembered with the up-close view I was getting. My lips would have to work to get all of him in, and I couldn't wait.

I pulled the underwear all the way down and rubbed my cheek again his hip while he stepped out of those, getting more of his precome slicking my face. Once he resettled against the wall, I looked up at him, knowing good and damned well how debauched I had to look, that close to his dick, skin shiny with his fluid, panting openmouthed like a bitch in heat. Dean gasped, the same lust reflected in his eyes, hands fisted at his sides. I wanted like anything to get those hands in my hair once I had him in my mouth.

"My lips are sealed." He grinned darkly at me, the look so sexy and sinister behind the glasses. I was so glad he didn't take them off. I wanted him to see exactly who was going to bring him off.

"Not for long." And then I gripped him with one hand, stroking him tightly, getting a feel for the size and weight of him in a way that I didn't the first time we had sex. This was far more intimate than that hot fuck, even though Dean had tried to get me to slow it down. Now I could appreciate what he wanted to do. This wasn't a performance, not when we were alone.

I took my time stroking, opening my mouth and just letting the fat, drooling head rest on my tongue, filling my senses with his rich, heady flavor. My tongue couldn't stay still for long, and I ran it against his skin over and over, giving the tip a dirty little french kiss, punctuating each pass with a needy moan. We had all night for me to decide between letting him come in my mouth or up my ass. Tonight, it was just a matter of what I wanted first. I was getting both, no matter what it took.

Dean kept his legs apart, giving me access to his balls as well, and I dipped low, bathing them with my tongue, taking them in one at a time, rolling my tongue around the sensitive skin there before replacing my still-pumping hand with my mouth. I heard a thump above me and looked up. Dean had his eyes closed, head flush against the wall with his mouth wide open, panting for breath, deep moans echoing with every exhale. Pride welled up inside me. I was doing this to him, making him feel that good.

I opened my mouth wide to take him in completely, not stopping, suppressing the gag, getting him to the back of my throat and farther. My lips stretched around him as I knew they would. I heard another thump and felt hands in my hair, hard and tight, and thank fuck I didn't have to let him go to ask for a harder grip. I felt weak at the sensation of his hips moving in and out, cock nudging the back of my throat, and was so glad I was already on my knees. My nostrils worked overtime to keep me from passing out at the thrusts. I felt light-headed, anchored by the cock in my mouth and my own arousal, bulging painfully in my pants.

My free hand got to work to relieve the pressure there, hauling my own dick out into the cool air of the house, but I remembered our little half-drunken conversation a few nights ago. I wanted him to fuck me, yes, but that didn't mean I couldn't play with him a little. I brought my hand up to my mouth and slipped a finger between my lips and his pistoning cock, getting it wet, and then aimed behind his balls, seeking and finding his entrance, though Dean had to slide down the wall a bit, and I had to work to find it. His whole body shuddered, and I pushed, getting in to the second knuckle. He picked up the pace with a raspy grunt, his grip even tighter, and my eyes rolled to the back of my head, giving me the barest glance of his face. He watched me take him, staring intently enough to bore right into my goddamn soul. I made the hand that was giving his balls a good fondle grip him firmly, and pulled down, just once.

It was enough.

"Oh God... Jon...." That was the only warning I got before the first hot gush hit the back of my tongue, then another, and I took him so far back that I could inhale his pubes and take every drop of him without having to swallow. I was still stroking myself, and slowed down, wanting to wait, to save my orgasm until I had him where I wanted him even more, not just standing in front of me, but lying next to me. I could do it, exercise some self-control, whether my dick wanted to or not.

He didn't look away, letting me see his face twist with pleasure, mouth falling open, giving me those loud, hard moans, his entire body shaking and sliding down the wall until I had to stand up and wrap my arms around his shoulders to steady him. His head rested on my shoulder, and I kissed his cheek and ear and his hair and anywhere my lips could reach as he calmed, my mouth murmuring things I had no idea I was even saying.

Soon, he held me by the waist, pulling me against him, returning the neck kisses, and I was the one trembling with held-back release. He did this to me. With one touch he could ruin my plan and throw me off. I liked it a lot.

"You officially have permission to call me Jon. Especially like that." I had no idea why, of all the things I could have said, compliments on taste and thrusts and the tenor of his moans, I settled on the way those three letters sounded to my ears, like a caress. I wanted to hear them all the time.

"Thank you." He kissed my neck firmly before pushing me back just enough for our eyes to meet. "Ready for a shower?"

I laughed, leaned in and gave his neck one long swipe of my tongue. "You're not the only one who likes a little sweat, but I'm down for some good clean fun."

He stood up from the slump against the wall, his hands moving to my ass, giving me a hard squeeze. "I'll call you next time I'm done with a workout, then."

"Mmm, jock sweat." I mirrored the ass grab and squeeze, adding a light smack before I pulled away completely and started walking toward the bathroom.

I'd barely noticed it the last time I was in Dean's house, too busy with a quick piss to have a look around, but I swore I heard angels start to sing the second I stepped inside. It was clean, no towels on the floor, and it smelled a bit of ammonia, like he'd made the effort to neaten it for me. Whether or not that was true, I was touched all the same. The tub was full size, could easily fit the both of us with a minimum of elbow and knee bumping. Did I mention it was clean? Compared to the biohazards I've washed up in over the years, this was heaven. It was nearly too clean for me to strip down and leave my dirty clothes on the floor.

I did drop my dirties on the floor anyway and slipped under a strong, hot spray, the force bearing down on muscles I'd forgotten were achy from dancing. I let it hit me for a while before finding a bottle of orange shower gel that smelled citrusy and musky—no surprise there— and an honest to goodness mesh puffy thing. I didn't know they made them in gray, and it was both endearingly cute and achingly manly. I lathered up and rubbed the puff over my body, the same way he probably did twice a day. I shuddered at how squishy the thought made me feel inside.

Just when I began to wonder where Dean had run off to, the bathroom door opened and I could see him through the foggy glass shower door. No glasses, not a stitch on him, so much pale flesh, and in a few seconds I would have all of it to touch. My dick, which had relaxed a little in the aftermath and the shower, twitched like a hunk-seeking dowsing rod and reminded me it was there and liked what I saw.

*Don't worry, little buddy. You'll get yours very soon.*

"I could sooo get used to this," I called out, sliding the door open for him. "Get in here before all the hot's gone."

Dean slipped in behind me and closed the door, settling right up against my back. The skin-to-skin contact was glorious. "I put your bag in the bedroom before we forgot again. What the hell do you carry in that thing?"

"Everything." I rested against his chest, giving his neck a nuzzle and getting shampoo lather all over his shoulder.

"Like a hermit crab?"

"Hermit crabs aren't this sexy." I turned around and leaned my head back to rinse my hair clean. My bend shoved our stomachs together in a slick slide. I felt him shudder, and I couldn't help but do the same.

His hands landed on my waist, supporting me, though I didn't think I'd need it. "I don't know. Some of the ones in the little kiosks at the mall have really hot pinchy claws."

He was asking for it. I stood up straight and went right for his nipples, pinching them hard enough to make him gasp. "Mine are hotter."

We switched under the spray so Dean could get wet and even more delicious looking than any fantasy I could conjure up. The bite marks on his neck were starting to go from red to bruised. Water ran down his body, turning his hair dark enough to match my own and making paths down his chest that I wanted to follow with my tongue until I was back on my knees. After a few very thorough visual sweeps, I noticed Dean watching me watch him, smiling shyly, with a hint of a promise.

If I didn't want to blow that promise, quite literally, I had to move fast.

He went for his puff, but I was faster and got it first. "Hands to yourself for now. Let me show you some appreciation."

"The blowjob in the hallway wasn't appreciation enough?" Dean chuckled quietly and clasped his hands behind his back, shielding me from the blasts of water. His shoulders rolled with the motion, and I had to shake my head to remember what I had planned to do because damn, I wanted to trace those muscles with my tongue.

"I lied. Getting my hands all over you is more of a treat for me." I added gel to the puff and squeezed up a pile of lather that I happily dragged over his chest. "You have no idea how badly I've been wanting you this close."

He stayed quiet, saving me the indignity of having to hear his response to my mouth running amuck again. No ruining sexy time with silly talk. I took my time washing him, following each swipe with the puff with my free hand, spreading the suds around. To my delight, all that rubbing was getting him at half-mast by the time I'd gotten to his hips, matching my own. The groan he let out when I washed around his cock, deliberately ignoring it for now, made me grin wickedly.

We switched places, and I told him to turn around to face the wall, giving me an eyeful of the very definition of "bubble butt," soft, round, begging to be bitten or spanked or even fucked. Shit, I had the urge to plunge my dick inside of him, and I'm mostly a bottom. Struggling to keep on task, I pressed in close to wash his back, biting back my sharp gasp as my cock slid between those perfect cheeks. Dean, the bastard, apparently wasn't going to even attempt to have any control, with the way he moaned out loud and pushed against me.

"Aren't you eager?" I squatted down to the level of that tantalizing ass, rubbing lather over each cheek, then down his thighs. Dean groaned and managed to spread his legs a little more, and that gave me access between, to give his sac and inner thighs my close attention. Some of the lather had dripped off his ass, giving me a clean patch of skin to kiss, smooth, and wet, hints of soap on my lips and then in my mouth when I opened it and gave the muscle a bite.

He tensed with a low grunt and a tremble, and I couldn't keep hanging on to my control for much longer. I stood up, dropping the puff behind me, eager hands running up his sides, around his waist, clinging tight as I rubbed my cock across the cleft that had to be made just for it. "Now I'm all conflicted," I confessed, breathy in his ear. "I was all ready to have you screw me silly when we got out of here, but then you had to show me this ass, fuuuck."

"Anything you want." Dean cupped my hip firmly and pushed me even harder against his back.

We went quiet then, slowly rocking and sliding together, harsh breaths competing with the sound of the still-running shower. Thank fuck, I needed the time to get my thoughts together.

My hand glided over his abs as I made my decision. "I bet my come would look perfect right here, and this"—my other hand gripped his heavy cock gently, enough to earn me a low, growly moan— "belongs in me."

"You got it, Jon." Dean gave my hip another squeeze and opened the shower door, the blast of cooler air helping me focus enough to let him step out of the shower and for me to turn the water off. Him saying that added fuel to the fire of my need. Anything I wanted from Dean, I had it.

Drying off went faster than our shower, rough and fumbling in our haste and the hungry looks we gave each other. I snatched away the towel he wrapped around his waist, used it to squeeze more water out of my hair, and cursed its length for the first time in a very long time. "Go on and get ready. My hair's gonna need a few more minutes to be less drippy."

He leaned forward, giving me a quick and hard kiss before leaving the bathroom. I couldn't dry off fast enough, thinking about him waiting in bed for me. So perfect that he'd just left, doing as I asked without question. It was almost as sexy as him saying my new nickname.

Once my hair was as undrippy as it was going to get, I stalked down the hall and into the room, to discover the picture in my head was not nearly as vivid as the one before me. Dean lay on his side, facing me, one hand slowly stroking his cock, already sheathed in a condom and shiny slick with lube, glistening in the low light of the bedside lamp.

"Damn, condom on and everything?" I stood next to the bed, stroking myself in return, taking the view in completely. His eyes widened a bit; a flush crept up his neck. I couldn't tell if he was really, really turned on or embarrassed until his smile dimmed.

"You wanted me ready...." I wanted to kick myself for doing anything to make him unsteady. It had been two years for him, I reminded myself with a growl, before giving him a slow smile that I hoped was reassuring as I crawled onto the bed.

"I love the invite, baby. Think I'll take full advantage."

Relief made the man melt onto his back as I climbed over him, draping my leaner body over his. His arms wrapped around me, pulled me close, and our kiss went from a light brush to hungry possession in barely a breath. I plundered his mouth, only backing off to run my tongue over the corners of his lips, nibble each side, then plunged back in to do battle with Dean's tongue. His hands gripped my ass hard, grinding our cocks together as he kissed me back.

His left hand moved up my back to cup my head, and I gave up control of the kiss to him, allowing Dean to slow it down, remind me that we had all night. It became soft and wet and seductive, a SuperKiss, doing all the things to me I couldn't put into words yet, but I accepted it, reveled in the tenderness. It may have been two years since Dean had put his cock to proper use, but I'd never had this sort of attention ever. I craved it. I craved more.

"Get me ready too," I gasped when he released my lips for just a second between kisses. Dean whispered a "yes" against my mouth before diving back in, one arm extended for the pump bottle of lube. I didn't pay any more attention to what that hand did, because I was more into his lips and tongue, until one slicked-up finger circled my hole in long, lazy swipes.

I broke the kiss with a needy cry, as if he'd skipped all ceremony and speared me open with his cock. "Jesus, Dean, hurry!"

He'd gone temporarily deaf. It was the only explanation for why he kept his slow pace, rubbing me until I accepted the digit easily, then another, despite my pleas and outright demands for him to hurry it the fuck up. The angle was strange with me sprawled on top of him, my legs draped over his hips, bucking, writhing against his fingers. We humped madly against each other, erections gliding, wet with his lube and my own precome.

Finally, I couldn't take any more. My balls were so full they hurt, and my hole clutched at his fingers in waves. I lifted up over him, gripping the base of his cock with one hand, hot and throbbing even through the latex. He didn't argue, taking my hips in both big hands as I steadied myself, aimed the tip where it needed to be, and lowered myself down on him. The burn was sharp, but quickly gave way to the full sensation I had been craving. So weird—I'd been screwed just a few days ago, the quick tussle with Patch after the picnic, yet Dean's girth made me feel like it had been much longer than that.

Oh God, I hadn't been good at all for Dean. He'd been good, probably. He hadn't mentioned having any other lovers since he ended his dry spell, while I'd been fucked and sucked to oblivion. He'd been exclusive and I hadn't, and the realization filled me with shame I hadn't experienced in years. I had to close my eyes, bow my head, let my hair shield my face as I tried to stuff the weirdness back under control, to use his cock to shove it all away for now. This wasn't the time for it, not stuffed to the gills and riding this paradox of a man, physically strong, emotionally tender, mentally fragile. I was supposed to be giving him a better memory of the night, not wallowing in my own stupid issues.

"Jon?" Dean's clean hand parted the curtain of my hair and cupped my face, his body straining with barely contained control. "You all right? Am I hurting you? We can slow down if you need to."

We hadn't moved since I fully seated myself on his shaft. No wonder he thought something was up. I shook my hair out of my face, gave him a wicked smile, leaned down until our lips touched for a sec, then rose, hands on his chest, and began to ride him, hard and fast, like a jockey racing on a stallion. His concern quickly dissolved into the need I wanted to see. Fingers dug into my thighs, his breath came quick, making his chest heave over and over again with loud grunts that filled my ears.

That was more like it, and it all felt so good. I bounced and wiggled my hips, driving us both insane with the sensation, my head thrown back, just letting it all go. I knew I was yelling at the top of my lungs, his name, "yes," "oh God," and lots and lots of "fuck!" but I knew we were acres away from the next neighbor, far enough that no one would hear me. It was good, being able to really let loose like that, knowing my voice would reach the only person who needed to hear what his cock did to me.

Dean bucked below me, matching my thrusts, adding the slap of our bodies to the sounds bouncing off the walls, ruining the effects of our shower with our sweat. His eyes never left my face, and I gripped his shoulders hard, feeling his heat brand into the palms of my hands. My cock dripped and ached, needed attention, and I grabbed it to stroke hard and fast, aiming each drop to pool in the valley between Dean's abs. He moaned even louder and snapped his hips up into me, and I rode him until my strokes became more and more jerky, release boiling deep inside of me.

"Don't stop," I demanded, spots dancing in front of my eyes with each sharp thrust.

"I won't, baby." His hand covered mine, stroking right along with me, quick, gripping pulls. "Do it. Come on me, just like you said."

His voice was the last straw, all growly and rough, scratching my senses like sandpaper, and I came hard with a moan pulled out from my toes, shooting where I'd wanted to, all over his belly and chest, a drop hitting his chin. The look on his face, concentrating on not stopping and yet still full of pride and bliss at my orgasm, could have made me hard again in an instant. I liked that look; it made him dangerous. Fuck, there was a lot to like about him, and that thought made it hard to breathe, the rush of completion battering the shield I'd held up to keep how I really felt at bay.

I stared down at him, confused, mouth still open and gasping with each of his thrusts, now slowed down to let me catch my breath. He was still rock hard and buried deep. "Don't you dare stop," I protested, needing that slide to ground me before I did something I wasn't prepared to handle.

The bastard chuckled, cupped my face with both his hands, and pulled me down for another deep kiss. The world upended itself with a tumble of thighs, and I lay on my back, Dean on top. Missionary was a position I usually avoided with casual partners. Too close, too intimate, too much lover, not enough fuck buddy. My arms wound around his shoulders anyway.

"You called me 'baby'," I accused. Hypocritical of me, yes, but I didn't care. He called me "baby," and it was perfect.

"You said it first. Should I take it back?" He rocked inside me in slow, deliberate, shallow pumps, crumbling my resolve.

No, I didn't want him to take it back. He could call me anything he wanted right now, while I lay beneath him, feeling all kinds of vulnerable and fighting the burn behind my eyes. Fine, tomorrow I'd get the defenses back up. Just let me enjoy what he was doing to me. "Shut up and fuck me, Dean."

That earned me a SuperKiss as he got back into the groove, one arm snaking beneath my shoulders, the other on my hip, holding me close. I expected a hard ride to his orgasm, but he took his time, slowly stoking the fire. My hand gripped his hair hard, but eased when it was damned obvious that I'd given him the reins. He wasn't going to speed things up. The kiss ended softly, and then there were lips on my neck, tongue licking at my skin. That freed my mouth to groan with each lunge. "Fuck, what're you doing?"

"You."

I turned my head to bite his earlobe hard, growling, "Smartass."

He retaliated by shifting his hips and lunging, hitting my sweet, still sensitive as all hell, spot so solidly that my eyes rolled back and I let go of his lobe.

"Don't like it?" He stroked it again and again, until I had to struggle to remember how to make words over all the goddamned cries and groans.

"More!"

He took pity on me then, keeping up the faster lunges. I locked my legs around his hips and sank my fingers into that incredible flexing ass, refusing to let him go. He smashed our lips together again, the kiss messy and wild, exchanging grunts of exertion. Our bodies, slick with sweat and my come, smacked against each other as the bed began to rock. I heard the banging distantly, the headboard smacking against the wall with the force of our sex. All of my senses opened and fired and focused solely on Dean.

It didn't take long after that for Dean to bury himself deep, deeper than I've ever felt anyone inside me before, and spill. Okay, watching him come from a blowjob had been hot, yes, but having a first row view of him losing it like this, so close that my ears rang from the cry tearing out of his throat that sounded so much like my name, topped it by far. I hung on tight as he bucked mindlessly, reveling in all that wild strength moving around me. I kept him close until he was completely spent and lay boneless on top of me. I could barely breathe, but I loved the feel of him on me, so sated and drained.

"I'm staying the night," I gasped, kissing his temple, the gesture tender, my attempt to be sweet. I didn't want to go, didn't want to leave this delicious weight on my body. Not this time, anyway.

"Good thing I stocked up for breakfast," he murmured against my neck.

I chewed my lip, trying to figure out what to say in a moment like this. The burny sensation behind my eyes faded as we sank back to earth, and I had the urge to tell him… something. Anything. Put words to the emotions I damn near drowned in just moments ago.

"I don't eat beef, pork, or chicken."

Dean's chuckle was more a breath against my skin. "That leaves eggs, dairy, and fish. Anything else?"

I thought I had to have come half my brains out to be having this weird post-orgasmic conversation. Then I added, "Or asparagus or broccoli. Or goat."

That got an honest-to-goodness laugh, and he squeezed me even tighter. Why did he have to be so damned agreeable? I was honestly expecting derision for being such a picky eater, for mentioning it now, of all times. Of all the things he could find messed up about me, my not eating meat except for fish was low on the weird scale.

We lay there for long, quiet moments, the air around us chilling our skin save for where we touched. When I shivered despite his warmth, Dean kissed me once more, then moved off my body to do away with the rubber and slipped out of the room. I missed the contact instantly and promptly pouted. Great, two good fucks and I was turning into a whiny baby. Was I gonna cry until I got more cuddles next?

I heard the sink turn on, then off again. Dean came back shortly after, warm washcloth in hand, cleaning himself and then me. That sure felt nicer than the wad of tissues or paper towels or discarded clothing I usually used for a come rag. He didn't let me take the cloth to take care of myself, happily wiping the mess from my stomach and chest and ass before tossing that toward some hamper. I eagerly accepted him back into my arms, and he pulled the covers over us. Tucked against him, I inhaled the scent of Dean and sweat and our sex, committing it to memory. Call this one Eau de Freshly Fucked Hot Guy Number Five, and put a big bottle on my bill.

My mouth didn't seem ready to ease into sleep, however. "Jesus, Dean, how'd you learn to kiss like that?"

Dean froze for a moment, long enough for me to instantly regret the question. Did he have to think back that far? Couldn't remember? I've shoved my tongue down a lot of throats, and even I could tell you who taught me how to kiss decent: Greg Alverez, my seventh-grade crush. Before I could tell Dean to forget I asked, he replied, "I'll tell you later."

Later. Better than none of my business. Everyone had a reason to keep something back, and we'd only been together, no, just fucking, twice, so I had no right to expect an answer, even as curiosity gnawed inside me. I kissed his jaw to reassure him I wasn't going to press anything more than my body to his as we settled into sleep.


MORNING came soft and quiet, warm sunlight, soft mattress, smooth sheets, hot body pressed all around me and moving. A hand, gliding up and down my back, smoothing down my hair, gentle pets that slowly brought me out of some of the best sleep I'd had in a while.

No, I didn't want to leave this dream. It felt too good and real. I could even smell Dean, feel that hand that could almost be his, big and strong. The touch was gentle, teasing, exploring, running through my hair and then moving down to cup my ass.

The hand squeezed, and I tensed, ready to fight to keep the dream for a few seconds longer. "Patch, let me sleep, jackass."

"Wrong guy."

My eyes popped open, and all I could see was the pale shoulder that I used as a pillow. Either I was having a very vivid lucid dream, or I'd just called my bed partner by the wrong damned name. And there were no stitch tattoos anywhere on that shoulder. Oh shit.

"Nope," I murmured, my face getting annoyingly warm, hiding in that neck, soaking up some warmth before I ended up getting tossed out for my faux pas. "Right guy. Wrong name, but definitely the right guy."

The hand on my ass squeezed even tighter, drawing me closer to his side. That was as good as saying he forgave me. "Still want me to let you sleep?"

Let's see, go back to sleep and dream of being snuggled against Dean, or stay awake and enjoy the real thing. No contest. "Nope. Where's my good-morning kiss?"

My reward was one hell of a good-morning kiss. Dean grabbed my ass with both hands and hauled me up and onto him, our lips smashed together. It was slow and sweet and hungry, our tongues tangled together like our legs. We rocked against each other, and I spread my legs wider to straddle and grind my groin into his. I think it had to be the fastest I've gone from sleepy to horny to ready to be mounted and stuffed.

"Shit, baby," I moaned against his lips when we finally pulled apart. I found the bruises I left on him the night before and revisited each one with a kiss. "When you said breakfast, I thought you meant food."

"I did, but you were so hard up against me, and I'd be a bad host if I left you like that."

His hands gripped my hair lightly, enough to bring my head back up for a bunch of light, teasing kisses all over my lips and cheeks and nose. This was a hell of a lot better than my dream, and no one else needed to know that I just relaxed and enjoyed it. "So far, you're being a damned good host."

Dean chuckled, tilting us to the side and rolling over until I was on my back under him again, pressing down on me with all that sweet weight to the point that I could have melted into the mattress. He rumbled into my ear, "A good host takes care of his guests."

I wrapped my legs around his waist, continuing our rocking and loving his deep moan, lifting my chin in challenge. "Are you going to take care of me?"

His eyes looked golden in the light, golden and sincere as he looked down at me, the passion easing into something more serious. I realized then how many ways anyone could have taken my teasing. I swore I'd meant taking care of me in bed.

"If you want me to." The heat returned as quickly as it left, and he buried his face into my neck, running his nose down the curve to my shoulder. I could feel the warmth in his face, see his neck redden. Thank fuck we were both feeling a bit awkward at that moment.

I attempted to recover the mood—grabbed two of the iron bars on the headboard, held on tight, and damn near purred "Yeah, I really want you to."

His shiver was the reaction I wanted, bringing us back to the flirty, teasing precoital banter we had enjoyed. He ramped things up by stroking my cleft, fingers finding where he'd been last night, rubbing my tender hole. "I wasn't too rough?"

I let my body answer for me, opening up to accept the digit as he pressed inside. I probably still had hints of lube that didn't get wiped away, so his entrance was a lot smoother. One finger became two, and I squirmed against him, my hands tight on the bars, inviting him to take whatever he wanted.

He apparently wanted to lean over and nuzzle one of my armpits, running his tongue over the furred skin and making me shudder despite myself. There was another one for the new-experience memory banks. No one had ever done that to me before, and it felt strange and tickly and yet made my dick jump.

"Get the goddamned lube," I growled, not bothering to hold back my desperation. I didn't want to be lovingly teased until I was a babbling wreck on a Sunday morning. He'd done enough damage to my control last night.

"You in a hurry?" he replied right up against my pit before using his teeth and sucking hard as he probed my needy ass with three fingers. I arched up against him, lust shooting from that point of contact to wash all over my body. Holy hell, I didn't know that could feel so good.

"No, I just… Jesus, Dean!"

I sank my fingers into his hair to move him somewhere, anywhere else, anywhere that would get him closer to screwing my brains out, but he caught my wrists, one at a time, moved them back to the bars, and turned his attention to my other armpit. I shuddered, realizing he was actually taking control again, and I had given it to him. What was more surprising, I liked it. I wrapped my fingers back around the bars and relaxed.

"The bars are a very nice touch." I chuckled, breathless, as I kept squirming. "I think I like your bed."

"I think I like you in it."

Any reply I could attempt was quickly squashed when Dean licked farther down my body, from my arm to my side, the licks becoming kisses, then a mixture of both, kissing each inked star on my flanks before licking the outlines, slowly, his touch designed to drive me fucking insane, and I told him so with each ragged gasp.

Then he had the nerve to stop, resting his head in the crook of my thigh, so close to my straining cock that I could feel his breath. If I'd had enough presence of mind, I could have twitched my muscles to make it smack him on the nose.

"For. Fucks. Sake." My eyes opened into slits, making me wonder when I'd closed them. "Why did you stop?"

He smiled up at me, that same adoring gaze that made my heart feel utterly wrecked two weeks ago, so naked that I wanted to look away before I turned into stone, unable to leave. "I mean it, Jon. You look really good in my bed. Wish I could see this all the time."

I needed to head this off before he said too much. My lips curled into a half smirk, my entire body feeling boneless and lazy. "I look really good anywhere."

That smirk vanished when Dean stuck out his tongue and ran it up over the side of my dick, chasing away my cockiness and about half my mental functions. To my infinite frustration, he didn't linger there, but went back to kissing where he'd rested his head and up my inner thighs, adding tiny bites. I know my mouth moved, I was sure I made noise, but I'd be damned if I knew what I was saying between moans and curses and pleas to just… God… fuck me already.

The bastard kept moving down my body, sitting up to hook my legs over his shoulders to get to my knees, then kissed down both until he got to my feet. I still had no clue what the appeal was for him. They were ugly dancer's feet, calloused on the soles from years of being on stage barefoot, my little toe on the right crooked from when I broke it and it healed wrong, but he was lavishing each one with the same worship he'd given the rest of me.

I'd had enough. I needed him in me or I might explode, and I knew just what I had to do to get him on board with this idea. Well, I knew what worked before, at any rate.

I whispered his name to get his attention. Once I had his eyes on me, I took myself in hand loosely, planted my feet on his shoulders, and pushed my hips up off the bed, fucking into the circle of my hand. From the spread-open view he had between my legs, he could see it all, my leaking cock, my stretched and hungry hole, the desire in my face as I stared up at him. When his eyes darkened to deep amber, I knew I had him.

"I think I'm ready for the goddamned lube," he growled, rubbing my calves, each dig of his fingers hard. I made a mental note to ask him for a damn massage one day. Even horny as all hell, he knew just where to touch.

"You in a hurry?" I taunted, and moaned when I rubbed my foreskin, pulling it up until it covered the tip completely, then pulling back to reveal the entire crown. I shook my head, not waiting for a response from him, at least not verbal. "Fuck it, I need it too bad. Need you, Dean. Come on!"

He suited up and got lubed in record time, and he prepped me with more lube just as quickly as I grabbed the backs of my knees, bending myself in half, presenting my hole for two slippery fingers. The prep didn't last more than a few seconds. He didn't skip a beat or pause or ask if I was ready, and I sure as shit didn't want him to. He slid home after only a few finger strokes, and I threw my head back and let loose a rough gasp.

My legs rested against his shoulders as he wildly pumped into me, and I brought my hands back to the bars, loving the feel of implied surrender. It was glorious to see that all of his teasing had driven him as insane with lust as I was. I became a gibbering mess as he snarled and growled and pounded into me.

We weren't going to last, not after all that foreplay and his fucking and my jacking. I came first again, an agonized, primal cry bursting out like I was shooting my actual brain out through my dick, and this time I didn't mind or care, the release so sweet. My body was angled so that I ended up hitting my own damned neck and chin with each warm, wet pulse. Dean stared down at me, grinning at the sight, then bent his head, licking the drops off my chin, the sensation of his tongue on my stubble drawing out more shivers.

He leaned back, keeping my legs draped over his arms, and began pounding with hard, quick thrusts, now watching where we joined, and it was enough to bring him off. I tightened my legs around him, letting go of the bars, crushing him against my chest as he roared and trembled.

"That's it, baby," I urged him on, tightening my muscles around his spasming cock, still buried so deep I could feel it pulsing his load into the condom. "Give it to me."

"That's... that's all I've got...." He moaned, letting my legs down around his slowing hips, and leaned forward into my embrace, rocking easy and slow.

I kissed his temple, holding him close, riding out the last of his thrusts. "I'll take anything you give me."

I wasn't even sure what that meant, wasn't sure what he had meant. It sounded like the right thing to say, and once I said it, it felt like the right thing to say. We clung together in the aftermath, trading long, lazy kisses, his cock still inside me, and everything was all kinds of perfect. I liked it entirely too much. In a perfect world, there would be a lot of Sundays just like this.

"You don't get to fuck me again until you've fed me," I joked when we finally pulled apart so Dean could throw the condom away. "I don't think I'll survive another round before that."

"If I must." He sighed dramatically, standing near the bed, still looking at me tenderly once he had his glasses back on. I returned the favor just as openly. God, he was beautiful in the morning sun. "Guess I can't talk you into joining me for another shower, hm?"

"Hell no. We'll end up ravishing each other again, and I'll die in your arms of exhaustion. Go on and let a man rest."

Yes, let me rest and get another eyeful of his perfectly rounded ass as it and he left the room. Getting my hands, mouth and/or cock on that was definitely on the list of things to do as long as Dean still wanted me around.

And, God help me, I wanted to be around longer. I should probably head back to the House, take my licking for yelling at Rach and probably "ruining" the party, and if I was lucky, get my self-righteous rant on in return. But I really didn't want to go, not yet. Rach and I needed more time apart to cool our jets, I told myself. I'd be bullshitting if I didn't admit that the more time apart from her meant more time with Dean, though. I seemed to be bullshitting myself more often than not lately, and caring about it even less when it came to all matters Dean.

Dean came out of his shower, clean and smelling like his gel. He opted to wear just a pair of sleep pants to start breakfast, while I grabbed my own bathing supplies and the army of hair products out of my bag and took care of business in the shower. Once under the spray, I decided to use Dean's gel instead, wanting to carry the scent around with me if I decided to leave today.

Technically, it wasn't even my decision. Dean had work tomorrow. There was no way he would be willing to have a lay hanging around past Monday morning. I could see us getting together like this for weekends, certainly without the drama of going to parties first, but to hang out during the week? The walk to his place wasn't too bad if I could catch a late bus to the city border, I guess, so it wasn't impossible. I really didn't mind the walk last time.

Resolved to ask him his opinion on the matter, I stepped out of the shower, rubbing leave-in conditioner through my hair. I'd forgotten to grab something from my bag to wear, so I slipped into the tan bathrobe hanging on the back of the bathroom door. Not surprisingly, it was big in the sleeves. From the outside, I could hear Dean's voice.

"Yeah, I'm fine. Everything's okay. I had my inhaler and found a place to be alone until it passed."

I paused before opening the door. He had to be talking about last night, but to whom?

"Of course he was there. It was nice. Actually, Doc, he's here now." A pause. "Yes, I know, there's a big risk of rushing into intimacy. But I like him, and he didn't freak out when I was having my... moment...."

Well, didn't that just make me feel all kinds of warm. Wait, "doc"? Was he talking to Spauldy? Shit.

"Could we talk about it tomorrow? He's in the shower, and I should get breakfast in the oven."

Curiosity flooded me as I finally opened the door. Had he talked to her about me? Why was he seeing her in the first place, and, again, what business was it of mine? Most importantly, why were they talking on a Sunday morning? Didn't shrinks take days off?

I stepped into the kitchen, toweling off my hair as he ended the call. He set his cell phone down and graced me with a smile. "Morning." He motioned to the phone before turning to look at the oven. "My psychiatrist asked me to call her after the party to touch base, if I, um, cracked."

Of course he was embarrassed, and I couldn't tell him that he had no need to be, or that he could have told her I said hello. I mean, she was bound to confidentiality and couldn't tell him I was a patient, if she even knew we were... whatever we were. "No worries, baby. What's cooking?"

His face lit up, and he went to the coffeemaker, poured two mugs, and brought one to the breakfast bar for me. "Quiche, and I remembered what not to put in it. Want cream or sugar with this?"

I shook my head, taking the cup gratefully. Fresh brewed coffee was a rare treat, and given the other crap I poured down my throat, I could handle it strong and black. The sleeve of the robe swallowed my hands as I blew on the brew and sipped. "Today's usually laundry day." I lifted my shoulders, as if that would explain why I wore it.

"It looks sexy, like all I have to do is yank on a sleeve and you're naked again." He made stripping me bare sound so damned casual as he sat his own mug down on the bar and doctored it with an open carton of half and half and a few spoonfuls of sugar from a ceramic container. "You can help yourself to the washer and dryer in the garage. It'll be about forty-something minutes before breakfast is ready."

It was a nice gesture, but I couldn't just take advantage. "You sure? I could kick you a few bucks for the trouble, since you're saving me a trip to the Laundromat."

"Keep it. It's no trouble."

Sharing his bed, his body, and I suppose his cooking was one thing, but it felt like he was trying to do too much for me. All of the stupid resentment that I hoped the great sex would have washed away came back in a huge, ugly rush. I didn't need his fucking pity.

"I don't do charity. Take the fucking cash," I snapped suddenly, turning to head into the bedroom and find my wallet, immediately regretting my tone of voice the second I couldn't see his face. I don't know why the hell I was suddenly so defensive. Dean had been nothing but nice to me. It had been too much for my pride, but the hurt in his eyes when I came back with a few bucks crumpled in my hand brought me up short.

"Jon, I'm sorry. I didn't mean it like that. The machines are here, I did my clothes yesterday, it's no trouble."

And then I felt like a total dickbag, like I'd kicked a puppy. A Great Dane puppy, huge and sweet and only wanting to help. Since I couldn't explain why his generosity bothered me so much, it was better to simply apologize. "Sorry, I mean, thank you. I'll um…. I'll be right back, then."

Dean offered me a little smile when I returned without the money and with an armful of nearly all black clothes. Without thinking, I returned the smile before opening the kitchen door with one hand and stepping into the garage, around the car and the fitness equipment, and starting up the machine. I didn't have much—I usually wore stuff more than once to keep laundry cheap, and washed it all in cold so the dark colors didn't fade too much. I'd take care of my costume pieces, the silks and stuff, later in the week in one of the bathroom sinks at the House.

When I came back inside, Dean was standing in front of the shelf of DVDs near the TV. I gave into the temptation to stand behind him, slide my arms around his waist, and lay my head against his shoulder blades. Words, honest ones, came more easily since he couldn't see my face. "I didn't mean to sound ungrateful. I really appreciate it… you… everything."

Dean's big hand closed around my hip and held me close. "What did you say last night, 'it's not quid pro quo'? I do it because I like you."

"I just don't want to overstay my welcome." I steadied myself and leapt off the figurative edge. "I don't think I'm ready to face the music back at the House yet."

"Good, because I don't think I'm ready to let you leave. I'm sorry that you even have music to face."

I kissed his shoulder, loving the soft skin under my lips, and imagined for a second that all of him could be mine to kiss for longer than the weekend. "It wasn't your fault. If anyone's apologizing, it should be me. I shouldn't have left you in hostile territory. I should have known the territory was hostile, or was that hostile or... dammit Rachel." I sighed, resting my forehead against his back. "That was a really shitty thing she cooked up, and I'm sorry."

"She planned that?"

"Yeah, I think I let it slip that you weren't cool with big crowds before the party, and I guess she wanted to show just how not cool you were. Sorry."

"We could exchange apologies all day, or we could let it go and find a better way to spend the time. I like having you here, and we both agree that what happened was crappy. All right?" He gave my hip another squeeze. "Help me pick out a movie to go with breakfast? I've got a lot...."

I kissed his shoulder again and moved around Dean until we switched places, my back against his chest, his arms around my waist, and his nose against my damp hair. "Smells nice."

"With all the crap I put in it to look this good, it better." I relaxed against him, reveling in the fact that he wanted me here. "Let's see, Streep, Streep, Streep...."

"I like her movies," he murmured sheepishly against my hair, and I swore I could feel him blushing. It was the cutest thing ever, and I moved my finger away from the spine of *The Way We Were* to gently stroke his warm cheek.

My eyes continued the search. "Oh, here's a change, The Divine Miss Midler... wait...." I pointed my stroking finger at a DVD spine two rows down from where we searched. "*Tromeo and Juliet*? You watch Z-grade movies too?"

"When they're so bad they're good."

I kissed his chin and laughed. "And here I thought you only worshiped the divas like a good fag. Keep surprising me like this and I'm never leaving."

Dean's sudden puff of laughter felt warm against my cool, damp hair. "Don't worry. As long as I make the yearly power brunches and keep having sex with men, I get to keep my gay card." He reached around me and down, tapping a spine on the same shelf as *Tromeo*. "Have you seen *The Room* yet? It's not an oldie, but it's well on the way to being a go-to 'so bad it's funny' movie."

He pulled the case out and let me see. I cringed at the terrible design of the cover and the dead creepy eyes of the lead actor. "Holy shit, it is a zombie flick? This dude looks half melted."

Dean took the case out of my hands, his eyes dancing with glee that bordered on demented. I was beginning to really like this side of him, all relaxed and easygoing and generous. "Let me check on breakfast and we'll pop it in. You're in for a treat."

The couch was just as soft as it looked, and I sank into it, curling my legs under me. Dean returned with both our mugs and stopped at the coffee table, looking at me as if he liked me right where I was. I squirmed like a bug under glass and felt my own face get a little heated. It was like every second I remained there, it felt more and more right. He liked the way I looked in his bed and in his clothes and on his couch, and God help me, I was beginning to like it too.

HAPTER EIGHT

# *Not Cool*

THERE was no way in hell I'd be awake and functional early enough to catch a ride with him back into town Monday, so he told me I was welcome to stay at the house while he went to work. I did, soaking up the quiet and all of the space. Three hours later, I was bored with the quiet and the space, so I grabbed a nap, texted Dean about what he wanted for dinner, then out came the toolbox, and by the time I heard the garage door open, I'd made some serious progress on Spauldy's tunic, well, enough for her to try it on when I met her next. Dinner was my attempt at a stir-fry (excellent), with a side of some movie called *Birdemic* (hysterically awful), and a mutual hand job for dessert, since I was a bit sore from the several rounds of sex that had made up the rest of our Sunday.

Tuesday, I locked up Dean's place behind me and walked back to the Tribe House. Time to face that music. Just my luck that I was due back at Spauldy's right after. I would need the shrink time.

Rachel stood in the kitchen, alone, a cup of instant coffee in hand. She raked her eyes over me before setting the cup down. "Thor. Now."

Oh, this was going to be a doozy of a discussion if we were having it in the van. I didn't even set my bag down, just turned and headed back out the door. Her MP3 player was already plugged into the radio, and she turned it on to play Mindless Self Indulgence low enough for us to speak normally.

We sat quietly in the driver and passenger's seats for the first two short songs, not looking at each other before Rachel finally spoke. "It took two days to calm him down?"

"Nah, it only took the ride home. We screwed the rest of the time, and boy does my ass...."

"I don't want to know!" she snapped. "You left us. You left us for days, with not even a damned call to make sure you weren't dead in a ditch or some shit. And for who?"

I glared right back, not wanting to give up a single inch, remembering Dean's panicked face as clear as day. "Not for who, because of who. You. What you did wasn't cool, Rach. I didn't want to come back after that. At least not until whatever bitch vibes you were on cleared up. That wasn't cool."

She slammed her body back on the seat and crossed her arms. "I told you. I was doing you a favor."

"Oh, you mean like the same favor you did when you nearly got me beheaded with a fucking hoop? Not doing me any more favors would be a really good favor."

"You mean Lala? Fuck her." Her face screwed up in distaste. "Skinny bitch needed to be taken down a few pegs, with her going on about how many people showed up to see her. Like we care."

Oh, Rach cared all right. I should have seen it coming. Lala was competition. Lala didn't dance, but she was well known and cute and knew what she was doing. With her in the picture, Crimson Dream Tribal could not be the best in this town. At least that was Rachel's point of view whenever shit like this came up. She didn't handle competition well.

"Why switch up the set list right then?" I sighed, leaning on the window. "And why drag me into it?"

She shrugged a shoulder. "The look on her face was priceless? Why not? Doesn't matter anyway, we got a great crowd, they loved us, we're doing it again in a few months, without or without Miss Lala. We'll be bigger than her in no time."

She pulled out a small baggie from her pocket with a few tabs of what I knew was E. "Wanna roll for a few hours? You know I hate it when we argue. Patch is out with Cindy getting groceries, but they should be back soon." She gave the baggie a shake, her expression growing dark. "You should be more concerned with Patch. You don't know what could happen to him when you're not there. Make it up to him when they get back."

"Make what up to him?"

"I saw him after you left. Seriously, Jonathan, could you have acted more of a dick? I'm half tempted to shove something down your throat to show you what it's like."

Oh, right. Shit. Looks like our little ruse worked perfectly, because she looked pissed, not even looking at me anymore. "Yeah, that was real shitty of me, I know. I wouldn't have been so... rough... if I didn't hear you guys trying to mess with Dean."

Rachel gave the baggie another shake. "I wanted him gone. Not my fault he ran into the bathroom instead." Her mood lightened, and she chuckled softly, eyes full of mirth. "Did he ever play football? He almost knocked Cindy on her ass."

"Rachel, this is fucking serious. We don't do this shit. We never do this shit. Don't you get it?"

She rolled her eyes. "Yeah, we didn't do this shit the last time some mundane started sniffing around your ass, and you remember how well that ended."

My back stiffened with shock and the memory. That was a low blow, but I couldn't blame her. She was there for the whole Rafe drama and the aftermath. My fury melted away, and I murmured contritely, "That's not even fair. I didn't know Rafe would do something like that. Dean's not like that at all."

Her face hardened. "You don't fucking know that."

"I know he's not in the closet, for starters."

"And you know that how? Because he told you? You know people say all kinds of shit to get laid, and you won't know the truth until he starts smacking you around like a fucking football player's wife. Why won't you trust me on this?" She gave a disgusted snort and shook the baggie at me again, quickly changing the subject. "Just take this shit already. It's the real thing, not the DXM bullshit."

Because nothing would thrill Dr. Spaulding more than having me walk into her office high on Ecstasy. I shook my head, looking back out the window at the house next door. Vacant again. We were shitty neighbors, with the parties and all. Anyone living next to us had to be exceptionally tolerant. "He won't be coming back here."

"Good. And you should stay home tonight. I need to know that you're safe."

I had no idea where I was crashing. Dean's bed was damned tempting, and I'd slept like a baby the past couple of nights, but my friends lived here, and if there was one thing lacking in Dean's world, it was other people. The days I was over, no one called, and the only phone call I heard him make was to Dr. Spaulding on Sunday. He didn't mention hanging out with other people, though apparently Bette from work really wanted to meet me again. He worked out at home, talked about going out to eat solo, and seemed really content living like some kind of hermit with one very sexy exception. It was exotic and weird and sad, all at the same time.

We were quiet through "Dicks Are For My Friends" and then "Faggot." Words bounced around in my head, words I should be saying to her, but I couldn't. She'd reminded me that she was there for me at my worst, and I couldn't blame her for being a bit wary about this new "outsider" when I fucked up so royally with Rafe. Even if her wariness really hurt Dean, I understood where it came from. So I remained silent. When it seemed that she had nothing else to say either, I opened the door to get out. "I gotta go for a bit, Rach. I'll be back in a couple hours."

"Go where?"

I was glad I wasn't looking at her, knowing exactly which piercing gaze I'd be up against. I had to get going so I wouldn't be late for my appointment, and I couldn't stand sitting in the van with the seductive prospect of wasting the day away wasted, all open and empathic and finding myself agreeing to all kinds of shit. I could see the setup clearly. We were alone, one of my favorite bands playing, with one of my favorite indulgences at the ready in that little baggie. Add Patch returning, ever ready to get between my thighs, to that brew, and it would be like old times. Rachel wanted things to get back to normal, wanted me back to normal.

"I need a walk, you know, clear my head a bit." I let my legs dangle out of the door before pushing out, dragging my bag behind me.

"You're going to see him, aren't you?" she grumbled, looking crestfallen. I'd seen right through the setup, and she knew it.

Thankfully, she gave me the perfect out. I smirked, slinging the duffel over my shoulder. "You know me too well. I'm gonna introduce him to the concept of a nooner. If I don't get us arrested for indecent exposure, I'll be home tonight, okay?"

She grunted sourly and looked away, giving me the time to close the van door and head for the bus stop around the corner.

I insisted Dr. Spaulding try on the partial tunic first to make sure I got the fit right around her arms and chest. Thank fuck she was as flat as a board, since making space for a large pair of ta-tas would have been a big pain in the ass.

"Make sure you're wearing something underneath this, okay?" I chided as I helped her out of it. "Or you're risking some serious pinching."

And talking about pinching and chests made me think about Dean's pinchable, chewable, oh-so-sensitive nipples, and I had to shake my head to focus on stashing the work back in its own Ziploc bag and then back into the toolbox. I almost wished I had convinced him to sneak out of the office for a nooner. We were both sore and a bit bruised (my hips looked covered in leopard spots from his fingers), but I wanted him again. I never stopped wanting him.

Which got me worrying about running into him on the way out from my appointment. How had I never noticed someone that tall and hot before?

"Jonathan?" Spauldy's voice brought me out of my thoughts. "Did you hear me?"

"Oh, sorry, Doc, zoned out a bit… what did you say?"

"Your show? How did it go? And afterward, of course." She was already breaking out the notebook.

I wanted to be very proud of the fact that I didn't get shitfaced at all last weekend, kept myself occupied and away from my major vices, but that would out me as the mystery guy Dean had taken up with, and I'm sure there's rules about that. "The show was great, tons of people, no one exploded or broke anything. We even left the stage as clean as we found it."

"And after?" she pressed.

"Didn't get drunk, if that's what you're asking. Or stoned. I...." I looked at my open bag, at the toolbox, and thought about what I could be working on to distract me. "I didn't even stay at home most of the weekend."

She leaned back, eyebrow going up. "Your new guy? You had a second night."

"And a third, and a fourth, and if I head over there tonight, a fifth."

"And he was just as respectful as the first night?"

Fuck it. I could use another chain belt. Or a bracelet to make up for the one I'd yet to get back from Dean. I grabbed the Crown Royal bag and was busily looping away with a simple four-in-two pattern, linking two rings to two other rings, before I answered. "Yeah, he's a great guy. Really. I like him, and I think we'll be seeing more of each other."

Dr. Spaulding smiled and crossed her arms. "It's okay, you know. You can tell me you're seeing Dean Winton."

My head shot up. I thought it was against some sort of shrink code to look so damned smug. "How'd you guess?"

She pointed to the short length of chain in my hands. "It was easy. For starters, Mr. Winton was wearing your work when I saw him last. And unless there's another guy around town who belly dances...."

"There could be." I swore I wasn't pouting, trying to shove back a bit of irrational jealousy that Dean would be seeing anyone else, even my hypothetical doppelganger. "Fine. I am, and I don't have to go into detail about how great he is, okay?"

"So defensive, Jonathan. Don't worry. I can't tell him any more about you than I can tell you about him. Patient confidentiality and all."

"Yeah, surprised the fuck out of me to see him walk in here two weeks ago."

Spauldy looked confused for a second, then laughed. "Oh, two weeks ago? We had to reschedule our Monday appointment. I'd twisted my ankle out in the field that weekend, so I thought it would be a good idea to let it rest for a day. By Tuesday it was good enough to walk on."

The mental image of my shrink dressed as an elf and running around someone's acreage with a duct-tape sword was enough to bring me out of my funk, and I looked up with a sly smile. "Hope the other guy looked worse."

She made a dismissive motion with her hands. "I'm afraid the ground won that skirmish."

I guess if I wanted to know more about Dean's freak-outs, why and where they came from, I'd have to do something crazy like talk to him directly. The thought sobered me up and brought me back to reality. "I'm sorry about Saturday night. Shit got all messed up. Rachel really doesn't like him, and I was the asshole who told her about him, and she... dammit. And she isn't even sorry."

She looked confused for a moment before nodding. "Ah yes, the episode. I did ask him to give me a call when he told me he was considering attending that party. It wasn't your fault, if I've got the details right—as he could remember them."

I wanted to know what he remembered, because my memory all pointed to this being my screwup. "If I didn't get distracted by Patch...."

"Patch, the young man you've been sleeping with?" A frown crossed her face. She had never really approved of me fucking Patch. Mostly because I couldn't help but feel a little guilty whenever I brought him up. Consenting or no, it was damned clear sometimes that he considered keeping my balls drained and my ass filled part of the rent.

"He tried," I replied firmly. "He tried to distract me, and I didn't go for it. What kind of a dick would I be if I left Dean alone to fool around with someone else, knowing that he 'sucks at crowds'? I'm a fuckup, not an asshole."

I hadn't even told Dean about the nature of the "problem" that took me off his lap and into the house, or even that Patch and I were fucking, or had been fucking. How that was going to go down, I didn't know and didn't want to find out.

"I think you're neither." She picked up the notebook, jotted down a few things. "Actually, the way you handled Dean's episode was close to perfect. And that you liked him enough to still see him again, well, that's not exactly what an asshole would do. Or a fuckup."

My nose wrinkled, like it did every time she quoted one of my own curses. Drunk sailors with stubbed toes didn't have a potty mouth like mine, but it was unnerving to hear it come out of her mouth. "You should warn him off me, you know. I'm no good for him, and he's still being entirely too sweet about this whole thing."

"Jonathan, this 'dating' thing might be strange to you—"

"Dating? What?" Now my entire face wrinkled and my denial poured right out. "We're not dating, we're having sex. There's no feelings in this."

She stared at me until I realized my face was blazingly warm. Her bullshit meter was pinging so loud I could hear it. I looked back down at my rings, annoyed and wishing the hour was over so I could slip out before I made myself look like a bigger asshole. Fuckup. Whatever.

"What is it, Jonathan? Last time, you had a hard time dealing with someone treating you respectfully. Are you having that same hard time dealing with someone who thinks you're good for more than what your body can do?"

I frowned at the links in my lap. "I suppose you can't tell me how he feels about me, huh?"

"I'd rather you do the grown-up thing and ask him. Or, even better, pay attention."

Pay attention? To what, the way I could picture Dean smiling at me if I closed my eyes? Or how his hand fit so perfectly on the small of my back when he showed me around the huge honking hunk of land his tiny house sat on, the way it screamed "I'm right here," and how good that made me feel? How about how he never pushed me to do anything I didn't want to do, in and out of bed? Or hell, should I pay attention to the way my heart shimmied like a drum solo whenever I thought about him? She wanted me to pay attention to him. It was impossible not to, and I loved and hated what he revealed to me without having to say anything.

One of the steel rings tumbled out of my hands, bouncing off my lap and onto the carpeted floor right at her feet. I stopped, watching through my lashes as she picked it up, set it back in the Crown Royal bag, and took one of my hands in hers, stilling me before I even realized the drop was because my fingers were shaking. I needed a drink. Several of them. Now. I knew I should have taken Rachel's advice and rolled instead of being here.

"He's insane," I said roughly, in that way I hated during these little chats. Dr. Spaulding was there for all this soul-baring bullshit, I knew that, but it didn't mean I had to enjoy the process. I hated feeling like this, like my stomach was all knotted up, and all I wanted to do was hide. Spauldy keeps calling these moments proof that I've got some anxiety issues I self-medicate with alcohol and drugs and denial, but that's bullshit. I saw real anxiety a couple of nights ago. This was me being a pussy. "He's nuts. And a hermit. Doesn't even own a pet. He's too quiet. I mean, what is a guy with decent breeding doing wanting me for more than a good fuck. I mean, I'm an irresistible lay, but... fuck!"

That one attempt to summon up my bravado just pissed me off even more. The word "irresistible" sounded wrong in my mouth, lacking all sorts of sincerity. "I should go... is my hour up?"

"Take some breaths, Jonathan." Spauldy squeezed my hand. "Give him a chance. Give yourself a chance. You've gone so far in recovery, you know. It's not going to be smooth sailing, so perhaps you need someone on your side, someone you can be honest with and trust."

"I thought you were on my side...." Yep, I was pouting, stalling long enough to quickly rebuild my walls.

"You know what I mean, Jonathan. If you want, I can make sure that your appointments never cross if you don't want him to find out the way you did. Though telling him about this part of you might help with developing some real intimacy. When was the last time you've been more than physically intimate with anyone?"

Oh hell no, Dean was not going to know how his "Jingle Boy" was one hot mess. He had enough to deal with. Ignoring that suggestion, I shrugged and packed my rings away. "If you could, you know, with the appointments, that would be awesome. Thanks."

Her raised eyebrow pretty much told me she knew what I just did, but she rounded her desk to glance over her calendar. She still used a datebook instead of that clunky computer that took up most of her desk. "Not a problem, Jonathan. Before you go, though...."

She came from around the desk and rifled a stack of pamphlets near her door, pulling one out and handing it to me as I stood up. "If you decide to keep seeing Dean, it would help to understand his condition a bit more than he could explain it."

"Understanding Social Anxiety" was the title, large and red in a weird graffiti font on a white background. "You're gonna hand him one about me? Would only be fair."

Though what would she give him? Understanding Drug Addiction? I didn't think I was an addict. I only jonesed when stressed out, or when it was around, or when I felt like partying. I was sure there wasn't one for "Don't Date That Fuckup Esteban Jonathan Mendoza."

Spauldy shook her head and held the door open for me. "Protecting your privacy is my priority too, unless you want me to tell him what I know about you." At my look of utter horror, she smiled and shook her head. "I'll see you in two weeks, Jonathan."

"YOU owe me big time for this, *papi*," Patch growled softly, arms crossed like a bratty toddler, as we sat in the worst waiting room chairs that ever existed. And I've been in my share of clinic waiting rooms.

"You owe yourself for this." I smirked, not looking up from the wirework in my hands. This one was for one of Lala's coworkers, for another twenty-five bucks. Pendants were a lot more portable than my chain mail.

If I kept my thoughts mostly on the wire and pliers in my hands, and less on Patch's bitching, I wouldn't have time to worry about waiting on test results. Better he be bitching than the weird silence he had going on all the way here. He wouldn't tell me if anything was up when I asked, and something had to be up. Patch was usually only quiet when he was sleeping or had something in his mouth.

"And quit with the *papi* bullshit. It don't mean 'dad' if we're fucking."

"Fuck you. I'm calling you whatever the fuck I want until the nurse calls our names. I can't believe you talked me into coming here. Twice."

"It's called leading by example, jackass. Might as well get used to it if you're going to keep using your dick."

So a week turned into a month that turned into a month and a half, and then it was time for our yearly crotch check. Usually "our" would have meant every standing member of the Tribe, currently the five of us, making use of some low-income clinic, because one of the many things Rachel and I had in common was a paranoia about catching anything that would put a damper on partying, from a cold to the clap.

"If they have to take more blood from me again, I swear…."

"Easy there, Scarlett O'Hara, and I still can't believe you're afraid of needles. How'd they get your ink on, permanent marker? And the piercings?"

I reveled in his righteous flush. It was downright hysterical to see him squirm and whine when they had to draw blood. He acted as if it was some sort of violation.

"That's different and you know it. No tat needles go that deep."

"Patch, you have a barbell below the head of your dick. That's damned deep." Hell, he was more proud of that extra bumpage than the one in his tongue.

The flush on his golden beach-boy skin could have melted the metal on his face and clashed with a brilliant tinge of green. "It's just a frenulum piercing. Right under the skin is completely different, and it didn't take too long and I was high and why the fuck are we even talking about this right now?"

A nurse stuck his head into the waiting room. "Patrick Mulhaney?"

Patch groaned and stood up, bending over to growl into my ear. "And the nurse is hot. I swear to God, if I get told that you gave me some sort of Mongolian crotch-rot by that hot nurse, I'm coming back out here and shoving my boot up your ass. Sideways."

I looked up to verify Patch's assessment. The nurse, tall, handsome, hair in dark curls that tumbled over his forehead, nice bod even in the scrubs, looked older than me by at least a decade. Goddamn, did Patch have it bad for older guys. There had to be a name for it, some reverse of "robbing the cradle."

I set the pliers aside and smacked the kid on the ass. "Go on, you big baby. You'll be fine."

He had to be fine; I was sure of it. And even though we weren't having sex anymore, I still wanted to make sure he was taking care of himself before releasing him out into the wild world of cock. If he was clean, I would be too, and nothing said "I've been a good boy, now please blast a load in my ass," like presenting a clean sheet of results to the guy I was now fucking. It was an extra benefit for this yearly trip.

What was really different was that this trip didn't have Rachel and the girls along. At the very least, Rachel and I always came together to these things, mutually supporting each other through rounds of tests and pills and devices and that one time she thought she was knocked up but was just freaking out so badly about an upcoming show that she skipped a period like a busted typewriter. Those were the times we felt like the closest of friends, through sickness and health and swiping pocketfuls of condoms for a water balloon fight or a piece of subversive art that got us in so much shit with the dean of our art school. Those were the days.

Now Rachel told me the ladies had already attended our safe-sex mecca weeks ago, leaving Patch as my sole moral support. I was acting more like his moral support, though. I hoped it got easier for him to deal when I couldn't be there to hold his hand and make fun of his weirdly selective needle-phobia.

Patch was back in a few minutes, coming toward me with a lanky, sexy swagger, looking more than calmed down, smirking, clacking the tongue ring against his teeth. The only red was slight, on his cheeks.

"Good news?" I asked, watching around him as the nurse closed the door slowly, eyes glued to Patch's ass. Well, I had to give the man props. At least he'd know if his quarry was clean or not if he pulled from patients.

Patch, oblivious to the stare, took his seat next to me and waved the paper in front of me. "Great fucking news, and great news for fucking." He stilled the paper, and I could see something written in ink at the top of the page. "Dave gave me his number."

I had to laugh and shake my head at him. That was my boy. Good thing that would never change. "You gonna call him?"

The smile faded off his pretty face as he folded the paper and tucked it into his pocket, bright blues hooded as he took his seat next to me again, as if he'd forgotten about this quiet mood until now. I'd seen that look when we met up. It was brief, he covered it up quickly by grinning and making some crack about how I wasn't walking with a limp, but it was there. "I don't think so. You know, given all the crap you've had to deal with from Rachel. I doubt anyone at the House would care who I fuck as much as they care about you. Wouldn't be fair to him, just in case I'm wrong."

"Yeah." Patch had a point. Despite how well things were working with Dean, it was hard to ignore that things were deteriorating between Rachel and me. I barely saw Patch at the House anymore, save for parties, and it seemed clear that he wasn't sleeping over when I was spending the night with Dean. When I asked Rach about it, she ignored me. Tam and Cindy had no clue about where the kid was crashing. "You can borrow my cell once we're out of here. Call him."

"Really?"

Just then, the door opened again, and Dave poked his head back out, looking right at me. "Esteban Mendoza?"

One of these days, I would stop tensing whenever a stranger used my first name. That was not today.

Patch patted my thigh as I stood up. "Tell 'em I give great head, will ya?" he teased with a wink. The smile didn't reach his eyes.

To my surprise, Lala waited outside the clinic, standing next to her tiny Mini Cooper. She gave Patch a warm smile, and me the mother of all side-eyes.

"It's cool, Lala." Patch moved toward the passenger seat. "*Papi*'s always cool."

"Hey, dollface." I even held my hands up to try to show that I was harmless. For some reason, I had assumed we were all kinds of cool after the fiasco at the show. "I'm making good progress on Marisa's pendant, wanna see?"

"I'll wait for the finished product, Jonathan," she replied quickly, opening the door for Patch and turning to get in on the driver's side. "We've got to get going. Patch is showing Mark the basics of not setting himself on fire while playing with poi."

Between the chilly response and the kinda funny crack about her husband not torching himself, I didn't know how to respond, so I looked at Patch. He sat passively, as if he didn't know I was watching him, and I saw it in the tension in his shoulders, the way he jerkily toyed with an unlit cig with long, delicate fingers that were normally way more graceful when they played with fire toys. Something was amiss, and it might have been my fault. Did my stupid little "played too rough" ruse go too far? Did I actually hurt him? Hell, was he feeling upset that we weren't fucking anymore?

"You couldn't get a better dude to show him the ropes," I finally said, glancing back over to Lala. "See you at the next shindig?"

"Maybe," Lala mused, then got into the car. As I watched them pull away, I couldn't help the creepy discontent that welled in my stomach. I couldn't understand why I gave that much of a damn about anyone or anything not Tribe, but I was really shaken by Lala's apparent disapproval, even if I wasn't clear about what she was so not happy with. With Rach, I knew what her deal was. She was jealous of anything that took my focus away from her and the Tribe. I knew that. With Lala, and the way she seemed really kind to Patch, I felt like a real dick, for whatever reason.

Until I could talk to either one of them to see what was up, I realized there wasn't much I could do.

HAPTER NINE

# *My Brother's Keeper*

MY PERCEPTION of Dean changed the longer I stuck around. First of all, I learned that my sexy hermit was not only far from boring, but also wasn't that much of a hermit. He didn't stay home all the time. Sure, our outings happened at strange times, midnight grocery runs at the local twenty-four-hour big box store, movie screenings days after the movie was out and always a matinee, visiting art galleries hours before closing time, and early dinners at restaurants that piqued his fancy. But he got out, and when I was there, we got out. I had no cause to complain. I couldn't remember the last time I'd been inside a museum or a theatre I wasn't performing in. Being near broke and putting all my spare cash into the Tribe's pool for booze or pills or weed kinda got in the way of any other sort of entertainment.

Dean was more comfortable in his house, though. We talked more there, and he had tons of movies and a DVR packed with shows I'd only vaguely heard of. The land the house was on was mostly wooded, with a lake that bordered several other properties. And it was oh-so-swimmable on hot days. Dean really loved the house. He maintained the place well, hauling out a riding mower for the grass, doing minor repairs when needed, keeping the inside neat, and I found myself helping out the longer I stayed. It was so weird. I wasn't used to living in a house long enough to care. Then again, he owned it. I guess it made sense to take care of what was yours.

We shared stories and experiences. I got a new appreciation for terrible, terrible movies, made more fun when watched with company who mocked them mercilessly. Dean got introduced to a few of my favorite bands, and when I heard him belting out "Neuer Wind" in the shower in German, I knew my efforts were not in vain. He sang in a nice rich tenor, the sound ringing out of that lovely chest of his. Not understanding a word of German myself, I didn't join in the song, not even to garble along phonetically, but when I slipped into the shower with him, I managed to keep up in... other ways. By the time we finished and the water was starting to run cold, I had completely forgotten to ask him how many other languages he knew, and how he had learned them.

I gave the pamphlet thingy Dr. Spaulding sent me home with one look and tossed it. The last thing I wanted was for it to fall out of my bag where anyone could find it. Dean would be embarrassed, and anyone at the House would find another reason to mock him. Not only was I hanging out with them less, but spending my time with someone who didn't appreciate the joys of a good drunken party. It was like a crime against fun.

I felt the rift every time I showed up, less and less with my bag on my shoulder, since I'd taken to leaving it at Dean's place. We still did our weekly dances at Kouzina, but it was hard to keep in the groove with the troupe when my best friend wasn't speaking to me half the time.

I didn't find out that she'd had my mattress moved out of our shared bedroom and into another until Patch told me. He didn't seem to care about the change in sleeping arrangements, but he wouldn't say anything more about what was going on with him. When Dean surprised me with a new phone, a freebie he got when he updated his own plan, I gave Patch my old one, with the order that he was to keep in contact with me.

One Saturday, about a month since my triumphant test results and the messy-fun celebration, I gave Mama a call for the most recent update on the condition of her wonky liver. She was still working and treating patients, but taking her meds like a good girl. I asked for more details, exactly what was going on, but she refused to tell me, still refused to let me go and see her. She'd always been so fiercely independent, refusing to let anything slow her down or stop her. Having and raising me was only a slight setback in her life as a traveling nurse. I knew it was her way, but it goddamned hurt that she wouldn't lean on me just a little. Now that she was sick, I really missed having her around like I did as a kid.

The only update on my life I felt okay telling her was that I had a regular paying gig and was seeing a professional about that whole "slowing my partying down" deal because, like a good boy, all I wanted was for my mother to (a) not worry about me and (b) say "*Qué bueno*" so I felt like I'd actually done some good. She didn't need to know that I had practically taken up with a man, or that Rachel and I were having issues. Maybe I was more her son than I thought, and the last thing I wanted her to do was worry for me or try to help.

After that conversation, I needed distraction. Dean was in the garage, doing that thing where he lifted dumbbells over and over again until his arms bulged in a way that made me sit up and beg. That would be a lovely distraction, but I knew his exercise time was important to him. I tried to dance outside near the garage while he was busy with the weights a few times, but apparently, unless I was on stage, Dean took my shaking and swaying as a mating call he couldn't ignore. So, for the sake of both our exercise routines, we worked out in different rooms.

I went to the office, hooked up my little music player to Dean's computer speakers, and hit shuffle, ready to dance to whatever came up, clad only in my boxer briefs and a coin belt.

When I brag that I can belly dance to damn near any song, I mean it. I practice to anything that pops up on the player. I chuckled my way through Shakira—indeed, her hips don't lie, and mine don't either—slithered past Nightwish's "The Siren," and popped it to "We Will Rock You" hard enough to nearly sprain something in my right thigh. That song ended, and the player switched to some spoken word, so I shimmied over to the desk to press the forward button. "Damn near any song" required at least a beat for me to dance to it. I zigged instead of zagged at the wrong time, and my hip slammed into the desk hard enough to shake the monitor on the computer, ending the "scenes of nature" screen saver. If I hadn't been leaning over to steady one of the speakers from toppling, I would have missed it.

It was a picture of Dean, one of several of a set from the looks of the files behind the window. Unlike the ones hung up in the house, this one didn't look quite safe to post on the wall. He looked younger, not by much, a lot less buff, and there was so much skin. Normally, Dean wasn't all about showing off the goods outside of the house, but that photo was not at home. You know, unless there was a stable somewhere on the property I didn't know about.

Dean, without his glasses, grinned back at the camera, wearing nothing but a cowboy hat and jeans slung low and made even more indecent with the open zipper, showing off a tuft of bright-red pubes. I'd seen the look on his face before, many times, when we were alone and getting sexy, and looking at that picture I was stuck between allowing my cock to try to split my own shorts and wondering who the hell he was modeling for. This wasn't a casual shot; it looked too professional.

Throwing all caution and common sense to the wind, I rounded the desk and clicked on the next photo in the set. Same Dean, same smile, those pants hanging a little lower, and he was holding a hunk of coiled rope in one hand, the other on the hat, dipping it in a way that screamed "howdy ma'am." The others were of him in the same location, various poses, all accentuating his best features, ending with one shot that made me moan aloud.

He was just in the hat and the smile, sitting in a trough, legs spread, that glorious cock I worshiped lazily flaccid, lying on his thigh. That pose and grin screamed invitation, and if I could have jumped through the screen to bury my tongue below his balls and down his crease, I'd have been there in a heartbeat.

The file name of each of those shots had the date included, and they were four years old. He was as old as Patch and already looking damn fine. Something had to have happened to take him from posing with all his business out to getting shaky if there's too many people in the line at the grocery store.

Why did I care so much about this? Couldn't I just enjoy the naughty pics, tease him a bit about them later, let him know I saw them and would love to take him up on the invites they promised? It was another part of his past he had never shared with me. We'd exchanged crazy party tales, most of his from college. He'd told me stories of growing up with kinda rich parents and traveling around, and then stuff about work. It was like he was born, grew to age eighteen, and emerged full grown as a twenty-six-year-old adult with a steady job. Everything else got an "I'll tell you later" dodge.

I heard the kitchen door close, and I jumped up, turning the monitor off, and was on the other side of the desk in time for "Let the

Music Play" to start. Dean poked his head through the office door and gave me a tired grin. Sweat made his gray tank top cling to his chest, turning my thoughts away from wondering about the man's past to wanting to yank that shirt off and lick him all over. Mmmm, jock sweat.

"Hey, Jon." His eyes were locked to my swishing hips. "How does Kouzina sound for dinner tonight?"

Making myself look casual was easy since he was so distracted. I did a few spins as I answered. "Don't I perform there damn near every weekend? Why would I go there on an off day?"

"Have you tried the food? I think you'll love it."

He had a point, the fucking foodie. Some Fridays, I was grateful for the loud music drowning out my occasional stomach rumblings. The food sure smelled amazing, but the prices were prohibitive on the Tribe's budget. Between the way he cooked and our restaurant outings, I was going to look like a blimp. I danced my way over to him, all smiles. "Sounds like fun, baby. Can I have this dance, first?"

Dean arched his eyebrow at me, but I already had his hands in mine, pulling him into the office.

"I haven't danced in a while, and you're better at it. I'll just trip over you."

"Like I'm gonna complain if you end up on top of me, Dean. Besides, with the way you move in bed, you'll be fine."

I placed his hands on my hips and slowed my shimmy down. With one hand on his shoulder, one cupping his bright-red cheek, I forced him to look at me instead of his own feet.

"Don't get mad if I step on your toes," he muttered, hands moving down to cup my ass.

"You'll just have to kiss them and make it better then, won't you?" I purred into his ear and got the shudder I wanted. He did very much enjoy playing with my feet, and I enjoyed the attention. The man was a massage god.

His eyes met mine, fingers tightened on my ass, and he moved with me, in time, in step. Surprise, surprise, my hypothesis was correct. At least he could move and not look like an idiot, and my bare feet stayed clear of his gym sneakers. He sure danced like someone who'd seen the inside of a club more than twice.

When "Let the Music Play" changed into a club remix of "Somebody Told Me," his eyes lit up, but he made as if to leave the office. Knowing The Killers were one of his favorite bands, I grabbed his arm and hauled him back next to me. "One more song and I'll join you in the shower."

"Now you're playing dirty," he breathed, and we started dancing again. I simply laughed and drank in the sight of this man in motion. My heart swelled with pride, and I wanted more. Not a dance in bed, but I wanted to go out with him, take him dancing, show off the sweet, shy man with the bright, happy eyes and the sexy moves—and then take him back home because he was all mine-mine-mine. It would kill two birds with one stone, ease my restlessness and get Dean outside.

I hadn't set foot in a club in years, at least one we weren't performing in, and my suggestion made him go pale, the arms around me going lax. "You're kidding, right? Clubs have really, really big crowds."

"So we don't go on a really, really busy night. How about just an hour or two during the week? I want to ogle you in public." And ogle without anyone's disapproving glances or words.

His frown was at odds with his grinding hips as we kept dancing. I didn't blame him—our last public outing was the House party, and that didn't end well. I added, "It'll be neutral ground, and the second you're not cool with it, we're gone. I promise."

I was about to mention that we could keep Dr. Spaulding on call just in case, but I still wasn't supposed to know that. We never discussed our damages, other than Dean's obvious one, with each other, and I was okay with that for now.

"Fine," he sighed, pulling me against him completely, murmuring the final chorus of "Somebody Told Me." The very moment the song ended, I dragged him to the bathroom to make good on my promise and to distract him from any nervy thoughts about this upcoming outing of ours. I'm quite good at distraction tactics.


WE SEARCHED the local free paper for the names of any clubs that catered to the queerer set, since we were both clueless whether any existed in Belle Point. We clearly made horrible gay men. There were two, a kind of pub that advertised itself as for the ladies and a small dance club called My Brother's Keeper. We picked My Brother's Keeper for that next Wednesday night, and Dean managed to surprise me yet again by not needing that much help with picking out what to wear for clubbing.

I had stepped inside the bathroom to line my eyes when I saw him already in front of the mirror, peeling a black Under Armour T-shirt down over his chest. It clung tight to his skin, defining his pecs and making his chest look like someone painted it all black. "Is that new?"

He glanced at his reflection, his skin looking a touch pale. One deep breath brought back some of his color. "Nope. Haven't worn it in years, though. Might be too tight...."

My first thought was to ask him did he buy it to pose near naked long ago. Instead, I stepped in, hand on his back, rubbing the slick fabric, trying to ease him. I was ready to do this most of the night if need be, as long as we got out of his place for a little while. "Is it going to cut off circulation anywhere?"

He shook his head, then looked down at the bracelet I still hadn't taken back after all this time. Face the fact, boy, it was a gift. I didn't want to take it back. Even thinking about asking to borrow it made my heart hurt. It looked made for him now. I wrapped my free hand around that wrist, pressing the metal into his skin gently but firmly, reminding him that it and I were both there.

It seemed to soothe him. "Remember. Say the word when you're ready to leave."

Dean nodded, closed his eyes, and took another breath before pulling me to his chest. "Let's go before I completely lose my nerve."

From the outside, the club looked like a hole in the wall, but the inside was a lot nicer, throwing off vibes of "don't judge a book by its cover, bitch." The very feminine Asian man guarding the door let us both in, eyeing my ID a few ticks longer since it was very much out of state. I think we got them renewed in Florida some years ago or something, and I hoped it hadn't expired with all of our moving around.

Lights swirled, and the DJ was already cutting loose with the dance mixes for the handful of couples grappling on the floor. I bounced on the balls of my feet, ready to storm it like the beach at Normandy, when common sense told me to check in with Dean. With the small crowd, he looked a lot less shaky, but he stared at the bar like it was the answer to all of life's questions.

"Come on." I took his wrist and pulled us there, my order for a scotch and soda already on my lips. Dean didn't get his usual red wine, opting for a shot of Grey Goose. Well, if it was like that, then it would be perfectly okay for me to join in for solidarity. I added another shot for myself to our order. We took the shots first before I downed my drink. The hit of booze to my system felt like a homecoming, and I ordered a refill on the vodka before I knew what I was doing. I drove here; Dean could drive us back.

Speaking of, I had to keep an eye on his intake, all part of looking out for him. I had to keep an eye on him period, but the shot seemed to further relax him. I could feel his eyes on me as I took my second shot, and I knew I needed to get us both away from the bar. We were there to dance, after all, not get utterly shitfaced.

We probably looked quite the odd pair as we got out on the floor and began to groove together—Dean in his tight-ass T-shirt and loose blue jeans, me toning down the Goth look in a green V-neck shirt, ass-hugging tight jeans, and the silver coin belt and my hair left all loose and long. The glances I noticed were appreciative, and even more so when Dean finally relaxed into the rhythms. It was some sort of 90s dance music night, the DJ feeding my sense of nostalgia. I was a twinky little teen back then, too young to hit up the clubs that played this sort of music, so I was living it up to old hits from bands like The Real McCoy and La Bouche.

When "Livin' La Vida Loca" came on, we both stopped dancing and cracked up laughing at the same time.

"You had a crush on Ricky Martin too, huh?" I yelled into his ear. The mirth in his eyes was amazing, lighting them up under the swirling club lights, once again confirming the fact that a relaxed Dean was a damned sexy one.

One of Dean's hands squeezed my waist, the other grabbed my arm, and Dean spun me around until we were grinding back to chest. We swayed back and forth, my ass fitting against his hips like two puzzle pieces, perfect. "Broke my heart when he came out."

"Why?" I grabbed his hips, making him slow down until our motions matched, a sensual rock side to side.

"Was easier to crush on him when I thought he was straight. Forbidden fruit and all that. It wasn't so much fun when I knew he batted for the same team."

"Good for me, then." I nuzzled against his cheek. "I'm much less forbidden than he is."

"Yeah, I hate to break Ricky's heart, but I've only got room for one handsome Latino in my life."

The warmth that welled up in my chest wasn't just the alcohol I'd slammed, I knew that. I didn't want to acknowledge the feeling behind those words, despite knowing he was speaking his truth. I leaned my head back and distracted him by rolling an "r" right into his ear, turning it into a deep purr.

That got me held even tighter, and since he wasn't dead, I felt him hard against my ass. This was working beautifully. I was triumphant. Project Take Dean Out was so far a success.

We rocked out like that for "Ray of Life" and "Missing" before he tugged me back to the bar, claiming a parched throat. We stood close, waiting for our drinks, his a glass of some type of red wine that I didn't catch, me another S and S. Our arms wound around each other, and we slowly moved back and forth, exchanging kisses. His joy tasted delicious on my tongue. His eyes locked on mine, and I couldn't look away. There was something in that gaze. Something inside me warmed, and it scared the shit out of me. I didn't want to know exactly what he saw when he looked at me that way, and fear crept up my spine, attempting to spoil tonight's bliss.

I needed to back off and regroup, and, thankfully, the rental on the drinks I'd pounded when we first arrived was up, and I needed to hit the head. I pointed out the exits to Dean, mostly for my own peace of mind, reminded him to let me know if he'd had enough, even if he had to come into the bathroom and grab me halfway through my stream. He rolled his eyes at that suggestion, kissed me on the cheek, and shoved me toward the bathrooms.

It was a weekday night, but even so the bathroom was cruisy as hell, hotties hanging on the walls, taking their sweet time to take care of business. As I stepped up to a urinal, I noticed two guys in the corner exchanging cash for a baggie of pills.

Sure, it looked like a handshake, but I'd done that more than once to know what I saw, and a brilliant idea popped into my mind. The dealer met my eyes, his a foggy gray, barely hidden behind dyed black bangs, and I held the gaze until he moved to the urinal next to me and whipped his piece out.

Yeah, I looked at it. I'm longer. Dean's bigger. No contest.

Satisfied, I was the first to speak. "Got any favors left?"

"I might," he murmured, voice pitched low. "Interested?"

Sure, I could have used the cash in my wallet to buy something more worthwhile than two tabs of E, but I had a plan, and it was worth the money I'd paid. If I felt this good with Dean and a few drinks, I would be over the moon with Dean, a few drinks, and Ecstasy. Over the moon, more relaxed, and since Dean was having such a great time, it would be okay for me to relax a little and have a great time too. And nothing got me there faster than a few tabs of E. It was a celebration. No one could fault me for celebrating this monumental moment. Dean was in a club, dancing, with me.

Ignoring the teeny little voice in my head that sounded suspiciously like Dr. Spaulding advising against my plan, I popped the pills dry on my way out of the bathroom and walked around to find where I'd left Dean. I didn't think he'd be that far from the bar, and I was right. What I wasn't expecting was the *Jersey Shore* reject all up in his personal space. I would have probably been less miffed if they were flirting or making out, but I could see Dean's pale, stony face from a mile away. Someone was fucking with him. Again. We go for a nice night out, and someone was fucking with him. Someone was going to get his teeth knocked in, because, unlike my dear best friend, I had nothing to lose by lashing out at this spray-tanned asshole.

I stalked up to the two, and Dean saw me first, shoving the dickhole away, his voice clear as he pushed his glasses back on his face and held them there like a shield. "You've got the wrong guy."

Mr. Guido shook his head. "Hey, baby, I know I've seen you around town before. I'd know that face anywhere. Just one dance."

The asshole didn't even notice my approach, which was really pissing me off. As I got close, my steps got even slower and I cursed the effect of the pills I'd popped, the edges of my vision already getting fuzzy. Give me a second, E tabs. Let me get all righteously furious before turning me into happy jelly, okay?

Dean looked over at me, his jaw set to the point that the muscles jumped. "I don't know what you're talking about. Leave me alone."

Finally, Mr. Guido noticed me, since I practically bullied my way between them. He didn't look too impressed, given that I was inches shorter than both of them and didn't look like I mainlined creatine for breakfast. "This scrawny shit's your boyfriend?"

I heard Dean's "Screw you" at about the same time I brought my knee up to slam into Mr. Guido's possibly spray tanned business. It felt like a love tap on my end, but he was stepping back with that look that said I totally got him good. Score one for the cavalry.

"That's Mr. Scrawny Shit to you, *pendejo*," I growled, watching the bodyguard float in out of nowhere to drag his ass away. Dean said some other stuff to the man, I guess to keep me from joining Mr. Guido on the sidewalk. Everything was fuzzy and far away, and I wanted the guard gone before he noticed I was rolling. It was a weird sort of roll, though. It came on fast, and while I usually got the fuzzy wrapped-in-cotton-wool effect where everything was so sparkly and bright, this felt like I was swimming through slow-setting concrete. No brightness at all. Arms wound around me, and I leaned back against a chest. I knew it was Dean. I knew his scent too well. My head lolled back to rest against his chest, and I closed my eyes for a moment, willing my heart to stop thudding so hard. I'd solved the problem and Dean was okay. Time to dance some more.

"You... all right?" Dean's voice wavered at my ear, and I slowly, very slowly, turned in his arms and looked up at him. Yep, I was all right, and everything was nice and fuzzy and perfect, dammit. Now to get him back on the floor. His mouth opened, and I very carefully placed my hand on his lips. I didn't want to hear about anything, not about the douchebag who couldn't hear no, not about how unsporting it was to knee another dude in the junk, nothing. I wanted to move, to move with Dean, to ride the floaty feeling to the end.

It was a weird sort of roll.

"Jon...!"

I stepped back, grabbing Dean to try to pull him to the floor again, certain that my smile was oh so seductive, tempting enough to get him to not worry. I didn't want him to worry about anything tonight, because if he wasn't worried, then I could actually relax.

I must have miscalculated something, because the pull ended with the world tilting over, and it finally dawned on me as I contemplated what kind of weird roll was this. It felt like I had a lot of time before I hit the floor.

But I didn't hit the floor at all. The world tilted again, and I was stopped short. Dean's dim and fuzzy face came into view, lip-blurs moving. "... what... wrong... Jon...."

Wrong. Yeah, this was all wrong. This wasn't an E roll. I wasn't trying to bounce off the walls or rip his clothes off. I shivered all over with the sick feeling that the shit I'd paid for and swallowed wasn't E at all. That fuckheaded dealer in the bathroom was selling ketamine or DXM or something and calling it E, and no one would know the difference until they'd taken it. And whatever it was, mixed with all the booze I'd poured down my throat... no wonder it hit me fast and hard.

I opened my mouth to explain to Dean that we had to get out of here right the hell now, that I'd taken some bad shit, but nothing came out but the contents of my stomach: chicken piccata, minus the chicken, several shots of vodka, and two and a half scotches and soda. Panicked sweat beaded over my body, making me feel warm in the places my vomit didn't reach, and my chest ached from the force of my heart slamming against it. I wanted to scream and claw my way back to total awareness, fear churning my empty guts as the entire world got fuzzy, and I was overwhelmed by the urge to just let go and float away. Dean was there, close, clutching me, and I tried to cling to him like a lifeline. I didn't want to float away.

"Fuck... help!"

This was one massive screwup if it got Dean dropping the f-bomb outside of bed. I'd never been so stupid, never been so careless. Was I that rusty at partying that I would fail this badly? Rachel would have a fit, if she didn't die laughing of "I've told you so." Never take shit from people who aren't vouched for. We'd rammed that into people's heads. I didn't want this. I just wanted to relax. My lips moved, and I wasn't sure if words came out. At least it was not more puke. I thought. I hoped.

We moved, but I couldn't feel much in the struggle, and my mouth kept moving, but I couldn't hear it over the pounding of my heart. The pain spread from my chest, radiating out to my entire body. I hoped I was apologizing, or telling him to look away or leave me there so he wouldn't have to deal with it. This was my fuckup, not his. As much as I liked his company, he didn't deserve to deal with this shit.

Now there were blinking lights, flashing, blinking clouds of lights dancing over the blur that was Dean's face, and suddenly I wanted to see him clearly, hating the effect of whatever it was I'd taken for stealing that view from me. My hand felt like it weighed a ton, but I managed to get it up and on his face to make sure he was really there. Wet. His face was wet, his lips moved, there was shouting. Was he shouting at me? Good, baby, be angry with me. Now give my neck a good jerk and I can stop struggling.

"… don't… dare… pass out, Jon!"

More blurs joined Dean's, blocking out the blinky light clouds. The world shifted one more time and then went completely black.

HAPTER TEN

# *Enabler*

I CAME to a few times. Noise, darkness, pain everywhere, and then I was gone again. No stupid tunnels or lights or anything awaited me when I left the world of the conscious. Next time I saw some New Age hippie gassing on about near-death experiences, I was going to punch them in the throat. Fucking liars.

I woke up slowly, my hearing switching on first. People, lots of people, beeping machines, some brat crying in the distance. My body wouldn't move, and for a second I thought I was waking up at my own funeral. Mama did have a big-ass family, though it didn't explain the beeping and shit.

On the other hand, that would explain the Spanish I was hearing.

And thinking about Mama was enough incentive to get the rest of me in gear, slowly. There was only one voice speaking in my native tongue, fairly fluently.

Awareness slowly dawned on me at the words. The voice kept talking about someone's "hijo," speaking to a "Señora Mendoza" and then quickly, bashfully changing it to "Mama Carmen." The "Señora Mendoza" could have made me laugh, if I could have made my mouth function. Mama hated being called Señora or Ms., even if she was this close to sixty.

Wait. Someone was talking to my mother, and I was lying down. Okay, I wasn't dead. I was probably on a stretcher. The beeping was probably my own stupid heart. Heart monitor. It was the heart monitor.

Hearts don't beep. It was overwhelming, keeping up with all the sudden realizations. A hand was wrapped around mine, and I squeezed it involuntarily, interrupting the flow of the one-sided conversation.

"I think he's waking up." That voice sounded so deep and so familiar I wanted it to curl around me like a blanket and hide me from reality. Did I suffer some sort of brain damage in the place that figures out languages? I mean, other than whatever was wrong with me that got me in the hospital in the first place. Dean was speaking to my mother. "Yes, yes. I have to get a doctor to him. I'll make sure he calls you the second he can. I'm so sorry."

I wanted to ask him since when did he learn to speak goddamned *español,* but my throat was Gobi desert dry, and only a croak came out. A cup was pressed against my lips, and I gratefully drank, letting the water do its thing. My eyelids, coated with gravel from the feel of them, slowly opened to show Dean kneeling next to my stretcher, snapping my phone shut. His face was the picture I will always conjure up to invoke guilt for the rest of my life. Drawn, worried, but with fury in his golden eyes, blazing amber.

I wanted to ask him a lot of things, "What happened" being tops on the list. Was he okay? Did he have a freak-out? How badly did Mama want to strangle her only child? When could we leave? How soon did he want me gone? Because having me bumming around his place for months on end was one thing, but late-night hospital trips on a work night might be too much even for his infinite patience.

What did come out of my mouth, however, was "Where'd that guy know you from?"

He reeled back, his eyes flaring with anger, and the set of his jaw was so hard I swore I heard molars crack. I wanted to take it back, but he was faster. "I haven't exactly holed up in my house until you showed up, you know. I'm sure he'd seen me around once or twice. I'm going to assume, after a couple of seizures, you're not in the right state of mind, if that's the first damned thing you're asking. Let me get a doctor over here."

Wait, seizures? In plural? Like, I had more than one? Granted, even one was a big deal, but I wasn't some old fart in a nursing home. He got up and moved away before I could get my mouth to form a better question. With his back turned, I did a very quick wiggle test of my fingers and toes to make sure I hadn't suffered any sort of paralysis. Nothing screamed "broken moneymaker" like partial paralysis. I'd be no use to anyone in that case.

Wait, it was strokes that had the risk of paralysis, right? Whatever, I wasn't going to risk anything.

My toes were still going when some lady in a white coat stopped by my stretcher. It was then I realized I wasn't in a room at all. The stretcher was in a hallway, which would explain the racket all around me. We had to be close to the waiting room. Good, less of a bill for me to pointedly ignore later. I didn't have insurance, and we, we being the Tribe, tended to avoid hospitals like we avoided calling the cops, only in life or death or broken bone emergencies.

I hoped like hell Dean hadn't tried to call Rachel.

Speaking of the man, he reappeared next to my stretcher as the doc asked me a bunch of questions and poked at me and shone a light into my eyes. What happened and what did I take? Apparently, I wasn't the only one put on his ass in that club thanks to the asshole dealer and his not-E, just the one that got it the worst, because of all the booze I had poured down my throat. She helpfully pointed out the IV that I somehow hadn't noticed stuck in my hand that was busily making up for the serious dehydration I'd done to myself.

I'd had three drug-induced seizures, one while Dean held me outside the club, two in the ambulance. I was lucky to still have all of my faculties, though my shirt was a lost biohazard.

All the time, Dean gave me a few glances, and I could see his panic. Of course, we're in a fucking ER. Surrounded by people rushing about. Way to really mess this up, Jonathan. As soon as this lady was done bugging me, I would send him home so he could relax.

Before I could speak, she was gone, after talking about some sort of brain scan, "MRE", or something I didn't care about because I was going to march right out of here before she returned. Dean glanced at me, giving me the full weight of his stare.

"Let me try this again," I croaked. "Go home, Dean. You look like shit."

"You look worse." His tone was harsh, and those eyes got glassy. "Special K, Jon? Really? Was I that bad for company?"

I tried to cringe, but everything hurt. "Not bad, I just wanted… fuck, I was having such a great time, and I wanted to make it better."

"And five drinks weren't enough?"

There was nothing I could say to justify myself. He was right. "I fucked up, Dean. I know that, and I'm sorry. I'm sorry you had to see that, sorry you had to call my mother—"

"She called you, actually. I was talking to Dr. Spaulding when it rang." His eyes narrowed to slits. "She wants you to call her too."

"Mama?"

"Spaulding." If he could remember that growl when we were in bed, I'd be a puddle every time.

Oh shit. She couldn't have told him shit about me. "What the hell happened to patient confidentiality?" I sputtered, feeling upset and knowing good and damn well I had no right to be.

"You should thank her, really. I was about to make a run out of here, for air, so you wouldn't see me lose it, and she convinced me to stay. Convinced me that you had been doing so well, that there had to be a reason behind this." He found a chair near the foot of the bed and sank into it, big body slumping with exhaustion, and my own guilt ratcheted up by leaps and bounds, more so when he laid a hand on my leg. "Substance abuse and anxiety? Why didn't you tell me any of this, Jon? Aren't we… something?"

He thought we were… something. That made my tired-out heart want to leap out of my chest with glee and stop in shock at the same time, even as I growled right back. "Anxiety? There isn't a damned thing I'm anxious about."

"Not even lying in a hospital bed after three seizures? 'Cause I'll be damned if it's not making me a little jumpy."

"Dean, too many people in an elevator make you fucking jumpy."

I regretted the words the second I heard them. For a second, I denied they were mine. It sounded like I said those words. My mouth did in fact move, and there was no more chicken-less piccata to pour out. My regret grew when he flinched, hard, and pulled that wonderfully large hand off my leg.

Way to go, King Dick of What an Asshole Mountain. And I couldn't stop myself from digging that knife in deeper.

"It's not like you're exactly Mr. Forthcoming yourself, you know. If I had a nickel for every time you've said 'later' when I ask about something, I'd be able to pay this bill." I motioned to the ER around us. "The only thing you've been straight up with me about is the panic thing. No details, not why or where it came from. I know enough to try to not trigger anything, but fuck...."

"It's a big part of my life," he replied, voice hard and brittle. "You would have noticed it eventually."

"It's not just that, you know. Did you go to school or something? What happened to your folks? How the hell do you know Spanish that my mother could understand?" I knew, like all good mothers, she was probably a nervous wreck knowing that her grown son was laid up. Or she was waiting for me to call so she could rip me a shiny and well-deserved new asshole. Perhaps a bit of both. I should be calling her instead of having this conversation. Call her, and beg to join her so I wouldn't have to have this conversation. Or any other conversation with anyone. I didn't want to talk to Dr. Spaulding. I didn't want to explain to Rachel why a hospital bill would be making its way to the House in a few weeks with my name on it. I wanted my metal rings to play with and a strong drink. My stomach rebelled against that last idea, but fuck it. I was supposed to be in charge here, not it.

"What about you?" He still wasn't looking at me, still very pale and stiff. "You think a little problem with the booze and the drugs could have been something to mention before we started this? I feel like some kind of enabler. How much was too much? Should I have been looking out for you better tonight?"

Enabler? Yeah, he'd surprised me a few days ago by asking Mike from Kouzina what brand of scotch I usually got when I had those free drinks made and buying me a bottle for home. It sat on the little wine rack in the kitchen, nestled next to the reds he was so fond of. I'd never taken more than a glass or two with dinner, or whenever Dean opened a bottle of his drink of choice. It had been months since I'd overindulged in anything until tonight. If anything, he'd been enabling me to have some fucking restraint.

And yet, I heard the guilt, and I didn't understand. What did he have to feel guilty about? "I'm responsible for this shit, Dean. It's not your fault. Hell, I'm surprised you're even here."

Now he looked at me, hazel eyes wide behind the reflection of the lights off his glasses. "Where else would I be, Jon?"

"It's a work night."

"I've already called out for tomorrow. Today, actually. You were unconscious for a while."

Fuck, I was messing him up already. "I'm sorry. You don't have to look out for me. This was my fuckup. I was due one anyway. Go home, all right? I'm so not worth this."

The angry glower was back, searing into my eyes and rooting me to the bed. I couldn't move or look away. "Shut the fuck up, Jonathan. I get to decide who I care about and how I care about them."

Care. He cared about me, enough to drop two f-bombs in one night. Jesus.

He hadn't called me by my full name… middle name… whatever, in months. He cared about me.

He was taking the day off because of this. Dean cared about me.

Anger and possessiveness warred in his eyes, and whatever was growing warm in my chest before this fuckery, pulsed and grew even warmer. I didn't want to deal with it or see what it was. Please let it be a nerve failing to fire. I'd be happy with another seizure right about now. Do seizures happen in the heart or in the brain? I'm an art school dropout, not a medical student. I don't know this shit.

He raised a hand to keep me from talking, adding, "And don't you say another goddamned word to tell me you're not worth it, or why I shouldn't care, or whatever is going on in that head of yours, 'cause I'm not listening. You don't think I've noticed the way you try to deal with my shit, how you go along with all the crazy things I do to keep from freaking out? You deal with it with a smile, when you could have walked away. I've all but kept you from your friends and your parties, but you keep coming back. I've been avoiding things I know you want me to talk about, but you keep coming back." That hand returned to my calf, grounding me to that spot as effectively as his eyes. "I noticed, Jon."

And it wasn't because the sex was great. I wanted to say it was, make light of this, piss him off enough to leave me before whatever it was inside me got hot enough to melt me completely, but it kept heating up, my heart hammering loud enough that I was sure Dean could hear it. Why did I keep coming back to him? Coming back? I practically lived with him, visiting the House for practices and increasingly futile attempts to get Rachel to speak to me. Why did I give so much of a fuck about his attacks, or at least helping him avoid them? The memory of him on the House bathroom floor, red-faced, unable to breathe, broke me over and over again.

I didn't want to be the cause of that anymore. And tonight, I almost was. For all I knew, he could be lying and actually had a big meltdown in the ambulance that he wasn't telling me about. We needed to talk. I wasn't ready to put the feelings I had into words yet, but we needed to seriously clear the air, make things plain so we could decide what to do about this little whatever we had going on.

"Can I talk now?" I blinked dry eyes, dry because I'd been staring him down this whole time. Or maybe from the massive dehydration, who knew. At his nod, I continued, "You haven't enabled me to do jack. I don't know why I'm doing any of this shit with you. It just felt right, I guess. I expect tonight has completely messed all that up, huh?"

"Hate to ruin your expectations, but you're coming home with me, even if I have to lock you in the trunk to get there."

I closed my eyes, blocking out the annoying light over our heads and the sight of that possessive look. "You still want me?"

I meant "want me around" or "want me in your house" or "want me in your bed," but again, mouth was running before brain could catch up. Before I could revise my stupid fucking question, I heard the seat squeak, then a few steps, then felt Dean's hand on my cheek. I didn't open my eyes, and then there were lips on mine, soft, gentle, thankfully not too deep, because my mouth tasted like something had crawled into it and shat itself to death.

"You better believe I want you. Still. I'll tell you anything you want to know. I don't like talking about the past very much... but for you, I'll tell you anything."

"And I'm not all that fond of talking about why I see Spauldy. But I'll try to."

Lips on my cheek, then a hand running down my blanketed body, squeak of the seat, hand still on my legs. "Let's make a deal... question for a question? The doc isn't back yet. We have time."

"You mean, right now?"

"Why not? It's not like we can do much else while we wait."

"Fine. I'll go first." It would pass the time before she showed up and I flatly refused to get into the brain-scan tube. The weird radiation might mess my head up even more. "You've been on your own for a while. So, why me?"

"It wasn't like you gave me much room to refuse, with your threat to ride me in a bathroom stall. I was taking small steps to socialize, and I got invited to dinner with my coworkers. I wasn't expecting to run into the likes of you my first night out with people, and when you made it damned obvious you were interested, well, I decided to go with it. Thanks for giving me time to stall with an easy question, by the way." He squeezed my calf. "Why are you seeing Dr. Spaulding?"

"She told you half right." I refused to acknowledge that I was in any way anxious about anything, and she was going to get her ear chewed off when we spoke next. "I liked to get fucked up a little more than I should. My Mama's real sick, and she asked me to slow it down to make her feel better. I'm a lot better than before. I used to be much worse. It's not easy, 'cause no one at the House even knows I see Spauldy."

"So they keep carrying on while you try to quit?"

"Yes, and that's two questions. My turn, and I have a request."

"Does that count as a question?"

I opened my eyes to look at him with a smirk. "No. Move your chair closer."

"Gonna ask me a hard one, aren't you?" He knew me too well. He got up, and after dodging a passing stretcher, he placed the chair at the head of my stretcher. This meant I couldn't see his face, but he could put a hand on the one spot on my chest that didn't have a sticky monitor thing on it.

I covered it with mine. "What happened?"

It was open-ended enough. He could tell me anything he wanted, and this way he didn't have to see me react. I knew what I wanted to know, but I didn't want to pressure him. Too much.

Dean laced his fingers in mine. "I better start at the beginning. You wanted to know where I learned to kiss like I do. Well, I'm not as innocent as you think I am."

"Innocent? Whose tongue was in whose ass in the shower hours ago?"

"Complaining?"

"Not in the least. Go on."

A squeeze. "Let me try again. I'm sure you don't remember when we first talked on the phone, but I do." Another squeeze and a long pause. "You said something about paying to see my face. Well, would you be surprised if I told you that one time, for the right price, you could have seen a lot more than my face?"

Yes and no, I wanted to say. I mean, Dean's major-league hot with an athlete's body. He'd had those nude photos, and that was hard enough to reconcile with the man I knew. Speaking of those pictures, "Dean, wait, I gotta tell you…."

Another squeeze and a chuckle. "Hold on. Let me finish. My folks weren't exactly pleased when I told them the truth about why I never had a girlfriend. They cut me off completely. Second semester of my freshman year was already covered, so that gave me a whole three or four months to figure out how the hell was I going to finish school. I was in Spain on a student visa, for crying out loud. No job meant no money, no college, no education, and my folks were pretty upset with me."

"Spain…." I repeated. Of course I couldn't keep my mouth shut for long.

A chuckle and another squeeze. "Did that take care of your 'how did I know Spanish' question? I know enough languages to get me through most of Europe: Spanish, German, French, Italian. I got my bachelor's in linguistics, minored in sociology, but it was rough for a few years. I played rugby, was pretty good, but there aren't any sports scholarships in Europe. But I was damned determined to get my education without my folks' help, because the best revenge is living well and all that. I found a card advertising for nude modeling work in the bathroom at some gay bar I'd been drowning my sorrows in. One thing led to another, and the right person found my photos and offered me a place in his stable of escorts. I accepted and soon I was making decent cash, enough to finish my education. It was high-end, really classy stuff. Did you know there was a market for fresh-faced American boys in Europe? I sure as hell didn't."

That would explain the cowboy motif.

"I bet you made a fucking killing." That wasn't the response I should be having. If I were doing this right, I should have been super jealous. So many men had gotten a piece of the body I now coveted like mad. But that hand in mine grew cold and clammy as he spoke. I raised it to my lips. I had no right to judge him, tried to imagine how scared eighteen/nineteen year old Dean was when the people he'd come to depend on let him down. I couldn't imagine what it was like. When I came out, at the tender age of thirteen, Mama was only grateful I wouldn't be knocking up some chick. Then she promptly seared the fear of AIDS into my soul as only a trained nurse could, because not wearing a condom wasn't an option for her little *maricón*.

"I got through school. It took years. Sometimes I had to go part time because of all the traveling and doing locations. I got a lot of offers to do more than model and escort. You know, porn, live shows, dancing, but I was making enough cash. The job was great. I managed to do shoots and finish school and made decent money. I thought about doing it full time for a while after I graduated."

I gave his hand another kiss, and it warmed as he relaxed, and then promptly tensed up again when I asked, "Until?"

"That your second question?"

I nodded against his hand. "You don't have to answer it. I could ask something lighter, like 'how much did you earn?' or 'did you know keeping your naked pictures on your computer is a bad idea?' or something."

He peered down at me over the head of the stretcher, eyes narrowed. "I knew you saw them. I keep copies there as mementos. I couldn't bring myself to mention it yet, and when you didn't bring it up, I hoped that meant you were fine with it. It feels so long ago, you know, like I'm looking at a different person. Are you even okay with that, with what I did?"

I waggled a finger on my free hand and winced as the motion made the stupid IV needle move enough to pinch. "Answer my question first. These are your rules."

His head disappeared from view with a low sigh. "I graduated and I wanted to celebrate that and leaving the stable, so a bunch of my friends from school and I paid out the nose for tickets on this cruise liner that went around the coasts. We'd hit Ibiza and a bunch of other hot spots and dance the nights away. Diego, that guy that offered to blow me back in first year, came on to me again, wanted to go back to his room. I was all about that. I'd never stopped wanting him, but when I started working with the stable, it didn't feel right to ask him out properly."

He paused, and I imagined the worst before I could feel a hint of jealousy. The other fucker abused him, maybe even raped him. It was a trap, and he was savaged by a bunch of homophobic assholes he thought were his friends. Someone hurt him, and hurt him bad, turned him from the sexpot in the cowboy hat to the sexpot prone to panic attacks, and I wanted to find that someone and Riverdance their balls into mush.

It wasn't until I felt his hand on my cheek, rubbing with his thumb, that I realized I was the one tensing up. It was his trauma, and he was comforting me. There was so much wrong about that.

"We were in an elevator, heading to his room, me and him and a few other people that didn't like that he already had a hand down my pants. Funny, I can actually remember that."

"Were they jealous because you're part horse from the waist down?"

A pause and a soft chuckle. "Thank you, baby." I took his hand again and squeezed it when he continued. "The cruise liner hit something. All I knew then was suddenly we got thrown around like rag dolls. The lights went out. I landed hard enough to crack my shoulder blade and dislocate the joint. Diego, I don't know, the doctors said he had some sort of defect in his heart." His next breath was deep, ragged. "There was something really surreal about a dude your own age having a heart attack on top of you in the dark, while people are screaming around you, when you can't get up."

"Holy shit." My non-IV hand almost clawed up his arm to cup his face and pull it into my view. I didn't know what else to do. Ship crashes didn't have balls I could stomp on and make it any better. "How long were you in there?"

Those eyes had the same haunted look, like another panic attack, but they stayed steady on me. "Five hours, but it felt like more. They didn't think of looking for anyone in the elevators right away. The ship kept lurching to the side. It was gravity that got Diego off me, but then some lady in there with us started having a panic attack… she found me in the dark and held onto my arm, freaking out… and I had my first one. It was like we fed off each other. If it wasn't for the pain, I probably could have been calmer, but I hyperventilated and screamed until I passed out." He closed his eyes, mouth opened as he started to pant, his hand on my chest trembling.

"Dean, look at me," I murmured and cupped both his cheeks with both hands this time, damn the needle pinching, forcing Dean to look at me, thankful for the first time that night we were in a hospital. If he couldn't control his breathing, help was a yell away. "It's okay. You're not there anymore. I've got you."

The words tumbled out in a rush. "I was catatonic when they found us, stayed that way for about a week. Then they had to sedate me because I couldn't stop screaming. The doctors wanted me to see a shrink due to PTSD. It was such a crock. PTSD is what soldiers get seeing their buddies blown to bits. I was just some dumb whore that was trapped in the dark for too long. I shouldn't have been so messed up from it, right?"

I gripped his face harder. "They were fucking right, Dean. That kind of thing would mess up anyone."

"After that, recovering from the trauma was like chipping at a rock. Once I could handle the dark, being touched still made me freak. Then it was just crowds. The other boys were fine. They got out safely. I stayed in a facility for six months, had my diploma mailed to me there, then I found out about my folks. Plane crash in Thailand. I'd had no idea where they were stationed, but the estate lawyers found me."

"Stationed?" He relaxed some more, and I let his face go, holding his hand in both of mine. "And I thought they cut you off."

"Mom was a diplomat's assistant, and Dad traveled with her. We all did when I was younger. Either they hoped I'd change my ways, or they forgot to take me off the will. I didn't want their money, but I took it because I needed it to pay for a place to stay. I moved back to the States. Dr. Spaulding is well known in the field for treating trauma-related disorders, and I wanted to be near someone who could fix me. The lawyers helped me find land and everything I needed to have the house built while I holed up in a hotel room until it was finished. The rest of the cash is still in investments, because you know, I won't be young forever, and I hope to be well enough to really live, maybe get a master's degree, maybe travel around the world again."

Wow, he'd had years with Spauldy. No wonder he had her number at the ready. He'd been working on this a long time, creating this life where he could be comfortable, living in a house far away from other people. And then I showed up and shoved myself into his life.

"I'm so sorry, Dean," I murmured, looking up, wanting him to meet my eyes again. "That's a lot of shit to have to deal with." Then I remembered getting on his case about the elevator, and I cringed even harder. "I'm such an asshole."

"You don't have to apologize. I didn't tell you. And it's my turn. Are you okay with me telling you this?"

"I have another request before I answer that. Come closer, will ya?"

I wanted to hug him, actually, but the monitor and the IV and the fact that we were in a damned hallway kinda made that impossible. Despite that, Dean moved the chair next to me, rested his head on the pillow so I couldn't miss his eyes, and kept his hand on my chest. No one I knew was around. I could happily, openly express this strange attachment I had to him, and accept his in turn.

"The only difference between those pictures and your not-so-innocent past and all the crap I've gotten up to is that you were smart enough to get paid for it. Hell, compared to me some months ago, you're a saint."

"A few months ago? What happened then?"

"I hooked up with Patch and got the call from Mama. But that's not the point I'm trying to make. Why would I think differently of you because of that? I get the benefits of so much practice." I grinned and wanted to ask for another finely crafted SuperKiss, but again, funky mouth.

Apparently that didn't matter to him, because he lifted his head and kissed me firmly. It felt like my heart was going to explode from the barely hidden hope and gratitude in that kiss.

"You are coming home with me, right?" he asked against my lips.

"That's two questions in a row," I teased, giving his lips a lick. "And yes, I am. They're not going to release me by myself anyway."

Before I could ask my question, the doc came back and insisted on my brain scan. My argument to decline died on my lips as Dean asked if he could come with me for moral support and added if I dared mention the cost, he was going to put me over his knee. I told him to get a better threat, but went along without any more argument.

After that terrifying exam (do they really have to make the damn tube so small? I swore I felt the upper walls brush against my dick—and not in the fun way—and the techs weren't nearly as amused as Dean was when I asked to be lubed up before they inserted me), Dean asked for a semi-private room while we waited to see if I'd permanently fucked my brain over.

"So"—Dean leaned back in his chair next to my honest-to-goodness bed—"what's the deal with you and Rachel?"

I was tired, gagging for a nap and a shower and another nap, but I owed him an explanation. "Other than we've been friends since art school and founded the Tribe together?"

"Yeah, other than that."

I leaned back in the pillows and wriggled to get something like comfortable. Sure, the mattress I lay on was more comfy than a stretcher, but not by much. "We met in freshman Art Comp 101, second day of class. She was a shy, mousy, chubby little thing,"

"Shy? Her?"

I chuckled. "Work with me here. I was in metalworking and jewelry design and so out of the closet rainbows flew out of my mouth whenever I spoke. She was a painting major who'd apparently never seen a guy in eyeliner before."

"How is that even possible?" Dean interrupted.

"Really sheltered upbringing? Her family's real conservative, really cold, and they were all worried about her going off to heathen art college, like she'd take one sip of beer and immediately end up pregnant with a coke addiction or something. Anyway, she couldn't stop staring at me. Didn't stop staring when I made out with some guy after that class in the hallway. Finally I asked her what the fuck her problem was, and that started a very interesting conversation."

That made him laugh. "I'm still having a hard time imagining her as shy."

"When I got my hands on her, it was like night and day. I helped her with a lot of firsts. First drink, first toke off a joint, I helped her dye her hair the first time, showed her how to put a condom on a guy. I mean, she went hog wild, and I was there to make sure she didn't lose her damned mind."

"Kind of like you and Patch?" He arched an eyebrow at me. "Minus the sex."

"Not exactly. She didn't really believe I was into guys until she walked in on me fucking a few times. We watched each other's backs. We were inseparable at first. No worries about suddenly having feelings about someone who knew me that well, you see. And besides we totally rocked the whole 'too young to commit' vibe. Hell, what did I need a boyfriend for when I had this awesome *chica* who knew me better than I knew myself? She showed me off to her folks to scandalize them, we donned drag and went out dancing together, just doing some crazy shit together. She'd make a really impressive bear if she could grow more body hair."

Now the other eyebrow was up. "Drag… both of you?"

"I have pictures, actual ones on paper. I'll show you when we get home. It was easier when I was all younger and skinnier."

"So, what changed? You guys don't seem all that close right now."

That gave me pause. "I don't know. It wasn't even sudden. I think it was around when we brought Patch along. I was recovering from my last attempt at something more than friends with another guy." I shuddered, not wanting to think about that massive fail.

"I thought you were too young to commit…."

I swallowed heavily, and it was Dean's turn to hold my hand while I spoke. "I thought Rafe was the exception. He thought he could smack the faggot around once he realized his friends might notice he liked dick. We were both very wrong." I shook my head to get the images out of my head. "He made a shitty mistake in letting Rach see him put his hands on me. By the time we were done with him, well, we had to load up and get out of town right away."

Dean squeezed my hand. "Left him bleeding, huh?"

"Yeah. I'm sure he survived. She had to pull me off him at the end, and then deal with me mourning. I was a mess for weeks. I was angry, I was hurt, I thought I'd screwed up big time. But you know, she was there the whole way, like things were supposed to be, right? We cared for each other the only way we knew how. I'd get her weird kinds of booze to cheer her up; she'd get me high as a kite and introduce me to new dick. So, Patch comes around, barely legal and down with anything we could think off. That made me scared for him at first. I saw way too much of me in him. I think Rachel even saw that. He needed guidance, the same way Rach had needed it, and it gave me something to do. Fuck, Patch is a foster brat, no guidance, no family looking out for him. I didn't really argue when she all but ordered him into Thor and we took him away, all on the promise of easy drugs and parties and lots and lots of chances to play with fire and access to my ass."

"That's guidance?"

I shrugged. "Hey, better he party with people who at least try to look after each other than ending up OD'ing with a group of strangers who'll just leave him to die or something. I tried to keep an eye on him all the same, but it became obvious that I couldn't do it stoned off my ass."

He moved his head to the pillow. "So you wanted to change, to take care of another friend. And to make your mother happy. And you changed to take care of me. Jon, when was the last time you've been taken care of?"

"Look, baby." I smiled to dial back the venom, barely. "You're not Spauldy. Don't ask me the 'shrink' questions. I've been mostly self-sufficient since I could make a PB&J and wipe my own ass. Mama made sure that I could take care of myself, because there wasn't a lot of time for babying with how much we traveled. I understood the deal. She had to work a lot of hours, and sometimes we couldn't get a babysitter. She had to trust me to watch myself."

"So, that long, huh?" He kissed me again. "I won't let you down."

"What?" I blinked at him, sure it was exhaustion messing up my hearing.

"I'm going to take care of you. Get some rest." He kissed my cheek and pulled back, tucking the blanket over my body.

"You don't need to."

"I want to."

"You wouldn't be in this fucking hospital reliving your worst memories if it wasn't for my fuckup." My eyes were quickly losing the battle to stay open.

Another kiss on my forehead. "I wouldn't be outside my house except for work, period, if it wasn't for you. Thank you."

My body answered for me, shutting down under the weight of those kisses. We'd argue about the specifics later, I promised myself before dozing again.

HAPTER ELEVEN

# *Broke the Knob*

I'D LIKE to say that the scan found nothing and Dean and I went home that night and had hot sexy sex, reconnecting and forgiving and making everything hunky fucking dory.

I would like to say that, but the doctor informed me that something didn't look right in the scans, that I would have to see a neurologist for more tests, and that Dean was to keep an eye on me in case I seized again in the next twenty-four hours. Which meant no sex that morning. We didn't get home until well after dawn broke, and I was too damned tired to do anything but sleep. He stayed with me as I got over the massive hangover, and even took that Friday off to be extra sure. He took this whole "take care of you" thing to extremes, and I told him so. He told me that I was welcome and to have another glass of water. I neglected to tell Dean that I had no desire to call any doc for more tests on my head, because I didn't want to see him whip out his credit card again to pay for it like he did my middle-of-the-night visit. That made me feel just as guilty as getting fucked up had in the first place. So as long as he didn't mention it, I wasn't going back to the damned hospital.

I didn't get to make those phone calls I needed to make until Friday afternoon, due to Dean's babying. First one was to Mama, who spent about thirty seconds being all *pobrecito* before launching into a lecture of epic proportions. Spanish auctioneers didn't speak the lingo that fast to say so freakin' much. If she wasn't stuck in Peru, she told me, she would have taken a red-eye to deliver a boot to my ass. Dean was a nice boy I should keep if he was willing to put up with my irresponsible ass too, even if his from-Spain Spanish sounded weird to her Mexican ears. I took my medicine like a good boy, wincing all the way, and let her be all worried Mama until she ran out of steam.

"You are entirely too grown for me to be this worried about you," she finished tiredly.

I rolled my eyes and sighed, though I couldn't fight the guilt. She had her own shit to deal with, and I was a complete bastard for adding me to her troubles. "I know, Mama, I'm so sorry. I fucked up bad. I've been trying so damned hard, and I fucked up bad."

"You can stop beating yourself up, boy. Nobody's perfect. I just worry about things, like you getting sick or hurt without anyone there to give a damn. You're not getting any younger. The body wears out. I like this Dean. He gives a damn. Not like those lowlifes you travel with."

"Hey, they're not lowlifes!" I knew I shouldn't sound so defensive, but Crimson Dream Tribal was my troupe. We were decent enough people.

"Esteban, you tell me about your travels, and the story sounds the same. You arrive in a place, you stay for a while, you leave with so much bad blood. How long do you think you will last with so many burned bridges?"

She was right, as always. Even when I tried to hide the situations around our travels, she got them out of me no matter what. We would win gold if group bridge burning ever became an Olympic sport. I couldn't let it go, though. "We did it, you and me. We traveled, never stayed in one place, and we did fine. Hell, you still travel alone now, until your liver started acting up."

"Alone? *Mijo*, I've got people all along the way other than you that I can call if I get in trouble. People and connections I have made everywhere we've been and everywhere I go. This life doesn't work without connections. Haven't I told you that already?"

It was an argument we'd had over and over again. She didn't get that it wasn't how the troupe worked, that as long as we had each other's backs, we'd be fine. Before we went around with that argument one more time, I told her I loved her and hung up.

Dr. Spaulding spared me a lecture, thank fuck, when I called her. I got more questions about what drove me to think drugging up was a good idea, and I still didn't know why, even now that I was as sober as a judge. We would talk next week, and she was glad that Dean knew I was getting her help.

Rachel was last on the list. I wasn't going to dare tell her about my hospital adventure, not wanting two "you damn idiot" conversations in the same day.

Luckily, she was too distracted to pry. "We've got SummerFest in two weeks. We still running the table? It's too late to get that deposit back."

Oh fuck, I'd nearly forgotten about it, and it was me that scrounged up the cash to rent a table to sell my shit months ago when we heard about it. SummerFest would be at Atterro Park, since it was large enough to handle booths and concerts and dancing and a drum circle. The plan was to sell craft stuff and make a presence with the dancing. The theater hadn't contacted us about a date for another show, so we'd be talking up our Kouzina appearances.

"And is he coming along?" She sighed, sounding bored and rushed.

I didn't have to ask whom she meant. "I'll have to ask him."

"You know, there will be a lot of hot guys out there. Make him stay home and find yourself a new one."

I wanted to tell her that I had a brand-new fetish for hot guys who will still kiss me after they've seen me puke and who would do bedside duty when I really screwed the pooch, but talking about that would be as pointless as ever. I didn't even know how long I was going to be able to keep him with me in the first place.

"Not happening, Rach. How's the house? What's Patch up to? You seen him?"

"Hell if I know where the useless fuck is. The mattress was too good for him, so I haven't seen him since. We're not taking him with us when we go, you know. He's too much trouble."

"Seriously?" I frowned at the phone. I didn't want to think about moving. Not now, not while things were getting nice with Dean. And we didn't throw people out without talking to each other first.

"Well, yeah, he's all but abandoned us. I don't even want to talk to him if he's dumb enough to show up to this thing. You shouldn't talk to him either. We'll show him how he's messed up."

"What did he do that I'm not doing?" Neither one of us slept over at the House every night anymore, if I had my guess right, so what was the big deal?

"You're the exception, Jonathan. I still like you. For now. Things will be much better once we're on the road again."

I heard her throat hitch over the phone, like she was about to cry or something, and my outrage turned into worry. "Rach, you all right?"

She suddenly sounded rushed. "I'm fine, gotta run. Stop by the House before SummerFest, will you? You need to show up for more than just Kouzina dances."

And just like that, she was gone, leaving me worried about how things were affecting her. Granted, after I showed her the ways of the world, she took charge and I simply followed, but I never stopped worrying for her. I couldn't stop her from drinking or smoking herself stupid, and in the past would opt to join her in the mayhem. In the cold light of sobriety, it was clear that something new was up. What was even more worrying, she didn't want to tell me about it. The chasm between us yawned even wider, just like the one between me and Patch and Lala, and, before my fuckup, between me and Dean. I worried that it would it take another massive fuckup to find out what was rotten in the state of Crimson Dream.

I really hoped things would improve when we moved on too. If we moved on. I mean, Dean was awesome. If Rachel could just relax a little bit and find someone awesome too, she wouldn't have a reason to leave so soon. And maybe while I was on the subject of useless wishes, if I hoped hard enough, Dean would split into two Deans for sexy threesome fun. And I'd get a million dollars. And never go gray, unless it was that sexy silver fox sort of gray.

To the surprise of absolutely no one, Dean declined SummerFest outright, though he offered to drop me off and pick me up. I respected his choice and planned to miss him terribly. I needed the time to reconnect with my friends anyway, and I hoped that minding my table would mean I would be too busy to even be tempted to get fucked up again.

So that's how I ended up at my table with my very grumpy best pal two weeks later. Even with the stink of pot on her clothes, she looked utterly unhappy to be there. On a high note, I got some sales, a few bracelets, a necklace. When Dean finally brought up scheduling a follow-up appointment, I used "updating my inventory" as a successful excuse. Those two weeks were spent creating some really unique pieces. I'd even had very simple cards made up with my name and number, which came in handy when I got an offer for another honest-to-goodness chain mail bikini top. I think they're really, really cheesy, but I could get decent cash for the work, especially for this woman with an impressively large rack. I could charge her by the square inch and make a killing. I told her to give me a call after the festival and we could talk rates.

Rach rolled her eyes and took swigs from her flask as I schmoozed and sold and adjusted lengths of chain to fit their new owners. From the sharp scent each time she opened it, I guessed it was more brandy. The frown on her face deepened each time she offered me a sip and I declined for a swig of my bottle of unadulterated Sprite. We should have had water or even some munchies packed up under the table with us, but *someone* had spent this week's mad money from Kouzina.

"And you're not going to tell me what you got with it, are you?" I muttered after waving good-bye to another pair of browsers. I quickly eyed the selections that were left to make sure no one had made off with something.

"It's none of your business, Jonathan." She took another drink. "How much of this is going to the House, by the way?"

"Same as usual, Rachel, I keep 20 percent." My stomach rumbled. Damn thing was too used to regular meals. "Minus whatever we get for food while we're out."

"Could you take 10 percent this time? We're a little short on bills."

It was time for my eyebrow to arch. "Something up at the House?"

"Well, since that useless little fuck isn't in the picture anymore, that's less cash for the coffers. That's where the mad money went, by the way, making up for his share. Since it's your fault, you should pony up."

"How the hell is that my fault?" I didn't want to sound as snippy as I did, but fuck, being hungry and in poor company made me less accommodating.

"You fucked around, he left. We don't need him. Jugglers are a dime a dozen, and he wasn't that good with fire anyway. We could have you do more fire prop sets to make up for it."

Patch had potential, creativity, and the wiliness to risk immolation to give the people a good show. Any claim that he lacked skill was complete bullshit. That kid could do anything once you got him focused enough. I knew I had a bias here, but he was a crowd pleaser. "And does he know 'we' don't need him, since 'we' aren't talking to him?"

"Well, I'm not talking to him. I think it's best if you tell him. I can't stand to look at his fucking face." She was seething, and I felt that curl of annoyance that seemed to like making an appearance whenever we spoke lately.

"Then it should be easy to tell him off. Why is this my job?"

"Because it is. Also, tell him to keep his goddamned mouth shut. We don't need his rumors fucking us up."

Okay, that got my attention even more than the thought of us not "needing" Patch anymore. "What rumors? I haven't heard any rumors."

"Of course *you* haven't." The "you" was dripping with contempt as she peered down the row of booths. "He got drunk and imagined some shit, told somebody, and you know how these losers talk. I hate this town."

"Which means we'll be leaving soon." That was how these moves usually started. First it was someone hating this town, then it grew and grew until we all were grumpy, or some shit happened and then we fucked off elsewhere. The curl tightened inside me, and I wanted to tell her I didn't hate this place at all. I wasn't ready to leave yet. Maybe Mama was right about the cycle we'd set.

"You're surprised? This is what we do, Jonathan. Wrap things up with your little friend. Get it over with now so we can make a clean break."

"That's gonna be hard, Rach." We were friends, I told myself. I could be honest with her. That's what friends are for, right? "I kinda like Dean. A lot."

She peered at me again, but two chicks stopped by to gaze at my merch, so I had to give them my full charming attention. Once they'd walked away with two coins belts, and I tucked the fifty bucks for both of them into our money baggie, I noticed that she was still staring at me.

"What?"

Her voice was high and tight. "You kinda like him? Are you serious?"

I nodded. "Yeah, we get along great, and he's good to me, better than I deserve, really. So yeah, I like him."

I wasn't being entirely honest, mostly because I couldn't quite face the full brunt of how I felt about Dean myself. It was too huge, and I wasn't ready to see it all, no matter how good and warm and happy I felt whenever I thought about him. It was as if that trip to the hospital gave me a revelation. Life was too short and blah blah blah. All I knew was that I wasn't ready to walk away from this, from him, just yet. Maybe not ever.

To my surprise, Rachel laughed, the sound sharp and bitter to my ears. "Not this shit again. You're unbelievable, Jonathan. You can't possibly think he feels the same way. He must have a dick the size of Texas for you to be this blind."

"Gee, bitch, thanks for the vote of confidence."

"I'm serious. Look at you, Jonathan. You're hot, you can dance, and you can make and push these things"—she motioned to the jewelry on the table—"like no one's business. Do you honestly think a guy like that wants anything more from a guy like you than your ass? Really? Come on, you're usually smarter than this."

She reached for my hand, and I moved it away before she could grab it. She hadn't said anything to me that I hadn't thought myself in my darker moments of self-flagellation. I didn't know if Dean was the sort of guy to think that way of anyone, but hey, he had a colorful past that I probably wouldn't have known about until that night at the club. I mean, he'd been wonderful to me after that, but Rachel's words just fed into my own worry. Could he have been keeping the details of himself away from me because I was really not a long-term prospect? Never mind me. Did he even do long-term prospects?

Rachel leaned forward so I couldn't get away and wrapped an arm, jingling with coins and bells from her bracelets, around my shoulders. "You're getting it. I can see the little gears going round in your head. I'm gonna go dance for a bit and have someone bring Patch over. Later, you can end things with the Boy Scout, and we can go home and get wasted. I'm sure we can find you someone way more suited for your awesomeness." She hugged me tighter and murmured. "I've missed you so much, Jonathan."

To be honest, I did miss the crazy party scene sometimes. It was my life for ten years after the nomadic existence that was growing up with Mama, and until now it had fit me. I shouldn't tempt fate and go out drinking, however. Not after what happened at the club. My tolerance was shot, and with endless access to all sorts of intoxicants, I could successfully kill myself completely by accident.

Mama would hold a séance specifically to kick my ghosty ass if that ever happened. I was pretty sure Dean would miss me. How he managed to skirt his way past everyone else on the list of People I Give a Fuck About to land right behind the woman who gave me life was scary as shit. I was attached to him. I'd grown a connection when I didn't mean to. And Rach had reminded me why that was a bad idea. I wasn't his type. He'd be bored with me eventually. Who knew, I might get bored with him if my new dance with clean living got too hard to keep up.

She gave me a big hug, tugged on my ponytail, and made her way out from behind the booth and was gone. Dammit. I should have asked her to bring me back something to eat. It would have cut into housing funds a little bit, but man cannot live on air, Sprite, and repeated refusals of brandy forever. God, she was persistent. I was so into my own thoughts that I'd forgotten what she'd said she was going to do until I saw Patch walking my way.

One look at the kid completely derailed all thoughts of eating. Patch didn't look right. For starters, he wore a shirt, an all-black raglan. In the late summer sun. Even his unibang drooped. He looked unhappy. No, not unhappy. Scared. The closer he got, the more I could see it in his eyes. The sun had turned his bared decorated arms brown as nuts, but even that looked off, a sickly pale sort of tan. Before he came around to sit, he looked up and down the row.

"Patch?" I murmured as a few more browsers walked by. "Did someone mess with you today?"

I'm sure "kicking some fucker's ass what deserved it" was not on the list of vices I was supposed to be avoiding.

"Nah, man." He didn't look at me, but pulled a small bag of sour cream and chive potato chips out of one of the pockets of his cargo shorts and passed it to me. "You never eat during these damn things."

Usually because we couldn't afford to bring snacks, and I was usually the only person to sit at the table all day. I happily tore into the packet, still watching him, until my stomach stopped bitching. "Thanks, kid. Where are you staying now?"

He blinked in confusion, then gave a short bark of laughter, knocking him out of his fear for a second, to my relief. "With Lala and Mark. They're good people, you know. Been real nice to me, even with shit happening."

Oh yeah, the shit no one's bothered to tell me about until today. I leaned back in my chair, waited for a few more browsers to pass, and then said, "Be straight with me, Patch…."

"We've swallowed each other's loads, *papi*. There's nothing straight between us."

I rolled my eyes. "Point taken. You're my bud, right? Formerly with benefits? So, what's going on with the Tribe? Why am I throwing you out?"

He snorted and took a few chips out of the bag. "Throwing me out? Is this the part where I say 'you can't fire me, I quit'? 'Cause that ship sailed a while ago."

"Seriously?"

"Yeah, I moved out weeks ago. It was too weird without you there all the time."

"Weird? The fuck you mean, weird? And why didn't you call me?" God knows Dean had a spare bedroom that could totally hold one more squatter. The couch alone could seat a team of squatters.

His back curved forward even more, muscles flexing the stitching, and his bang fell over his face, hiding him from me completely. "I didn't want to bring the shit to you, man. I mean, you're doing all right with Dean. It wasn't a big deal. Something went down at the House, I didn't like it, so I got out."

I placed a hand on his back, the fabric warm from absorbing all the sun. "What went down, Patch?"

"Look, I'm sorry, okay? One night at Lala and Mark's, I was tossing and turning in my sleep, and Lala told me that I was screaming and freaking out before I woke up, and she had a guess about what was going on from what I was yelling. That's how people started finding out. I guess in this town, they don't keep secrets like that hidden at all."

I was starting to get frustrated because none of that told me the "what" of it all, but I let him continue and rubbed his back. "Better to get it out in the open, right?" I racked my brain for an example, and one popped up immediately. "Like if some dude's taking advantage of some other girls in a group, the group needs to know so they can deal with that dude, right?"

That made him go stiff, and he jerked out of my grasp. And then I got really worried. I was just rattling off a situation that was fairly common in our circles. We, the Tribe, were more vigilant with our parties and with who we considered "ours." I've thrown clueless straight dudes out for being drunk and clueless with a chick. The last thing any group needed was the rep of harboring clueless fucks or, worse, deliberate fucks that knew exactly what they were doing when it came to the dancing on the line between consent and rape.

"Patch...." I let it drag, and the kid shuddered hard. My mouth opened to say more, but more customers walked up in front of us, so I let him stew a bit while I exchanged a wirework pendant for fifteen bucks. Once they walked away with my best cheerful smile and a card, I sat back down and faced Patch, who hadn't moved from his slump. "Patch, what happened?"

"What if knowing ain't enough? What if... shit, Jonathan, this ain't easy. Nobody at the House believes me. They say I'm lyin'. Or useless."

He didn't flinch when I put my hand on his back again and rubbed. "You know me better than that, kid."

"Yeah, so why you playing Rach... 'her' hatchet man?"

"I can't toss you if you're already gone, and I won't toss anyone before I know why. There's rumors, they come back to you, and I wanna know what they are, especially if they've got you all torn up like this. Did you see someone take advantage of someone else?"

It was the softer of the two questions I wanted to ask. Patch went stiff again, and he turned his head, blond bangs moving out of the way to show me his face. Torn up didn't even describe it. He looked pissed off and scared at the same time, face red but lips pressed together in a tight line. His eyes were bloodshot and shiny, on the brink of tears.

The hurt on his face hit me hard, and I was done dancing around the subject. "Did someone take advantage of you?"

"I don't know."

Well, out of the two responses I was expecting, "yes" or "hell no and fuck you," "I don't know" wasn't even on the radar. "What the hell you mean, you don't know?" I wanted to sound less pissy, I really did, but I didn't understand what he meant.

His straw-colored curtain covered him again as he looked back down at his lap. Fingers traced over the stitch pattern around the opposite wrist. "I was drunk and hopped up. Totally wasted. I barely remember anything."

I grabbed the seat of his chair and yanked it and him closer to me, looked around for any browsers, and bent to meet his ear. Panic slammed my heart against my chest, fear and worry and rage brewing in a bitter mix in the back of my throat as I asked, "Patch, what happened? What do you remember happening?"

"It was that night you brought Dean over." His voice hitched, and he paused, taking breaths until he could speak again. "Remember? We did that thing to make folks... her... think I'd tried to fool around with you, like she told me to?"

I nodded, then realized he couldn't see that with his eyes down. "Yeah. That night was really messed up. It worked, right? Because she was pissed as hell with me when I got back."

"You got no clue, man. I heard you yelling when I went across the hall to take a leak, right? It was all quiet upstairs. Damn shame too, 'cause I just wanted things to go back to party time, right? I went back in the room and lay out on the mattress, to wait it out. I drank from the spray bottle while I was there, to keep my buzz."

"The one full of Everclear? You drank that?" And my throat clamped up in sympathy. That shit was harsh, never mind the crazy alcohol content. It could kill, for fuck's sake.

He nodded, the bang bouncing along like a horse's mane. "Wasn't like a whole bottle. We'd been passing the fire a bunch. But it was enough, more than enough. I passed out, fell asleep, something. Was gone for a while, I guess, 'cause the next thing I feel is somebody…."

Suddenly, all my rage and worry and shit vanished in a wave of "I don't want to know." I soldiered on, though, because the kid needed this out more than I needed to wallow in my own sudden case of chickenshit. "They got in you, kid?"

"No!" He recoiled, sitting up and scowling at me with red-rimmed sapphire lasers for eyes. "Hell no! I don't even know how that shit even happened. How could my dick even be hard? I was passed the fuck out."

"Patch, you're a nineteen-year-old kid with a pulse. Of course you get hard in your sleep." God knows I'd felt it, sharing that tiny mattress with him for as long as I did.

He huffed, looking away. "Still no excuse for anyone to… do that. They got on me, and I couldn't move. Tried to talk, but I dunno what came out of my mouth. They rode me, and I passed out when I came. If I didn't wake up the next morning with my pants still open, and smelling like… ugh…. I'd be damned sure it never happened."

I let what he said sink in for a few long seconds. "Damn, Patch. You didn't tell anybody that morning?"

"Who's gonna believe me? 'Yeah right, someone got a free ride on the Patch-pole and you're sooo traumatized, poor fucking baby.' You wanna know the really messed up thing about it?"

"What?"

"What I could remember of it, one thing just stuck in my mind. It wasn't ass. It couldn't have been ass. I know what ass feels like, and this—I mean, even your ragged one's got some tightness, and there wasn't…."

I couldn't help but recoil, letting the pieces fall into place. "You think it was a chick? All the available dick at that party and someone fell on yours?"

"You think this shit's funny?" With one sentence, his panic turned into ice and quiet outrage, daring me to agree because he was close to exploding.

"No, man, it's not funny at all."

"You're damned right it's not funny!" He stood up, fists balled, and I expected him to throw a punch. He had gotten loud too, people quickly walking past the booth, rubbernecking assholes. "Can't sleep no more, not without some damned nightmare or someone moving around waking me up. It feels like I'm going crazy, and Tribe wants me out? Fine! Fuck them, and fuck you too!"

He was already around the table before I lunged over it to grab one slim bicep to keep him from tearing off. "Whoa, kid, hold on. I'm sorry, I really am. I didn't know."

Patch yanked his arm out of my grasp, his entire body shaking as he noticed the rubberneckers, and his entire face, neck, and forearms flushed deep enough to show through the tan. "Shit, *papi*, I-I gotta go."

"Call me!" I yelled out as he took off in a blind run. I could have followed him, I should have followed him, but with my entire inventory and about three hundred bucks in profit at the booth, I couldn't leave it all. I wished he'd hauled off and punched me instead of looking with those scared and pissed-off eyes. I could deal with angry ex-Tribe members lashing out and everything, but this wasn't some lazy bitch unwilling to show up to practice or some fucker trying to make meth in the bathroom, this was Patch. My friend, my little buddy, my protégé, and it felt like I'd let him down when he needed me the most.

Word must have spread about our little altercation, because I got only a few more sales before it dwindled to nothing. It looked as if my take-home was going to be even smaller than I hoped, which wouldn't even cover basic supplies to replace my stock. To make matters worse, no one from the Tribe came to the booth to relieve me of minding-the-shop duty so I could go eat, pee, or dance for an hour or two. My text to Rach to get someone over here got ignored. So I sat, hungry, antsy, and miserable, until I did the only thing I knew to do.

*How's business, handsome?* My heart leapt at Dean's answering text.

*A gigantic ball of shit and drama. I can't wait to close this booth and go home.* I couldn't tell him anything more, not over text.

*That doesn't sound good. Need to leave sooner? I can be there in half an hour.*

I leaned back in the chair and smiled a little to myself at the text and loved him just a little bit more. My Prince Charming, ready to whisk me away to his castle by the lake, ply me with bad movies and too much popcorn and a warm body to lie against, then later fuck me until I spoke Swahili and forgot this day even happened. It sounded damned good, but I'd run away from my responsibilities, what few I had, long enough. I had things to do. I needed to make sure Patch was all right. Okay, who'd be really all right after shit like that, but I hoped he ran to a safe space. I had to see if I could scare up a few more sales. I had to rip my best friend a new one for wanting him gone after what he'd been through.

*I'm good, baby. Keep the couch warm for me until this is over?*

*Always.*

Things seem to improve in about an hour, customer-wise anyway, and I scored a few more sales before my phone rang. The display was Patch's number, so I quickly snatched it up. "Hey, kid, look, I'm really sor—"

"So you haven't seen him either?" I barely recognized the voice as Lala's husband. Mark's deep Middle American voice was tinged with worry, and my empty stomach started churning. Fuck.

"He left his phone with you?"

"Yeah, I'm at the first aid booth. I told him to have a lay down on one of the cots, but he blew up again and left about an hour ago, said he was having a smoke."

"So either he's having the entire pack, or something's up." God, kid, don't be off doing something stupid. I never understood the concept of being tethered to your cell phone (at least not the crappy flip thing that was formerly mine), but he wasn't in any state of mind to be completely without contact. Profit easily lost the battle this time. "It'll take me a few minutes to close this up, and I'll look for him."

"Thanks. I told Lala, and she's looking for him too. My shift here is almost over, but we're worried. He's been getting pissed like this a lot lately, and I don't want him blowing up at the wrong person and getting hurt. The only reason I'm calling is because he swore you didn't do anything to him."

As I placed my remaining stock back into the toolbox, going a little faster and a lot more sloppily than my usual tendency to be all OCD with it, my phone rang again. I remembered the little trick to flip it on its face to activate the speakerphone, but forgot to see who was calling. "Yeah?"

"Hey, baby, which booth are you again?" The tinny speakers didn't do Dean's rich tones any justice.

"Third row, tenth booth, wait, you're here?"

"Yeah, wanted to surprise you with dinner that wasn't fried veggie matter."

Shut up, stomach. "You sure you want to brave the crowd to find me?" It was pure asshole of me, but I couldn't deal with both my traumatized sleep-deprived friend with anger issues being God knows where *and* my traumatized prone to panic attacks boyfriend wandering around crowds. Damn, if I ever needed a drink, now would be the time. I could already feel cold sweat breaking out at the back of my neck.

"Actually," I interrupted his response. "I need a favor, Dean. I'll meet you at the food booths, but could you keep an eye out for Patch? You remember what he looks like, blond, skinny, stitch tats? He's gone missing."

"Gone missing?"

"Yeah." I shoved the now-full toolbox into my bag, folded the baggie full of cash and cards into my pocket, and did a quick look over to see if I'd forgotten anything. "He didn't take his phone, and there's some shit going on, and I'll explain later, but now we've got to find him."

"You got it, Jon. I'll meet you there."

Thank fuck, no more questions. Good man, that Dean. "I'll see you soon." He wouldn't be hard to find, unless he wandered into some line that only serviced tall hot redheads who wore glasses.

I scoured the lines of booths on my way to the circle of food carts. It was late afternoon, so the crowd was mostly at the stage to listen to the special guest rock band. I hoped Patch hadn't suddenly developed a liking for Bad Attitude covers, because we'd never be able to find him in the audience if it came to that.

He was nowhere to be found in the booths, and I ran to the center of the carts. Dean was scanning each line when he saw me, joy and concern blatant in his gaze. He bent down to kiss me briefly. "Looked all over, no sign of him."

"Fuck," I grumbled. "I can't remember where the drum circle was set up."

"Probably as far from the stage as possible." Dean pulled out a folded festival brochure from his pocket. As we looked over the map, my phone rang again. I didn't recognize the number on display, but I answered anyway.

"Jonathan, you really should get over to the circle. Things are getting rather unpleasant," Lala drawled tightly, each vowel pleasing my ears but making me feel even more queasy at the thought of what exactly was getting unpleasant.

"Have you seen Patch?" Dean held up the map and pointed to the little symbol that showed where the drum circle was. I motioned for him to lead on. He nodded, grabbed my hand, and we were off.

"Seen him? I'm hearin' him now. We're trying to hold him back, but he's on a real tear, love. Tried getting Mark over here, but he's got his nursely duties and all."

Shit. "I'll be right there."

If the number of people we passed bothered Dean, he didn't show it. His back was steady, and I could imagine anyone getting in our way would be tackled down like we were on a rugby field or pitch or whatever it was called. We ran from one end of the park to the other, the guitars of the stage fading to the sound of heavy hardcore percussion, and my belly and legs and everything cramped with the desire to stop the world and let me dance it out. If I couldn't drink or drug or drag Dean to the nearest tree to fuck the stress out, why couldn't I just dance for a while?

The drum circle got louder and louder the closer we got. My beeline there got redirected by Dean suddenly shifting direction to a cluster of people standing and sitting near the tree that I recognized as the one we chilled near when the Tribe took our one-day break. It looked like we'd claimed it again, from all the familiar faces. Familiar, uncomfortable, and angry faces.

I ran around Dean to get a better look at what was ahead. Patch stood stock still, shaking with rage and staring angrily at a very bored-looking Rachel. Lala stood next to him. Tam and Cindy were next to Rachel, all in some very strange Mexican standoff.

And here I was, about to add more "Mexican" to the mix. *Ay, Dios mío.*

We heard Lala first. "For fuck's sake, Rachel, it wasn't his fault you guys are harboring a rapist. Why are you being such a bitch about it?"

"Rapist? Get real. No one else mentioned anyone trying anything with anyone else, and all we've got's the word of one drunk little liar."

"Could we not call it that? I never fucking called it that." Patch sounded ragged, and the closer we got, the more I could see that he was close to tears. I wanted to go to him, but by then, everyone had noticed mine and Dean's presence with some confusion and, from Rachel, outright disgust.

"What's he doing here?" She held up a hand to keep either one of us from responding. "Never the fuck mind. Jonathan, I need you to tell this useless little fuck to stop lying. He even said you believe him. Can you believe this shit?"

Technically, she was right. I hadn't said outright that I believed him, but I wasn't running bitch over his story, either. I guess that counted as belief, if this was the reaction he got.

Dean grabbed at my duffel without a word, and together we got it off my shoulder and on his.

"First of all, how the fuck did we get here?" I looked from one faction to the other.

Rachel was first, looking at me expectantly. I knew we were supposed to agree in front of the "others," and that was what she wanted me to do. "You know how this started. This stupid twink hallucinated someone touching him in the dark. Now he's running around telling people he got raped or something in our House. You know what that kind of rep does to us, right? Point Theater isn't inviting us back because of this shit. Did you know that?"

"Just listen to you," Lala clipped right back, her accent strong in her anger. "Flip the bloody genders, and we'd be trying to lynch the fucker, not blame the victim. Jonathan, love, you can't stand there and let her say this kind of crap, can you?"

"I can say whatever the hell I want, and he started it!" Rachel roared right back.

"You don't think Patch has a right to be angry?" Lala's accent plus anger made it hard for me to understand what the hell she was saying.

They went back to bickering again, and I watched the bystanders look even more and more uncomfortable, a few backing off, hopefully to get security before this turned into a fistfight. Patch stared at Dean and me while the ladies started up a good row (as Lala would have put it) that seemed like a long time in coming. They yapped about sexual assaults and feminism and who was the bigger whore and who needed to shut the hell up. The cool sweat from earlier oozed down my neck, and my palms got damp. I racked my brain to try to figure out just when had I been in this sort of situation before, having to defend the honor of the Tribe and choking like this. We'd never had an accusation this bad on our heads before, though we'd leveled more than a few at others before hightailing it out for safer climes. I didn't remember being this shaky about those conversations. And the cravings for anything that would ease the pounding in my brain were going to kill me. I would have taken one of Patch's cigs at this point.

Dean squeezed my shoulder, and I looked up at his concerned face and wondered what he saw in this little clusterfuck. I hadn't even had time to tell him what was going on before rushing off here to fix it, though now he got the idea, thanks to the bitchfest in front of us. Was it too much drama for him to handle? I could have thought about it more, but it was hard to breathe at the moment.

"Jon?" he asked, cutting through the shrieking near us. "We don't have to stay and hear this out. But your friend looks like he's going to fall over."

I nodded, but one look at Patch, who looked even worse for wear, like his legs weren't going to hold up if he so much as breathed wrong, and I knew I couldn't walk away. Dean squeezed my shoulder again and went over to his side before I could even form the words to ask the kid to come here. At Dean's touch, Patch fell to his knees and looked up at me. And the look was damned familiar. No wonder Dean booked it over there. He was too well aware of what a panic attack looked like.

And if he could break himself out of his social mind-fuckery to help some kid he barely knew, the ex-lover of his current lover, to be a help, to be a goddamned friend, what the hell was I shaking and sweating about? What was I feeling anxious about? Fuck, Spauldy was right. Maybe I can be anxious about stuff sometimes. I'd never had to deal with it before, because that's what fermented beverages and other intoxicants were for. It made it easier to be an asshole, but now I had sobriety and my conscience to show me the right thing to do.

I turned to the girls, who now stood in each other's faces, seconds away from tearing into each other physically, and lifted my chin, opened my throat, and let loose with a loud ululation better suited for rocking out with my belly. It was loud enough to make everyone stop and look. Hell, even Dean, who had Patch sitting on the ground and bending his head between his knees, looked shocked.

Yeah, because I don't make louder noises in bed, right?

"The hell is wrong with you?" Rachel rounded on me. "We wouldn't even be in this mess if it wasn't for you!"

"Now it's Jonathan's fault?" Lala shrieked.

"Everybody shut the fuck up," I snapped, ignoring my own private sweat bath. This wasn't going to be easy. "Rach, this is kind of a shitty way to treat anyone, especially since Patch left already."

"No need for him to spread lies. I just wanted you to see for yourself." She crossed her arms and glared balefully at Dean, who had gone back to helping Patch not pass out. "Christ, what a pair of drama queens."

"Rach, I'm over here." I even waved my hands in front of my face for emphasis, though the urge to loudly defend my boyfriend's honor was strong enough to make me forget why I even bothered to speak up. "What if he's not lying?"

"He's lying!" she screamed right back. "Not our fault he boned some bitch and regretted it. Guess he's really not all that gay after all, huh?"

"Fuck you!" Patch snarled from his kneel, and Dean had to hang on to his shoulders to keep him from getting up. Looked like that insult was enough to snap him out of it.

"Then who did it, Patch? Give us a name!" Rachel arched her chin up in a cold, cruel dare.

I could see the resolve drain out of him like someone had pulled a plug, and he looked back down at the grass and shook like a leaf. Dean's lips tightened in a rage I'd never seen as he pulled an arm around the kid to steady him.

It seemed to be enough for Rachel, who looked outright triumphant. "That's what I thought."

I couldn't stay quiet any longer. "You know, Rach, I'd tell you to tone the bitch down, but you just broke the fucking knob. Leave him alone. There's no reason to look at him, talk to him, or deal with him. And don't ask me to do it either. It's done."

"And what about Patch?" Lala added, going to the two kneeling men. "You didn't see 'im the first couple of nights he was at my place. What's he gonna do?"

I looked back over at Dean and Patch. I'd thought the sight of another man leaning on Dean's broad shoulders would fill me with jealousy. Then reality sailed back in and smacked me hard enough to see that I had one fucked-up young dude on my hands, and Dean was willing to help him. Warmth flooded me, battling and defeating the nerves and the anger. Even my hands felt a lot dryer.

"Right now he needs to go to the first aid tent before he passes out. We'll figure out what next after that." I met Lala's eyes with a tired smile. "You and Mark really stepped up when you didn't have to. Thanks."

"Unlike some people"—she narrowed her eyes at Rachel—"I'd like to think I'm not a selfish waste of skin."

"Fuck you, toothpick," Rachel snarled, then to me, "And you? We're not wasting our time on that head case, you hear me? You've been gone too long if you think we're going to deal with this bullshit."

"Not 'we'," I pointed from her to me, then to me and Patch. "We. Because that's what friends do. If it was me sitting over there, would you be acting this way?"

"You *were* sitting over here once, remember? So that's it? You're only 'friends' with guys you've spread your legs for? I gave you this piece of ass, and this is how you repay me?"

"Rachel!" I growled low. Broke the knob? Shit, she just broke the awful person scale.

"Don't come crying to me when that overgrown Boy Scout smacks you around, you hear me?" She was yelling loud enough to make my ears ache. "I will not put up with that shit again, not when you treat me like this!"

I heard what she meant between the lines. Her helping me with my stupid broken heart would break her again. I knew this, but I was so angry that she was bringing it up again like some sort of rolled-up newspaper to whap me on the nose to keep me in line that I couldn't really feel much pity for her at that moment.

"I wouldn't lay a hand on him." Now it was Dean's turn to sound outraged, still holding Patch close. "You really need to calm down. This isn't helping anything."

"Who the fuck asked you?" she spat out, her anger wild and spewing forth like toxic waste, looking for more targets to slime. "Shouldn't you be off crying in a fucking corner somewhere, you fucking crazy son of a—"

And that was it. My hand moved so fast that I didn't realize what I'd done at first. It was hot and it stung, and the smack rang in my ears. Rachel's cheek was bright red, and she stared at me like I'd just grown a second head. Hell, everyone was staring at me.

While everyone was quiet, I spoke. "Apologize to them. Now."

"Why should I?" she whispered defiantly and closed her eyes. Twin streaks of tears ran down her cheeks. "Screw this. Jonathan, I'm damned tired of you throwing the Tribe, throwing me, under the bus for every fuck that comes along. This town is poison, it's affecting you, and there's only one way to fix it."

"You could start by leaving," Lala quipped.

Rachel opened her eyes and gave her the middle finger, then looked from Dean back to me. "You're gonna have to choose, real soon, who you're really loyal to, your fucking family, or these losers."

We stared at each other for a few long beats of silence before she backed up and stalked away, Tam and Cindy right behind her. I knew from that tone that I'd sped up the day of my decision. She'd do it too. It could be tomorrow. It could be next week. But I'd get the text or the call and we'd pack up and move on. Just like we always had. I'd have to leave all of this behind. I hadn't wanted to think about it, but there it was.

I still didn't want to think about it, so I shoved it way back into my brain and focused on two of my best arguments for staying. Lala, not certain that I wasn't a complete douchebag and complimenting me on my fine slapping form, gave me her cell and their home number. I made her promise that she would call me the moment they got Patch back home, then gave the kid a head ruffle. Patch nearly jumped out of his skin at the contact.

"Sorry, Patch. I forgot to be careful again."

"Sorry," he muttered back, eyes on the grass as Dean helped him on his feet.

Lala looked at me, so helpless, and I wanted to hug her. So I did, thanking her again. She was a lot less pissy at me this time around, and it made me feel good that she wasn't upset with me anymore.

While Dean got Patch on his feet, I looked back to watch Rachel and the girls head off. Rachel had her head in a garbage can, losing what lunch she'd had. Concern and annoyance flashed through me. She knew better than to get so wasted in public, flirting with getting a public intox arrest and a visit from the boys in blue we hated getting visits from. How could she be so out of control? Never mind that I was flirting with assault for smacking her. We both needed to get out of the park.

I reassured Lala that we'd take him straight on to Mark and shooed her away to the circle so someone could have a good time in this clusterfuck of a night. With Dean holding Patch up on one side, I stood at the other, put my hand on his neck, and drew him to my ear. He smelled like he'd tried to inhale an entire pack at once and then run a few miles, and it had drenched him not in sexy post-set sweat, but sick, nervous funk.

"Sorry, *papi*." He spoke low. "I just wanted to talk, but I got so damn mad. It wasn't fucking fair. And I know it was a girl. I know it.

She don't believe me, and then I started yelling and Lala was there and then shit just got crazy."

"Easy," Dean said quietly. "You have to breathe slowly or it's going to feel worse."

"Trust him." I rubbed the skin on the back of his neck. The heat coming off him felt like it could scald. "Dean's old hat at this kinda thing."

We walked together, ignoring the few burners and jugglers and spinners and dancers, our people, who stared. Let them look. If anyone thought poorly of the Tribe after this, I can't say it wasn't earned. And the thought of leaving town added a layer of suck to the evening. Later, Jonathan. I'll angst about it later.

Now I explained to Dean why we were going to the first aid station, and he looked down at Patch, who staggered between us. "Yeah, an EMT is probably the best person to watch you."

"If he's not pissed at me for blowin' up and runnin' off. I can't help it. I just get so damned mad, and my mouth goes off before I know what I'm sayin'. Don't even know how he or Lala stand me."

"You think about getting help?" Dean asked.

That made Patch's head snap up. "I ain't going to no goddamned shrink! Do I look crazy to you?"

We looked over his head, and it was my turn to share. "Actually, kid, shit like this can make you kinda crazy if you keep it in. And you've been kinda crazy today."

"Fuck you," he growled, but there was no heat, and he didn't try to get out of our hold.

I hugged him to my side to show him I wasn't insulted, glanced at Dean one more time, and made another non-me decision. "I'm seeing one. Have been since we got here."

Tired blue eyes stared. "You? What's wrong with you?"

"So do I," Dean added, and if I could have jumped over Patch to hug him for the backup, I would have. "She's helped me get old hat at this sort of thing."

Now Patch's head swiveled to Dean. "But you still freaked out at the party, so what use is it?"

"Before I started seeing someone, I couldn't leave my house. With her help and some encouragement"—he gave me a look so significant that the weight of it crushed me—"I'm getting better."

"Oh." Patch regarded the grass for a couple of steps, the sound of the band getting even louder as the first aid booth got into view. "What about you, *papi*? What's up with you?"

"Criminal insanity due to being constantly called *papi*." Both men chuckled, lightening the mood. I swore I saw Patch's lips curl up for the first time today, just a little. Hell, for that smile, he could call me "papi" for the rest of his life. "Seriously? I told you about my Mama, right? I wanted to cut down on the drinking and drugging and shit for her, and I couldn't do it alone. Been seeing her for months now, before I even met Dean." It was important, for some reason, that I made that clear to Patch. I wasn't doing it for a man, no matter how good said man was. "Actually, we found out later that we're seeing the same lady. How messed up is that?"

"Very… wait!" Now the smile was gone and Patch panicked again. "Shit, you were trying to cut down and I was still offering you shit and, fuck, man, I'm sorry."

"Easy, kid, it's okay." I pulled him closer to my side, and Dean let him go so I could rub his shoulder to try to comfort him. "It was all me. I should have told you. I should have told everyone, most importantly Rachel. Maybe this shit wouldn't have gotten so bad if I did."

Dr. Spaulding would be proud. I was taking full responsibility. Go me.

Patch shook his head. "Can't believe you hauled off and smacked her like that. I'm surprised it worked."

My hand still ached. "I shouldn't have done that. I'll have to apologize for hitting her once she's calmed."

"Why?" Dean spoke up. "Not that I'm okay with hitting a lady, but she was completely out of line. Taunting Patch was just cruel."

I shook my head. I couldn't explain it to these two guys. They had no idea how things worked between Rachel and me. "It's complicated. I hope Tam and Cindy get her home right away. She didn't look too well in the first place." I petted Patch's head and tried to change the subject. "Anyway, don't worry about my boozing and drugging. You didn't force anything down my throat."

That got a loud snort out of Patch. "Yeah, nothing except my dick." He covered his mouth and looked over at Dean, who was barely holding it together, trying to hide a chuckle behind his hand.

I have no idea how Patch looked, but it was enough for that chuckle to force its way out of Dean's mouth. "Relax, I know. And I suppose there wasn't a lot of forcing going on."

"Hey! Way to make me sound easy, assholes." I lightly shoved the kid in Dean's direction, who caught him, and they both laughed. It was the most awesome sound I'd heard all day. "And speaking of things we shouldn't be taking, where's your Valium?" He was usually good with a tab or two for me, and the boy could have used a few earlier for himself.

Patch shook his head, and we kept walking. "You know I was getting that shit with a forged script, right? If it got around that Mark was lettin' someone usin' prescription drugs the way I was live at their place, well, he could lose his job just by association. So I stopped. I haven't been able to get drunk either. I don't wanna be out of control again. Wish I didn't have to stop, though. I miss getting some sleep."

I replaced my arm around his waist and hugged him to my side, wanting to ebb the dark, sad clouds that threatened to return in his eyes. He used to fall to sleep so easily, look so innocent doing it. I couldn't imagine the hell he had to be going through whenever he closed his eyes. "I understand."

By then, Mark was striding out of the booth, all tall and lanky and looking scared out of his mind when he saw us. Patch slid out of our grasp and was in front of the man in two steps, yet another "sorry" on his lips. Mark shook his head and rested a hand on Patch's shoulder, giving it a squeeze before hugging him tight. It seemed that Mark was playing double duty in the physical touch department, making up for what his wife couldn't do for the kid. I had to smile and glance up at Dean, who tugged me to him. I went willingly, happy to have him close, to rest my head on his shoulder, to feel his hand rest at the small of my back.

I made Mark promise me to call the second they got home, and Patch had to promise to never leave his phone off him ever before we left the park. As we walked away, leaving Patch at the booth, I felt a little jealous. Patch had made a connection in Lala and Mark, and that connection was there when he needed it. Lucky bastard. He could make a clean break, even tainted by what had happened to him. I wanted to consider the house where Dean and I were headed my home too, but I couldn't stop thinking about my longtime friend. For ten years, Rachel and I were each other's families. Home wasn't a physical construct; it was a state of mind.

Technically, I could consider my duffel my home, since it carried my worldly possessions and my livelihood. The way Dean had just taken that bag off me without asking, and that I accepted giving it to him without complaint, really hit me as we walked hand in hand to the nearest crosswalk. He'd jumped in back there and tried to help me. He did more to help Patch today than I was capable of. The man got under my skin in a very good way. It was scary as hell.

"You didn't freak out once," I pointed out as we crossed the road.

"Patch needed help more than I needed to notice there were so many people around, I guess." Dean shrugged and squeezed my hand.

That got him a kiss. Shit, this guy was too damned good for the likes of me.

We quietly crossed the road from the park, toward the Trenton Enterprises parking complex, a five story building only a few blocks away from Atterro. Dean had obviously totally abused his parking privileges and used his work badge to access employee parking on the weekend. The downside was that employee parking started at the third floor, which meant we had to climb the stairs.

"I didn't want to have to look long for parking to see you." He squeezed me once before unlocking the car. "You want to go somewhere to eat?"

"Nah, I'm too damned tired to deal with a restaurant. Let's go home." I opened the passenger door and waited until he had slung my bag in the trunk before I spoke again. "Thanks."

"You're welcome. For what?" His eyes danced with amusement as he stood near the driver's door.

"You know for what. For coming when you did. For being there. If it wasn't for the damned money, today would have been a total disaster." I looked out at the park. The festival was winding down.

Another band was playing on the well-lit stage. People down below us were still having a great time, and I hated them for it. I could even see the lights surrounding the drum circle on the other side of the park. "I didn't even get to fucking dance."

We got into the car, and Dean started it up, but we idled long enough for me to look over at him to make sure he was all right. I'm sure he didn't want to hear me whine more, especially since we knew damn well that someone down there was certainly having a worse time of it that I was.

"Hold that thought." He backed up, and instead of driving toward the exit arrows, aimed the car toward the fifth floor. He parked, the only car on this level, and opened his door. "Come on out."

"Dean?" I did what he told me, eyebrow arched as I closed the door.

Dean was standing at the back of the car, eyes closed. I joined him, and he opened his eyes and looked at me. "Listen."

All right... I heard the cars on the street passing, the audience below us, and the strains of the band's cover of "November Rain." It had to be an encore or something to play a song that freaking long.

"Okay." I let the word drawl, still confused. "It's got a nice beat, but I don't think I can dance to it." At least I hoped that was where this was going. Unless he wanted to fuck me to the beat, that is. A nice slow screw against the car's trunk sounded damned good too. I could forget about what a terribly inappropriate tune it was if Dean was putting it to me.

Dean pulled me into a warm embrace, his arms around my waist. "And here I thought you could dance to anything. Besides, I want to dance with you, and I don't shimmy."

"Oh God, if you could, with that ass, I'd need to carry a change of pants everywhere we went." I wrapped my arms around his neck, still looking into his open hazel eyes, and together we rocked back and forth, slowly.

His chuckle was warm against the top of my head, and his kind murmur had an edge. "Welcome to my world. I get hard just thinking about you dancing."

It was then I noticed the rest of the world around us. Strange, I know, but we were five floors up, stars shining above us, the moon battling with the dim lights of the parking lot to illuminate everything. The late summer heat was long gone, replaced with cool evening, but I barely felt the chill being so close to Dean, our foreheads pressed together. I closed my eyes and just felt, let him lead, his touch, his breath, his steps all washing away the stress of the day, and what couldn't be dealt with at the moment was given notice to temporarily get the fuck out of my mind. Yes, it wasn't the frantic sways and dips and shimmies I'd craved, but it was motion, and it was enough to allow me to melt against him, feel him all around me.

The song ended and there was applause down below, and the keyboardist must have called in a favor with the band, because the next tune was "Enjoy the Silence." I laughed a little against Dean's chest, and he shushed me as we moved together again, bidding me to do what the song said and enjoy the freaking silence.

And then he had to break my little bubble of joy by moving his lips to my ear in time for the chorus, and sing along. Damn, he sounded better than in the shower.

"All I've ever wanted, all I've ever needed is here in my arms...."

Shit, I didn't need to hear that. He was already screaming it loudly with everything he did by putting up with me. I *knew*. I knew, and the fear crept up my spine, threatening to ruin this sweet little gesture. I needed to best him, keep him from saying anything more that could break me. I turned my head and rested my lips against his, just far enough to whisper, "Baby, words are very unnecessary."

And I didn't care if I was completely out of turn or that I spoke instead of sang along, but it worked, and his kiss was the sweetest thing I'd tasted all day.

CHAPTER TWELVE

# *The Power of Good-bye*

MY PUNISHMENT began that Monday, when I stopped by the House to deliver the baggie full of cash, three hundred and sixty dollars to be exact, once I took my ten percent out. There were only boarders about downstairs, and I sure didn't trust them to hold it for Rachel and company. I headed upstairs, and Rach's bedroom was locked. Okay, so maybe she had a friend over for sexytimes, but the exclusively feminine voices beyond were a dead giveaway. She was one of the straightest women I knew, wouldn't even make out with another chick drunk.

"Hey, Rach, you wanna open this thing so I can give you this money?"

There was silence on the other side of the door. Then I heard it unlock and it opened, barely. Tam stood in the little sliver, extending one brown hand for the bag.

I handed it over to her. "Secret girls-only meeting, or can I come in?"

The answer came from behind her, in Rachel's voice, low and sick and strange. "No." So much for "missing me so much."

Tam gave me a sheepish little smile, and the door was closed and locked in my face.

I ignored the little spike of annoyance. "Hey, Rach, are you all right?"

My question and my knocks after that were both ignored.

"Look," I started, "about SummerFest, I'm sorry I hit you." I would not apologize for coming to Dean and Patch's defense, but I was still feeling guilty for raising my hand to a woman. Mama taught me better than that.

I waited a few minutes more for some sort of reaction, and didn't get it. There was silence on the other side of the door as well. So I left, willing to have her be mad for a little longer. I had an appointment with Dr. Spaulding anyway. Her tunic was all ready to go.

Tuesday, I got a call from Anah of the Caress troupe wondering why she'd gotten a message from Rachel saying that we wouldn't be doing Kouzina shows anymore. I told her it was news to me and that I would talk to Rachel. My calls got sent straight to voice mail, my texts ignored.

On Wednesday, I got a call from Lala. She and Mark both had to work late and wondered if I could keep an eye on Patch. Dean and I came over to their apartment with pizza and a sampling of Dean's Z-grade movie collection. Patch was unusually quiet but appreciated the gesture, especially after watching *The Room* twice. No calls or return texts from Rachel that whole day.

By Thursday, it was pretty clear to me that my fellow dancers were avoiding me. I broke down and tried to call Tam or Cindy to get some answers, but the calls went to voice mail. I went over to the House and got the silent treatment at Rachel's bedroom door again. I asked Dean if I should consider myself paranoid. He told me it's not paranoia if they're actually after me. I told him to shut up or no stuffed shells for dinner that night.

By Friday, I was going a little nuts. Was this some sort of trial run, where I got to find out what life would be like without the Tribe? Whatever it was, I didn't like it.

That night, I got the call. Okay, it was more a very terse text, but it was a response.

*Last chance. We leave first thing in the morning.*

The three texts I sent back, questions, what time, when should I come to help pack, and whatnot, went unanswered. There was to be no argument; Mama Bear had spoken. I understood why, especially after the shitstorm at SummerFest. It was time for the Tribe to take a bow and slink out before things got worse.

And I was expected to go with them. And I was going to. Because that was our way. I couldn't think of anything else other than the way we'd been living. It was habit, it was tradition, it was what we did. I couldn't stay and be Dean's kept man forever.

Unfortunately, that left me with a very difficult conversation to have. See, I'd been getting very comfortable with this whole idea of being with Dean, not as his kept man, but as his lover. The idea was so comfortable that I was afraid I might just be in love. This was both new territory and a very bad idea. It didn't make sense for any of us to get attached to people, not in the way I got so happy with Dean near me. And Dean, heart on his sleeve and all, seemed to care for me right back. This would break him. I knew it.

Best to go for the sticky Band-Aid approach in sharing the bad news. I thought about slinking out in the wee hours of the morning, even slinking out the second I got that text while Dean was on his way home, but Dean deserved better. He deserved better than me; that was for damn sure. I needed to think about this as me giving him that chance to find better, giving him some room to find someone way more stable and more deserving of his devotion.

And as long as I could keep the aching heart from exploding out of my chest until we got past the city limits, I could get through it.

I waited until he got home from work, sitting upright on the couch when he walked through the kitchen door. My bag was already packed up tight, leaning against the front door, ready for a quick getaway should he very rightly throw my ass out. As long as my legs and shoulders stayed intact, I'd keep walking right out of his life. My stomach was in knots, and I couldn't even think about eating or making dinner, which was a shame since before that text, I had the fixings for the world's most awesome stir-fry this side of Shanghai sitting in the veggie crisper.

"Hey, baby," he rumbled, walking around the couch. He leaned down to kiss me and stopped short before our lips could even touch. I could be a good actor if I wanted to, but dammit, Dean at least needed to know how much this messed me up. "What's wrong?"

*Yank the bandage off, Jonathan. Man up and get it over with.* "Tribe's leaving tomorrow."

My knees became the most fascinating things in the room with how hard I stared at them. I heard a whoosh of a sigh from above, then felt him sit down next to me in his casual-Friday jeans. I didn't look up farther, but I knew the green of the polo shirt really brought out the greens in his beautiful lion eyes. "How soon tomorrow?"

"First thing." I leaned back on the cushions, now finding the blank television more intriguing than my damned knees. "That could be 6:00 a.m., could be anytime before noon."

"I see."

And we were quiet for what felt like forever. I dared peek at his lap, where both his fists lay curled. His breathing was high and tight, sounding like he was close to his first panic attack in months. That shook me out of my pity party, and I turned to look at his face. His eyes were closed, but the repressed fury painted a red flush on his cheeks. That wasn't going to work. Didn't Dr. Spaulding tell us both that repressing is bad or something? "Dean, I'm really...."

"Don't." It was a quick, harsh puff of breath. "Don't apologize. I've known they'd be leaving eventually, and that you would probably go with them. It's your way, like you told me."

That made me angry for some stupid reason. "So what the fuck was this all about?" I waved my hand in the space between us. "You knew I'd leave, so you take me home and do all this caring shit anyway? That doesn't make any goddamned sense!"

Dean's eyes flew open, returning my anger with his own. Finally! He needed to get this out, and better it be now than when I was gone. "I choose who I let in, Jonathan, not you. Haven't you heard of 'it's better to love and lose than not have loved at all'? I chose to love you anyway. I hoped it would be enough to get you to stay, but I can't force you to."

I didn't know what shocked me more, the pain of him using my full middle name for the first time since the hospital, his mangling of the tired saying "tis better to have loved and lost, blah blah blah," or that love was even in this conversation. It sounded so easy coming off his lips. He thought he loved me, despite this impending fuckup.

I looked back over to the TV. "It's okay to yell at me, you know."

"Just tell me why you're leaving. I think I'm owed that much."

"Why? Because they're my family. And we need to go, to get away from all of this. Because I think Rach isn't okay, and once we're in another town I can try to make it better. Because I don't want to look at Patch's face again, knowing we've completely fucked him over. Because...." I looked at him, the words sticky, lodging in my throat. *Because I love you, but all the love in the world isn't going to make me less of a fuckup, and I don't want to hurt you like I've hurt my friends.* I couldn't dare tell him how I felt, not now. "Just tell me to go, and I'll be out of here tonight."

Dean moved so fast, like a large angry blur, tackling me to the couch and pinning me there like a hungry predator. It was damned scary, the furious look in those flashing hazel eyes, but it was okay. I'd rather be devoured than walk out that door. The kiss he planted on me sure felt like I was going to be eaten, all lips and teeth.

Once I was properly quieted, he growled against my cheek. "We've got one more night, and I'll be damned if I'm going to spend it fighting with you. If you want to leave right now, fine, I'll let you go, but that's *your* damned choice."

His eyes glinted with anger, but were also clouded with a need I'll never forget. He wasn't going to ask me to stay past tonight, he wasn't going to make me choose between him and my "family," and that reality made relief and disappointment meld inside of me in a solid, sour lump. I wasn't sure I would be strong enough to say no if he asked. He was right, though. I'd rather be doing a lot of things than have a big blowup.

"Fine, just promise me you'll hate me when I'm gone. You can't keep it in, okay? You just can't."

I needed to know he was going to be okay. Well, not completely okay, but at least not repressing or anything. I should have him promise to call Dr. Spaulding too, but I couldn't think about anything else after he kissed me again, fierce and bruising.

We didn't make it to the bedroom, which was for the best. The bedroom was full of great memories that I didn't want to spoil. I wish I could say that our fucking was nice and slow and passionate, but it was none of those things. Dean said he didn't want to waste time with a fight, and he didn't waste time with being gentle. I wasn't gentle with him either. I'm sure I drew blood once or twice, scored his skin with my nails, made my mark. I would have bruises and bite marks, and I memorized the sound of his snarls as he took me aided with only spit, my very well-trained hole opening up to take him one last time. His orgasm seared me from the inside out, and I came screaming his name. Then we did it again.

Was it good? Far from it. I've had better sex with near strangers, and the looming departure darkened everything about our grapple. We didn't look at each other, even when we were face to face. Being turned around and taken from behind for round two was a relief, a blessing, even though he growled his love for me into my ear when he came again. I was going to be a sticky mess, and I didn't care about come drying on my thighs or on my barely removed clothes. It was hard enough for me to keep from breaking down. He didn't need that. I didn't need that. If I had broken down, I would have done something stupid, like beg him to make me stay, force me to stay, take the decision out of my hands completely.

I didn't sleep a wink that whole night, just lay in his arms on the huge couch, listened to him breathe, memorizing the sound and the way he looked while sleeping. We didn't even bother turning off any lights, so I got the best view of the man I'd grown to love in his natural habitat, at home, horizontal, and sated. The furrow in his brow was the only indicator that anything was wrong.

He stayed with me the entire night, which made extracting myself from his tight embrace once the sun peeked over the horizon difficult. Thank fuck he still slept like a rock, since it spared us both another good-bye. If he told me good-bye like that again, I'd be too sore to walk out the door. My ass ached enough, and I welcomed each twinge. I took a quick trip to the bathroom to pee and splash water over my face, and readjusted my mussed, sexed, and slept-in clothing. I didn't want a shower, leaving my hair all wild and unconditioned. I was going to leave as grungy as I first showed up, give or take the dried semen on my ass and thighs. Romantic or creepy, I didn't care. I wanted as much of his mark on me as humanly possible. I would be his always. I'd never feel this way for anyone else ever again.

I gave the stupid bracelet on his wrist one last look as I unlocked and opened the front door slowly, minding the creak. The thought of taking it back made me ill. No, I wouldn't take it. Who was I fooling? It was as much his as I was. He could toss it, sell it, keep it.

With the aching echo in my chest, I knew it wasn't the only thing of mine I left behind when I closed the door behind me.


MUCH to my surprise, Thor was the only vehicle packed up and ready when I arrived at too damned early in the morning. Rachel was standing near it, arms crossed, waiting for me impatiently. The only thing in the back of the van was stuff, not people.

I pointed to Loki the station wagon, still in the driveway as I got into the passenger side, letting my curiosity keep my self-imposed grief at bay. "The girls joining us later or something?" Cindy owned Loki, and we usually caravanned together for these moves.

Rachel slammed the door way too hard after she climbed in. "They're getting the last bit of our crap into Loki. We'll call them once we stop somewhere. I've got to get out of here."

Everything about the woman screamed tense and angry, and I was wary. Occasionally, the Thor and Loki caravan got delayed or split up during these trips, but nothing seemed right here. "What happened with them?"

"Don't matter now, we're leaving," she snarled, taking the turn out of the neighborhood a little too quickly. Her face went pale behind her makeup, and she reached between her legs and pulled up a child's sand bucket. When we got to the first of many red lights out of town, she ducked her head and was sick. Loudly.

"What the hell, Rach?" I recoiled, the sound of it threatening to set off my own stomach, though it'd been empty since yesterday afternoon.

She said nothing, grimly taking the roads out of Belle Point. Thank fuck that was the only time she lost her lunch on the way. Since all of the gods above apparently had shitty senses of humor, our path led us to the two-lane highway I'd walked miles on, always leading me to the man I loved. Still loved. I'd completely forgotten that was how we got to Belle Point in the first place. I used to get all kinds of happy approaching that oversized metal mailbox with "Winton" written on it in bold red letters, but now, watching it zoom by physically hurt. Sorrow closed my throat, and I blinked away tears I refused to cry. I wouldn't dare let it show. Rachel wouldn't have understood.

It was better to focus on why my best friend was puking her guts up and looked ready to do it again at any time. "Seriously, Rachel, what's going on? If you weren't ready for the drive, what was the rush to get out?"

"We had to go," she repeated. "I couldn't stand to be in that house another second. Wish you had been there to help me pack, though, but I got the important shit."

Granted, most of the crap was hers. I wasn't even sure my mattress was back there among the bed frame, boxes, and chests of our props. "Are the girls gonna have room to carry the rest?"

She shrugged. "Not our fucking problem anymore."

"Well, unless you want me bunking in the same bed as you until we get me a new mattress, it's kind of our problem." I shook my head and tried to get both our minds on troupe matters. "So, we're back to being just a dance troupe...."

"We're rebuilding. We'll be stronger for it, get rid of all the dead loser weight with better people."

I kept watching the rearview mirror knowing we had driven miles and miles away from the mailbox, miles and miles away from our fuckups. Sure, I wasn't bored and grumpy with the local crowd or dealing with the fallout of vicious rumors like she was, but I had a good thing and willingly let it go. A rebuilding season meant we would gather more people, who obviously wouldn't have heard about our dramas. Start over.

The thought of starting over made my gut churn all over again.

An hour of silence passed, Rachel still looking pissed as hell and me being morose while yelling at myself to buck up. I'd made my decision, no time to whine about it. Emo was so last season. Buck up, asshole. On a high note, the long, flat highway meant her skin didn't look so damned green.

"There's a bottle of Jack I took with me behind your seat." She broke the silence, her voice a rasp from the earlier puking. "Might as well start this road trip right."

"You're driving, dear."

"Not for me, jackass, though don't drink it all. I'll need it when it's my turn to sit and stew."

My hands moved automatically to the net pocket behind my seat, that crazy little part of me that apparently forgot I was supposed to be mostly sober now screaming like a hungry babe presented with a tit. I stopped myself, folding my hands in my lap, thought about sitting on them to be extra sure they wouldn't grab the bottle of their own volition. "Nah, I'm good."

Rachel proved it was possible to keep a van on the road, keep a handle on her next gag, and keep an icy glare on me all at the same time. "Boy Scout's not here anymore. You can go back to normal now."

"I said I don't want a goddamned drink," I snarled right back, outraged she would even invoke his unwanted nickname to me right now. My stomach fucking cramped, as if it didn't believe the words coming out of my mouth either.

She snorted. "Give me a fucking break. You can't be that broken up about him. Take a few swallows, relax. You'll get over it soon enough."

"Seriously, Rach, I don't want to talk about it." I winced at the embarrassingly high octave I reached at the end of that and prayed to the Gods of Testosterone that I wouldn't suddenly burst into tears.

"What would you like to talk about, then?" She sounded sweet and cheerful, but that quickly ended with a deep groan of agony. Good. I wanted to splash her with holy water to see if she would tell me my mother sucked cocks in hell or maybe start melting and give me back my real friend.

Two could play at this game, though. "I got a better topic. How about why the hell are you so sick? Stomach flu? Bad Chinese? You knocked up? What?"

"I don't want to talk about it."

So we didn't talk about anything for another half hour. I made a suggestion about stopping by a McDonald's for food that she promptly shut down with a groan and more dry heaving. Then I suggested we pick up some Dramamine for her and let me drive. She also refused, which got me checking exit signs for hospitals. Maybe her being so damned sick was the cause of her flip-out, and I couldn't fix that shit without medical intervention.

Finally, she growled, "You're a real bore sober, Jonathan. You're not going to mope the whole way, are you?"

"Not my job to entertain you."

"Of course it's your job to entertain me. It's always been your job to entertain me. Until your mom got sick, you even liked it." She rolled her eyes and fiddled with her music player, hooking it up to the radio.

I winced. Hard. "Really, Rach? Are you seriously going to bring up my Mama right now?"

One of her thin eyebrows arched. "It's true, you know. Before that call, you were my Jonathan, my normal Jonathan who knew what fun was. With that Jonathan, I knew everything was going to be all right, no matter what shit got thrown at us. We had each other's backs. After that, you... you...." She sighed and shifted and licked her lips. "You know I thought for a while that you were, like, mentally depressed or something. You stopped drinking so much, quit smoking up all the time, you weren't all there anymore. You even tried dating that dickhead Rafe, for Christ's sake. Dating? You? I didn't know what to do with you anymore."

"We're not talking about Rafe. He's in the past. And how the fuck did you expect me to react, hearing that my Mama is sick?" I turned to glare at her. "Not everyone hates their parents, Rach."

Her lips thinned, and I knew I'd scored a hit. While Miss Carmen and I called each other once a month or two, Rachel hadn't spoken to her folks in the ten years we'd been dancing and partying. She acted as if she didn't care for them, but I knew it hurt sometimes.

"You don't think I know that?" she snapped. "I just wanted my old friend back to normal. I wanted you to feel better, so things could be all right again. Life was getting so boring with you in this stupid funk."

"Oh, and here I thought I was your friend because you liked me." It should have really hurt, but it was like adding a dropper full of hurt into a giant lake of hurt. I barely noticed.

"That was before you abandoned me. Now here's your chance to be my best friend again. Have some Jack and cheer the fuck up already, or this road trip is going to be the height of suck."

Thankfully she had nothing more to say about Mama, as if she remembered I would kick even her ass for talking shit about Miss Carmen. But since there seemed to be no limit to the hurtful shit she was willing to spill out this far, maybe even that wasn't taboo anymore. "And where are we going?"

"Do we ever know?"

Point taken. We had a map... somewhere... that would at least give us a clue as to where we could go. An hour and a half's driving didn't take us far enough from gossip, I knew that. It would be a really long slog with both of us in crappy moods.

I turned my head to watch her drop the player in the middle console to clutch the wheel and straighten the van, still green around the gills. "Why are we leaving like this? Why didn't we wait for the girls? What happened?"

Her grip tightened. "Nothing you need to worry about anymore. We're taking care of it right now."

"What's this 'we' shit? I can't take care of anything I don't know about. I mean, look at what we're leaving behind. We had a house, and a troupe, and God, you know about what happened to Patch. How could we just leave?" I felt guiltier the longer I spoke, thinking about my traumatized ex-lover. Sure, he had Lala and Mark, but I was his *"papi,"* and I was running out on him. I didn't want to think about who else I'd run out on, not anyone tall with loving lion eyes and whose smile was burned into my brain forever. That wound was still too raw for me to keep poking at it as much as I was.

"Why do you even care? We're going to rebuild our troupe someplace else. It's not a big deal." Rachel's arms trembled as she gripped the wheel. "Fuck this shit, we can't both be sober. Roll me a joint. My kit's in the glove compartment. I wouldn't be so damn nauseous if I'd had time to smoke up before we left."

Fuck this shit indeed. Nothing would scream "make things worse" more than being stopped by the cops with the driver high off her ass. I didn't like this whole deal. It smelled as wrong as the bucket in the driver's well, and all the open windows in the world wasn't making it go away.

"Are you insane? Pull over, I'll drive, and you can smoke."

"No. Not yet. We're not far enough away yet."

I had so many questions, and they weren't being answered. There had to be a bigger reason why we were leaving it all behind. And I couldn't stand to go another mile without answers.

Suddenly, I grabbed the wheel with one hand and, with Rachel screeching at full volume, yanked the van toward the shoulder. Either she would hit the brakes to keep us from barreling into the ditch or we'd hit something hard enough to make the hurt stop for a little while. I'd be happy with either option.

She opted for the first, and Thor came to an abrupt stop, the nose of the van dipping into the ditch. Once I engaged the parking brake between our seats, I turned to my wayward friend. Her skin was completely pale, eyes wide and looking ahead. One hand on the wheel, the other clasped protectively over her belly. I stared at that hand until she noticed and let it slip away, and it all finally clicked in my grief-fogged brain.

"Protecting something in there?" I said flatly as I stared at her belly and saw something there I hadn't noticed until she had her hand pressed there. Was that a lump under her shirt? Was I seeing things? I was going to catch fresh hell if I was wrong.

The weeklong puking was morning sickness or some shit. We cut people out of the Tribe for a lot of reasons, drama being the most common. But we didn't have time to take care of any unexpected accidents either, so that was reason enough to leave someone behind too. No wonder she wanted to run.

"If you had fucking waited until we got far enough away, I would have told you," she whispered, her entire body trembling, and I felt like a right dick for scaring the hell out of her.

"Who are we running from?" Worry spiked up my spine for her, all sorts of reasons and thoughts filling and overspilling as to why we were running instead of finding the son of a bitch that got her *embarazada* and… shit, I didn't know what we'd do at that point. But anything was way fucking better than running away.

"None of your business, Jonathan. It doesn't matter anyway." Her hand rubbed at her stomach, and she shrugged. "We don't need anyone. Just you and me and this... whatever it is."

"What about Cindy and Tam?" I demanded, panic seizing my guts.

"They found out about... this... and they didn't want to leave. Fuck them, anyway. We'll start a new Tribe." Her voice became lighter, softer, almost gleeful as she looked at me, gray eyes glassy and dreamy and scary as fuck. "It'll be fine. We don't need any of those losers. This kid is going to be certified awesome with how we're gonna raise it. I bet they even make little belly dancer outfits for toddlers. We could teach her early. Or him. Think about it. It'll keep us together, the way things are supposed to be. Doesn't it sound awesome? We'd be great parents, especially without all of that sex shit to worry about."

I knew someone was certifiable, and it wasn't me or her impending spawn. "Are you shitting me? Rach, we can't run and not tell whoever spunked inside you that you're carrying his baby. And seriously, me? You're not even bothering to ask me first, just 'surprise, you're a daddy'?"

Both hands moved to her stomach, and I got the glare of doom. "It's my fucking kid, and I decide who's going to help me raise it. We don't need anyone else. No one else gets it. Not Tam, not Cindy, no one else. But you, Jonathan, we go way back, more than anyone else. I need you. I can't do this alone."

I was a few seconds from needing that damn puke bucket. My vision dimmed for a moment, and fresh panic swelled deep within me. "We can't travel like this with a kid, Rach."

"You and your mom did."

There was a serious difference, and I recalled the conversation I had with Mama after I got out of the hospital. "Connections, Rach. She had them, we don't. Hell, she needed them. We'd have to find work, real jobs." Fuck, why was I saying "we" like I was already on board with this insanity? "And my dad knew about me. He knew she was carrying his kid, and the asshole left anyway. This shit is way different. This guy should at least have the chance to step up before you shove a kid at me."

"Fuck him and his chances. You can't back away from this. It's your damned fault anyw—" She stopped talking, lips pressing together.

I pounced. Verbally, of course. Strangling a pregnant lady, even a pregnant jackass of a lady, would be a shitty thing to do. That stutter screamed "I'm not telling the truth."

"You said the same thing at the festival about Patch. How is this my fault? How, exactly, did I get you knocked up? We've never slept together. I wouldn't even know what to do with a vagina." Just call me 7UPwhen it came to pussy. Never had it, never will.

"You wouldn't listen to me." Those eyes got even glassier, a prelude to tears, and all my worry came rushing back. Someone had hurt another friend of mine. There were some scums of the earth running around, forcing themselves on people I knew and cared about. And we just left them to keep on doing it. They could do it to Patch again. Hell, they could walk up the two and a half hour jaunt and try to do it to Dean. Sure, Dean could put up a fight, but could he defend himself if he had an attack? Rachel was one of the toughest bitches I knew, and that didn't matter for shit.

We'd left them.

No, I'd left them.

In my worry, I nearly missed the rest of what she was saying. "And don't give me that crap about not knowing what to do with pussy. I mean, I'd never have you in bed, even if you begged me, but you gay guys react like any straight guy would if your dick's hard enough. Even the useless ones."

"And you know this… how?" So this Mystery Rapist was gay, or at least bi leaning toward dudes. But he attacked her anyway.

Wait, she called him useless. She'd used that insult before. Something else clicked, and I didn't want it to. If I could have made it unclick, I would have, to spare me the realization. It couldn't be who I was thinking.

I hadn't gotten to know this group of locals very well, but I thought if any dude there liked the cock besides me and Patch, me or the kid would have already fucked him. Patch, the kid that Rachel started calling useless.

"I just do. Can we go now?"

Her hand moved to the center console, and I put my hand over the parking brake to stop her from releasing it. "No. Do you know this guy?"

"And what if I did?"

"Then you know it's shitty to skip town without reporting him. We have to go back and do the right thing." The words "go back" felt like a balm for my aching soul. Sure, there would be no crawling back to Dean's with my tail between my legs, but doing a right thing would make this whole mess worth it.

"Fuck the right thing. I'm doing what I want. We always do what I want, so what's the difference now?" She seethed and tried to tug my hand off the brake handle. "If you had been there, he wouldn't have been... this wouldn't have happened. I wouldn't have been so pissed off and not thinking straight."

She used her sharp nails to get me to move my hand out of the way. It hurt like crazy, but I kept my hand there and hoped she wouldn't gouge out a chunk of flesh. What were a few more marks on me, anyway? "Rachel, stop and talk to me, for fuck's sake. When did this shit even happen?"

"After you dragged your loser Boy Scout home—fuck!" She screamed and smacked my hand hard enough for me to finally let go. She started to disengage it, but I opened the door to get out. She instantly let go of the brake. "Get back in the car, Jonathan. You can't run away from this! It's your fault."

It was all wrong. Patch's attack happened while I was taking Dean home. How the hell did Rachel get into trouble at the same time? I went over the kid's story in my head. He was too drunk to resist, never mind the guilt he had about being hard and coming when he sure as fuck didn't want to.

*It wasn't ass. It couldn't have been. I know what ass feels like, and this....*

"Are you fucking kidding me?" I spat, one foot out of the van. I had no choice anymore but to see exactly what was going on. "Did you have sex with Patch?"

I should have used the big four-letter scary word thumping about in my brain. But I couldn't. I needed to know what had happened in her own words.

She lowered her head, her voice a quiet rasp. "You know, when I first met him, I thought he was just like you when you were his age, you know, fun and horny and outrageous. And I thought he was just what you needed to get back to normal. But he wasn't. I gave him the chance to bring you back, but fuck, if he couldn't keep your interest, then he was more than useless." A dry, humorless sob of a chuckle coughed out of her throat. "He wasn't even a decent lay."

"Why!" My throat closed up, making the sound less of a roar and more of a squeak.

My best friend was talking, the words were in her voice, but my brain wouldn't allow me to associate anything I was hearing with anything I knew about Rachel. "It's really simple, Jonathan. If you would have let me get rid of 'him', if you would have acted like normal and just laughed at him and let him leave, if you hadn't gotten all in my face for trying to *help* you, I wouldn't have been so upset. And I had to do something with all that upset, you know?"

"Patch was wasted." Especially after having enough Everclear to pass out.

"So was I. I barely remember anything I did, okay? I was really pissed off and angry, and I hurt, Jonathan. You leaving like that hurt me. I didn't know what I was doing, and there he was, just lying there, no good for anything but the goddamned boner in his pants."

"You could have just smacked him around or thrown him out of the house." Not that I would have been A-OK with Patch getting the shit kicked out of him or tossed out on his ass, but God, anything but what Rach had actually done would have been better. I could only whisper, worry for her turning into rage, and I seriously reconsidered that whole "not strangling a pregnant lady" rule. I'd already smacked her without even knowing she was knocked up. Why would this be any different? "You knew he would do damn near anything you said to keep a roof over his head. You knew that. You knew he wasn't into girls, either."

"Not into girls? His dick said otherwise, as you can fucking see." She pointed to her stomach. "I feel like a reject from an afterschool special, hit the fucking rate-of-failure lottery on my pills the one time I... I... forgot...."

"Too angry to try to get a condom on him, huh?" I spat through the red sheen that coated my vision. She all but admitted to forcing

Patch into sex, and sex without consent was a word I still couldn't say out loud. She didn't even see Patch as human. It didn't matter how he was taking it, not to her. He was nothing. Switch the genders, and I'd be screaming the word bouncing in my head from the rooftops before shoving boy-Rachel into traffic, and the whole world would applaud me. But now, things were way more complicated. The mini-me in her tummy didn't deserve to meet that kind of fate. Also, Patch needed to know, not only who did this to him but that he was going to be a... oh God.

That was when I leaned out of the open van door and did some dry heaving of my own. We were running away so Rachel wouldn't have to fess up to anything, that we were throwing Patch under the bus like some kind of fucking broken toy she deemed useless. By her order, I was to be a father of a kid that wasn't mine, a kid that I would have to look at every day and see Patrick Mulhaney's face and try not to drown in guilt. Just my luck, it would be a blond-haired boy with big blue eyes, and we'd have to keep him away from matches forever. The antigay douchebags would prove to be right, and he'd be gayer than the month of June by virtue of his queer genes and having me for a foster dad.

"Close the damned door, drama queen." Her disgust was evident, her hand on the parking brake.

"We have to go back." And there was that weird soothing sensation at the thought of going back. Quiet, heart, this isn't about you. "He might not press charges, but he's got to know."

"Fuck him...."

"That's what got you into this mess."

"And fuck you. This is not just my problem. I told you, if you hadn't abandoned me, it wouldn't have happened."

I turned to her, pleading, ignoring the crazy talk about abandonment. "Come on, Rach, this isn't just your problem. You're recruiting the wrong fag to help you." This was going to be hard, and I steadied myself for what I had to say. "It's not right, and you know it, and I can't go along with this."

She looked wounded, and tears stained black by too much mascara fell down her pale cheeks, and she was my friend again, and I had hurt her. "You're going to abandon me? Again? You'd leave this kid without any kind of father figure?"

"You're making the choice to leave." I sighed, fingers closing around the straps of my duffel. For the first time in a very long time, I was grateful that my life was so portable. "And I can't go with you, Rach. Not this time, not like this."

She grabbed my arm tightly. "You're going back to him, aren't you? You should have listened to me! I told you that asshole was bad news, but no, you had to keep on seeing him. You care about him more than me. I saw that shit from the first fucking night. That fucking hurts. This is all your fault! Your fault and Patch's fault and that fucking Boy Scout's fault! If we'd done things the way we always had, none of this would have happened!"

All of our faults but hers. Lala was right. Her issue was getting even clearer the more she talked. Rachel had been jealous all along. All the snark and the incident at the house party, all of that had been her way to turn me off Dean and keep me with her, and when it didn't work, she took it out on Patch. I struggled to get loose and managed to, tumbling out of Thor, landing on my ass, the duffel thumping onto my lap.

Rachel was still ranting, completely out of my sight as I attempted to stand up, using the open door as leverage. "Do you think this is the first time I've tried my damnedest to keep you safe with me? It's not, Jonathan. I knew where Rafe was going to be that night; I asked him. I didn't expect him to hit you, but damn, when he did, I was a little glad, because that meant I could really teach you a lesson."

The shock of that confession landed me back on my ass. Rach had insisted that we scope out that sports bar, and me, trusting and stupid me, didn't even question it. She usually hated bars, with their stuffy mundane crowds and overpriced booze. "What lesson was that?"

"To listen to me. We've always trusted and depended on each other. That's how we work. I knew he was a closeted piece of shit, I could feel it in my fucking bones, but you were so stupid about him that you wouldn't listen. I knew he would hurt you, and I was right. I thought this Boy Scout asshole would do the same, and I was so angry that you made me have to do this again. The fucker's all fucked up in the head, and I thought you'd just reject him, right? Toss him on his freaked-out ass? I waited by that bathroom door, waited for him to start flipping out and kicking your stupid, soft-hearted ass so I could come to the rescue again. Maybe this time you'd stick with just fucking and leave all the emotional stuff where it belongs, with me. But that didn't happen. You left with him, and then you stayed away." A shaking sob made her words crackle. "All I wanted to do was keep us together, like a family. You're so used to me making all the decisions, and now you want to claim some kind of high-road responsibility bullshit? Fuck you, Jonathan. We're leaving, I'm having this kid, and we're raising it. So get back in the fucking van so we can go!"

I got to my feet, the handles of the bag in one hand and the van door in the other. I looked at her, all tears and makeup running down her blotchy, angry face. Who was this woman wearing my friend's face? Had I been so wrong this whole time? Now that I was out of Thor, I felt this crazy sense of peace, that what I was doing was right. "I'm going back, Rach. I don't want to be a part of this family, not anymore. You should come back too, for you and for that kid. That baby's got a daddy, and we need to go back and make things right."

For a split second, I thought I had gotten through to her. Her eyes softened, and we were back at college and I was asking her what the fuck she was looking at, and she was asking me if I was a girl, because only girls wore makeup. And by the end of the day, I'd taught her how to line those big gray eyes. We were taking our first belly dance lesson, and I was worried that I'd get stared at, that this was entirely too gay even for me, and she smacked me upside the head and told me get over myself, and we went and had a great time. She drew the snake design that encircled my navel and was so proud to see the finished work that I wasn't allowed to wear a shirt for a week. She had those eyes, bright and beautiful, and I hoped I was getting my best friend back as she once was.

Then it all closed up again, behind shutters of the woman she was now, maybe the woman she'd always been but I'd never noticed. "Close the fucking door, you sorry piece of shit. I never want to see you again."

Shocked, I leaned back and did what she said one last time. I watched Thor roar back to life and tear down the road, and I kept watching until it was just a little speck in the distance. Then I watched for a little while longer, my heart shattering for an entirely different reason.

CHAPTER THIRTEEN

# *Nobody's Friend*

So, THERE I was, miles away from Belle Point, miles away from anywhere familiar. Thank fuck our route had been mostly straight and still on the highway, or I'd be attempting to use the GPS on the fancy phone Dean gave me, and I didn't know if I had enough battery power to make it all the way back to town.

I'd made my decision, and it was time to go through with it. No use standing on the side of the road fighting the urge to scream, cry, or both. First thing I did was Frogger my way to the other side of the road. Then, as I walked along the side of the four-lane highway, I tossed Mama a text, asking her to call Rachel. Since Rach was all about wanting to repeat how I grew up, I hoped Mama would be able to squeeze some reality past her wall of crazy. I knew I couldn't do it.

Next was a text to Patch, letting him know I was coming back to town and that we needed to talk as soon as possible. And yeah, I guess I needed to stop calling him "kid," knowing he had one on the way. Talking to him felt like something I didn't have the right to do, that was none of my business, but it needed to be done, and the person who should have been doing this had just skipped town completely. I couldn't let the secret sit in my mind, even if Rach never came back or didn't have the kid or adopted out or something. Give Patch a chance to either step up or not. Was only fair.

I should have texted Dean next. Fuck, I should have called him and talked to him directly, or even asked for a pickup and talked to him in person. I couldn't exactly leave him in the dark about my return. It would be awkward to randomly run into him, if he ever decided to leave the house again.

I called Dr. Spaulding, and left a message when her voice mail clicked over. He would need her. I broke his heart, and he would need someone to help heal that, and that wasn't the jackass that broke it. Of course, if I didn't stay in town for too long, running into him wouldn't be a problem.

Two hours of walking in the heat quickly wore on me. We'd left without having breakfast, and it felt like lunchtime. I pulled my shirt off and tucked it into my belt to help ease the heat, though it did nothing for the hunger. The sun wasn't being kind, and I could imagine that if I didn't find a gas station or that exit with the Mickey D's to get indoors soon, I would be red as a lobster, even with my perma-tanned skin.

Another hour passed, and I began to have a new worry. In prepping inventory for sale for SummerFest and the drama of the following week, I didn't return to the hospital after my triple-threat seizures. What if the light-headedness wasn't just heat and hunger? What if I had another brain stutter right here on the road? I'd be useless to anyone, dead of exposure. So I did what felt like the smartest thing I'd done all that day besides get out of the van: stuck out my thumb and tried to hitch a ride back to Belle Point. Sure, I could be gruesomely murdered, but at least I'd be gruesomely murdered in a car with AC.

Cars passed. One trucker slowed down enough to cruise alongside me, making me worry he was going to up and snatch me while the cab was still rolling. He drove off after getting a closer look at his "prey." No, asshole, I'm not a topless, flat-chested chick looking to suck your cock for a ride. I've got facial hair, for fuck's sake.

A passel of college-age chicks were my salvation. They were giggly to the point of making my starved brain ache, but once I explained that I didn't bat for their team, they kept their hands off. Some of my faith in the breasted half of the human race returned.

Once we'd gotten onto the familiar highway and approached Dean's mailbox, I fell silent, distanced from the mindless banter. My heart ached to ask to be dropped off there, but I really needed to give my news to Patch first, and was pretty sure I'd be very welcome. That didn't stop my heart from wrenching like it was trapped in a vise when we sped by.

I asked to be dropped off at Atterro Park, and from there called Patch for Lala and Mark's address so I could find it by foot. The last time I was there, Dean had been driving.

They lived in a set of apartments not that far from Dr. Spaulding's office, but even if I wanted to pop in to see her, it was Saturday. And I had something important I needed to do, I kept reminding myself.

I was welcomed and told to take a seat the minute Lala got a look at my sunburned chest and arms. They had just finished lunch, but Lala shoved leftover sub sandwiches and a broken bit of an aloe plant at me. Once I was anointed, full, and had a shirt back on, Patch declared a severe nicotine deficiency, so we all headed to the back porch to have the dreaded chat.

From the moment we stepped outside until he sprawled on a deck chair, cancer stick in his mouth, Patch didn't look at me once. Lala and Mike took the opposite swinging porch chair, and I opted to stand between them, leaning on the porch railing. For a second, I wanted to ask for a cig too, just to get through this.

Before I could say a word, Patch grumbled unhappily, "You wouldn't be here unless she told you she did it, huh?"

Lala made a squeaky sound deep in her throat, so it was up to Mark to ask, "Wait, Rachel raped you?"

Patch's lips twisted into a sneer. "I never fucking called it that, okay?"

"What else do you call sex without your consent, Patch?" Mark sounded frustrated with Patch's denial, and I couldn't blame either one of them.

Patch took another long drag, taking half of the cigarette in one breath, blew out a long stream of smoke behind him. "I knew it was her the second she started talking." He looked directly at me, a wry smile on his face. "I've been called a lot of things while fucking, never been called useless before."

"She obviously don't know quality dick." I shared his smile and got a quick puff of laugh.

"I know, right? I ain't good at much, but I know I got fuckin' down, right, *papi*?" His next laugh was brittle, and it sobered me up, sinking the little smile off my face. This really wasn't very funny at all.

"Jesus." I put a hand over my eyes for a moment to hold back the fury at myself. No wonder he booked it out of the House with barely a word to me. "I'm so sorry, kid."

"And she dared you to call her out last week!" Lala finally got her voice back, but her eyes brimmed with unshed tears. "You could have named her right then and there."

"Yeah," Patch snorted, stubbing the done cig into an already full ashtray, then lit another one. "Then she might have claimed that I forced her, and who the hell do you think people are gonna believe?" He took a deep drag and kept talking. "I tried to get her off me that night. I did. I thought maybe she mistook me for one of her other fucks. But she knew. She goddamned knew. She told me if I didn't stop fighting, she'd scream for help."

"And who are they gonna believe?" I repeated and suddenly really wished I'd accepted the offer of a beer with lunch. Hell, we should all be drunk for this.

"That's bullshit." Lala leaned against Mark and visibly shook, the tips of her pink hair quaking with her. "That is so much bullshit. How is that not rape?"

"Because it wasn't, okay?" Patch was on cig number three at this point. I'd never seen him go through that many at once, like he inhaled them in one breath. His gaze stayed on the ground. "The next time you came by, I was supposed to try harder to get you to stay. Like, if I was a better fuck, you wouldn't want to be with Dean no more."

Mark wrapped an arm around Lala and pulled her close, and the closeness between them made my heart ache. If Dean were on the porch with us, he'd probably do the same for me. I would bitch about it, a little, but I'd take it. Besides, if anyone looked like they needed a hug, it was Patch. Pale, hiding behind his bangs again, eyes cast down, clutching the cig like it was the only thing keeping him sane. I would have offered, but I didn't have the right, not as the bearer of really, really, bad news.

"That's why she told me I had to make up with you, wait for you to return from the store when I got back?" I asked, my voice dry as fall leaves.

His blond bangs swished back and forth as he shook his head. "Hell no. Fuck no. I wasn't going back. I'd go back to being homeless first. I couldn't even think about fucking after that, you or anyone else. I can't even think about fucking now, shit."

"Man, I'm so sorry." It was all I could say. I walked to him, wanting to offer something, anything. In wanting to protect him from those who would use him, Rachel and I used him anyway. How he could want me breathing the same air boggled my mind. "We treated you like my personal dildo with legs. No wonder Rach thought she could treat you like that. I don't know what else I can say but...."

Patch lurched to his feet, fist rounding on me, and I didn't bother to duck or block. My cheek exploded with pain as my head snapped to the side. In shock, I stumbled, gripping the porch rail to keep from falling on my ass. I heard Lala scream behind us, and Mark was at Patch's side, holding his arms and telling Lala to go get some frozen packs out of the freezer.

Under the sudden chaos of the happy couple, Patch growled, "You think you're the only asshole I've ever fucked for a place to stay and a good time? I'm younger than you, but I ain't dumb, Jonathan. Fucking is what I do. It's what I did, anyway. I can't even do that no more. Just thinking about someone, anyone, near my dick makes me want to fucking puke or cry like a pussy. What the hell I got going for me now, huh?" His voice crackled, and he yelled, jerking against Mark's hold. "Huh?"

"Don't shake your hand, let me see if you broke something," Mark told Patch, who glared at me until I willed myself to face him. His eyes softened by a fraction, and I turned my head to offer the other cheek. If that was what would make him feel better, he got it. It was about time someone smacked me.

"Before you go to town on this side, I've got more news," I muttered, and then finally unloaded the burden that had been haunting me for hours. "She's knocked up, kid."

I didn't get punched again. As a matter of fact, Patch looked like he was the one who'd just gotten a knuckle sandwich. All the color and anger drained from his face. He slumped against Mark like a broken doll, eyes wide. I heard something drop, and two packs of frozen peas lay at Lala's feet as she stood at the open french doors.

"Are you saying it's his?" She was the only one capable of speech at the moment, and I nodded. "You're certain?"

I nodded again, finding words. "She didn't deny it."

"That doesn't mean anything," Lala insisted, coming closer to my side. "Not if she had her share of lovers in this town."

For a moment, I thought about censoring myself, but fuck it. "There was no condom, and we're pretty damned puritanical about that. Normally. And since he came...."

Patch let out a choked little sound, a mix of disbelief and maybe disgust, and Lala grabbed my arm and pulled me away, her eyes never leaving Patch and Mark. Mark had slumped down on the deck chair, his fingers pressing into Patch's wrist, checking his pulse, I suppose. Patch shook hard enough that I was sure his piercings were going to rattle off his face and ears. He looked like a scared nine-year-old instead of nineteen. *Way to go, Jonathan, you've just sent the poor kid into shock.*

"I think it would be best if you left, Jonathan," Lala told me once we were inside.

I nodded and looked around for my duffel. She was right. It would be best for everyone if I left, not just this house, but this town. I needed to go before I ruined someone else. In loving Dean, I hurt him. In loving Dean, I caused Patch to get hurt. In loving Dean, I caused my friend to go completely off the deep end. Rach had a point. If I'd just kept acting like "normal," none of this would have happened. This was completely my fault.

Once I had my bag properly shouldered, I turned to look through the back doors one more time, while Lala held the front door open. Patch was leaning on Mark, who had an arm around him, and my heart twisted again. Mr. "I don't cuddle" was accepting the comfort like the air he needed to breathe. Mark was straight, for crying out loud, and he was being a better friend to Patch than I ever was or could be. He would be all right with these two. They had more to offer than lame apologies.

"Take care of him, please?" I murmured to Lala, who was now stoically crying in the way that screamed "stiff upper lip." The lump in my own throat threatened to choke every breath I took.

"We've been doing that since I brought him here."

I paused, then took out my wallet, pulled out Dr. Spaulding's battered business card, and offered it to her. I'd been carrying the thing around since the doc and I first met. It was the least I could do. I mean, she obviously didn't help me very much, but then I was an unredeemable fuckup. She was obviously helping Dean. I hoped she could help Patch.

As the front door closed behind me, I heard the most heartbreaking howl from behind the apartment. I didn't know humans could make that sound. I wanted to turn around, throw the door open, see that sound being made, find out what emotion created that sound. Anger? Grief? Fear? A mix of all three? It faded into loud, broken sobbing, Mark's deeper voice rumbling over it, and I reminded myself that I was supposed to be gone. I'd done enough damage.

My legs felt like Jell-O from all the walking, so I sat at the bus stop near the complex, planning to take whichever one would get me back to the park. There I could figure out where I was going next. The folks at the House might take me back if I distanced myself enough from Rachel. Dean would... no. Dean would be well within his rights to tell me to piss off, and I sure as hell didn't want to risk him doing just that. I should just take my remaining funds and buy a Greyhound ticket to wherever it would take me. Learning how to live by myself would do me some good.

I leaned back on the bus stop bench, ignoring the cars that drove by. I looked up at the sky and considered taking my shirt off again and seeing if hitchhiking worked in town. I knew the buses ran on a limited schedule on the weekends, and I was dying to have a place to lie down for a little while, at least until the throbbing at the side of my face stopped. Patch had got me good, and I knew I'd be wearing a bruise for a while yet. I was so tired and wrung out I knew that not even dancing would bring back my spirits. In fact, I didn't even want to think about dancing or anything else that made me think of Crimson Tribe or Rachel or Patch or sobriety anymore. I was retired from all of that, effective right the fuck now.

The bench creaked as another body joined me. I closed my eyes, not wanting to deal with another person right now, not even a complete stranger. Better nip the expected social interaction in the bud. "Sorry, man, dunno when the bus is coming."

"Good thing I brought my car."

My eyes flew open at the sound of Dean's deep voice brushing over my eardrums, and I nearly fell over jerking my head up to look at the source. Dean sat next to me, hunched forward, hands folded in his lap, eyes on me. The red rings framing both his eyes didn't look right.

"No buses stop here on Saturdays."

"How... how the hell do you know?" I squeaked, those little pieces of my heart twisting at the drawn and exhausted expression clear on his face. *I did that to him.* "What are you doing here?"

"That's two questions, you know." He pulled out his phone. "Patch hadn't deleted any of your old numbers from his phone. He called about an hour ago and told me you were on your way here. Then Lala sent me a text telling me you'd just left. Got the bus schedule on my own phone, and I knew you'd try to run again. The rest was luck. I take it things went bad at their place?"

"It was Rach that fucked Patch. She's gonna have his kid." Good God, I prayed for a brain stutter just for the excuse to get out of reality for a little while.

Now Dean turned to face me, and I was thankful I was still sitting, my knees going weak as I got the full brunt of his attention. "How's he taking it?"

"Badly," I growled, mentally sealing Rachel's place on the short list of Really Horrible People for good. "Apparently Rach didn't bother with a rubber."

That made him sit back a moment with a long whistle. "Damn. Where is she now?"

"Somewhere between here and West Who-the-Fuck-Knows." I had to look away from his gaze and cling to the duffel between my legs like a kid's teddy bear. Dean was so close that I could smell sweat and grass and luscious man. From the damp shirt still clinging to him, I guessed he might have been working on the yard when he got the text.

"You didn't go with her?"

"That's three questions in a row. You still suck at this game."

That got me a deep chuckle. "I guess it doesn't count if one question answers itself, but go ahead, your turn."

"Fine." I doubled down my glare at the sidewalk beyond the bag between my feet. "Why are you here, Dean? I called Spaulding for you. You have to move on. This isn't good for you. I'm not good for anyone."

He grabbed my chin and jerked my head to look at him eye to eye before he spoke. I didn't dare fight, but I winced in pain as the motion made my head spin. "See, here's the thing, Jon. Like I told you last night, you can't make me feel anything I don't want to. I wasn't going to let this chance to have you back pass me by."

"Why?"

"That's two questions, and I wasn't finished answering the first one." His grip softened, and he cupped my shiner-free cheek. "You left me and then called my shrink to look after me. You always try to look after people you care about, even when you're being a bit of an idiot about it."

"Gee, thanks," I muttered. "I'm trying my best here, and you coming here isn't helping you."

"How about you let me figure out what's good for me, huh? Why do you think Patch called? I'm here to take you home. As for why I want that—" His thumb grazed my cheekbone, and a little sound of longing tore from my throat. "—I love you. I need you, Jon. Not in the same way Patch is going to need you, as a friend, but—"

"Friend? I'm nobody's friend. The only friend I ever had tore out of here instead of fessing up to fucking someone over, and for some stupid reason, I couldn't play along and go with her. I'm a fuckup, Dean. You'd be really smart to go back home without me." My eyes slid shut to avoid his penetrating gaze.

"Look at me," he growled, and I quickly obeyed. "That place I live in stopped being a home the second I woke up this morning without you. Where are you going to go if I leave you here?"

It was hard to get the words out with him looking at me like that, but I did. "That's not your goddamned problem anymore."

"So you're running away? You and your friends always run when things get rough. Do I have that right? But you came back, Jon. You came back. Aren't you tired of trying to do for other people, but not yourself? What do *you* want?"

To be honest, I was just plain beyond coping with everything and was ready to give up. I didn't know where I would go or what I would do, but it couldn't be here. "I want you to leave. You need me? You're fucking deluded. Why aren't you talking to your shrink? You need to talk to her and get over this... stupid whatever we've got. I'm no good for anyone. No one needs me, except to fuck up their life worse than it already was." I hoped if I ignored the twisting, wrenching feeling in my chest and annoyed him or got him angry enough, he would go away.

My phone buzzed against my thigh, breaking our little staring contest before Dean could respond. I thought it was Rachel finally pulling her head out of her ass and coming back to face responsibility, so I went for it.

It was a text from Patch's number. *Lala here. Patch is threatening to kick your ass if you dare leave town again. He says he needs you, no more face punching, and he'll call you when he's pulled himself together enough to operate the phone.*

"No one needs you, huh?" Dean whispered, reading the screen. "Maybe we're all crazy."

I was sure I was seeing things. My vision wavered, and I was damned sure it was a seizure coming on. It made it damned hard to see the words that I read over and over, and Dean took the phone out of my hands when my fingers went limp. I couldn't breathe all of a sudden, and he wrapped his arms around me, tight. I wanted to fight him, tell him that we had to get to the ER like now, I was seizing and it was going to be the big one and I'd wake up with one side of my body paralyzed and I didn't care if I was getting it mixed up with a stroke again and why the hell was Dean's shoulder so wet and why couldn't I get my lungs to work and help me take in air?

He rubbed my back in soothing circles, shushing me like I was a kid or something. Why Dean was doing this to me, I didn't understand at first. I wasn't scared. I was upset, hell, I was pissed off, thinking ungentlemanly thoughts of throwing Rachel down a few flights of stairs, of telling Dean to go the fuck away and leave me to figure out what to do next. But I was so tired, and his shoulder felt so good, and I couldn't stop the sobbing.

Sobbing? Shit, that was me making all that racket. The Gods of Testosterone had truly and utterly failed me.

"Fuck," I warbled, trying to pull away from Dean to compose myself, but he only held me tighter, and I had to cling to his shirt to keep the world from spinning.

"It's all right, baby. I'm taking you home, where you belong," he crooned into my ear.

"Why? I fucking left you!" Most of what I said was muffled by his tearstained shirt. Home sounded good, though. Home meant a bed and some sheets and maybe a whole tomorrow to figure out how I was going to be worth "needing" by anybody.

"You fucking came back." There was no malice there, even a bit of humor, and I wanted to smack him for it. "You're here now. I still love you. It hasn't been a day yet, and that house is so empty without you in it. You came dancing into my life, you saw me at my worst, and you stayed by me. Now the house feels like home, and with you I feel like I can really live. I need you, Jon, and I know you need me too. Stay with me. Let me be solid for you."

Dean took care of what was his—the house, the lawn—and it looked like he thought of me as his. I needed Dean. Dean was my rock, the calm, steady spot in my life when things got crazy. He'd chosen me, no matter what I thought of myself.

I struggled to get more words out, but lost the battle with another choked sob. Eventually, I lay limply against him and let the duffel fall, landing at our feet, in a sign of my surrender. I remembered that he'd seen me at my worst too, and was still here. The weight disappeared off my feet right away, and then he pulled me up, steadying me and kissing my temple. "Come on. I've got you."

"You... you've always got me." Surprise, surprise, I could actually remember English. "I don't deserve it."

Another kiss and we moved, my legs on autopilot. He kept me tucked at his side, and I could feel the end of the duffel nudging me with each step. "Hush. I'm going to make it my duty to show you just what you actually deserve, starting with some more sleep and an ice pack for that shiner."

"Little fucker's got one hell of a right hook," I muttered, managing a little painful grin.

We got in the car, bag tucked in the backseat. I waited until we were on the road to ask for my cell back. The text was still on my screen, and my fingers felt fat and graceless as they tapped over the teensy keyboard:

*Tell the kid I'm not going anywhere.*

THE ride home was a blur. I fell in and out of a doze with Dean's hand in mine. Dean helped me out of the car, into the house, and out of my clothes. He lay next to me, and in my slow drop to deeper sleep, I felt his lips pressing against every bruise and bite mark on my neck, shoulders, and chest, even brushing lightly against the newest shiner on my cheek, like he was trying to soothe them away. It felt so nice, and I made myself a promise to return the favor. Then I don't remember much else except for a soft mattress and a warm embrace, then nothing.

I woke up in that huge bed, feeling more rested than was possible, given the day I'd had. With the steady sunlight pouring through the bedroom windows, I couldn't tell if I'd slept for an hour or the rest of the day. I'd been stripped down to my boxers. Dean wasn't next to me. The pillow on his side felt cool, as if he'd been up for a while, but I could hear some grumbling outside of the bedroom that gave away where he was.

I stopped at the bathroom first to assess the damage. There was a bruise, all right, from my jaw to right below my eye, but nothing felt broken. I followed the grumbles to the living room. Dean, clean and showered and frowning, sat on the floor surrounded by squares and rectangles of pressed laminated particleboard, some loose, some partially assembled into something I couldn't recognize at first glance. He was using a little Allen key to screw some metal strips to a board when he looked up, his face melting into that smile that made me all soft inside. Jesus, what had I been smoking when I decided to walk away from that smile?

"What was more interesting than lying next to me?" I sounded a lot more stable than my little weep fest earlier. If I could manage to tease this freely, maybe there was hope for me after all.

He lifted the piece of particleboard for my inspection. "Thought you might want something a little more permanent to keep your things in instead of that duffel bag."

It was a drawer. The whole works would become a dresser. Black paneled wood, four drawers, silver-colored handles. "You got it while I was sleeping?" Fuck, how long was I out?

His cheeks went a little pink as he shook his head. "I bought it weeks ago. Was going to ask you to stay then, but I kept chickening out."

And just like that, my throat felt strained again. He'd told me he loved me, over and over last night and today, and the evidence was there, in his hands and all around him, hard proof of the depth of what he meant. He wanted to care for me as much as I cared for him, had been planning to make this house my home too. My words, so hard to say to him before, finally forced their way through the constriction in my throat. "I love you."

Dean put the Allen key down and stood up, walked over the wood flotsam with one long step, and into my waiting arms. We kissed, our lips seeking and finding, our tongues flirting and teasing. It was like bright sunlight, chasing away the rest of the dark shadows that clung to my mind from earlier this morning, or yesterday, or whenever, because once Dean got my mouth opened and took over the kiss, I could barely remember my own name.

Dean dragged his lips over to nibble below my ear. "God, Jon, you always smell so good. I missed your scent so much."

I chuckled huskily. "Really?" I hadn't had a shower since before our hot and rough good-bye on the couch, so I could only imagine what strange sweat/sun/grief/come combination I was rocking, but if he liked it, who was I to bitch about it. "Can we go back to bed?" I panted as the kiss moved down my neck. I cupped his ass, hard enough to get a sharp gasp for my trouble. That made me shiver, and I knew just want I wanted. "I need you."

"Haven't you slept enough?" Dean rumbled against my shoulder, deliberately flexing the hard muscle beneath my hands as he nipped at my skin.

I slid my hands under the back of his sleep pants to touch him directly. With our close press, I could feel both our cocks twitch at the contact. "Not talking about sleeping."

Dean moved his cock against me in a slow, dirty grind that made his ass flex wonderfully in my grip. He tugged at my boxers, freeing my cock to bob and drip precome against the front of his pants, exposing my ass to his touch. I could have freed his cock too, but my attention was shot the second his finger ran between my cheeks. Just that touch, and he had me panting for him.

He sure acted as if he knew what he was doing to me, grinding against my cock as he lightly fingered my pucker. I moaned into his neck, "Not gonna make it to the bed at this rate."

Dean pulled his hands away, laughing at my disappointed moan. "Then I guess you better get moving, baby."

We'd picked up this game where one of us went to the bedroom first to wait for the other and lay out all ready. It was so enjoyable that night after the House party that it became a habit. I grinned up at him before turning on my heel and slinking down the hall. Before I stepped through the bedroom doorway, I looked over my shoulder. Dean hadn't moved from that spot, his eyes glued to my half-exposed rump, his cock out of his pants, hard in his fist. Pride and happiness that all of that hunger and need was only for me made me fucking glow inside.

I hooked my waistband with both thumbs and started to slowly rotate my hips. My gaze didn't leave his body as I pushed the boxers down my legs until they could drop to my feet. "Don't make me wait too long," I purred, stepping out of the cloth and into the bedroom.

I listened for footsteps as I lay on my back on the bed, too horny to keep still. I'd been pretty sure that even his self-control couldn't take that bit of teasing, but he made me wait a good five minutes before appearing at the door, completely naked, glasses in hand, the sunlight illuminating every inch of skin and muscle. I wished I was a better artist, someone who could draw more than basic jewelry ideas, because not saving that view for posterity was a crime.

"Took you long enough." I grinned and closed my eyes, raising my hands to grip the wrought-iron bars and parting my legs in invitation.

I heard him move closer to the bed, heard the soft click of his glasses touching the nightstand. The drawer opened, then shut, and the familiar bottle landed near my pillow, then the squeak of bedsprings as a body sat near me. Then nothing but Dean's ragged breathing.

"Baby?" I whispered, finally looking at him. One glance at Dean's beautiful, open face, shining with the love he had pledged over and over again, and I was completely lost.

"You are so gorgeous, Jonathan." He stifled a choked gasp, leaned over and kissed me softly. "Almost too gorgeous to get all sweaty."

"Thought you liked me all sweaty." My chuckle was cut short when Dean grabbed my hands from the bars, pulled them off and then used them to pull me to sit.

He looked at our joined hands, then up at me, then took a breath. "I want you."

"Then you're in luck, big guy, because I want you too." I laughed softly, pressing kisses to his smooth cheek.

"Not like that, Jon. I *want* you." His glance moved down to my cock. "I want all of you, especially that."

"Oh hell." The moan poured out of my mouth before I could stop it. I couldn't blame him for the shyness. God knows I'd been shy about asking to top this whole time. "Then we'd better switch places. Now."

Switching took longer than "now" with us being unable to keep our hands and mouths off each other. Before long, though, Dean was on his stomach, and I was straddled over him, kissing his spine, up to his neck to nuzzle at the hairs at the nape before kissing my way back down. I moved slowly, reveling in the knowledge that it was this man who taught me the joy of taking my time with lovemaking. He would be getting the benefits of that lesson for the rest of our lives, as far as I was concerned.

When I got to the rising curve of his ass, I moved to kneel between his spread thighs, and he opened them more to show me his lightly furred hole. Stilling the urge to shove my tongue there, I concentrated on rubbing the corded muscles of his legs, nuzzling the backs of his knees until he jerked with a barely hidden gasp of laughter. His skin was so soft and felt so good against my tongue. I licked up his inner thighs, which quivered more the closer I got to my goal. The fold where his leg ended and ass began tasted delicious, the combination of Dean's skin and sweat, and I explored both sides for what felt like hours.

"Jon," he groaned low in his throat, the sound desperate. That moan became a sharp cry when I gave in to the urge to give one of his cheeks a bite, then licked the hurt away. I dotted the entire surface with kisses, my hands kneading the flesh, pushing together, pulling apart, then just holding him open as I let my thumbs pass over the crinkled skin between them. The moans got louder then, and I'd have bet every penny I owned that his monster cock was making a monster wet spot on the sheets below. I knew my own cock was hard enough to explode as I let my tongue replace my fingers. The stuttering groan I got was a sweet reward, and I dragged out more with each circle and lunge.

Dean tasted so damned good, hot and musky, even after a shower. I licked until the muscle gave, and pushed my tongue in for more. Each lick was an apology, *forgive me for being so stupid.* Each dip inside was a promise, *I'll do better.* He made sounds I'd never heard him make before, and I loved them all. Soft pants, long, loud groans, stuttering words that became my name, over and over. His hips moved, a slow rolling motion that ended in hard jerks.

"Fuck… Jon… please, baby, don't stop…."

I hadn't dreamed of stopping, wondered why I hadn't done this with him before, and I rimmed him until all of his noises melted into one wordless moan of need.

I got my fill of his entire crease, licking from the top down to the back of his heavy sac, and then licked it too. His ass flexed tight under my hands, and I had to let him go, sit back and grip the base of my cock before I shot too soon just from doing all of that to him. I felt pretty damned proud of getting Dean to sweat, a light sheen covering his back that I greedily tasted while I grabbed the lube.

The sound I got when I worked a lubed finger inside of him nearly made me lose it again. He was so hot and clingy, gripping the digit like he didn't want to let me go and then greedily taking another. I pumped him, nice and slow, moving with his shallow thrusts as I licked his back and shoulders, wanting to taste as much of him as I could. I gently spread my fingers, then dragged them over just the right place, and his bellow almost shook the windows.

"Right there, big guy?" I cooed into his ear, rubbing that spot again and again. Dean gripped my head with one shaky hand and pulled me down and over his shoulder as he strained his neck, turning to get to my mouth. Our lips crashed together. It was desperate and messy, and I swallowed his moans like they were manna from heaven. I loved doing this to him, making him start to come apart, his pleasure literally at my fingertips.

"We are so doing this again." I more rubbed the words against his lips than spoke them.

"Now," he panted back to me, and shivered all over as I twisted my fingers. "God, Jon, I need you in me right now."

Reluctantly, because, God, his hole felt so good to my touch, sloppy with lube and still so tight, I withdrew my fingers. Using my clean hand to balance, I pumped out a generous supply of the slick for myself. My slippery hand worked over my cock, prepping it until it gleamed. I had to close my eyes and not openly stare at his fine ass, or I'd have been finished just from looking at it. "Turn over. I wanna see your face."

He grunted and rolled to his back, bending his legs at the knee, spreading his thighs wide and giving me one of my new favorite views of him. Open, trusting, his face flushed, mouth opened, and his entrance, shiny, puckered, begging to be filled.

I nearly obliged, but there was something missing from this luscious view. It shouldn't take long, but one hand was covered in lube and precome, and my cock was hard enough to be a major distraction. Distractions be damned, I managed to urge Dean's arms to the headboard, just as mine were earlier, all while Dean lifted his hips and made our cocks bump and glide together like a teasing bastard. He wasn't cooperating, chuckling as I had to move up over him and wrap his fingers around the bars. He kissed my skin when our hips lost contact, hard pecks all over my chest as my fingers fumbled and slipped and stopped when a tongue circled one of my nipples and his teeth tugged. He was going to drive me insane before I even got inside him.

"If you make me shoot all over your chest before I get inside you," I growled softly as he bit my nipple again, "I'll tie you up and eat your ass until I'm hard again."

That got me the sweetest moan I'd heard, and he gripped the bars hard. I escaped his evil teasing, leaning back on my heels to survey the view in full. Holy hell and all the gods above. Dean was completely at my mercy, our fuck under my control as long as I avoided placing any of my body parts in range of that incredible mouth. He was stretched out, his arms flexing and bulging over his head. I watched him make a few teasing attempts to struggle before I pounced, returning the favor he did to my chest with licks and bites of my own. The valley between his abs was a good spot for my tongue, his nipples budding obscenely under my bites.

"Want to touch you," he gasped, rocking his body until the head of my cock brushed against his ready entrance.

I looked up at him, my lips curling into a wicked smile. "Later. Keep your hands right there."

I couldn't hold back when he returned the grin, and I gripped my cock to aim it and pushed into his heat. My eyes stayed on his face, watching the grin melt into surprise, then a pained wince that made me slow down. But a moment later his expression melted into so much *fuck yes*. My world flipped upside down the very second Dean's entrance gave up the resistance and drew me in. I thought I should take it easy, not try to completely bottom out with the first stroke, but his strong legs curled over my thighs and around my waist, and he pulled me all the way in. He was blazingly hot and tight and deserved a damn sight better than the few frantic pumps it would have taken me to finish in this state. I froze there, breathing, trying to regain some of my crumbling control, our eyes locked.

His eyes closed, head tossing side to side, his knuckles white around the bars as I sat still. "Move, Jon. Please."

I gave him a breathy snort. "Didn't know you'd be such a pushy bottom, baby... I think I love it."

"I learned from the best."

I brought up one of his heavy legs over my shoulder, kissing the knee, and groaned low and long as the position caused me to somehow go even deeper. My hips began to move, steady thrusts that only fed our mutual need. Being inside his ass wasn't good enough. I wanted to crawl into him completely, be a part of him, but this would have to do. One shift of my hips in the right direction, and the beautiful man below me keened, a deep, low sound that bounced off my eardrum to echo in my brain. I swore to God, I would do anything if I could hear those noises forever. They were quickly joined by a wild cry, long and loud, my throat aching before I could realize I was the one making that sound. Together, we competed to drown out the sound of the squeaks of the bed.

The view was breathtaking. He kept getting more and more gorgeous every second we fucked, all flushed and sweaty and panting, his head tossing back and forth. His cock was harder than I'd even seen it, curving over his belly, sweet drops of milky liquid damn near pouring out of the slit. His eyes opened again, his whole expression so dazed and so damned sweet. He'd given up the reins and trusted me to give us both what we needed.

And what we needed, as far as I was concerned, was more kisses.

We readjusted our legs to tangle together in the sheet with me still buried deep, allowing me enough room to bend down and dive into his mouth with the same hunger I sank into his ass. The close contact brought the head of his cock sliding against my stomach, and he nearly blew my eardrums out by yelling my name. For a second, I thought I'd hurt him, until I felt the hot pulses of his come between our bellies. He'd gone over without either one of us jerking him off, and I didn't know who to be more impressed with—his eager body or my skill. Both. Definitely both.

"Don't stop!" he sobbed against my shoulder, and I didn't let him down, fucking him through his orgasm and right smack into my own. I convulsed over him, hips shoving impossibly close as I filled him over and over, his tightness wringing me dry until I fell limp on his chest, my hips bucking as if I could stuff my release into him even farther, leave a part of me so deep inside, he would have me there always.

"God, Dean, touch me…." I gasped, and my reward was so quick I felt like weeping, being crushed to his chest with those powerful arms, held tight and nuzzled until breathing became a near impossibility.

I kissed his cheeks over and over. "I'm so sorry I left home." I could have said something witty or sexy in our afterglow, but screw it. I felt more than a little vulnerable, calling this home, but here with Dean I could be vulnerable. No one was going to laugh or call me a drama queen or ignore how I felt.

He was quiet a second too long, and I pulled away from my kissing to have a better look before he spoke. "No reason to be sorry. Just do one thing for me?"

"Anything, baby."

"Don't ever leave me like that again." He squeezed me even tighter, and it had to be the yelling during the sex that had his voice all rough and ragged. Had to be. "Don't just give up and leave me alone. Lie to me, tell me you want someone else, tell me I'm crappy in bed, I don't care. But never like this again. I don't think I could take it."

"Never. You're going to have to work hard get rid of me now. I love you."

I kept kissing his face, tasting the old salt of sweat and the new salt of... tears?

"I love you too," Dean muttered, so tense he shook. "Just don't go, not again. You're home to me."

The tremble I was feeling wasn't from sexy exhaustion after all. I rolled us over, bearing his weight on my chest, held him close, and he broke down. Today had to have been rough as hell on him, and God only knew how he'd been dealing with my leaving the way I did. But I was here now, and even as the muffled sobs tore at my heart and drowned me in guilt, I would stand firm for him. I heard him out, apologized over and over again, rubbed his back, and told him how much I loved him. We lay like that until we were both drained and spent and whole. Dean and I were together again, we were complete.

PILOGUE

As WE passed through the automatic doors of the inpatient ward of Carter Center, Dean pressed a large, warm hand on my shoulder and squeezed, freely giving me some of his strength. We'd been visiting almost daily for the past month, and it hadn't gotten easier yet.

Then again, I didn't want it to get easier. Maybe if I remembered the dread and fear and the sheer surrealism of it all, I could try my damnedest to make sure this never happened again.

The receptionist behind the desk perked up upon seeing us, and I didn't have to struggle too hard to recall her name without looking at the white tag on her blouse. "Hey, Mary, how's it going?"

The tiny older woman with brassy bottle-red hair sighed, then smiled up at us with carmine lips as she slid over the sign-in sheet and a pen. "Same stuff, different day, boys. It's not raining too hard out there, is it?"

Dean answered as I filled out my line with barely a thought. "It's not too bad for now, but we heard on the radio that it was only going to get worse after dark."

As they talked about simple, polite small talky shit, I wrote my full name and the date and the time and paused at the field for "Patient." You'd think this part would be just as automatic and easy, but my throat never failed to close up for a second before I started to write the name of the patient we'd been visiting so regularly: "Patrick S. Mulhaney." Hell, even writing his memorized patient ID number didn't take as much out of me as writing his name, like writing it made what had happened so real.

It wasn't even two weeks since my aborted attempt at leaving Belle Point when I'd gotten a frantic call from Mark at too-damned-early in the morning. He'd been transporting a cranky elderly woman with heart trouble to the hospital when a call from his own home address came through in the ambulance. Lala had found Patch on the bathroom floor, limp and almost senseless, and if it wasn't for the scribbled attempt at a good-bye note on his lap, we all would have just thought he'd fallen off the wagon and gotten a little too fucked up. Then again, who the fuck took a handful of Valium (from a stash he wasn't supposed to have anymore) and washed it down with half a bottle of Absolut vodka for shits and giggles and a good time? Okay, besides spoiled rich bitches who could afford fancy rehabs.

Later, Patch would admit that he was trying to punch his own damned ticket. He'd been pretending to be okay enough to be left alone that night. The long permanent nap was preferable to no sleep at all or being awakened by more nightmares, or jumpy anxiety, or dealing with the pain of living in a body that had betrayed him in the worst possible way. That night, the four of us huddled in the waiting room, all gut-punched with shock at just how Not Okay the kid actually was and how fixing him was too damned big of a job for us to try to take on. We waited for nearly four hours to hear from someone about whether or not he'd actually survived. The sick déjà vu of being a patient in that same hospital nearly made me puke.

Two days after he was cleared of the poison in his body, and another day after each of us begged and pleaded with him to give the okay to stay at a private facility with shrinks damn near around the clock, he was transferred to Carter Center, quiet, sullen, and so pale that the dark lines of the tats stood out in relief on his bared arms and wrists. Dr. Spaulding was a familiar face there and took him on as a patient, and the work only he could do began. It took a month before any of us could see him, before he was stable enough to handle company. Dean and I did our part with visiting and bringing him little things and decidedly not talking about what he was doing there unless he brought it up. He wouldn't allow Lala or Mark to see him, he was so fucking ashamed of himself. Cindy and Tam, still in town and very much pissed with what our troupe coleader had done, were also on the "no visit" list when they found out about Patch.

Well, former troupe. With Rachel taking damn near every prop we owned and Patch in the hospital and the very name of Crimson

Dream making me sick with grief at how everything had gone down, there really was no troupe at all anymore. Ten years was a decent run, I thought when I gave myself permission to think about it.

Dean paused in his and Mary's conversation to hand her back the sign-in sheet, his name and info right below mine. She quickly and efficiently strapped visitor's wrist bands on both of us and buzzed us into the facility proper with a smile and a wave. I took point, knowing by now what Patch's usual schedule was, and with the rain, he'd probably be in one of the common rooms right after a session with Spauldy. None of the nurses we walked by even blinked as Dean's hand never left the small of my back. Supportive, solid, quiet, his presence soothed some of the tension in my spine.

I'd learned more things about our little blond mental patient during his stay at Carter than in nearly half a year of us fucking. The *S* in his middle name stood for Shane, he never learned to drive, and he had the singing voice of a fucking angel. The first time I heard that voice was the first visit at Carter. Patch was sitting at the far windowsill in the common room, lost in thought, singing, irony of ironies, Gnarls Barkley's "Crazy." When I asked him why he'd never sung where I could hear him before, he gave me a sad, embarrassed little smile.

"There were better things to do with my mouth, remember, Jonathan?"

My laugh was brittle and laced with shame, and Dean had to drive us home that day because I was shaking with upset and a little self-loathing, slagging myself a little more for treating Patch less like a person and more like a "dildo with feet." Fuck, he hadn't called me "papi" since the overdose, and I fucking missed it. Now, Patch was at his usual spot, looking out at the rainy courtyard. Today's tune was Amy Winehouse's "Rehab." I was starting to sense a theme in his quiet little serenades.

"Think fast, kid," I called out before reaching into my messenger bag (old habits die hard in the "must carry a bag around" department, but it was much smaller than a duffel) and pulling out a red rubber ball. Before he could recover from the surprise, I'd tossed the ball in his direction, and then a yellow one, then one in blue. He caught the red, then the yellow, and was already juggling them both when the blue sailed over to him. His eyes lit up as he grinned at Dean and me, hands moving fast to keep the balls in the air.

"Told you, Jon." Dean chuckled as he took a seat in one of the big chairs near the window as I sat on the carpet next to it, looking up at both men. "They don't have to be on fire to be interesting."

And the facility frowned on live fires, for practical reasons. They also frowned on my idea of a music player, since the cord of the earbuds was considered too risky for a suicidal patient, as were drawstrings and shoelaces. We knew Patch was probably getting bored going on so long so sober, so when I mentioned offhandedly that he would start trying to juggle anything he could get his hands on, Dean suggested we get him plain rubber balls. My objection was that they weren't nearly interesting enough, no blinky lights, no fire fuel. Turns out I was wrong.

"Thanks, guys." Patch looked damn near entranced as I took out a fourth ball, this one in green, and pitched it toward him. With a grace that had to come from a ton of practice, that one was worked into the rhythm with barely a bobble. "You know, Dr. Spaulding thinks I could get out of this place in a few weeks, if I still go see her in outpatient."

Best news ever, I thought. This place was giving me the utter creeps. Patch wasn't the only patient here, and it never failed when we came to visit to hear someone having a really, really bad day, screaming or crying or wailing, the sound echoing down the halls.

"Great," Dean said. "We've got the guest room set up for you when you get back."

"That's good." Patch nodded, eyes still locked on the balls. "'Cause now that the Zoloft stuff's kicked in, I don't feel so pissed at everything, so me and Spauldy's been thinking of plans, for after I get out of here."

I perked up, sensing his excitement and being damned happy to see it. Seeing Patch in a month-long depressive state nearly did me in, so this was great. "What plans, kid?"

"I'm getting there. Hold on. Spauldy thinks maybe if I had something to do, something I gotta get up and do instead of lying around feeling like crap, that maybe it could help me deal with the shit going on in my head. So I gotta go back to school, don't even have my diploma. Get my GED, then think about going further than that. Maybe go to a NarCon meeting or something so I can stay on the wagon, but I dunno about that place, exactly. I've read the steps, and it's too…

religious-y for me, and I ain't never really seen the need for church, you know?"

Dean lifted an eyebrow. "I'm sure there's meetings out there that could work better for you. We'll look up some places when we get home. Oh, crap." He turned to me with a sheepish expression for a second, then back to Patch. "Lala and Mark said they would come by tomorrow. Are you okay with that? They really do want to see you."

Patch's pretty lips twisted into a frown, and much to my surprise, he kept juggling. "Are they mad at me? I mean, I know we agreed that I'm gonna live with you guys, but...."

Lala and Mark were more than happy to take him back to their apartment, even though they were upset about the presence of that much V in their home that Patch never told them about. Since we had the spare room, as opposed to a couch, Dean offered it and refused to take no for an answer. And since this stay was also on his tab, none of us argued too much. Dean kept blowing me away with his generosity, his open heart, and his willingness to help, wrapped around this iron will. He shamed me sometimes with how kind he could be, and I wanted to be worthy of his attention.

"They're not mad at you, Patch," I answered with a sigh. "I promise you this. They're worried as all fuck out, but they're not mad. Lala calls us every day asking about you. Give the poor woman a break and let her see you breathing, all right?"

Now Dean leaned forward in his seat and pressed his hand on the back of my neck. He was more used to this kind of place than I was, was a lot calmer. I wanted out, wanted Patch out of here and healthy and whole and better. Once he got out, then we could work on all kinds of things, his GED, getting both our slacker asses some sort of job, staying clean, and, when he was ready, consider finding Rachel and finding out about this kid of theirs. Right now, he couldn't even talk about that last one, and we didn't push.

But we could talk about our missing friends. Patch dropped one of the balls but kept going with three, biting his lip as he thought. "You're right. Sure, tell 'em to come on by. We can talk and shit. It'll be cool."

The ball rolled over to bump against my foot, and I picked it up, tossing it in one hand. "Yeah, it'll be cool. Think fast." I tossed it back at him, and it joined its siblings hopping around between Patch's hands once more.

"You want us to bring you anything when we come by next time?" I asked an hour later as we stood to leave. In that hour, Patch had managed to toss those balls around in ways I'd never seen before and keep up with the conversation at the same time. I made a mental note to ask him to teach me how once he was released, because it all looked awesome.

"I can keep these, right?" Patch replied, holding his new distractions up in both hands. "I mean, I can't really hurt myself with 'em."

"We called first and checked before we got here. They're all yours."

The balls were slipped into the pockets of his drawstring-free sweatpants. "I don't think I need anything. You guys have done way too fucking much for me already. Letting me stay with you, paying for this place. I don't even know if I can repay you—"

I held up a hand to stop him, because if he kept down that road and said what I thought he was going to say, guilt would have sent me to tears or to smack him. Maybe both. "Hey, quit that right the fuck now. You'll never have to 'repay' us, not like that. Never like that. Never again, I fucking promise."

His eyes widened in surprise, and Dean stepped in. "Easy, Jon. I don't think that was what he meant, right, Patch?"

Patch nodded quickly. "Yeah, I meant like rent money or something. I'll have to get a job, but I know I can't really repay you like that with any job I could get right now. Or ever."

Dean moved to Patch's side and curled an arm around his shoulders. "You want to thank us and repay us? Get better, and don't scare Jon and Lala like this again, especially Jon. You know how high-strung and bossy he gets when he cares."

A smile curled Patch's lips, and a little chuckle erupted from his mouth as he drawled, "High-strung should be his middle name."

They both started to grin, and my face heated up. Yeah, I wanted to care for my friend, and I was probably being an overreacting idiot.

"Fuck the both of you," I muttered, not able to keep from smiling right back. "And excuse me for giving a shit, Shane."

Patch's nose crinkled as he sneered. Shortly after learning his middle name, I learned he had a similar love/hate feeling about it like I had about my first name, with more hate. Which made using it perfect tease fodder. "Go home, Esteban."

"Okay, children, since you two can't play nice, I'm going to have to separate you," Dean deadpanned, acting like the best big brother ever, even though I was the oldest. He let Patch's shoulders go with a pat and then took me by the strap of my messenger bag and pulled me back toward the door. "We'll see you next time, Patch."

Patch waved at us both, looking a lot better than he did when we approached him. I dropped my own mean face and returned the wave, murmuring to Dean as we left the common room and walked into the lobby. "We'll be taking him out of here soon. That's the best damn news I've heard today. Are you sure this isn't going to be awkward, though? With the three of us?"

"Because you two were lovers and there's still some feelings there?"

"Wait, what?" I sputtered and stopped and stared at Dean. The desire to bullshit was pretty strong, but what fell out of my mouth instead was "How the fuck did you know?"

Dean glanced at the door of the common room. "I'd be pretty disappointed if you could just turn your feelings about anyone on and off like a switch. I'm not mad, you know. He does bring out the urge to protect."

"Yeah…." I squirmed a bit at the thought. I didn't regret my past, but the past month had revealed some really fucked-up shit going on in Patch's mind when it came to sex. Which made how I felt about him even more complicated. The way Dean stepped in, paying for this place, welcoming the kid into his—no, our—home made me ashamed of myself for not being able to help him on my own. "How about you?"

That got Dean's eyes back on me. "Me?"

"That 'urge to protect'? You're not doing this just for me, are you?"

"No." His answer was so fierce that I had no doubts about how true it was. That was Dean—he never bullshitted, and I loved him for it. "Look, take it from me, he's going to need a lot of time to heal. I want to see him through this mess too, okay?"

There was more to it, I could tell. Fuck, there was more to my own guilt. But now wasn't the time for either one of us to sort that shit out. "All right. We'll need to get him earplugs, though. Don't want to keep him up nights."

Dean pulled me into his arms and kissed me softly. "Good thinking."

Mary, who we'd forgotten was sitting at the lobby desk, cleared her throat. "You know what's a better thought? Not taunting a single nurse with the two of you kissing on each other in front of her, capisce?"

I covered my face with one hand, barely hiding the sudden laughter welling up inside my chest. Dean turned a shade of red that competed with his hair. I took his hand, then shifted my grip to the chain mail that still circled his wrist and squeezed. I winked over my shoulder at Mary, and we stepped through the door, into the rain and our future.

NICOLE FORCINE was born a strange child and former Georgia peach. When she was younger, she was never far from a composition book, a pen in hand, and way too many people in her head (she's even been known to talk back to them). When two or more of them talk loud enough to overshadow the rest, a story is born. After years of writing and storing her tales in those books, she had a revelation: man, there are a lot of dudes kissing in these stories.

Her stories include themes of creating families of choice, how love can come in all forms and supersede all boundaries, and the joys and sorrows of earning a happily-ever-after.

Currently, she resides in Minneapolis with one of the most laid-back men in history and his even more laid-back cat. When she's not writing (ha!), she's saving the world/galaxy/humanity as we know it in the world of video games and general geekiness and opening other people's mail for a living.

Contact Nicole by e-mail, littlewhatever@gmail.com,
on her blog, http://nicoleforcine.wordpress.com/,
on Twitter, @NikiForcine, or on
Goodreads,http://www.goodreads.com/author/show/7160783.Nicole_F orcine.

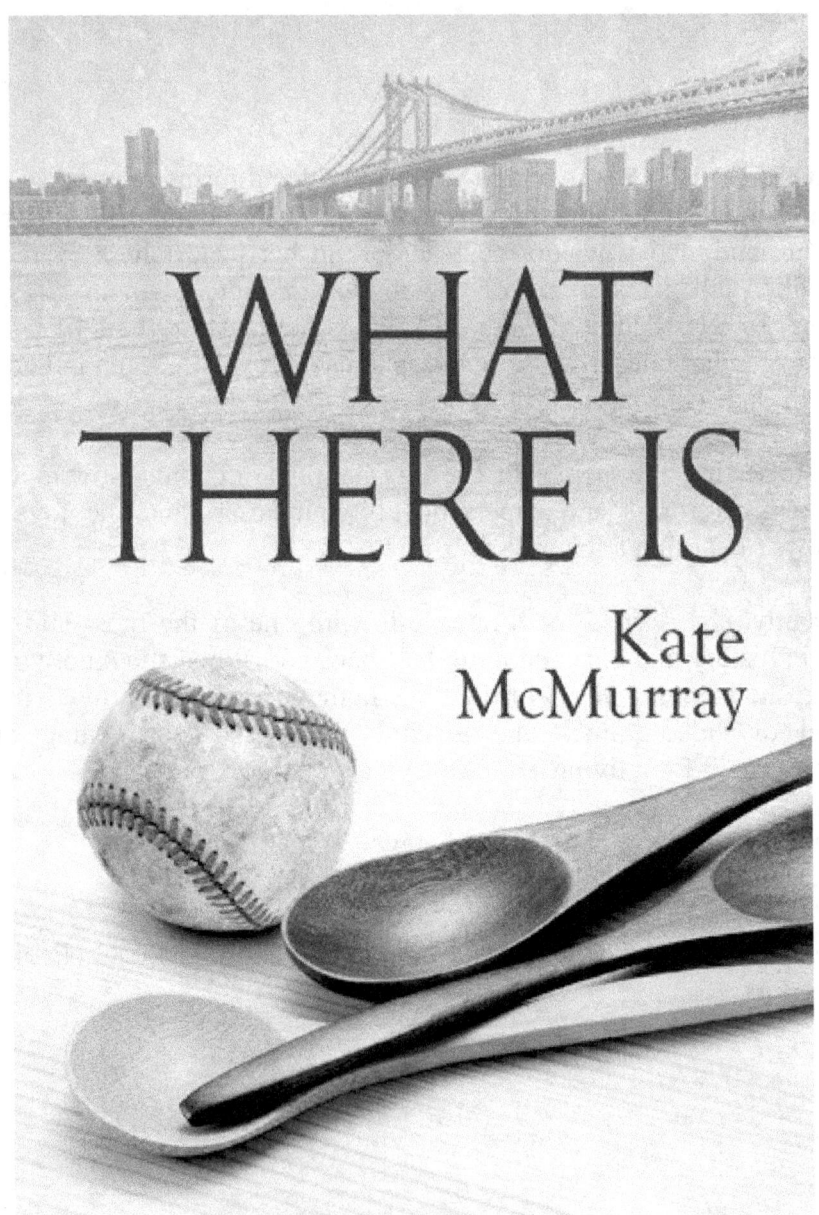

DETERMINATION

WAITING FOR FOREVER:
BOOK III

JAMIE MAYFIELD

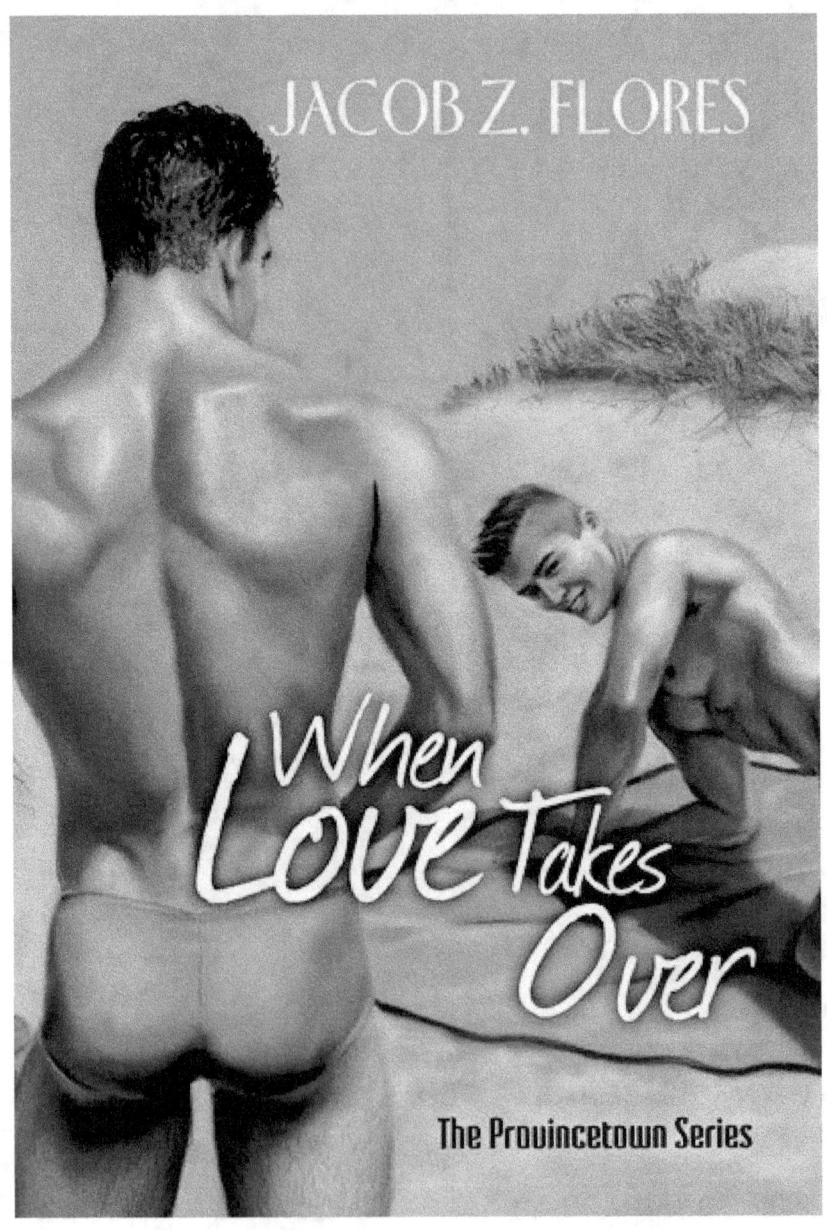

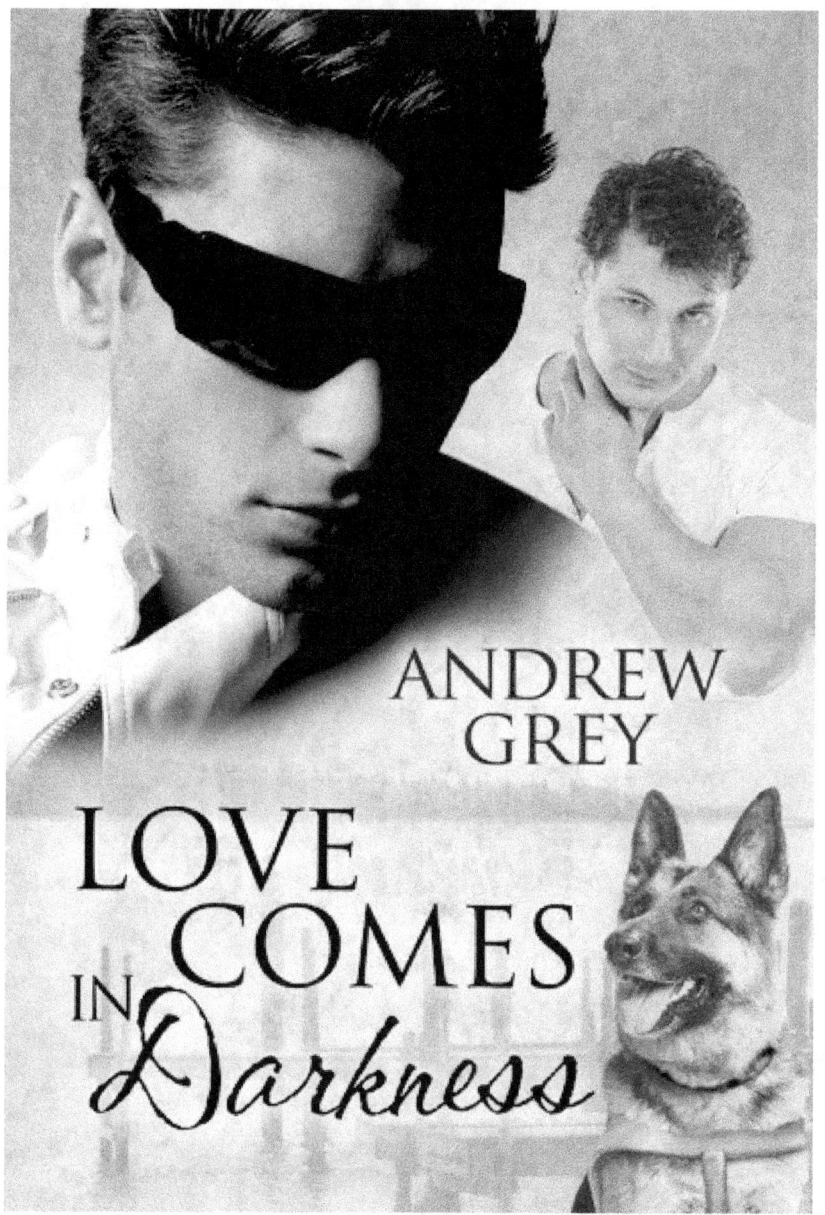